FIREBREAK

NICOLE KORNHER-STACE

SAGA PRESS

LONDON SYDNEY **NEW YORK** TORONTO NEW DELHI

SAGA PRESS

AN IMPRINT OF SIMON & SCHUSTER, INC.

1230 AVENUE OF THE AMERICAS, NEW YORK, NEW YORK 10020

This book is a work of fiction. Any references to historical events, real people, or real places are used fictitiously. Other names, characters, places, and events are products of the author's imagination, and any resemblance to actual events or places or persons, living or dead, is entirely coincidental.

First Saga Press hardcover edition May 2021

SAGA PRESS and colophon are trademarks of Simon & Schuster, Inc.

For information about special discounts for bulk purchases, please contact Simon & Schuster Special Sales at 1-866-506-1949 or business@simonandschuster.com.

The Simon & Schuster Speakers Bureau can bring authors to your live event. For more information or to book an event, contact the Simon & Schuster Speakers Bureau at 1-866-248-3049 or visit our website at www.simonspeakers.com.

Interior design by Michelle Marchese

Manufactured in the United States of America

1 3 5 7 9 10 8 6 4 2

Library of Congress Cataloging-in-Publication Data is available.

ISBN 978-1-9821-4274-2
ISBN 978-1-9821-4276-6 (ebook)

For everyone who's been here & didn't have the words.
I've spent my whole life looking for a few of them.
Here they are.

part one
toy soldiers

THE FIRST TIME IN WEEKS I SEE a SecOps NPC up close, I'm coming up on my daily thousand, my mind is long past numb from the repetition, and between that and the dehydration and the lack of sleep, I'm pretty sure I'm starting to hallucinate. Immediately I start second-guessing the figure in the distance, because what else can I do? Try to sprint over to it across a sea of mobs and wipe my thousand when I inevitably get pasted? That's six hours of work, and I'm getting really thirsty. Besides, power curfew is approaching faster than my kill counter is climbing, and if it's been weeks since a sighting, it's been a month since I've actually made my thousand, and if there's one thing I'm shit at letting go of, I'm staring down the barrel of it now.

The thing in the distance is another player, I tell myself, or some random unimportant NPC. Something in the scenery. Tired eyes playing tricks on me. There are upwards of fifty million people in-game at any given time. Be reasonable, Mal. Since when has getting your hopes up gotten you anywhere.

Except that this figure is *glowing*. Glowing in a very distinct way. A way that I usually see in other people's streams, or much more distantly than this. The beacon rises off it, a column of light stabbing the sky, close enough that my pointer finger doesn't eclipse it when held at arm's length. It can't be more than a quarter mile away.

From here I can't see what's at the base of that column of light, but I don't need to. Only one kind of thing in-game throws beacons like that.

But if it's what I think it is, there'd be a crowd swarming it. A couple hundred players easy. Trying to talk to it. Catching their glimpses. Streaming their footage. But there's nobody here except mobs and me. And the figure in the distance and the light spiking up from it, and both of those things moving off, one slow, sure step at a time.

"Hey," I call out, but whoever it is keeps walking, away and steadily, not so much as breaking stride. There's a field of gunners and mechs and an entire three-ring shitshow between me and it. One by one these mobs would be no effort for me to kill, but all at once it's another story. Which is, of course, the point of the thousand: it takes time. An ungodly lot of time.

Speaking of. Twenty minutes to power curfew, and my kill counter's stalled at eight hundred eighty-seven while I've been standing here like an idiot. My health bar is flashing ominously, but I'm down to four heal patches, and I have to be smart. I allow myself exactly one second to stand and squint after the retreating figure, but either the graphics resolution or my eyes just aren't that good. What's floating above its head looks shorter than a regulation username. It's a number. But which? There's only one that's going to make me cut bait on my thousand and brawl my way over there, no matter what stands in my way. One of twelve. The odds, again, are slim.

I just barely resist the urge to rub my eyes and risk accidentally dislodging a lens. Instead I slap a heal patch on an empty arm slot, reload, and battle my way up the landing strip, vaguely keeping note as the daily ticker climbs—eight hundred eighty-eight, eight hundred eighty-nine, eight hundred ninety—heading toward whoever it is I've seen, now receding in the distance.

I'm taking on bullets like a leaky boat takes on water, though, and my health is dropping fast. There might be heals on some of these corpses, but no time to loot them and see. Every second is a scramble. I need to duck behind something, just for a moment, to fix myself up. There's nothing to duck behind. There's nothing, period. The place is dead. Just the tarmac, and the purple sky, and what I fucking well hope is the remainder of my thousand, an untouched spawn from who knows how long ago.

I've never been out this way before, don't know the lay of the land, and I've been low on supplies for days because I haven't finished out a single thousand since I don't even know when, and I'm not going to get the time to try again—really try, out here on my own, no stream, no viewers, no Jessa dragging me off on side quests and wild-goose chases and fuck knows what to amuse the audience—until late next week at best. It wouldn't be the first time I lost a job because of chasing a thousand on someone else's clock. Free time's like free water, that rare.

It's getting dark, and worse, my timer's blinking: eighteen minutes to power curfew. If I don't make it back to a save point before those eighteen minutes are up—if I get disconnected here, in this mess, surrounded as I am—not only is today a wash, but tomorrow's not looking so great either. An uninterrupted loss streak like the one I'm looking at is a slippery slope straight to shutout city. No heals, no ammo, no credits to pay for more. And that's not a possibility I'm exactly thrilled to entertain.

But for now I've got to stay alive just long enough to make my thousand, set myself up for climbing the boards tomorrow, and get the hell offline before the power cuts and strands me here.

I call up my last ten-second cloak, load another fresh clip, slap on another heal patch, hesitate, then chase it with a third, nearly the last in my bag. It's getting dire. If you stood in my inventory right now and shouted, it would echo.

Even through the cloak I'm pulling aggro from all sides, and there are only three seconds left on the stupid thing anyway. Then the three seconds are up and the mobs pile onto me again and I have to blast my way free.

Single headshots when I'm lucky, multiple body shots when I'm not. Their health is dropping way too slow. Mine is having the opposite problem. I switch the blaster to auto and start strafing. It chews through my next-to-last clip, but at least they're going down a little faster. Nine hundred thirty-two, nine hundred thirty-three, nine hundred thirty-four. I'm running on autopilot. If I wasn't almost out of heals and ammo, I could do this in my sleep.

That thousand is my only ticket onto the boards, which is my only shot at something better than some middle-distance sighting, so I grit my teeth and keep grinding.

I blink at an empty corner of my visual field and pull up a chat window. Not overly concerned if I strike the proper half-joking-but-only-half tone when I project the message to Jessa: going to kill you when i get out of here

The reply pops up almost instantly: going that well, huh?

you said this place was safe. easy thousand, you said

i said it wasn't a pvp zone. forgive me if i assumed you could aim

I resolve to let that slide. i thought i saw one of them out here

I'm not sure why I tell her, and I immediately regret that I have. Apparently six hours of mind-numbing grind can induce even my thought-to-text interface to make small talk. Any case, the beacon was way too far off to investigate in the next—I check the clock—eleven minutes before cutoff. Power curfew waits for no one, no matter what they saw or didn't see.

This time the reply is instantaneous. wait, what? which one? where?

you know where i am, you sent me out here

I send over my coords. Back in real life my hand, curled around the invisible blaster, is starting to cramp. seriously though it was probably nothing By which I mean, of course, *there's no time*, but Jessa wouldn't buy that if I paid her.

it isn't nothing, nycorix, she says, and I roll my eyes a little at her chronic insistence on using my in-game handle. you're telling me you of all people don't want to go over there and see who it is?

Like I haven't thought of that. Like I'm not thinking it every second of every day I'm out here. Every time I see a beacon in the distance, its player crowd dense enough to spot a mile off, no chance of getting close and no real point in so doing, not really. Intellectually I know this. And yet. There's no *intellectually* about why I'm still squinting after that retreating figure, trying to make out the number above its head.

I'm starting to kick myself pretty hard for bringing it up in the first place. Jessa's great and I love her, but there's a reason I came out here alone. it's someone else, I tell her, willing the *just drop it* to come through in text.

A pause this time, which I realize is probably Jessa frantically checking the boards. Four years of being her roommate and teammate have endowed me with a pretty well-developed sense of what's coming. i'm staying here and finishing this out, I say preemptively. tomorrow's my only chance at the boards until my schedule calms down next week. i'm not wiping this thousand, jessa, i can't

nobody asked you to, comes the reply, which I immediately flag as bullshit. ok, so i'm looking at the boards right now and none of them are out that way. not remotely that way This pause is very likely Jessa weighing her options. Sighing. Crinkling up the corners of her eyes the way she does when her internal monologue is steering her toward a bad decision. Or in this case, steering her toward steering *me* toward one. Even odds, most days.

seriously, I repeat, just to head off whatever I'm about to have to refuse, probably just my eyes crapping out on me, i've been out here all . . .

I trail off, defeated, when I realize a reply is already inbound. which one did it look like? i'm guessing not 22 or your ass would've run over there fast enough to leave scorch marks

I grit my virtual teeth and elect to choose my battles. too far away to tell

but if you had to guess. how tall was it, how did it move, what was it doing? come on nyx, give me something

just walking, I tell her. But Jessa would be more likely to drop this if it were glued to her hands, so I add, no way of knowing if it's true, 02 or 21, maybe, just from the *way* it walked? But this is Jessa's field of expertise, not mine. I'm pulling guesses from the air. In some fucked-up way I *want* it to be one of those two. Then I could finish out this thousand in peace, well outside of this what-if fuckery in which I find myself.

Seven minutes. Nine hundred ninety-two.

Only a few mobs left anywhere in sight. I only *need* a few, but these are way off in the distance in the absolute opposite direction from the beacon, because of course they are. I cast one last glance toward that glowing figure. Then I slam a fresh clip into the blaster as Jessa yammers away on the periphery.

were they with a player? that isn't showing on the boards for either of them. i mean. not for *any* of them

I give my head a little irritated shake, like Jessa's voice is a mosquito in my ear. Apart from three or four mobs in the distance, the airstrip is deserted, and no telling how long it takes these things to respawn in this playfield. My health has bottomed out low enough that my vision is starting to go red around the edges, and I can hear the bass line of my heartbeat in my ears.

It's only when Jessa repeats the question that I make myself reply. not that i saw

reeeally

look, if it was earlier in the day i'd go check it out, but i gotta finish this up and get out of here before curfew

Another pause, and then: any chance it could've been 06? I can almost hear the fangirl fake-casual through the ten-point font. Like I have any room to talk.

like i said, I reply, marshalling my patience. A couple mobs are just about within blaster range, but barely enough that I waste half a clip trying to bring them down. Nine hundred ninety-three. Nine hundred ninety-four. Shot by precious shot I'm chipping away at the health bar of nine hundred ninety-five, but that one's in body armor with regen shielding, and my blaster slugs are pinging off it like rain. it was probably nothing

but you definitely saw the beacon?

i saw a light. it could have been a flare, or . . . Over a shoulder, burning a second I don't have, I glance back. No chance that's a flare. No chance that's anything but exactly what it is. Why did I even answer that much? I could have lied. I'm not streaming. She never would have known the difference.

but nyx. if it wasn't nothing . . .

She doesn't finish that thought and doesn't need to. I know, down to the credit, down to the milliliter, what might be at stake here. If it's one of them, and I'm the only one out here, and I haul ass over there and turn on the stream and get exclusive footage of whatever the fuck whoever the fuck that is is doing, by the numbers that's worth way more than any thousand, any chance at the boards, or what that might earn me.

But I'm too far off now. I won't make it back in time, not on foot and within licking distance of death as I am. I can't afford to chase some what-if down some rabbit hole. Not today. Not when I'm so close to that stupid fucking thousand and a long stretch of free time tomorrow afternoon before my whole next slammed week starts.

Do the safe thing, I tell myself. *Get the thousand and then stream your pathetic scrabble up the boards. The viewers love expressing their pity through company credits. It's a few ounces of water you didn't have before. Some noodles from the company store. Maybe even the good ones. Just walk away.*

I want to listen to that rational part of my mind. I swear I do. But part of me keeps coming back to the time last year that Jessa and I bagged almost ten minutes of footage of 33 not even really doing anything interesting in particular, and that kept us in food and water for a week. I've heard about bigger scores, of course, like the one last month where chaoslogic topped the boards and took 42 on a two-day spree while being hunted across three dozen playfields by a zillion other players, all of them streaming the chase online. That guy and whoever took him down are going to be rolling in cash and company credits for a while.

It's hard not to hear these things. It's hard not to be tempted against what remains of your better nature.

And then there's the little detail of 22. Out there, somewhere, complicating matters. The one-in-twelve chance it was his beacon I just turned my back on and walked away from. People beat odds worse than that all the time. The water lottery wouldn't be raking in millions by the day if they didn't.

That could be me and 22 on that two-day spree. It could be me and 22, period. If I make the thousand. If I climb the boards. If I get that top spot and my choice of the twelve.

Or. It could be 22 behind me, off in the weeds outside the airstrip with no one else in sight. Doing whatever the fuck he does in his free time, when players aren't pointing and shooting him like the weapon that he is.

It'd be footage-worthy, yes, but I'd be lying if I said that was my foremost motivation here. If footage-worthy was my priority, I'd be hoping that was 06's beacon, far and away the prevailing popular favorite.

No matter how hard I try to rationalize it, what this is is a personal project. There's a time to pursue this kind of shit, and six kills to go on my thousand is not that time.

I suck it up and focus on drilling nine hundred ninety-five's health bar down to the bedrock. Body armor. Why don't *I* have body armor. Except I know why I don't. It's because I keep dicking around like this, wasting time weighing cold hard numbers against something much less, well, like I said. Intellectual.

Fuck it.

i don't know what i saw, I tell Jessa, which is true. But deep down I know how this is going to play out. Maybe I can resist bait, but that's never been Jessa's strong suit.

yes, she replies, i'm getting that There comes a long pause, recognizable as Jessa's lens interface calibrating. stay put, i'm coming to you

I flick a glance toward the timer and apply the last heal patch. It barely takes the edge off. Honestly, I could use the help. careful. five minutes to cutoff

i'm. coming. to you

well i'm on the move now but if you drop to the coords i sent you i'll be

"—nearby," I finish out loud as Jessa crashes to the airstrip like a meteor, not twenty yards away, close enough to shave a few precious points off my health bar. Worse, the concussion of Jessa's impact deals the death blow to number nine hundred ninety-five before we get a chance to form an official team, so I get no credit for the kill. Outstanding.

I'm still taking low-key burn damage, and will for several seconds before the effect wears off. My health bar is running on fumes. I'm pretty much one gentle slap from death.

"Hey," I yell in the direction of the crater, backpedaling from that wash of heat. "Goddamn it, Jessa, watch it."

"Relax, I got you." Sudden pinch as Jessa slides a heal syringe into my upper arm. Virtual or not, the implant knows its shit, and that needle stings. "But look, no real names in-game, I keep telling you."

"Fine, QueenOfTheRaids," I say, shivering as the heal syringe goes to work, the equal of half a dozen high-grade patches. The implant tells my nervous system that there's top-shelf meds hitting my veins with delicious warmth. My vision begins to clear as the needle atomizes to voxels, and my health bar climbs. Still stuck at nine hundred ninety-four, though, and not so much as a lone infantry goon in sight. Four minutes.

Without a word, Jessa slides a second syringe into the pocket of my suit jacket. Familiar tiny ping as the syringe lands in my inventory. Tension drops from my shoulders. "Thanks."

"I said I got you." Jessa lifts her chin at the middle distance. "Lead on."

"Wait wait wait. I got six left on my thousand. Help me first and then we go."

"No chance. I just burned a suborbital drop getting to you. Do you know how long I've been holding on to that? Plus I just saved your ass. Those heals aren't cheap."

I consult my kill counter, like it will have budged spontaneously from six shy. I look at Jessa. She looks back at me, eyes gleaming silver. I do a double take before I can stop myself. "Are you streaming right now?"

"Of course I'm fucking streaming," Jessa says. "What you think I'm out here for, a picnic? Say hi to Nycorix, guys!"

A pause, which was probably exactly that, but I don't know, because I have them muted. Not that I'm about to tell Jessa that. "Hi," I say.

Jessa leans in close to whisper. The illusion of privacy. "Look, we've got three minutes and change before they cut us off. I'll make it up to you. Okay?"

Besides, it might be 22, she visibly chooses not to say. I have ground rules about what can and cannot be said on-stream, and this would top that list. It's nobody's fucking business, not even Jessa's really, but you try living and working with the same person in the same room for four years and see how many secrets you manage to keep.

I sigh, which apparently stands in for an answer, because Jessa is already pulling her hoverbike out of inventory, already slinging a leg over it as it blinks into existence. She throws a glance back at me. "Then let's go."

I'm torn. All my rational thought is still clawing after that thousand and the chance it represents. But I don't want to look like an asshole in front of our nineteen hundred subscribers, and asking Jessa to stop streaming would be like asking a hurricane to detour around your town. I've already got a reputation as the uptight one. No need to prove that point for them. Not when I can multitask my way out of this instead.

"Okay, but I'm driving. I'm going to try to run over a few more on the way."

Jessa pulls a face but scoots back. "No scenic route."

I raise my arms in a gesture at the blasted tarmac, now black with night, lit only by the smoking ruin of Jessa's crater. "Do you see anything remotely resembling a scenic route."

"I just hope you're right about what you saw," Jessa says, as if I've said I definitely saw *anything*, and I hammer down a little spike of irritation and goose the controls, and we're off, skimming over the peaks and troughs of the half-melted landing strip like a skipped stone.

I take out nine hundred ninety-five as it respawns a few yards away from the edge of the crater, banking the bike hard right and straightening out just in time to run it down as it raises its blaster toward my face. It thunks under the platform and is lost. One down.

It's almost fun this way. I should have thought of this ages ago.

We whir past Jessa's crater and on into the dark.

"Near those buildings?" Jessa yells over the onrushing of slag-scented wind.

"Just past them," I yell back. Then I spot a tiny cluster of mobs at maybe a hundred-yard diagonal from where I can just make out the thinnest silver needle of the beacon, meandering northeast. Jackpot. "Slight detour. Hold on."

"Make it real real slight," Jessa hollers. "Two minutes forty."

"I see it." I crank the hand controls and peel off eastward. When we're within range, I draw the blaster, wrangling the bike left-handed.

Behind me, Jessa is busily spouting reassurances to the ether. "Nyx is just finishing up her thousand, guys, be right with you."

"Four left," I shout as an exosuit gunner drops to a lucky headshot. As that one falls, I light up the demolitions bot behind it. "Three."

A message from Jessa pops up in the corner of my visual field. keep doing that crazy shit, they love it

you could be helping me shoot, you know

i didn't want to team in the middle of a shootout? remember that time we did that and the game bugged out and wiped my progress on my thousand? you're sooo close, it's fine, you got this

Yeah. Sure I do. Two minutes.

I've got a good two hundred yards of straightaway in front of me, so I take my driving hand off the controls to prop the blaster on the bent elbow of that arm. As I take aim, the bike skids over something and unbalances, whipping in a full, loose, wobbling one-eighty. I miss my shot, wasting seconds as I wrestle the bike back around. I can't see for shit now—it's fully dark—so I pull up a minimap and start firing in the direction of the nearest enemy dots. I luck out, and my counter goes up by one.

Too slow. Behind me, Jessa's clandestinely tugging on my sleeve.

just two left, I tell her.

no time

i need these last two

nyx there's just. no. time. ok? we have people watching. we land this, it's more important than your thousand and you know it

I think about chaoslogic and 42. By the end of that spree, he was streaming to over five million followers. By the end of that spree, he'd been hanging out with 42 for two days.

"More important to you, maybe," I whisper aloud, because I know Jessa can't hear me over the bike and the wind and the voices in her head. But there isn't time for both this potential footage and my thousand anymore—there really isn't. I rolled the dice on that one and I lost, and now it's time for damage control.

As always, I shut my mouth and keep the peace. I holster the blaster, angle the bike toward a slot between buildings, and jam both controls forward.

It's dark. So dark. The buildings we're between now look like some kind of warehouses, and if the lights are on inside, they don't make it through the windows. A crash would wipe us both, and then when the power comes back on tomorrow, we'll respawn here. We've fought our way out of worse together, but the bike's power cell is running low, my blaster is almost dry, and the syringe in my back pocket is the only worldly possession to my name. Unless Jessa has another power cell that I don't know about, or we score some footage in the next two minutes that by some miracle earns us one, we'll be slogging out of here on foot. We'll—

"On your three!" Jessa shouts, and I snap out of it and turn my head fractionally to see. A glint of something to the northwest, a spire of light stabbing upward from the field beyond the airstrip, half a mile off, easy. You always forget how fast they can move until you're tailing one. "Oh shit," Jessa is breathing. "Oh *shit*. You guys see that? Ninety seconds, Nyx, you gotta punch it."

I punch it. The hoverbike slingshots over the edge of the airstrip and into the weeds beyond. There's some junk here mucking up any chance we had at clear terrain. The ruins of a building, maybe, or some dead mech rusting in the tall grass. Whatever it is, it's annoying the hoverbike's delicate calibrations. The whole platform wobbles like a spinning top that's just been nudged.

Visibility is nil. Odds of a wipeout are escalating rapidly. But I race the clock toward that spike of light and, with thirty-six seconds left before cutoff, dump the bike into a skid that brings us within kissing distance of the figure's boots.

Jessa doesn't even seem to care that I've just dumped her bike, or that the power cell is now screeching angrily as the calibration systems try to get a grip on empty air, or that a third of her health bar has vaporized in the fall, and we have no back door out of this shitshow. She's scrambling up and tilting her silver eyes right into the glowing figure's face. "Guys," she's hissing. "Guys, you're not going to believe this. *Look who we found.*"

It isn't, I tell myself, *it isn't, it isn't.* Hoping that what I see when I look up from the controls will prove me wrong.

It doesn't.

It's a young woman in a dark uniform, brown hair pulled back in a ponytail. On her face is an expression of vague bemusement. The number 28 floats above her head in the place where a name would be if she were a player character or a standard NPC. Below that her health bar is full and so red it's almost black. I realize that she hasn't just been aimlessly walking, she's been reading meanwhile. Some comic book she must have picked up in one of the in-game vendors, or else, more likely, some player must have given to her for laughs. She pockets it without taking her eyes off us. I only catch the barest glimpse of the cover before the book vanishes into her inventory: several figures on a city street, their backs to me, facing down the vanishing point between two buildings and an unrealistically large mech emerging there. One of those figures is probably her.

28's eyes track back and forth between Jessa and me and the wreck of the hoverbike, and that is the only part of her that moves. Then she huffs out an amused little breath and leans in like she's going to tell me a secret. Jessa hustles out of the way and shoves me into her spot, eyes wide like that'll give our subscribers a better view of whatever comes next.

I spare a glance for the timer. Nine seconds. Eight. Seven. I look up into the amused set of 28's mouth, 28's single raised eyebrow.

"Someone should really teach you how to drive that thing," 28 says with cool derision, and I open my mouth to say something probably extremely ill-advised, but the cutoff alarm trills and everything goes dark.

0   0   0   2

WHAT I REALLY WANT IS TO RIP the blackout mask off my face, fling it across the room, and lie here in my bunk in the dark in this murderous mood until sleep takes me. But I can't afford a new mask if mine goes missing, and I *really* can't afford to miss my place in the water line, and I need to find Jessa at some point so we can strategize how the hell we're going to get off that airstrip and back to civilization when the power comes back on.

Besides, some of the other bunks are occupied. Tegan's, Talya's, Jackson's. I can see their still shapes in the moonlight across the room. Maybe people below me too. I'm in no mood to talk to anyone, and if I walk past them, they'll start asking how I did today, if I squeaked my thousand in before cutoff, whether I finally made the boards, and so on, and I'd really rather stay right here. Two seconds of shitty footage of 28 might net us a few more subscribers, a few more credits dropped into our accounts, but it isn't what I burned an entire evening for.

THANK YOU FOR DOING YOUR PART TO CONSERVE ENERGY, the display is flashing. It's the last thing it'll show me until the power curfew lifts in the morning. *WE APOLOGIZE FOR ANY INCONVENIENCE. SEE YOU SOON!*

So I put the mask away on the shelf, glance at the wall clock—the water line doesn't even open for another forty minutes yet, the cutoff ran early today—and lie there a moment in the comparative silence, mentally replaying what Jessa and I just did, or failed to do. Trying not to think about what might have happened if I'd cut my losses on the thousand just a few minutes sooner. Pursued that beacon when there was still time to get enough footage to be valuable. Here's the thing. 28 is a massive pain in the ass to find. She's easily in the top five for staying out of sight when she wants to, and arguably top three. Just now, out on that airstrip, I was the only fucking one there. I could have been streaming 28—exclusively, lucratively streaming her—for nearly twenty minutes.

Or I could have made my thousand and had a chance at the boards tomorrow. Like I'd come out there for in the first place. Instead I split the difference and managed to accomplish jack shit. For a reason that I fully realize makes zero sense to Jessa, or our viewers, or anyone but me.

And now I'm stuck until curfew lifts in the morning, and then it's off to work, and even if I make a thousand tomorrow, I have no chance to climb the boards before the grace period expires.

I know there are people who manage to sidestep power curfew. On the surface it's easy: you just figure out which neighborhoods go offline when, and you bounce back and forth staying ahead of the blackouts. But I don't have that information or the credits to make use of it. I can't even afford a hoverbike in-game, what chance do you think I have of one out of it?

I'm so thirsty. So, so thirsty. Hungry too, but that's a dull ache compared to the ashen wasteland of my mouth, the pounding behind my eyes.

I'm too tired to be properly angry, but that's there too. I lost my thousand. I haven't made a thousand since last month. And now my chance of climbing the boards tomorrow is shot. Instead I get to spend the afternoon trying to get out of that field where the game dropped us. Briefly I entertain the idea of letting something kill me out there, respawning at a save in the city proper, but nobody's going to sponsor our stream, Jessa's and mine, if we start taking the easy way out. It's just not interesting enough to watch, let alone pay for.

We fight our way out, though, me with my one heal and Jessa with her busted bike, dragging ass those overland miles back to the city? That's drama, and drama sells. It beats working the plastic digesters, anyway, or getting caught up in a blood-donor loop the way Allie did last year.

Small noises around the room as the others peel their masks off and climb out of their bunks. I close my eyes and pretend I'm taking a quick nap before heading down to the water line. One by one, they take their turn in the bathroom, collect their cups and bottles, put on their coats—an hour past power curfew in this weather, it gets like a refrigerator in here, especially down in the lobby—and leave, talking quietly among themselves.

Suresh pokes his head into my bunk. "Hey. Mal. You awake?"

For a second I consider doubling down on my fake sleep, but it's Jessa I'm annoyed with, or the game, or myself, and Jessa must have scooted off to the company store or wherever while I lay here pouting with my mask on like an asshole, and annoyance with myself is kind of my baseline. I open my eyes. "No," I say.

"I can see that," he says. "Well, if you feel like doing some sleepwalking, we're headed down to get early spots in the water line. They ran out yesterday, and I only got half ration."

I make a face. "Again?"

"Third time this month. I think it's a ploy to get us down there to buy shit in the company store while we wait for the line to open." Six floors up from the water line, he still says that part quietly. You don't usually see the water-line guards pull their guns on anyone, but then again, when they do, you can never quite tell the reason.

Just in case, I force a laugh, like I think for one second he was joking. "Well, don't wait for me. I'll meet you guys down there in a minute. Thanks for the heads-up, though."

"Yeah," he says, and leaves me alone in the dark.

Jessa's messaging me again, this time on the local channel and whatever power's left in her emergency backup battery, just tiptoeing around the razor edge of curfew violation. I'll deal with her in a bit. For now I pretend not to notice. I roll my head sideways toward the stack of bunks that goes: her on top bunk, then Keisha in the middle, then Jackson on the bottom. Jessa's bunk is empty, all her collector crap staring sightlessly back at me in the moonlight as if it's giving me both middle fingers and an I-told-you-so on her behalf.

Really, it's amazing how much kitsch she can cram into her regulation ninety-six cubic feet of personal space between her mattress and the ceiling. She's got posters on top of posters: 08 with 21, 05 with 11, 06 with 22, 28 alone, and so on, and then one with all twelve of them posed together, the living and the dead. She's got printouts of news headlines. She's got action figures stacked two deep on her little plastic shelf. She's got promo soda bottles and coffee cups and cereal boxes, and enough keychains and statuettes and god knows what that she could make a good-sized shrapnel bomb. She's got stickers plastered pretty much anywhere you might have otherwise glimpsed a wall or part of her bedframe through this forest of stuff, the jacket draped over her top-bunk footboard is encrusted in patches and buttons so thick it's like she's wearing armor when she puts it on, and she used to have a no-shit actual *body pillow* of 08, but that disappeared a while ago, either because someone stole it or sold it (likely), or she sold it (less likely) or threw it out (which I would personally bet my life against). She's even got this ridiculously detailed 1:6 model of 33 on a Parallax Instigator that's the newer, sexier real-life version of Jessa's hoverbike in-game. It's not even a smart model, just regular plastic, but it's got to be worth something anyway, because 33 has been dead in the ground since November '29, and the way Jessa tells it, she's been lugging this thing around with her from settlement to settlement since she was younger than 33 had been when he died. It's a miracle nobody's walked off with it by now.

28 locks eyes with me from the ensemble poster. It doesn't help that this particular poster was made in such a way that all their eyes literally follow you back and forth across a room. Normally I tune it out, but today, in the blue of the moonlight, it's getting under my skin a little. The look of contempt in 28's eyes is too much like the one she gave me in the weeds outside the airstrip when I dumped Jessa's bike at her feet.

"I lost my thousand because of you," I inform her. The moonlight ripples under thin cloud cover, doing weird things to her face. I don't let myself look at 22.

Whatever. Right now I have thirty-seven minutes until the water line opens, and it wouldn't kill me to have at least some faint idea of how I'm getting back to in-game civilization after work tomorrow. Jessa and I could pool our resources and replace the bike's power cell, or get a stack of heals and speed boosts and slog out of there on foot. We could—

The door crashes open in the dark. I shoot upright, startled, but I know it's Jessa because she's already running her mouth a mile a minute. She's out of breath. I can barely make out what she's saying. She clicks off her solar headlamp and flops down in the room's one chair.

"Breathe," I tell her. "What, you run a marathon before coming here?"

"I was up on the roof," she gasps. "In the greenhouses. My turn to grab the room's produce ration. Here." She tosses me something, and I catch it. It's a quarter of a lemon, wrapped in plastic. I've read that a hundred years ago, scurvy was mostly an extinct disease in this part of the world. Maybe that's true and maybe it isn't, but here and now, 2134 in New Liberty, this quarter lemon is all I get for a week, and you'd better believe I'll be licking that plastic wrap clean.

"Thanks," I tell her. "I'll just squeeze this into all the water I don't have."

She looks genuinely confused.

"What?" I ask.

"What yourself," she says. "Did you not notice—oh. You had them on mute again."

"I was trying to concentrate."

"You didn't get my messages a few minutes ago?"

This is easier to deflect than answer honestly. "What'd I miss?"

She doesn't reply. She just gets up and walks into the bathroom. There's no light in there at all because there's no window, but I can hear the distinctive beep of a water account being swiped at the sink, then the exquisite angelic choir that's a faucet being turned on at full blast.

If there's a sound in the world that can get me out of bed fast enough I almost trip over my own feet, that's evidently it. Jessa meets me in the doorway, holding out a much-reused collapsible silicone water bottle, full to the brim. I blink at it a moment, unsure it's entirely real. Jessa guides it up toward my mouth, and I drink and drink until it's empty.

I don't even know what to say. I look the question at Jessa, but she just grins back at me.

"Water line comes to us today," she says. "Check it out."

I narrow my eyes at her, but then I go over to the sink and press my thumbprint to the scanner. *GOOD EVENING, MALLORY,* the display reads. *REMAINING ACCOUNT BALANCE: 25.325 GALLONS*

This can't be right. That .325 gallon was my emergency stash, what little I've been trying to scrape back and save from each daily ration for pretty much ever.

The twenty-five gallons on top of that is new.

I've never had twenty-five gallons in my account at once. I've never had more than *five* gallons in my account at once. There is no way our subscribers donated that much. Our best single day's haul was last summer when we ran into 38 and 02 playing chess in the park for the three and a half minutes it took 38 to lose, rip the table out of its concrete footing, and hurl it into a storefront across the street. Even that topped out around a gallon. *Nobody* has that much water to just give away. And if they do, they don't pay streamers with it, they pay in credits or cash. At least in my admittedly limited experience.

Alarms in the back of my mind begin to ping. *It's too good to be true*, they're saying. *There are strings attached. You just can't see them yet.*

I realize I'm still standing in front of the sink display, like it'll start making sense if I just stare at it long enough. "Jessa," I say, "what did you do?"

"What did *I* do? You're the one who found 28 and beat the cutoff to get us there. I just turned on the stream." She grabs me and gives me a little shake. "Cheer up, will you? This is the best news we've had in months."

"You got twenty-five gallons too?" I ask, because my brain is going a mile a minute, but my mouth can't figure out a better question to frame.

"Sure did," she says. "And that's just the down payment. We start getting regular payments after we meet with the sponsor tomorrow. Which you would have known if you ever read your messages."

I'm barely listening to the I-told-you-so part of this. The alarms in the back of my mind are getting louder.

"Down payment," I say slowly, "for what?"

"Check your messages!" she calls out, halfway to the door. "I got some debts I need to repay before I spend all this by accident! I am going to take *such* a shower—"

"No, you need to *tell me what's going on*." I get between her and the door and lean against it, folding my arms. "This—" raising my chin toward the sink, where the display has finally timed out and blinked off—"looks like bait. Meet with the sponsor? What sponsor?"

"I don't know," she says. "They didn't say much. They said they wanted to congratulate us in person. Noon tomorrow. They're going to come pick us up."

"And that doesn't sound like a trap to you?"

"It sounds like twenty-five gallons down," she says, "and another five per week. Each."

"Per *week*? To do *what*?"

"You really shouldn't put people on mute," she says primly. "It's rude."

"And congratulate us why exactly? For doing our job? Why in person? Why can't they just message us like a normal sponsor? Why are they paying in water and not cash? Is this some creeper shit? Because if you got me into some creeper shit—"

Jessa makes a face like I just spat in her coffee. "The fuck? *No*. It's a sponsor, Mal. An actual sponsor like the big streams get all the time. This is a good thing. This is the break we've been waiting for." A pause, and then, because apparently she hasn't belabored this point to her satisfaction: "You could have asked them all this yourself if you hadn't—"

I take a deep breath, let it out pointedly slowly. She mistakes my silence for invitation.

"It's *five gallons a week*, Mal," she says. "It's the best sponsor we've ever had. By, like—" a nervy little laugh escapes her—"a considerable margin. In case you forgot, our entire business model is built on sponsors. This is how it's supposed to work. Do you think WhisperWalker would be living up there somewhere in orbit right now if he chased his sponsors away at the starting line? Do you think Ecclectricity and Anachronista would—"

Thunking commotion behind me as someone tries the door and fails. Jessa freezes.

"Guys, let us in," comes Tegan's voice from the hall. "I'm going to spill this."

Say nothing, Jessa mouths at me. I give her a do-you-even-know-me look over my shoulder as I turn to open the door.

It's Tegan and Talya, carrying their daily water ration two-handed in old disposable plastic cups with their names written in black marker on the sides. Not that it will end up mattering. One of them will swipe sips from the other's water, just like always, and there'll be drama and screaming and possibly a fist-fight in somebody's bunk. The most melodrama that happens in this whole room, nine people crammed into a fourteen-by-fourteen-foot space, happens between the two of them, and for basically any reason you can think of. Then again, none of the rest of us are related, so maybe that explains it.

"Hey," Jessa tells them, brushing past on her way out into the hall. Off to pay those debts to whoever, I guess. I don't ask, and she doesn't volunteer the information.

I leave too but go the other way. Down six flights of stairs to what was once the lobby when this place used to be a hotel. I'm going to hit the water line before it closes up for the night. Sure, there's twenty-five gallons in my account today, but you can't just look at now, you have to look ahead. You have to be careful and calculating. You have to play the long game. As much as I want to, I can't bring myself to share Jessa's optimism. As far as I can tell, no good thing lasts forever, and there are always plenty of bad things waiting to take its place.

0 0 0 3

MY ALARM GOES OFF AT SIX THE next morning. For a moment I leave my eyes shut and enjoy it. I have it set to Woodland Serenity, so whatever I've been dreaming changes over to this huge redwood forest that I'm walking through, and all these birds are singing and the sun is rising in the distance between massive trees. It's peaceful if you don't think about it too long, about how the forest it's based on is gone, and most of California with it. Here, now, in this crappy endless winter, it's a nice enough way to wake up.

Usually at this point I stay in bed for half an hour or so, pull on the blackout mask, and try to put a dent in my thousand before I have to get ready for work. But today I'm waiting for Jessa, because I'm not going to make it out of that playfield on my own with a dead blaster and one heal. And even if I wanted to stay in bed, my bladder has other ideas. All that water I drank last night.

All that water.

I'm wide awake now. I kill the alarm and check my messages since the power's back on. There's the daily public safety announcement: *PHASE YELLOW—NO IMMEDIATE THREAT—*

EXERT CAUTION—ENJOY YOUR DAY, which is exactly what I need to see, because I work outside today, and I'm down to my last two masks. I make a note to pick up more downstairs and delete the announcement.

Next is a whole wall of messages from Jessa, dated to last night, which I ignore. Trying to rope me into conversation on the stream, probably, in tones of increasing outrage. I'm sure I'll be hearing from her any minute now, live and in person, so I slide all those into the trash along with the PSA.

I poke my head real quick into BestLife. Not to play—I don't dare log Nycorix back in to that death trap on her own, not without QueenOfTheRaids there tanking—just to see what our followers have given us for last night's session. There's a little gift box icon in the corner of the lobby screen, which I always take a moment to savor before opening. This usually turns out to be the best part of my day, and I want to make it last.

Today there's a tidy pile of stuff, none of it amazing, but it all adds up. I open the items one by one, glancing at the little notes people left with them. *gg tnite nyx* and *don't die out there!* and *it is my fondest hope that this token aids you in your journey* and so on. There's a little cash, a little more company credit. A few ounces of water. I swipe all that over to my account and then check out the in-game items.

"Come on, power cell," I whisper, like I can summon one by force of will alone. "Power cell power cell power cell." Though I know it's not going to happen.

There's some ammo for my blaster, though, and a bunch of low- to mid-grade heal patches. A helmet that's the next level up from the one I've got on now. A shimmering, blue-black, crow-colored cape that does nothing whatsoever except look cool, which I am absolutely going to put on the exact second I log in. Some kind of shitty mesh boob-armor thing that I toss directly on the market because no.

No power cell for the hoverbike. Unsurprising. This last one cost us thirty thousand credits, and while there are plenty of streamers out there who would happily blow their noses on thirty thousand credits, Jessa and I are not among them. If they're top shelf, we're maybe two shelves from the ground. So it looks like we're on foot today.

On the bright side, if we get our asses handed to us out there, people might give us more stuff. I never know why that happens, whether it's that they want to help us out or that our suffering is quality entertainment worth paying for, but it happens.

For now I close the game and climb down out of bed, careful not to wake Allie and Suresh in the bunks below. I grab my clothes and stumble into the bathroom to pee and get dressed as quietly as the quickprint jumpsuit fabric allows.

The sight of the sink stops me in my tracks. I didn't dream what happened yesterday, I'm upwards of ninety-five percent sure of it. The fullness of my bladder a minute ago, if nothing else, is proof. Still, it could have been some sort of elaborate prank. From somewhere, ancient stories pop into my head. Gold turning to leaves in your pockets overnight. I press my thumb to the scanner.

GOOD MORNING, MALLORY. REMAINING ACCOUNT BALANCE: 20.885 GALLONS. Then the company mascot pops up on the display, cartoonishly eyeing me with gentle reprehension. *IT LOOKS LIKE YOU'VE BEEN USING MORE WATER THAN USUAL, MALLORY. REMEMBER: STELLAXIS INNOVATIONS WELLSPRING™ WATER DISTRIBUTION PROGRAM SAVES LIVES, BUT WE ALL HAVE TO DO OUR PART TO CONSERVE THIS PRECIOUS RESOURCE!*

I wait for it to clear, then scan again. Same result.

Last night, when I got to the water line, they were already on their last barrel and put up the cordon right behind me. One of the guards came around from the distribution side to man the cordon with his semiautomatic, facing backward toward the remainder of the line. I glanced over a shoulder. There were still seven people behind me holding their empty cups and bottles, and they all looked just as thirsty as I'd felt before Jessa had handed me that bottle. So I got out of line, gave the person behind me my spot, swiped a half gallon over to the accounts of each of the other six, and left without saying anything. Then I came back and washed my face and hair in the sink—really *washed* them, with soap and shampoo and hot water, like I haven't done in the better part of a year—and filled up another bottle at the sink and drank it slowly, sitting on the floor with the door locked. I didn't even care that it tasted like purification chemicals, or that it left my face papery and dry. It was water and it was mine.

Almost twenty-one gallons left. After all that. It's not that the math doesn't add up. It's just . . . the kind of thing you hear about happening to other people.

In the background, part of my brain's already scheming. This, plus five gallons a week as long as this mystery job lasts. If I'm careful, and add my daily ration to it, and don't do anything stupid, I won't have to pay for water, at least not to the tune of somewhere north of forty percent of my income, the way it is now. Some for laundry, maybe, and showers, and my share of the gardening water, but I'd have more than usual to drink. I could cut back on my jobs, make enough to pay for food and my space in the room, leave more time for the game. Get my thousand. Make the boards. Maybe even start to climb them. Any *and then* beyond that is the worst kind of self-indulgent daydreaming, therefore unproductive. First things first.

I sneak out of the bathroom past the sleeping bodies, shrug on my coat, shoulder my backpack, and close the heavy door quietly behind me. The elevators haven't worked the whole four years I've lived here, so it's six flights down, just like always. I cut across the lobby, trying not to trip over the holes in the carpet, and on into the company store, which still has the CONFERENCE ROOM C plaque up by the door, just below the stars-and-arrow Stellaxis Innovations logo rendered in slowly rotating holo. I guess the company left it there to look retro. Above the door itself is more retro, neon this time, letters the size of my head: COMFORTS OF HOME.

The store's almost deserted this early in the morning. Just a brisk-looking woman selecting a donut, a couple of teenagers with obvious hangovers arguing over what painkiller to buy, and a man eating from a bag of chips as he walks it past the checkout scanner.

I weave my way among winter coats, designer sunglasses and sneakers, plastic water bottles, candy bars, lens-cleaning kits, a whole shelf of dry shampoo and another of disposable face wipes, toilet paper, multivitamin tabs, batteries, makeup, a display of Stellaxis SecOps action figures, a self-serve ten-flavor soda dispenser, and so on. Your basic company store.

This one's out of filtration masks, because of course it is. I make a note to check again tomorrow, and wander over to park myself in front of the coffee machine.

I fill up a medium, dump three sweeteners in the cup, buy a four-hour energy bar, and head out into the street, where the wind hits me like a cheese grater to the face. My coffee has gone cold before I so much as get it down the front steps onto the sidewalk. I finish it anyway—water's water—then get my bike out of storage and head to my first job of the day.

Like pretty much everyone I know, I have a bunch of different little jobs, some of which pay in cash or credit, some in water, some in random barter. I've had as many as seven at once, but right now I'm holding down four. The game is the most time-consuming one, obviously, but I don't even know anyone who can maintain their expenses on one job alone. Last I heard, Tegan was juggling eight.

So my other jobs right now are: I switch off days with Talya walking dogs. And Tegan and Suresh and Jackson and I shovel snow for people who still live in actual houses. Then on my own I've got this thing I've been trying for a few months where I add yeast to soda to turn it into something like beer for barter with other people in the hotel. I just threw out my third failed batch, but it's not like soda costs much of anything, so I'll probably try again someday. My bottles share windowsill space with everybody's solar chargers and Keisha's sprouting jars.

Today I'm walking two dogs for the Carvalho family, who live in the old high school near the park. It's cold, but the dogs are friendly, and it's a hell of a lot better than a job that keeps you cooped up inside all day. All those office jobs they have down in the city? Sitting at a desk for eight-plus hours? I'd be climbing the walls.

Jessa hates living in old town, but I like it. Whatever town this used to be, forty–fifty years ago before it was abandoned and they built New Liberty City on top of it, is cute in an old-timey kind of way. Sure, living in a hundred-year-old hotel can be loud and crowded and annoying, but it's safe. There's no fighting in the streets, no air strikes, no bombed-out buildings. Old town is neutral territory. Most days I don't even need a filter mask to go outside.

I get to the school quickly, lock up my bike, and let myself into the Carvalho family's room. They're off at work, as usual, so I gather up the dogs and walk them around the back field of the school. I'm not supposed to let them off-leash because of all the tents and garden plots and little kids running around, so I just take them to where there's the remains of an oval track and jog them for a few laps, my mind busily gnawing away on the mystery of whatever Jessa's gotten us into with this new sponsor. The sun is just coming up, not even pretending to take the edge off the cold.

I'm a little over halfway through my paid hour when Jessa calls.

"Change of plans," she says without so much as a hello. She sounds like she's been awake for about thirty seconds. "They want to meet with us as soon as possible. Where are you?"

I'm too tired for sarcasm. "I'm at work," I tell her. "Just like I am literally every other weekday at this time."

"Well, get your ass back here. They're sending a car for us. Don't make them wait."

"Don't you think we kind of need to get out of that field before we start streaming for big sponsors? We're not going to look super impressive if we get our asses handed to us on—"

"We're not going to *have* big sponsors if we piss them off, so get a move on."

I open my mouth to reply, but *CALL ENDED* is flashing across my field of vision. I blink it away and sigh. "Sorry, guys," I tell the dogs. "I'll make it up to you next time."

As I run them back toward the rear doors of the school, it occurs to me that this is the same thing Jessa told me yesterday. I hope I'm more convincing.

THE CAR IS waiting when I get back, idling by the sidewalk, Jessa making hurry-up eyes at me through the rear window while I walk my bike around to the lockup. It's a battered old electric car done over at least twice in flaking suntouch paint, for all the good it's doing in this weather. The sun hasn't come out in days. The fact that they've left the car running on last week's battery charge suggests extravagance, probably deliberate. It's at odds with the general condition of the car itself. It looks like somebody's DIY project. For all I know, it is.

Jessa reaches across the back seat and opens the door for me. I realize why when I get in and see there's no driver. For such an ancient-looking car, this is faintly surprising.

I settle in, trying to calm my nerves. The car's interior is aggressively nondescript. Like it's been expressly calibrated to make it impossible to remember in a witness deposition. Which does wonders for my mood.

"Please fasten your seatbelt," the car tells me, and once I do, it takes off at exactly the speed limit. "Would you like music?"

"No thank you," Jessa says. Then, quieter, to me: "It's just a meeting. Sponsors meet with players all the time. You know this."

"I didn't say anything."

"You were thinking it."

I don't seem to have anything to say to that, so several minutes of silence ensue, both of us looking out our windows. The car pulls out onto the highway and through an underpass, then on past the old mall. People still live there, although it's older than our hotel, and one whole wing of it has totally collapsed, and there's a sinkhole in the parking lot that's visible even from three lanes away at high speed. People live in the lot, too, of course, in tents and lean-tos and campers and cars, just like in the back field of the high school and the old supermarket's parking lot and anywhere the ground is reasonably open and levelish and not too prone to floods big enough to make the news.

Like the hotel, the mall has no name anymore. Nobody knows if the signs just broke or vanished with age, or if Stellaxis had them removed when old town was turned into housing and they didn't want any other brand names appearing on their turf. Probably that.

Jessa and I exchange a look as we whip past the mall and away. We're maybe eight miles from the hotel, and I'm officially the farthest I've been from old town since I came out of the camps and got relocated there four years ago.

Maybe five miles after the mall we start slowing down. Traffic's backed up ahead of us. I see the party lights of cop cars, the gigantic silver-black lump of a roller mech. A checkpoint.

A little noise comes out of Jessa, and she immediately starts twisting around in her seat to get a clear view. "They're not going to post any SecOps out here in the middle of the road," I tell her, although they've certainly done weirder. "It'd be a—" I dredge my memory for the newsfeed phrase—"a disproportionate response."

"They sent 33 and 38 to sit on the checkpoint out by the Monument that one time," she replies.

"Yeah, and 33 and 38 are dead now," I say, as if there's an existing crumb of SecOps trivia on which Jessa needs reminding. "They're not getting sent anywhere."

Jessa isn't listening or doesn't care. She rolls down her window to crane her neck, but right then the potential reality of the situation hits me, and I reach across her to roll it back up. "The air might not be safe," I hiss at her. "This thing is driving us into a *war zone*, Jessa."

I mash my sleeve against my nose and mouth like it's any kind of filter. With my free hand I dig the last two masks out of my backpack, pass one to Jessa, slip the other over my face.

Waiting for the smart paper to adhere to the shape of my mouth and nose, on full alert for whatever might have already come through the windows and landed in my lungs. The soldiers at the checkpoint ahead are in full filtration gear, but I have no idea if that's just checkpoint regulation or if there's an active crisis. Up until now one hundred percent of my checkpoint experience has been from watching news feeds, and one hundred percent of my airborne-chemical-agent experience has been from reading the daily safety announcements and staying inside until the warnings are lifted.

It could be paralytics, it could be hallucinogens, it could be interface scramblers, it could be anything. I strain my senses for vanguard symptoms but come up empty-handed. No tightness in my throat, no warbly feeling behind my eyes, no pins and needles in my scalp, no phantom tastes in my mouth, and my lenses are still online. And there are no public safety warnings flashing on my display.

Which just means it could be something new. Something so new that its clinical presentation doesn't yet trigger an announcement. But I feel fine. Not take-the-mask-off fine, more like barely-avoid-the-inevitable-panic-attack fine, and that's fine enough for now.

Jessa, to my horror, hasn't put her mask on. She's twirling it on one finger, watching me with one raised eyebrow. "You finished?"

"What?"

She rolls her eyes. Rather than deign to reply out loud, my inbox chimes as she forwards me the realtime air quality location tracker so I can lay eyes on the all-clear for myself. "Have a *little* faith in people, Mal, god."

Okay, fine. Point taken. "Sorry," I say. "It's just . . . this is kind of a lot."

"Right? Tell you what. If you get killed out here, you have my permission to haunt me. And, like, I mean, really fuck with me. Go nuts. Make the walls bleed."

Under the mask, my mouth quirks up a little. "Noted."

But we've reached the checkpoint by now, and we both shut up fast and do our best to look like people who know exactly where they're going and exactly what they're planning to do when they get there. Wherever we're going, whoever we're meeting with, whatever we're supposed to do, I'll take my chances with it over an interrogation cell any day. They've got one over by the roller mech, a pop-up prefab gumdrop shape with the Stellaxis logo on the side and a sentry posted at the door. The faint screams I think I hear are probably just in my head.

We roll through the scanner field at walking speed and then

stop while a soldier analyzes the readout and another soldier inspects us through the windows. I do my best to look bored. Jessa is attempting the same, though it lasts about three seconds before she's twisting around to stare some more, like she really thinks she stands any chance of spotting 06 or 21 or whoever out here scanning traffic at the ass crack of dawn. I try to ignore how nervous she's making me. "You look like a tourist," I mutter at her.

"Well, we kind of are," she replies.

I guess they're used to this kind of thing, because nobody flags it as suspicious, at least not visibly. Almost immediately there's a soldier waving us on. The car speeds up and joins the stream of traffic exiting the scanner fields in other lanes, and within a mile we're in among the glass and steel and concrete of New Liberty City. It spreads around us exponentially like something unfolding.

If we might have looked like tourists before, we probably definitely do now. We both used to live here, of course, just like Tegan and Talya and Suresh and Jackson and Keisha and Allie and Ryan, and everyone else in the hotel and the mall and all the schools, all throughout old town. But it was so long ago most of us don't remember. Or if we do, we remember the *idea* of the city more than the real thing. The version that's on the newsfeeds and the entertainment feeds and in the movies. And, of course, in the game.

The real thing looks both shinier and dirtier, bigger and smaller, safer and more dangerous, realer and more fake. Which of course makes no sense. But I can tell from Jessa's face that she's thinking pretty much the same thing.

Weird to think how we used to live here with families like normal city people, before our families died in the war, one way or another, and we were relocated from camp to camp until we washed up in old town. I haven't seen my family since I was eight. That's twelve years ago. Of course, I'm not supposed to think sad things about the war dead. I'm supposed to think about how they died for free trade and liberty and American values, like they stood on the front line themselves and laid down suppressive fire on the enemy.

Except they didn't die fighting. They died halfway through Friday pizza dinner because somebody's smart bomb wasn't as smart as they thought. I'm only here in this car in one piece because my parents took the ninety-second warning the proximity alert gave them and spent it tossing me in the bathtub with a blanket and a bottle of water and some granola bars and my favorite stuffed dog and then piled in on top of me and told me bad jokes to keep me from crying.

I don't even remember my mom's face that clearly, but I remember the last joke she told:

Why don't you ever see elephants hiding in trees?
Because they're really good at it.

And I remember the sound of that bomb. It came down on us like something singing. Like a bird. It took the rescue team two days to find me, and that sound stayed trapped in my head that whole time, echoing.

Sometimes I wonder where all our dead families are buried. Somehow I can't picture a graveyard here, not like the one near the diner in old town, with the moss on the gravestones and those huge, ancient trees.

Not that we all had bodies to bury. Keisha's family was vaporized in a nano strike. Suresh's grandmother caught a resonance grenade at a protest and was reduced to a puddle of sludge inside a minute. Tegan and Talya's parents were crushed like mine, but in the lobby of their building, with three hundred apartments landing on top of them. It's only because Tegan and Talya were out playing on the sidewalk that they survived.

My mom didn't even have time to tell me that punchline herself. I came across the same joke one time by accident, years later, somewhere online.

ONCE UPON A time I guess there was a government that did things. Once upon a time it had its own military, took care of the country's infrastructure, education, that kind of thing. I wonder if the government would have fought the war the way the corporations do. I wonder if it would have been more careful.

Once upon a time there were lots of corporations. Hundreds. Thousands, maybe, I don't know. Once upon a time the government decided to give fifty-one of the biggest corporations control of the fifty-one states there used to be. They just auctioned them off, the way Jessa auctions off her duplicate SecOps merch online. But the corporations merged with each other and bought each other out and took each other over, and when they did, they took control of those corporations' states at the same time.

Once upon a time Stellaxis Innovations didn't control upwards of ninety percent of the country's water. Once upon a time Greenleaf Industries didn't control upwards of ninety percent of the country's agribusiness. They didn't even start out as water and agribusiness companies. They grew and rebranded and renamed and sucked other corporations into themselves like black holes—biotech, pharma, entertainment, communications, defense industries, you name it—until there were only two left standing. Stellaxis and Greenleaf.

At the time of the last merger, a few years before I was born, there were forty-five states left that didn't belong to the ocean. Stellaxis Innovations had control of twenty-three of them, and Greenleaf Industries had the other twenty-two. Then I guess they decided they weren't going to merge anymore, just divide what was left of what used to be a country between them.

One of Stellaxis's states used to be New York. One of Greenleaf's states used to be Massachusetts. But their original company HQs have been sitting under a few dozen feet of salt water along with good-size pieces of their company-states since the late twenty-first century, long before the last merger. So, at the turn of the century, when New Liberty City was built along with the other amalgam supercities, it was built as kind of a mash-up of the two.

There are nine supercities in total. All huge, all built on the same principle as a kid putting her sandcastle well back from the tide.

But either the other supercities didn't spark corporate turf wars or they settled them some other way, but in any case, right now Stellaxis and Greenleaf each own four. I've heard it's because Stellaxis was founded in New York City and Greenleaf was founded in Boston that they both kind of took the idea of controlling New Liberty a little more personally. Of all the supercities, it's the only one that's been sparking and smoldering its way through civil war for longer than Jessa or I or anyone else in our room has been alive. Stellaxis HQ on the west edge of the city, Greenleaf HQ on the east, throwing punches at each other like a couple of cage fighters trying to get control of the ring. The outcome of which makes more or less fuckall practical difference to the forty-eight million people who happen to live in the cage.

I don't know anyone old enough to remember the prewar world. We all make vague when-it's-over noises, sure, but nobody really has any kind of clear sense what that might imply. What the world might look like without Stellaxis Innovations SecOps and Greenleaf Industries mechs kicking each other's asses in the streets every day. Without water rations and air quality alerts and checkpoints and housing lotteries. We've seen old movies, seen people living in houses with lawns, water that runs out of the faucet for free. Traveling wherever the fuck they like.

When Stellaxis wins the war, things will be better. No more fighting. No more power curfew. No more water rationing. The cost of food will drop. Travel restrictions will lift. Where I come from, you learn that around the time you learn your ABCs.

It sounds . . . if I'm honest, really truly brutally honest with myself, I don't even know. A world without all those things is hard to imagine living in. It might as fucking well be Jupiter.

THE CAR SLIDES through traffic in silence and eventually stops across the street from a park. It's not much of one, just a rectangle of grass maybe the size of the company store. No playground for kids, not like the one near the old town high school. All there is is a statue, dusted with either old snow or pigeon shit or maybe both. Too far away to make out what it's even a statue of. Some people standing together around something. There's a sign at the edge of the dead grass that reads PROSPERITY PARK.

"Here?" I ask the car. "Are you sure?"

"Positive," the car replies. "Look to your right. Two hundred yards."

I look. Past the statue, way back at the rear of the park, I spot a woman sitting on a bench, her face obscured by steam from a dispenser coffee. She raises her chin incrementally in my direction.

"Game on," Jessa tells me, which doesn't strike me as being nearly as funny as she probably intends.

We get out of the car. As soon as we shut our doors behind us, it leaves.

JESSA AND I WORK OUR WAY THROUGH the park, following the clear trail of a paved jogging path through the snow. Our route takes us past the statue, close enough to make out what it represents. It's a group of figures posing in a ring, young people in clean-cut uniforms, holding the broken earth between them like they can push it back together by force.

The statue looks brand-new, or like it's been here forever. It looks like something out of the game. In fact I'm pretty sure I've *seen* it in the game. I feel momentarily dizzy.

I count the figures as I go past, although I already know how many there'll be.

Beside me, Jessa gives a little gasp. "That's *When All Else Fails*," she says, pointing to the statue. "I've only seen it in-game." She elbows me. "Look, there's your good friend 28."

I glance up. From this angle, 28 is beaming down at me beatifically. *Someone should really teach you how to drive that thing.*

"Whatever this is, it better be good," I say. I shove my hands in my pockets and walk faster.

When we're maybe twenty feet from the bench, the woman doubles over cursing, messing with her face.

I hurry the last few steps. "Hey. You okay?"

"It's the grit in the air," she says, blinking hard. "It's screwing with my lenses. This happens almost every day lately. Don't you notice it?"

She removes one lens, then the other, and pops them in their case. She looks back up at me like she's trying to project a thought into my head. Which is strange. If she'd just kept the lenses in, she could have messaged—

Oh.

Here's the thing, though. Do I trust this random stranger?

I hesitate, but just for a second. Whatever this is, it's shaping up to be more interesting than whatever I'd be doing back home. Besides, I have my taser in my backpack in case things go wrong.

"Ow," I say. "Oh wow. You're right, it's pretty bad here." I swing my backpack around to get at my lens case. "Oh well, I needed to clean these anyway." I pop the lenses out of my eyes and into the case, making sure to position myself in full view of Jessa while I do it.

Lucky for me, she's smart. She takes about point-five seconds to catch on and take her lenses out too, muttering about air quality and half-assed public safety announcements, a continuous stream of self-righteous irritation that stops abruptly as soon as she shuts the lid on the case. She folds her arms and watches the woman on the bench with the dialed-back aggrievement of a person who really wants to protest a situation and equally really does not want to screw up a potential future situation by doing so.

Her mouth works. Eventually she settles on: "Anything else? You want us to dig out our implants while we're at it? Burn off our fingerprints, maybe?" With this weird pasted-on grin that's not fooling anyone. She's shaken.

The woman smiles. Gets up off the bench. Throws me a wink. "I thought you were supposed to be the uptight one," she tells me. "This way. Do me a favor and don't follow too close." She takes off, out of the park and down the sidewalk.

Jessa and I exchange a look, then follow, talking to each other in low tones like somebody's listening. This no-lenses thing has got me paranoid. Who *takes out* their lenses? Why?

"No real names," I whisper, not that it'll really end up mattering. If we're walking into something shady, our in-game handles will tie us to it just as effectively. To say nothing of the twenty surveillance cameras that probably have eyes on us right now.

Jessa nods, a compressed gesture that could have been a twitch.

"She say anything last night about the no-lenses thing? I swear, if this turns out to be creeper shit—"

"I've got my taser," she says.

"Me too."

"We could just put our lenses back in," she says, nodding to where the woman's orange knit hat is bobbing in and out of the crowd ahead. Still whispering, like we're within anything resembling earshot to anything short of a SecOps operative. Whoever this woman is, she is definitely not that. "She's way up there."

"Don't you even think about it," I tell her. "You wanted to do this, we're doing this. You dragged me out here. I'm out here. Now we see how it plays out."

How it plays out is the woman leads us to a hole-in-the-wall coffee shop wedged in between a lens outfitters and a hair-and-nails place, so tiny it doesn't even have a proper sign, just an old-school chalkboard out front that says, imaginatively, COFFEE.

Inside it smells amazing. Real coffee, or maybe just better dispenser coffee than what I'm used to. I'm not exactly an expert. All I know is that I want to get a bucket of it and stick my windburned face directly inside.

By the time my eyes adjust to the cozy lighting, the woman has seated herself at a far table, back in a corner but with a clear view of the door. That uptight part of me I keep getting called out on wonders dimly if that's relevant, but I shrug and head over to the table with Jessa.

The woman stares at us each in turn, like she's reading some kind of deep meaning in our faces. "QueenOfTheRaids," she says. "Nycorix."

"Morning," I say with forced casualness. "And you are?"

"Call me B," the woman says, and I have no idea if she's saying Bea or Bee or that her code name handle is B, the way we don't know anything about the SecOps operatives' names, if they even have names, just the numbers they were assigned when they passed quality control and were declared fit for duty.

"Please," B says. "Order anything you like."

I'm still running on my crappy coffee and my energy bar, and I don't need to be told twice.

I swipe the table to bring up a menu, and Jessa and I spend a few minutes perusing it before settling on triple hot chocolate with soywhip and rainbow sprinkles (Jessa), extra-large dark roast coffee with soy creamer (me), and cookies the size of our faces for both of us (chocolate chunk for Jessa, oatmeal raisin for me). I also throw in an orange juice, because I don't think I've had a real one since I was a kid. Jessa makes a little *ooo* sound when she sees me doing this, so I tap the icon again.

I gesture like I'm going to spin the menu around to B, but she waves it off. "They know me here," she says, and right on cue the server hovers over with a coffee and muffin on its little tray.

So I hit send on the menu, then swipe it away. Jessa and I sit and try not to look awkward while B goes through some kind of breakfast ritual of situating her muffin precisely in front of her, sweetening her coffee one fraction of a teaspoon at a time, and so on.

Jessa's foot nudges mine under the table. If we had our lenses in, she'd be screaming at me in messages right now. I nudge back, as if to say *I have no frigging idea. Just ride it out.* As if I'm the one who wanted this.

B takes a calculated sip of coffee, a measured bite of muffin, while we try not to stare. Our order arrives. I apply myself to my coffee, counting seconds in my head. I get to thirty-five before, without so much as an *I apologize for being less than forthcoming in messages* or a *sorry for making you take your lenses out with no warning* or a *my regrets about making you sit here waiting for answers while I take the longest amount of time humanly possible to arrive at some kind of point,* B says, out of nowhere: "How much do you know about Stellaxis's SecOps operatives?"

Jessa nearly spit-takes her soywhip. Usually, spouting Sec-Ops operative trivia ends with pillows being thrown at her head. Clearly, this is her time to shine. I don't even bother opening my mouth.

"Oh," she says. "Well. Where to even begin. It's probably fastest if you tell me what kind of stats you're after. I can give you height, weight, rank, blood type, hours in the field, notable engagements, favorite food, date of death—for the ones that applies to, obviously—preferred fighting style, date of deployment, favorite pastime . . ."

B is staring at her with open fascination. She cuts a glance at me, and I shrug, helpless. "She's the expert."

"Oh, don't sell yourself short," Jessa says. "I know for a *fact* that you—"

"Or did you mean the in-game versions?" I ask B. Not loudly enough to draw attention, I hope, but loud enough to cut Jessa off midsentence. "I mean, it's our stream you're sponsoring." I pause fractionally, waiting for her to contradict this. She doesn't. Which does little to take the edge off my confusion. "Right?"

"Of course," B says. "And I suppose the most accurate answer to your question is *both*. Both the real and the in-game versions. As the one is so firmly based on the other."

"Well," Jessa says, and you can pretty much see the fangirl dynamo reignite behind her eyes, "the in-game versions are high-level NPCs whose personalities are patterned after the actual operatives. They update them periodically as the operatives get older—well, *older* isn't exactly—never mind—so they stay accurate for a *more immersive experience!*" This last in a breathless voice that could have fallen out of an ad. I know her well enough to know this tone was aimed at irony, but sounds more like irony that's crawled far enough up its own ass to come out the other end as sincerity. "It's all from some huge database Stellaxis keeps on the whole SecOps program. I guess they get the info from the operatives' implants or surveillance cameras or something? Nobody really knows. Anyway, wherever they get it, they have it, and it all goes into the in-game ones. Dialogue, mannerisms, fighting style, all of it. Some of it, like the blood type, they have to make that up, of course, but when it's all put together like that it makes, like, a story? All the way down to what they do when nobody's interacting with them and they're just, like, minding their own business walking around or whatever. Really intricately detailed stuff."

She pauses for air. B makes a go-on face. Jessa runs with it.

"*Really* intricately detailed. Super sophisticated. One time me and Nyx found 17 just sitting on the edge of that statue out there, you know, the one in the park we just came from? He had this whole bag of donuts he'd gotten somewhere, and he was just stuffing them into his mouth one by one, whole, like he'd never had donuts before and he was never gonna have them again. And there were all these pigeons, just coming out of nowhere, and he was throwing pieces to them, even though you could see in his face he really didn't want to share . . ." Another pause. "I mean. Maybe the real 17 never got to *have* donuts, not in real life, you know? He was so young when he died." She looks down at her cookie and hot chocolate, the rainbow sprinkles bleeding into the melty soywhip. "He probably would have loved this stuff."

The silence stretches.

"Like when we found 28 last night," I cut in. "Nobody was using her, so she was just wandering around reading, killing time."

The phrase sounds weird even as it's leaving my mouth. Killing time. Especially when you consider how the 28 we found is nothing but information coded into a game, and how the real 28 is dead. And was never even really *alive* to begin with. *Dead* is just shorthand that feeds the same narrative as *blood type* and *favorite food*. Damaged beyond repair, I guess. Destroyed.

"And what she said to me when she saw me, that's different from what 17 would have said if we'd found him instead, or 02 or 33 or any of them."

"33 tried to chase us off that one time," Jessa says, brightening again. "With a sword."

"That happens," I agree, and sip my coffee gratefully while she takes the conversation back over.

"So," Jessa says. "Whoever has the top position in the day's leaderboard can recruit one SecOps NPC of their choice to be, like, an ally? And that NPC stays with their player until someone knocks that player off the top of the leaderboard and gets to choose their own operative NPC instead. That—the real high-level stuff—is the bread and butter of a lot of top-tier streamers because whoever's got the operative is scrambling to keep him or her, and everyone else is trying to knock that player off the boards, and there's millions of people watching this play out. Having an operative on your side makes a huge difference, of course, but it paints a giant target on your back at the same time. It's like a whole other game inside the game."

"They don't just use the operatives to fight, though," I say between sips. This coffee really is very good.

Jessa pulls a face. "No. You earn the favor of one of the NPCs, you get them all to yourself until you lose them, but there's nothing saying what you can or can't do with them during that time. Some people get . . . creative."

"Sex stuff," I say, nodding at my coffee.

"Don't listen to her," Jessa tells B. "I mean, yeah, okay, *sometimes*? But it's not allowed with any of the operatives who are underage. Or whatever the equivalent of that is for them. Or whether you even count as underage if you're dead. But okay. Sex stuff aside. Though those streams are exactly as popular as you'd expect when they *do* happen, they don't happen *often*."

I snort. "I think you'd be surpri—"

"*Most of it* is intended-use gaming. You get your fighting buddy, go fight, rack up a zillion points, try to stay on top of the heap. Good clean fun." She eyes me pointedly, then rolls her gaze back to fix on B. "Sometimes it's just random stuff that's supposed to be funny. One time I saw someone put 38 in a frilly pink dress and set up this little-kid tea party with her and some stuffed animals and dolls they found in some bombed-out building somewhere. She was so confused. It lasted about two hours, and it's all anyone was watching that afternoon. It was absolutely massive. 38 just kept saying, 'I really don't think this is authorized.' Nyx, remember that? It turned into this huge meme for like a week, nobody could shut up about . . ." Jessa trails off. "Where was I going with that?"

I spread my hands at her expansively.

"Anyway. I forget who did that, the thing with 38, but who-ever it was, they're set for a while. I've seen streamers go from zero to superfame just by getting their hands on these guys, even if they only keep them for five minutes."

"But first you have to get on the boards," I say.

Jessa nods. "First you have to get on the boards. In case you don't know," she tells B, "you get on the boards by killing a thou-sand mobs—um, nonplayer enemies—in a given day. That gives you access to try to climb the leaderboard for the next twenty-four hours. You make your thousand every day, you keep that chance every day. You don't, you fall behind. It's really time-consuming and *really* hard to actually climb the board once you get on it. Nycorix here could tell you all about that part."

I busy myself with a bite of my cookie, because it's either that or I kick her under the table. She doesn't seem to notice.

"Anyway, in terms of keeping a SecOps NPC away from other players, the standing record is still from '31, when GeneralRei managed to hold on to 11 for *nine and a half days,* and *she—*"

Left to her own devices, Jessa would plummet straight down this rabbit hole and drag us both with her. Her enthusiasm is one of the things I like best about her—I find it baffling and ad-mirable in pretty much equal measure—but once she gets really spun up, it can be hard to shut her down. I can't tell if B is too polite or too awkward to interrupt this force-of-nature mono-logue, so I do us all a favor.

"She knows all this," I tell Jessa. Then, sliding my gaze over to B: "You *must* know all this. If we're not here because of the footage we got of 28 last night, then—"

B has no trouble cutting *me* off, at least. "I saw. Impressive driving."

"Thanks," I say. "But we're not here because I trashed the bike to get like three seconds of dark footage of 28 on a nature walk."

"No," B says. "You're not."

Jessa looks up from her hot chocolate.

"Okay," I say. "Then why?"

"Because you fit all of our criteria," B says.

"Criteria for wh—"

"You're solid middle-of-the-road streamers. You have a following, but a modest one. You're capable enough, but not star players. You're not famous enough to draw attention, but that means you have more potential for an upward trajectory. With the right sponsor, of course." She smiles. I'm trying to squash down my cynicism long enough to fail to translate all this as *You're small enough to buy.* "And you were local enough to meet up with in person. I always prefer that."

"Wait," I say. "*Our* criteria?"

"Is that why you had us take out our lenses?" Jessa asks over top of me.

B's pause is almost imperceptible. "Call me old-school, I guess." Then, to me: "My family and I are sponsoring you jointly. My brother's account fronts your payment, but it comes from all of us. This is my sister's place we're sitting in. She helped me set up this meeting."

I don't know anyone with that much surviving family. Not by a long shot. I assume she must mean *dead sister, inherited coffee shop,* but B is pointing toward one of the baristas behind the counter. She's got a MANAGER pin on her apron. They don't look much alike, but that doesn't mean anything. Maybe one of them's adopted. Maybe they both are. They look to be wearing matching earrings, and at the moment that's good enough for me. The moronic notion takes sudden root in me that the sister's name might be A.

"Okay, but this list of criteria of yours must describe a thousand streamers just like us in a five-mile radius. Why us? Specifically."

For a long moment B says nothing, just holds my gaze. Under the table, Jessa is grinding her heel into my instep. I pull my foot away and kick her.

"Well," B says. "You *did* find 28. If I recall correctly, 28 doesn't really tend to make herself available to *be* found. She avoids interaction."

Beside me Jessa is nodding furiously. "Almost as much as 22 does, which is saying something. We picked up another couple hundred followers for last night's session," she says. "Might even be more by now. I'd know if I had my lenses in."

"Why don't *you* play?" I ask B. "It's not like we find 28 on a daily basis. This is the first time I've ever seen her close up. She's a real asshole, too, by the way. Who knows, maybe you'd make the boards and get her all to yourself for a while. Do whatever the hell you want with her."

Another long silence. On the one hand I'm starting to regret continuing to dig this hole. *FIVE GALLONS A WEEK* is blaring through my head in neon two-hundred-point font. Jessa will murder me in cold blood if I blow this, as she should.

But on the other hand, I've always been crap at letting go of things I don't understand, and that doesn't seem to be suddenly changing today.

"I would if I could," B admits eventually. "If I didn't still have three-plus years on my interface lockout, you wouldn't be sitting here. Anyway it's not 28 I'm after. *Specifically.*" This last comes out with obvious mockery, but mild enough, and no more than I probably deserve.

"*Three*-plus years?" I sputter. "What'd you *do*?"

"Domestic terrorism," she says. "I was collecting rainwater on my roof and purifying it. Giving the extra away in the camps. I didn't last two weeks before they caught me." She catches the look on my face and is hasty to clarify: "That's not where we got the water we sent to your accounts. We pooled our money and bought that. This is all aboveboard, I promise."

"Nyx was wondering why you didn't pay cash," Jessa pipes up.

B grins. "I was hoping to get your attention. I assume it worked."

Jessa raises her cup a little in acknowledgment, then gives me a double take when she sees I'm not doing the same. I don't know. It feels a little too much like we're being handled.

B notices. "Don't worry. Future payments can be made in cash or company credit, if you prefer, and after today, there's no need for us to see each other again, if that concerns you, which I can tell from your face that it does. After today, I will happily sponsor you at an anonymous distance. I just wanted to see who I was working with. Whether you seemed reliable. For the record, you make a good first impression."

Jessa nods sympathetically. "There's someone upstairs of us who's serving a one-year lockout for something like what happened to you," she says. "He stole a bottle of water from the company store. Just stuck it in his pocket and walked. Nothing in his account for the scanner to take."

"No wonder they hit you so hard," I add. "Processing your own potable water, that's a hardcore offense." I hear a note of admiration in my own voice that I don't fully understand. I change the subject. "So, what? You watched our stream on a public computer somewhere?"

"Sure did. It is exactly as laggy and awkward as you're imagining. Hey, at least nobody's bombed the library yet. Then I'd really be in trouble."

"So wait." I lean forward. "Back at the park. You didn't have any lenses to take out. You're locked out. Why wear lenses that don't interface?"

A smile tugs up the corner of B's mouth. "That's right. I'm still allowed to use public computers, and I can sponsor who I want. I have a job, I have an income. It's all on the level. But the fact remains I'm on a list, and I figured you didn't want a whole conversation with a convicted terrorist on record." She holds up both hands palm out. "Don't worry, though," she continues. "Like I said, this place belongs to my sister. Nobody's listening."

I mentally probe this, rolling it around and around in my head, trying to gauge my level of shock and upset at what B's said. Minimal, honestly. I'd probably run out of fingers before I listed all the people I've known who've gone down on terrorism charges at one time or another. The water bottle guy, sure, but also a family at the school who was recycling their wastewater, a woman who hacked her water account to get into rationing lines at three different buildings, a group of teenagers who were filtering and selling river water, a couple who straight-up rolled a keg off a ration truck, that kind of thing. I bet on the Greenleaf Industries side of the city they bust you for keeping a garden instead. Keisha's sprout jars would probably be enough to put her away.

Periodically, Suresh and Keisha and Tegan will get drunk and take their lenses out and have this big whispered cooperative rant about the merits of a corporation that supplies neonatal brain implants and interfaced lenses for free but charges more for water than most people can begin to afford. "They position themselves as gatekeepers for this whole world," Keisha will say, tapping her forehead like she can touch the implant through her skull and two inches of brain tissue.

"And they lock people out of it for being *thirsty*," Suresh will add. "When they're the ones keeping the water, too."

"So have a march or something," Talya told them once, and Tegan rounded on her.

"A *march*. And that would accomplish what exactly? They'd blockade us in the street and jack up the price on the water they sell us. Think about it. This is the same company that owns the record labels that sign the artists that write the resistance songs. Protest as a form of war profiteering. They love every minute of it."

I realize Jessa is looking to me for a reaction. I nod once at B decisively. "We're good." But I'm a long way from putting my lenses back in. "Still confused, though. What exactly is this all about?"

"You know a lot about the SecOps characters in-game," B says immediately, like she's been waiting to drop this on us the whole time. "What about the real ones? Where did they come from?"

This knocks Jessa back a step. Me too, if I'm honest. There's a trick hidden somewhere in this question, otherwise why would she be asking it? Even though on the face of it the answer is painfully easy. It's as if B asked us why trees are green, or why this city was built, or why it's Tuesday.

"Stellaxis made them," I say slowly, trying not to let my impatience show. "The SecOps program. They're synthetic humans, they're weapons, they grew them in a lab somewh—"

"No," B says. "They didn't."

Something happens to her voice when she says this. It makes me think of movies, how you have this perfectly still body of water that gives this single ominous ripple that promises that within the next five minutes, somebody's getting dragged in to die.

A red leather wallet has appeared on the table where B's muffin used to be. She's opening it up and turning it toward us to show us an actual printed paper photo behind clear plastic. Old-school indeed.

B waits wordlessly as Jessa and I lean in.

The girl in the photo is maybe seven years old. She's on the roof of what's probably an apartment building, somewhere in the north end of the city. In the background you can just make out the Monument, glinting silver in the sun. It's not a snow-man the girl is posed next to, but something like it. A snow . . . dog, maybe? Something she's built and is in the process of being photographed next to. She's wearing a blue snowsuit and no hat. There's snow melting in her hair. She's grinning, but that's for the camera. There's something else entirely in her eyes.

"I took this picture almost thirteen years ago," B says qui-etly. She taps the girl's forehead, just above the left eyebrow, where a glaring white strip of smart bandage catches the cam-era flash like a bike reflector. "I was babysitting while her par-ents were at work. She was so excited to get out in the snow that she tripped coming out onto the roof and fell on the edge of the snow shovel she was carrying. Gashed her forehead open. Bled like you wouldn't believe. I asked her if she wanted to stay in and watch cartoons, but she said no, so I put this bandage on her and she ran straight back outside. It's the only picture I have left of her. The only proof I have that she even existed."

B's hands have taken to swirling her coffee absently, round and round. I glance into the cup. It's empty.

"The next summer this building was gone," she says. "Dropped into the street by some mech gunner's bad aim. The warnings always say to stay inside when the fighting reaches your street, but what they don't tell you is that a direct hit from a plasma cannon will bring a thirty-story building down like a house of cards, and that everyone in it dies anyway. At least, almost everyone."

Her gaze sweeps upward and pans back and forth between Jessa and me, expectant. I have no idea what she wants, so I nod. This seems to disappoint her.

"You have to give them credit," she says. "They were care-ful. They must have picked them up from hospitals or shelters or something. Little kids who had no families left. Nobody to

know or even suspect they might be still alive." She chuckles a little to herself, humorlessly. "What they didn't count on was the *fucking babysitter.*"

This monologue isn't really giving us anything else to work with. We're both frozen, staring, essaying polite nods like we have the first faintest clue what she's talking about.

B's disappointment visibly deepens. I begin to kiss my five gallons a week goodbye.

"Do you remember when the operatives became overnight celebrities?" B asks abruptly. "The company started making all the t-shirts and posters and soda flavors and action figures, and put their virtual analogues into the game?"

Relief radiates off Jessa as she finds her path again. "Sure," she says, sketching a fake-casual shrug that almost sends her elbow into my side, she's that tense. "About eight years ago. When they came out of their growth tanks and passed quality control and were sent out to the front to fight for our economic freedom. The action figures and stuff came first, though. Almost immediately, really. The game wasn't until a few years later. And it wasn't just a case of putting the operatives in. The game already existed. They designed the whole war module. There are I don't know how many of them in BestLife. Modules, I mean."

"A bunch," I say.

Jessa nods. "I want to say at least a dozen? There's a space one, a fantasy thing with dragons, a time travel one, I think? The war module is just one of them. That's where the SecOps NPCs live."

Then, a smidge defensively to my ears, she doubles back. "Yes, okay, the marketing stuff looks tacky, but it's genius if you think about it. It makes people care, you know? People like to feel involved. This makes them feel like what they're doing is, I don't know, relevant somehow."

"By buying t-shirts," I say dryly. I know it's not the time or place, but this is a long-standing thing between us, and it's out before I can stop it.

"By *taking* an *interest*," Jessa sniffs. "Lack of complacency is a political statement."

"Collect soda cups to support the war, that kind of thing?"

"Please. It's not like *you* don't—"

"Growth tanks," B echoes, like we haven't moved off on this whole other stupid tangent by now. "It's amazing what total media consensus will make people believe."

We look at her. She's gazing down at her picture of this random girl. We wait for her to say something else, but she's gone quiet. Sad because this girl died, I guess. I mean, it *is* sad, but honestly, who doesn't have a story like that? My whole family died in this war. And Jessa's and Keisha's and Jackson's and everyone's. And no amount of t-shirts and action figures is going to bring them back.

B is sliding a second photo out from behind this one. Concealing it in her hand like a card trick.

"When they brought the operatives out of the Stellaxis labs," she says softly, "I heard about it vaguely on some newsfeed. I was walking down the street when the first headlines broke. I only really paid half attention to the news clip. A superweapon that could stand up to Greenleaf Industries' infiltrator mechs and resonator ordnance and mantis drones, really turn the war around."

This time she goes quiet long enough that Jessa leans in and touches B's arm gently. "And?"

"And. And then I saw the ads. They were everywhere. All of a sudden. I don't know where they came from so fast. Within an hour they were on every display. Every billboard, every taxi, embedded into every article on my newsfeed. I didn't look too closely at them at first. And then when I did, at first I didn't believe what I was seeing."

"That they looked like kids?" Jessa supplies, nodding know-ingly. "I remember there being a lot of debate about that at first, but it settled down after—"

"No. Not that they *looked like* kids. That they *were* kids. That Stellaxis Innovations was lying through its teeth about where they came from. The operatives didn't come out of any growth tanks. They were stolen. They were orphaned and vulnerable and had no families left to look for them, and so Stellaxis took them and put them in their labs for years and *changed* them. Turned them into tools to fight their corporate war. Until it killed them. One by one by one."

"Wait," Jessa says. "What? That's not—"

B doesn't seem to hear her. "They're celebrities, but we don't know *anything* about them. Height, weight, blood type. Those are collector-card stats, not information. Nobody *knows* these people. They don't have friends or families to go home to—hell, they don't have *homes.* They live in Stellaxis HQ. We get the version of events Stellaxis feeds us. Online profiles and news clips and airbrushed posters and I bet you know someone who has a story about seeing 33 up close at some checkpoint or 06 pulling some civilians out of some wreckage, but that's it. Everything about them—everything that matters—is classified. They're somebody's lab project. And we don't even know what they called that project, back when it was an experiment not yet ready to be announced to the world as the wildly successful, tide-changing, table-turning, war-winning *Stellaxis StelTech SecOps program.*" B does something annoyed with her eye-brows. "Some stupid name, probably, if historical precedent is any kind of indication."

She's lost me, but I don't dare admit it. I nod like I under-stand. Beside me, Jessa is doing the same. A moment passes while B fidgets with the photo in her hand, cupping it like if she held it to her ear she'd hear the ocean.

"What kind of celebrity is kept that locked down? They live in that lab. They come out and fight, they go back in. Rinse, repeat. We get the news footage of them working, we get the announcements when they achieve some kind of victory, we get a remembrance flare when one dies. Sometimes, here in the city, you'll see them out there fighting—" here Jessa perks up and is met by the wall of B's gaze—"but if you're close enough to get a good look at that, you've probably got bigger problems. The collateral damage projections in their typical workplace environment are, shall we say, not encouraging. But for the most part, the only versions of the operatives we have easy access to are the in-game analogues."

Whatever rail her train of thought is barreling down, I can't see where it's headed. Glimpses of the photo make it through her caged fingers. B catches me looking, raises her hand a little. Does not open it.

"So I went home that day and I dug this old picture out of storage, and I ran it through one of those extrapolator apps that shows you what you'll look like when you're old, or what your new baby will look like as an adult, or . . ." She trails off. "I guess part of the reason I approached you two is that you remind me of her. I looked you up after watching your stream." *So much for no real names*, I think. "She'd look a little like you now, and she'd be pretty much exactly your age if . . ." B gives us a once-over. "Nineteen? Twenty?"

We nod.

"Well. This is about as old as she got."

B opens her hand.

The other picture is of a girl maybe fifteen years old. She's got slightly wide-set eyes, roundish cheeks, raised eyebrows, lifted chin. She looks like she's just asked us a question and is waiting with a dwindling supply of patience for our answer.

The app has erased her grin and replaced it with a neutral

closed mouth, deleted the smart bandage, and given her a scar in its place. Thick brown hair falls heavily past her shoulders.

I swallow. The app has messed up the hairstyle, but as for the rest—

"That's 05," Jessa says, and her tone is a perfect distillation of my thoughts. She blinks across the table at B in confusion.

"No," B replies evenly, and I realize I've been utterly misreading the quiet in her tone. It's not shyness or nerves or worry or even sadness. It's anger, curled and ready like a fist. "That's Elena."

IT'S ANOTHER TWO HOURS BEFORE JESSA AND I are home. We say nothing of the meeting the whole way back to the car (which has reappeared exactly where we left it earlier) or on the long ride back through the darkening winter afternoon to the hotel. It's not a taxi, but that's no guarantee the car isn't recording. I have no intention of reinserting my lenses until I'm back in my own space, around people I can trust. Not that I plan to relay to them everything I've just been told, either. The basics will do just fine. New sponsor. Weekly swipes to our water accounts. We'll do something to celebrate, probably, like always when someone in our room picks up a sweet gig. Get some snacks from the company store, a few buckets of soda, and put on a movie. Nothing big. We all have to get up early tomorrow anyway. New job and all.

Not that we've been asked to do anything illegal, anything that will land us on a lockout list like B. Just . . . keep doing what we're doing, basically. Same stuff, better pay. And the one condition: we get as much detailed footage of as many operatives as possible. Get right up in their faces. Look for distinguishing marks like 05's—Elena's—scar. While B, from her library or wherever, collects screenshots. Takes notes. For some reason I picture her tacking all these up on the walls wherever she lives, running strings between pushpins like she's living in some old crime movie.

We're just doing what we always do, I remind myself. She's just a sponsor. She's paying us to play the game. Whatever she does with our streamed footage is her business. We don't have to meet with her again. We play the game. We run our stream. We collect our water. That's all.

If I thought about it, I might be insulted that B knew she could buy us that easily. Small-time streamers who have to hold down four jobs and wait nicely in line for their daily water rations like good patriotic customer-citizens. But a job's a job, and water's water, and I'm reasonably sure B's weird suspicions aren't anything that can incriminate us if she decides to go off the deep end somehow. We're just playing the game.

On that long quiet ride home, I go over bits of the meeting in my mind.

After showing us the photo of Elena, she gave us an envelope. When we opened it, I began to understand more than ever why she wanted to meet in person. It wasn't the sort of thing I'd email someone over trackable channels.

It was a list of names. Descriptions. Ages, all varying between seven and nine. Identifying marks. A few sketches of faces done with varying levels of artistic ability. Only a couple of photos, both untouched and run through the same aging-extrapolator app, then printed. Neither looks like any of the SecOps faces in the ads. In the news. In the game.

"Who would have photos of these kids?" B said when I asked. "Their families are gone. Most of the schools were destroyed. They have nobody to look for them, to even know there's someone there to look *for*. As far as the system's concerned, they're ghosts. These—" pointing to the couple of photos—"are the exception, not the rule. Situations like mine. The Martinez family—Elena's family—was close with ours. That's how I kept getting roped into babysitting. But for every twenty-thirty vaporized families, there's maybe one school bus driver or librarian or friend of a friend of a friend who's alive." She tapped the list without looking at it, somewhere between *girl, age 8, dark skin/brown eyes/black hair, bitten nails, mild eczema* and *boy, age 7, light skin/blue eyes/red hair, scar on right knee (bicycle accident)*. "And remembers."

Something shifted at that, way in the back of my mind. Whatever this was, it wasn't just B and her family. What I was walking into was a full-on conspiracy theory. In which I was being invited to take part. The kids on this list could be bones under a ruined high-rise. They could have been on one of the airplanes Greenleaf shot down into the sea. They could be anywhere.

I looked again at the two extrapolated photos. They could have been anyone. But they looked nothing like any of the twelve SecOps operatives. Of course they didn't. Thousands and thousands of children have died in this war. To expect those faces to match up with the ones in the newsfeeds was the worst kind of wishful thinking. Making up part of a collateral damage tally is way less glamorous than being kidnapped and secretly turned into a superhero or whatever it is B thinks happened to this kid, but believe me, it's the only option pretty much any of us are going to get.

"Why wouldn't they remove those things for the in-game analogues?" I asked, shitty stand-in though it was for all my other questions. "Distinguishing marks like Elena's scar. If you're right, and the real-life operatives were stolen as kids, why give people ways to identify them now? Wouldn't that just be asking for trouble?"

"Well," Jessa said slowly, thoughtfully, like she was actually lending credence to this fairy tale, "the game's whole thing is that it's hyperrealistic, right? That's why it's so popular. Like you're right there on the front lines with the real 28 or 33 or whoever and not some random cartoon who's dressed like them."

I knew she was playing devil's advocate, that she didn't believe this conspiracy theory stuff any more than I did. Still, though.

"Historically it's always been easier to fight wars that people support," B said. "What Stellaxis did is genius. The SecOps operatives put a face on it. Twelve faces. With trading-card stats and action figures and t-shirts and *fame.* You can root for them in a way you won't root for a mech or a smart bomb or a grenade. You care about them." She searched our faces, and I looked away. "Caring about them keeps you caring about the war, at least abstractly. You don't want them to get hurt. The irony is that it's Stellaxis who hurts them. Keeps them imprisoned. Uses them up. Every minute of every day." She raised her coffee spoon toward Jessa, then toward me. "But that's not the part you see. You see the part that keeps you *taking an interest.*" She snorted. "The part that keeps you busy looking at it. So you don't pay too much attention to what's really being done to them and to the rest of us."

I thought of yesterday's wiped thousand, six hours out the window, and I cringed.

"I mean. You've seen the war approval ratings. Twentieth-century wars, twenty-first-century wars? Nowhere near this popular. Read up on some history sometime. It's fascinating. Hearts and minds, you know?"

I didn't know. It sounded like a quote from somewhere. But I didn't want to look stupid in front of our new sponsor, so I just shrugged and made a third pass for missed cookie crumbs on my plate. There weren't any.

"Besides," B went on, more lightly now, "you're assuming that an all-powerful megacorporation is remotely likely to be bothered by anything I can do, no matter what I know or don't know. But there are others out there like me. Other people who knew the operatives when they were young. If we combine information, work together . . ." B trailed off, blew out an exasperated breath. "I don't know. Maybe it won't turn up anything. Maybe none of them will match up. Maybe it's a dead end. But I've spent years just sitting on this knowledge, keeping my head down, trying not to draw attention, scared of what would happen to me and my family if I did."

Jessa furrowed her brow. "What changed your mind?"

For a second B looked like she was actually going to laugh. Then I realized that whatever her face was doing, it was closer to a snarl. "They're dying. All of them."

Beside me, Jessa was nodding. 06, 08, 22. The only ones left.

"I can't sit on this anymore. I have to do *something*. Elena's gone. Most of the others, gone. I'm running out of time. If we expose the company's lies, they'll have to shut down the program. Let those last three go. Maybe one of them is on this list. Maybe one of them has somebody out there somewhere. Someone who knew them well enough when they were little to recognize them in something we find now."

"A fucking babysitter," I suggested, earning me a little coffee-cup salute from B.

"Hey," she said. "If I suddenly disappear, at least we'll know I was right."

BY THE TIME we get home, everyone except Allie's back from work, so the room is packed. There's a bit over three hours left before power curfew, which means everyone's busy catching up on all the various self-care and housekeeping tasks that require electricity before putting on their blackout masks and settling in to run out the clock before the curfew drops them.

We walk in to well-ordered chaos, if such a thing exists. People are weaving in and out of each other's way with the grace that comes of long-term cohabitation. Keisha and Tegan are taking turns microwaving their company-store noodles and tea water. Jackson is putting grounds into the coffee machine with one hand, swiping water over from his account with the other. Talya and Suresh decide they want in on coffee, so Jackson adds more grounds while they swipe their water over. Then they go back to the fold-down table where they've been assembling their peanut butter sandwiches.

There's laundry strung up across the closet door, barely damp and smelling of badly rinsed hand soap, and a huge tangle of devices and accessories piled around the charging station with a whiteboard indicating who still has how much time left on which slot. Ryan unplugs his self-warming coffee cup, checks the whiteboard, and plugs Keisha's headlamp into the vacated slot. The bathroom's empty, so Jessa and I duck in there to put our lenses back in before someone asks us why we're offline.

"Last call for coffee," Jackson calls over when he sees us emerge. Checks the volume of water allotted to the coffeepot against its potential capacity. "Got eight cups left."

"Fill it up," Jessa shouts back. "Mal and I got a new sponsor. Coffee's on us today." She works her way over and swipes water to the pot amid cheers.

When it's done and divided among everyone except the tea drinkers (with a cup left for Allie when she gets back tonight from the drug trial she's working), Jessa and I put together some half-assed dinner for ourselves and climb up to our bunks one-handed with sandwiches balanced on top of our coffee cups. Some of the others have already settled in, blackout masks in place. Not sure who's playing today and who's just messing around online. Not that Jessa and I tend to run into any of them often anyway. It's a big game.

I load the game, and the login pops up, overlaid on my field of vision. A few seconds pass while my lens-implant interface verifies that I'm me. Then the login screen vanishes, replaced by the stars-and-arrow Stellaxis logo, which fades out through the BestLife title screen and on to the game lobby. I select Nycorix, put on the new cape and helmet, and pull on the blackout mask to double-check my newly earned stash of ammo and heal patches while I work my way through my sandwich and coffee.

Two hours forty-eight minutes before power curfew. No way am I getting anywhere near today's thousand. But of course, I remind myself with a stupid little pang, that's not what we're here for. Not anymore.

Jessa's team request is there, blinking, and I hit accept. In the corner, she's already messaging away.

so. about today. do we really believe all that stuff about the you-know-whos being you-know-what instead of. um There's a moment while she tries to gauge what she does and doesn't want to risk being recorded and kept by the game, then settles on: instead of the other thing

Easy enough to translate, not that I really have an honest answer. Do we really believe that Stellaxis's operatives were kidnapped instead of made? I don't know. I'm not even entirely sure it matters. Five gallons a week is a lot of water, and B's photo could have been of anyone. The real 05's been dead for, what, almost six years now? All we have to go on is old news footage and internet videos and poster close-ups. Sometimes one of them will get hauled out of Stellaxis HQ to do some kind of photo-op or product sponsorship, and sometimes there'll be a commercial in which 11 drinks a soda or 38 models some smart mascara or 06 talks about how, despite her best efforts, the war zone is a dangerous place and we should really think about optimizing our health coverage. There was one a few years back where they had 22 pushing some kind of frozen dinner thing, presumably under duress, and while on the one hand it made me want to murder people, on the other hand I watched that piece of fuckery more times than I care to admit.

For all we know, the 22 in the commercial, or the 06 or the 11 or whoever, might not be *them* them at all. They can practically clone the operatives down to the mannerism for the game, why not for TV?

What I'm getting at is that, while the operatives' faces are plastered pretty much everywhere, that's as far behind the curtain as we get to see. We don't *know* enough about them to have handholds on the question: no, they can't be lab-grown AI. Only a real human could have done such-and-such. We don't ever *see* them doing any of those favorite pastimes or eating any of those favorite foods listed in such loving detail in the wikis. They do that stuff in the *game*, sure, but is that the same thing? I don't know. It's not like they're in the habit of turning the cameras on the operatives for interviews. The whole defense division of Stellaxis Innovations has been classified forever. The mystique is part of the SecOps allure.

Still, all the no-lenses, meet-in-my-sister's-coffee-shop, never-need-to-see-each-other-again secrecy has me on edge. I mean, B's whole if-I-disappear thing feels melodramatic. Along the lines of those fan theories that pop up regularly, the ones where people are convinced there's some higher purpose to the game. Top players will be recruited and trained by that same corporate defense division to fight for real in the real war in the real city—that's a popular one. Or that they get taken to live in fancy suites in the Stellaxis building, where they drive the real-life operatives remotely, bonded to them in some kind of prototype bleeding-edge fully immersive interface. You get the idea.

Point is, if Stellaxis locked up or murdered everyone who had a pet conspiracy theory to air out, our hotel room would be a whole lot less crowded. More likely, if we somehow man-

aged to annoy someone in power, they'd slap us with a terrorism charge and an interface lockout, and we'd be as good as
disappeared.

dunno, I reply carefully. but we listen to the requests of generous
sponsors. that's kind of our whole job. let's get in there and earn our pay

I hope she takes this as it's meant, namely: *shut up before
you say something that gets us put on a list, and we'll talk later
if we can find someplace that's not listening.*

There's an ominous pause. Before Jessa can open her virtual
mouth and bury us both, I turn Nycorix around on her booted
heel and walk her through the door at the back of the lobby
and into the game. Jessa's teamed with me, which gives her a
ten-second window to get her shit together and follow.

The door leads, as it always does, to wherever we were when
we left the game. Last night's power curfew dropped us without
a proper logout, which means our characters lingered around
for the minute or so it takes for them to time out after a connection goes dead. Usually this is something you'd try to avoid
in a hostile area like this. Especially a hostile area that isn't pa-
trolled often enough by other players to keep it cleaned out of
fresh enemy spawns. We could be logging back in to the middle
of a world of trouble, surrounded and unprepared. I've already
got the heal syringe free of my back pocket, already cleared and
reloaded the blaster, on my way through the door.

But it seems fine. Dead empty, in fact. All except a lone
spidermech in the distance among those warehouses, stutter-
ing in place like it's stuck in the scenery.

When I got here last night, this playfield was swarming. I
made my almost thousand in the absolute horde of enemies
that had spawned here. Today? Nothing.

Immediately it's clear why.

Jessa's got QueenOfTheRaids coming through the door
behind me, double-fisting her plasma guns, already gluing her

back to Nycorix's like we're going to have to mow ourselves a clear perimeter and then inch our way out of here shot by shot. Probably would look good on the stream anyway, for the twenty seconds it'd take us to die.

She takes in the scene and wilts visibly. So much for looking good on the stream. "Where the hell're all the—oh."

The answer to her question is: dead. There are at least a dozen teams out here canvassing the airstrip, blasting anything in their path. "At least it's not a PvP zone," I mutter.

"Why so annoyed? This is, like, the literal opposite of what we were afraid of happening when we got back in here."

"Yeah, no, it's great." I shade my eyes against the sun. What are they all *doing* here?

Why *am* I annoyed? No good reason. There'd be no chance of making a thousand today anyway, sea of mobs or no sea of mobs. And even if I did, that's on the back burner now. Water is the thing. Reliable, easy, no-strings-attached, enough-to-live-on-if-I'm-careful water.

"What's that?" Jessa is saying to someone unseen. "Oh. *Oh.* That makes a lot of sense, guys, thanks for the heads-up!"

Even as she's saying this, a new message lights up in the corner of my view. you didn't get any of that did you

I pretend I don't see it. Dawning on me is a pretty solid guess as to what these other teams are doing out here. If I'm wrong, the timing would be highly coincidental at best.

will you pretty please. take. the stream. off mute

Fine.

I blink at the icon to unmute it and am hit with the exact wall of noise I was hoping to avoid.

"—out here all morning waiting to see if she pops back up again—"

"—seen her in months, she's like some kind of fucking ninja or something, she just straight up *disappears*—"

"—doing when you found her anyway?"

"Nyx found her," Jessa tells them, and turns her gaze on me like a magnifying glass with the sun behind it. *Engage*, she mouths.

"She, uh." I clear my throat. I hate this part of the job, I truly do. It's public speaking and performing in front of an audience and hanging your entire livelihood on the approval of strangers all rolled into one tidy panic-attack-inducing bundle. "She was over there." I raise one hand vaguely toward the warehouses. "Walking around."

"Coordinates?" someone asks.

"I don't know."

"Distance?"

"However far those buildings are."

"What about before QueenOfTheRaids started the stream?"

"Same thing. I caught her beacon in the distance. Literally just wandering the airstrip and off into that field over there."

At least one of our viewers is obviously following one of those other teams as well and relaying info, because within two seconds of my saying this, over by the warehouses one guy whips around toward the field and signals his team to follow. *I never said she's still there*, I want to yell after him.

Understandable, though, really. Jessa checked the forum this morning, and it turns out nobody's logged a 28 sighting in the past two and a half weeks. Someone in the top spot apparently nabbed her a few days ago, but it's not the same. It's when you catch sight of them in the wild, as it were, that they're said to act like the purest analogues of their real-life selves. I don't know who actually has any basis for comparison to verify this, but it's internet gospel, and so this place is slammed. Especially for a dead one, like 28, or a hyperpopular one, like 06, any intel you can get your grubby little stream on is gold.

Speaking of. I check the time. Two hours thirty-nine minutes.

"How's the bike?" I ask Jessa pointedly, and she breaks off whatever chat she was having with whoever and takes the bike out of inventory for inspection. It shimmers into existence beside her. She powers it on, and nothing. The power cell spins up and drops back juddering.

General background chorus of advice and sympathy from our viewers. Mostly advice.

"I'm walking," I tell Jessa.

Walking where? is a question that neither of us really has an answer for. There were dozens of kids on B's list, none of them at a glance any more or less liable to have grown up into supersoldiers than the others. As for the SecOps NPCs, where they are now is anyone's guess. According to the boards, someone's using 21 at the moment, but the rest of them are out there somewhere, wandering, reading comics like 28, or eating donuts like 17. It's just a question of finding them. Which is easier said than done.

"Hold up a sec," Jessa shouts over a shoulder at me. I turn. She's pried the power cell out of its casing and is shaking it hard between both hands. "Read about this—trick—in the—forum. Here we go." She pops the cell back into its casing and powers up the hoverbike. The connection flares up, fizzles wetly, and dies. "Hmm."

"Worked better in the forum?"

"You know, it *did*."

More advice coming in, getting louder as people disagree and advance countertheories and generally make an outrageous mess of noise all over our stream.

Two hours thirty-four minutes.

I can barely hear myself think over this. I message her directly.

we have to get moving
i know i know. watch my six i'm gonna try some—

She freezes as something else yanks her attention away. Maybe some of these advice givers have taken to direct messaging. She lets way, way too many random people into her personal space. There's a reason why none of them are hassling me, and that's because they're not any of the dozen roommates and employers in my filter.

Dutifully, I watch Jessa's six. There's not much there to watch. The airstrip is deader than it was when I left it last night. Periodically a gunner or mech or whatever will pop and get obliterated in the crossfire of at least three canvassing teams, but no major spawn appears. They must have done a sweep here real recently, and it takes some mental rearranging to perceive that as a good thing. *Let it go*, I tell myself. *Start early tomorrow.*

Sudden shadow overhead. I glance up. A breakaway nanodrone is hovering above me, freshly spawned, just outside aggro range. I take aim and blast it out of the sky before it notices me there. My daily thousand counter skips up from zero to one. The resulting happy little sound effect adds insult to injury.

I loot the downed drone real quick while Jessa does whatever. Nanodrones take a handful of seconds to decay, but the flip side of that is the loot is good. This one has almost a dollar's worth of credit and a half dozen bio-freighted fléchettes, which I can sell to someone tradeskilling dirty bombs. I drop the fléchettes in my inventory, dump the credit in my account, and turn my attention back to Jessa.

Jessa, who is pulling a fresh power cell out of inventory like a magic trick and slotting it home. The hoverbike spins up to an audible purr and holds it, running lights flaring as the skirt clears the airstrip.

"—so much, you guys!" she's saying. "Wow, this is a real lifesaver!"

I realize I may have been tuning out something of import.

is that from you know who? I ask her as we hop on.

nah. bunch of them got together and bought it used on the market-place. still runs though. you going to thank them or

"Thanks!" I say, and I do mean it. Reputation notwithstanding, I don't hate them. I just don't know what to do with them. But this is why Jessa and I make a good team. We know how to do maintenance on each other. I watch her six when she bites off more multitasking than she can chew, and she handles the people end of things, because she knows I'd rather have my fingernails pulled out than make small talk with strangers. It's stupid and sloppy, but it works.

"Anytime," somebody says. "Gonna get that thousand today, Nyx?"

This catches me up a second. "Gonna try," I say, recovering hopefully quickly enough to be convincing. "But we want to see who we run into on the way, y'know? See if our luck holds."

Jessa flashes me a look of pure gratitude. Scoots back from the controls. they wanted you to drive, she says. told you they were into that crazy shit

I slide the controls forward, and the bike glides eastward like butter on a hot pan.

SO HERE'S THE THING ABOUT THE GAME. Like the ancient joke about space, it's big. Theoretically this module is supposed to be a near-exact replica of New Liberty City and its environs. Old town is there, and the hills and struggling forest and parched farmland that surround it, but either they've taken some serious liberties or else the actual city is bigger than I thought.

Although, I mean, it's called a supercity for a reason, and of a certainty it's crowded as fuck. And like I said, the game tries hard for realism. Streets are packed, not only with players but with window-dressing NPCs, only there for flavor. Buildings number in the tens of thousands, easy. Fighting and protesting shuts off entire zones of the city at a time. In real life this means they send out alerts to cordon those zones off to civilian activity and send in a dispersal bombardment to flush out the protesters, but in-game it just means huge player-vs-player free-for-alls that usually end in widespread storefront looting and a surge of high-end in-game items on the marketplace, priced to sell.

Finding one of a dozen free-roaming NPCs running wild in their natural habitat is going to be like finding a needle in a haystack the size of the moon. A haystack that is probably also on fire. Getting up in their face enough to try to match their features with someone from B's list . . . is going to look exactly as weird as it is. Our audience's reaction to that weirdness is a bridge we're just going to have to burn when we get to it.

"So what's the plan?" Jessa yells up to me over the velvet buzzsaw whine of the hoverbike. "Where to?"

Like I know. Like anyone knows. Twelve operatives, dozens of kids on B's list. Or, not even kids. Those descriptions are to actual kids what a chalk outline is to a corpse. This is some Cinderella's-slipper shit. I haven't the first fucking clue where to start.

Statistically, according to the forum, each SecOps NPC has a preference, but only statistically. We wouldn't be the only assholes hoping to ambush one of them by the numbers, and by the numbers spectacularly fail. "Taking suggestions," I shout back. "For now, just trying to get off this airfield before one of these teams recognizes us from last night and starts asking questions." Then, as an afterthought that they really do deserve, I address our viewers: "Thanks for not giving us away, you guys. Really appreciate."

Still, once we've zoomed off the airfield and into the outskirts of the city, I swing the bike ninety degrees to cork it in between two buildings, in an alley just wide enough to hold us.

Two hours twenty-six minutes. I get my legs under me and kneel on the seat facing backward, resting my chin on my hands on the backrest, eyeing Jessa. we can't just drive around aimlessly burning through this power cell, I tell her. we need a plan. but it has to not look weird, they'll notice

relax, i got it

"So, guys," Jessa calls out, "curfew really screwed us last night, huh?" Over the noises of solidarity this elicits, she goes on. "Been a while since we've gotten decent footage of a sighting, and this three lousy seconds of 28 is like, I dunno, blood in the water. I'm thinking we go find us some more. What d'you think, Nyx?"

Is it really that easy?

"Yeah," I say, chill as chill. "Sure." Then, in a flash of sudden uncharacteristic people-skills inspiration: "Taking requests." And about fifty people start shouting out the numbers of their favorites.

I guess it is.

Jessa gives them a moment to shut up. They don't. "Wow, okay, guys, your enthusiasm is amazing, but I think we need a more official vote. Let me real quick throw up a poll for you."

She does, and we spend a few seconds watching it fill. 06 is the runaway clear winner, followed (unsurprisingly) by 28 and, more distantly, 33. Not that we have any real way to find any of them in particular beyond consulting some fan-made algorithm that might tell us who has a marginally greater chance of showing up where.

I've tried that before, on my own time and without Jessa. A lot. It doesn't work.

"All right," she's saying. "We'll see what we can do. So. Looks like whoever had 21 just lost her, so she's up for grabs somewhere."

I nod. B seemed to want to prioritize IDing the living operatives, but there are only three of those, and we're going to have to work with what we can. "Who got taken instead?"

"Let me double-check, but it *looks* liiiike . . ."

"22," supplies someone from the audience.

Jessa gives me a look. I refuse to react. It's bad enough that I felt myself startle a little, like every goddamn time 22 gets brought up in conversation. If there's any justice in this world, nobody noticed.

Fine. So he's out of the picture right now. Probably being made to do some behind-closed-doors shit with some player who's going to make bank off that stream. Just fucking whatever. That still leaves eleven. Not that we have any idea where any of those eleven are. Already my enthusiasm has tapered drastically, and I'd be lying if I said I didn't know why.

I've seen 22 three times before. All briefly, almost all from a distance. It's always faintly depressing in a way I can't begin to quantify. The fact he's off the table today is disappointing and relieving in equal measure, because I am a sadsack asshole who can't leave a side project alone.

Not for the first time I wish the operatives behaved like NPCs in most games, just hanging around in a given location until someone rolls up on them looking for a side quest. Except then some tens of thousands of streamers would be straight up out of jobs. Not for the first time I wonder if this whole offshoot subculture of spying on the operatives, trying to piece together what the inner lives of honest-to-shit superheroes must be like, was intended when they made the game, or whether it just kind of sprang up around it after the fact. Jessa and I have only really dabbled in this corner of the fandom, getting what footage we can get but not making a serious go of it. But here we are now, turned virtual paparazzi with the rest of them.

Except the in-game NPC versions of the operatives *aren't* real people to be spied on, no matter how much they may look and act like the real people on whom they're so closely modeled. They're information. And unless we're swallowing B's whole story now, which I for one am not, the real ones aren't *people* exactly anyway. They're property. They were made in the Stellaxis labs, and they are Stellaxis assets. They just also happen to have a massive fan base that drinks up the barest scraps of information like water on a double-ration holiday.

And it's not like Jessa and I exactly have a burgeoning job market to select from. At least we're not out working the desalination plants or the plastic digesters. At least we're going to have enough water to drink this week. I can swallow a whole raft of skepticism if it keeps my kidneys functioning, turns out.

"All right," I say. "Let's check the map."

I pull up an overlay of the in-game city. Jessa and I are both running crowdsourced variants that filter for past locations of given operatives. A lot of streamers swear by this method for finding given targets, but as far as I can tell, it's about as reliable as flipping a coin.

On a normal day I would be busy chipping away at my thousand right now, and any SecOps footage I happen to come upon would be icing on the cake. But I can't fall back on usual routine today for the same reason I can't flip that coin now. Even if we end up finding nothing for B, I want to at least make it look like we're giving it all we've got, while also keeping it interesting for the audience. Pay is pay, whoever it comes from. Company credit from regular, everyday footage-hungry fans is going to keep us out of the rehydration clinics just as effectively as water from some well-meaning conspiracy theorist with high misguided notions of avenging the dead.

The map overlays look like the kind of thing conservationists use when they track the migratory patterns of butterflies or whales or whatever. Colored lines—some curvy, some squiggly, some as perfectly straight as if they've been drawn with laser guidance, some tacking back and forth like a switchback mountain road—litter the streets and parks and ruins around the edges of the city. You can set the filter for time: last hour, last twenty-four hours, last week, last thirty days. Obviously it's not comprehensive. There are gaps of minutes, hours, days, even weeks, when nobody has any goddamn idea where a given operative NPC is. Hence the fifty-odd guys out there scouring the airstrip right now. Like I said, 28 is a massive pain in the ass to find.

For ease of use, each operative's line is a different color, and you can filter for whichever ones you want to reference. 28's, for instance, is red. The entirety of it for the better part of the past month consists wholly of the line between the airstrip warehouses and the field beyond, where I caught sight of her last night. You have to zoom way in on the map to even make out that it's a line. From the default distance it's a dot, small enough to make you assume 28's filter is bugged.

"This is kind of a lot," Jessa says, with the thousand-yard stare that says she's laboring to parse an overlay.

I nod in agreement. I don't pull this map up often enough to know what to make of it. It's like someone unraveled twelve balls of yarn the size of roller mechs across a five-hundred-square-mile spread.

Except for 28's, of course. And 22's, equally to be expected. His filter is a hot mess. His dark gray line just pops up randomly and then vanishes for long stretches at a time. I can't shake the sudden idea that he goes back to the Stellaxis building when nobody's using him and sits on the edge of his cot or whatever—perfect posture, sword across knees, staring at the floor—until a player summons him again.

There's no pattern to what any of them are doing, at least not one I can figure out. Most of them have these meandering, touristy walking habits, like they've woken up to find themselves in a new place that they're bound and determined to explore, thoroughly if utterly randomly. Which, I suppose, they pretty much are. Their intelligences are artificial, decanted or distilled from the real thing, but all machine intelligences can learn. Medbots and teachers and even Stellaxis's old surveyor probes wouldn't have gotten very far if that wasn't the case.

And some of them seem to have developed definite preferences as to where they spend their infinite supply of time.

"Looks like 17's still hanging out a lot at the park lately," Jessa says, characteristically reaching the same conclusion as me around the same time, just from a different direction. "And

11 really likes the Monument for some reason." She shakes her head. "They're all over the place. I mean, look at 06: she's taken up, I don't know, *hiking* or something—"

I swap to 06's filter. There she is, an unmistakably orange line doing what looks like laps around the city limits, out in the woods and deserted farmland and whatever else is out there.

Two hours nineteen minutes, and it has not remotely escaped my notice that my daily thousand count is still sitting solidly at one while we burn time here in our alley as red blips of enemies respawn out in the street, full of points and loot that somebody-not-me is going to add to their score and inventory. On top of that, we're absolutely going to start losing subscribers if we just stay here with our thumb up our ass all session. If I know Jessa, and I do, she'll overanalyze all the data she can get her hands on, right up until power curfew drops us. As for me, I'm not confident that the map is even the answer. High-probability sighting spots just mean over-camped crowdedness, and some of these are PvP zones that will get our faces murdered off on sight. We're probably more likely to snag footage by accident, like I did with 28 last night. But that would fly for shit with our viewers, not to mention with B.

I'm this close to just flipping a coin for real when I remember something B said.

Maybe one of them is on this list. Maybe one of them has somebody out there somewhere. . . .

Well, *that* narrows it down.

Out of the twelve real SecOps operatives, only three—06, 08, and 22—are still among the living. The other nine—05, 28, 02, 33, 38, 11, 21, 42, and 17—are dead. We lost 11 and 21 late last year: 11 just after Valued Customer Appreciation Day and 21 just before Halloween. And we could probably have eliminated 05 from our list in general because there's probably not much we're likely to learn about her that B doesn't already know, or think she knows.

Definitely not for the first time I wish Stellaxis had bothered to stick some name tags on the SecOps's growth tanks. I'd settle for pet names. Hell, *consecutive numbers.* Something.

Except if B is right, they *do* have names. Or did.

I push that aside. Like Jessa said about the map, it's *kind of a lot.*

pick one of the living ones, I message Jessa privately. i don't care which one as long as they're not dead

She doesn't bother messaging me back, just sings it out like it was her idea. "Let's go take a look for 06 in the outskirts. Won't be too far if we don't have to sidetrack around a raid. I have a side quest to wrap up out there anyway."

Your side quest but not my thousand? I stop myself from saying. It's as good a place as any, really. I wouldn't take the odds on finding 06 out there, any more than here in this alley or back at the airfield or anywhere else. It looks good, though. It looks like effort. It looks like we have some idea of what the hell we're doing. And the fields outside the city are usually crawling with stuff to kill—not only mobs but players, too—so at the very least we can put on a decent show for our subscribers.

I gun the bike north.

WE TAKE THE big roads where we can. They're choked with the traffic of other players—on hoverbikes, on foot, in transport trucks, even a few high-level guys clomping around in mid- to high-range mechs—but it's more efficient than navigating back-alley barricades. Anyway, this crowd moves fast. Upwards of ninety-five percent of this server's population has a power curfew that's going to kick in sooner or later, and everyone has somewhere to be.

This section of our route isn't flagged as PvP-designated right now, so nobody starts shit with us, but I keep my blaster drawn, and I know Jessa has her guns out too. Not being shot off our bike by player characters does not for one second mean we won't get painted and pasted by an orbital laser or peppered by some drone's fléchettes, or round a corner straight into some mech fight's crossfire or a resonance bombardment. Not a lot my blaster and Jessa's plasma guns are going to do against an orbital weapon, of course, or citykiller mechs for that matter, but it helps keep up appearances.

"Something big going on over there," Jessa says, throwing down coordinates for me to check. Maybe half a mile south-southeast, pretty much the opposite of where we're headed. I turn my head as much as I'm able while also leaning on the accelerator and trying not to eat it on the personnel transport in front of me, but all I see is buildings. I slow down fractionally, squint down the next alley. More buildings. Skyscrapers laid out in their rows and columns like a bed of nails, each glassy surface reflecting off the others. An infinite mirror.

Whatever's going down behind those buildings, it's blanketing my minimap with the pale blips of player characters in neutral territory. If those blips were red, I'd think raid and steer clear. This is something else.

Then I see it. Reflecting off the buildings' glass exoskeletons, too high up to be some kind of weird light-show effect from a player's outfit. Barely visible in the low-contrast daylight, wavery like I'm looking at it underwater, but just *there* enough to catch. Even so, at first I think I'm seeing things, but that mass of blips on my minimap tells no lies.

Jessa sees it at the same time I do, messaging me so as not to draw the crowd's attention, shaking my shoulder furiously to make sure she's drawn mine.

nyx that's a— but I don't even need to read the rest of it, I already know, I'm already kicking the bike in a hard hundred-twenty-degree arc back toward the side street we've just passed.

It's a beacon. Fainter than 28's was last night, but that golden upstabbing of light is unmistakable.

I wrangle us across the paths of half a dozen other players while Jessa yells apologies on my behalf and the power cell chirps its outrage, and slew us into the side street at such a sloppy angle that I clip the decorative railing of the shallow front steps of some bank or something on my way.

Behind me, Jessa has taken about one nanosecond to ramp up to full presenter mode. Effortless, as always. Like she's flipping some switch I wasn't built with.

"Okay, guys, sliiiight detour real real quick here. Check this out. Nyx is on *fire* this week, two sightings in two days, you can't *make* this shit up. Wow, what a mess over there. There's gotta be two, three hundred people between us and whoever's throwing that beacon."

There sure are. The bike slogs to a jog, then a walk, then a crawl, as we hit the ragged edge of that packed mass of bodies. I can make out the beacon clearly now, rising up above that seething, jostling horde of bodies and vehicles and augment rigs in every variant of the biotech rainbow. But I can't see whose it is.

Normally I'd have given up by now. Correction: I'd've checked the forum, seen who was throwing that beacon, and then almost certainly given up by now. A crowd like this means we have zero chance of bagging any kind of footage that our audience couldn't see just as well if not better from any one of three hundred other streams. Last night with 28 was an utter outlier, statistically, because the only person who was there was too fucking stupid to start streaming. Generally people make better decisions, and the site gets mobbed, and *they* start streaming, and then you have a situation like pouring sugar water on an anthill. Like the old news clips you sometimes see about the water riots, back when there was enough of the stuff that it came out of your faucet for free.

I've seen plenty of swarmed beacons in the distance in my day, and usually a crowd like this, even in virtual, is enough to turn me on my antisocial heel and send me far, far away. Today, though, I don't get to be picky. I get to suck it up and soldier on.

This crowd is insanity. It's counterproductive, of course. All these people trying to capture the inner secret lives of Stellaxis operatives in their natural habitat, and in so doing, utterly prevent them from whatever they were trying the fuck to do in the first place. Which is why I generally wouldn't waste bike battery and heals and ammo and *time* on trash footage. Whoever's at the glowing core of that beacon is stuck in that crowd like a bug in amber. Not exactly putting on a show.

In favorable conditions, the hoverbike is omnidirectionally maneuverable. In *these* conditions we're cemented in place. We may as well get off and walk. So I do. Jessa follows, the bike shimmering out of existence as she stows it in her inventory.

Walking isn't much better. It just puts us within range of everybody's poky elbows. I brace myself and shove through, but I'm taking damage now. The hell?

I check my minimap. Sometime within the past thirty seconds, the random zone designator has decided this one is now PvP. Of course it has. Already people are noticing the change. There's a general background noise of weapons being drawn, teams gathering together in formation, bodies hitting the ground.

"Anybody got eyes on who that is?" I ask, because most of our subscribers are probably watching several feeds at once, and as the crowd starts battle-royaleing it out around me, I find myself thinking about discretion and valor and getting the fuck out while the getting's good.

"Looks like 08," someone answers.

I blink. "Really?"

"We going for this?" Jessa asks. She has to shout to be heard.

Elena's gone, B says in my head. *Most of the others, gone. I'm running out of time.* Earn your fucking keep, Mal. "Yeah."

"Then let's do it."

She holsters the plasma guns long enough to pull two cloaks out of her inventory and toss me one. The design realism is so top-notch that the thing almost blows away before I can catch it. "Cloak up and bolt. On three," she says.

I look at her doubtfully. "This is going to suck."

"Sure is." She's grinning. "Three."

I toss the cloak over my head and run like hell.

There are a few ultra-top-shelf items in this game that could get us there without a scratch. A suborbital drop like the one that got Jessa to the airstrip yesterday. A permeability shroud, which would interpose our virtual atoms among and through the other players' like breeze through an open window. An invincibility shot.

The smart camouflage cloak is none of these things. Best it buys us in a situation like this is a few seconds of confusion. Ten seconds, to be precise.

I push and dodge, trying to shoulder people out of my path in a minimally damaging way. It's not easy. I've lost sight of Jessa. Which is unsurprising because she's invisible. I could try to track her by the trail of annoyed players she leaves in her wake, but it wouldn't necessarily be her. We won't be the only ones pulling this trick.

The drain on my health is steady but slow. No lucky shots have found me yet, just incidental impact damage from body-slamming my way through other people's power armor. I duck under someone's pet spidermech's autotargeting perimeter turret, I backpedal out of an all-out firefight, I burn my boots on the area-of-effect nuke radius of a lobbed grenade.

The beacon's close now, though. Real close. I can make out the number hovering over 08's head. Not sure from here what they've interrupted him doing, and I kick myself for not getting that footage, even though I know I'd be the six zillionth dumbfuck to try to profit off it, well beyond fashionably late to that party. Now that they *have* interrupted him, though, he's just standing there, chatting with the crowd. He's holding something, or has got something propped up against him?

People are talking to him and he's talking back, but it's just the one of him against the horde of them, and they're all screaming to be heard over one another, shooting at one another, climbing over one another to get a better vantage point.

The little cluster of people right in front of me all drops together and lies there, quivering. Resonance grenade. If this was the real war, their insides would be jellifying right now, but as it is, they just sit there for a few seconds and then blink out of existence, dead, to respawn wherever they last saved. I dart into the opening where they were—and in that instance my cloak expires and blips out, leaving me exposed.

At least five different blasters swing round to bear on me. "Watch out, Nyx!" someone shouts at me from the audience, but I'm already on the move. My emergency shielding system is on its last hoarded gasp, but it's not going to do me much good when someone loots it off my corpse, so I power it up and accelerate out of the gap and back into the comparative clusterfuck safety of the crowd, the shields glimmering around me like soap bubbles.

Another few feet and I'll be right up in 08's face, just like B wants. I'll snag some extreme close-ups of the pores in his nose and the capillaries in his eyes if that's what she's after. From the sound of things, Jessa's already there. She's managed to finesse her way through the waves of players breaking against the impassable glowing cliff of 08's beacon. She's out of close auditory range, but her voice comes through clearly on our channel, presenting 08 like he's a wild-caught specimen of some critically endangered species. Which isn't really all that far from true.

"Say hi to 08, guys! I haven't gotten close to this dude in a while! Love how he's taking the time to stand here and hang out with us, seems like a cool guy. He's saying something—see, you can see his mouth is moving—but there's just too much background noise here. Sorry, 08, we can't hear you! I've always liked him, though, always follow his missions on the news. Who am I kidding, though? I follow all of them. We love you, 08!"

I risk peeking at Jessa's visual feed in the upper right-hand corner of my field of vision. Somehow she's gotten *right* up in 08's business and is peering directly into his face at a distinctly unflattering angle. He's still talking, but it's impossible to make out. Which is a shame, because voice data would probably be useful intel for B's collection.

I shove forward, trusting the last long-suffering tatters of the shields to carry me. I scramble over corpses too freshly dead to have despawned yet and pop through the far edge of the crowd to land at 08's feet. The shiny toes of my boots are grazing the edge of the beacon. It's an old-fashioned skateboard he's got, the kind with wheels. He's standing there with it leaned up against one leg. Out of nowhere it occurs to me that the in-game versions of the operatives probably have a lot more fun than the real ones.

"Hey, 08," I say. "08, hey, over here."

It's dangerously tempting to start waving my arms to get his attention. As it is, I'm presenting something of a target. Someone at my five o'clock unloads a blaster in the direction of my center mass, but the iridescence of the shield not only absorbs the fire but deposits its alloyed charge into my inventory for sale as repurposed tradeskill materials. I am for sure going to miss this shield when it blows.

All at once 08 catches sight of me. He looks straight at me looking straight back at him, and I can only hope B's watching. There's nothing distinctive there, though, nothing on the order of 05's—Elena's—scar. He just looks like some guy about my age, like someone I'd walk past on the hotel stairs without giving him a second thought.

He's about my height, which also seems strange for the meticulously designed, lab-grown—stolen and lab-developed?—superhuman that he is. Somehow I expected him to be taller. Jessa could probably give me his height to the millimeter.

Another shot, this one a bullet from a standard pistol, sizzles away into my shield. Jessa, angel teammate that she is, returns the fire for me.

Not knowing what's going to come out of my mouth until it does, and even then I realize it's probably a bad idea, it's the kind of thing that either has no result at all or gets you put on the kind of list you *really* don't want to find yourself on, but it's just hit me, all my doubts about B's story coalescing into this question I have to ask 08 while I have the opportunity, even as I immediately regret it, syllable by syllable, real time.

"Do you know a girl named Elena?"

Behind me, Jessa gasps. "Dude, *what*—"

At first 08 doesn't react. He looks at me blandly, much as 28 did last night, but then his forehead creases in something I wouldn't hesitate to describe as confusion, if this were a real person in real life and not a glorified fanservice artificial intelligence based on the cached personality of a corporate-war superweapon, programmed into a hyperpopular massively multiplayer game.

At first he doesn't react. And then he does.

"Elena?" he says, and shakes his head. "Sorry, can't help you."

He says something else after that, but whatever it is, it's annihilated, instantly, in the screaming liquid rainbow fire of a suborbital drop.

I don't even see it coming until I'm lying twelve feet to the left of where I was, at the edge of a smoking crater that's aligned with the former dead center of 08's beacon projection. I sit up amid a general flickering that I soon realize is a mass despawning of player corpses. Where the hell is Jessa?

"She's okay!" someone from the audience shouts. It takes a second to realize she's talking about me. "Raids, man, that was a thing of beauty."

"Aw yeah," Jessa says from somewhere. "Get it, Nyx! Do me proud!"

Later I'll replay the footage and realize that Jessa bodily shoved me out of the way just as the drop obliterated the twenty-foot radius of city street I was standing in. No: she put on some kind of power glove and *punched* me out of the way, fist to sternum, sending me rocketing backward ass-first into a bus-stop sign. Which explains the hit to my health bar, but at least I'm alive. Which is more than I can say for Jessa, who's way back wherever we last saved. Her corpse, along with 08's and easily three hundred others, has already vanished.

"Oh wait," Jessa says, watching my stream from her respawn point wherever. "Oops. I guess 08 ate that drop with the rest of us. Shit." A pause. "Wait. Who the hell is *that*?"

I'll pick all this up later also, because I'm really not paying much attention to her now. Because I've already seen what Jessa is looking at, and it's engaging the absolute entirety of my focus.

I'm looking at what came down in that suborbital drop.

It's 22.

He's not off doing behind-closed-doors stuff after all. He's standing there in the smoking pit of the drop crater along with whatever player has use of him. Someone high level, whoever it is, come to crash the party and rack up player kills in a high-density area. Predictable, as tactics go. Sort of a cheap shot. The suborbital drop was a nice touch, though. Effective. He's just standing there with 22, blathering away to his unseen audience, one hand resting lazily on a holstered beam weapon like he's waiting for someone to issue him a challenge but not expecting it to be much of one. His health bar is almost as dark red as 22's.

"The fuck is this asshole," Jessa is hissing. "Lay a blast radius down on a crowd like that on purpose. Talk about a dick move."

I don't care about that, or literally anything else about this new-arrival player. He wrecked my shot at getting decent footage of 08—who was *answering my questions*—and now he's killed my teammate and jacked up my shield and generally pissed me off. My interest in him begins and ends with the idea that if I follow him around long enough for him to die, I might be able to loot his corpse.

I do, however, give somewhat more of a shit about 22.

There's nobody else here. I mean, there's a few, but new guy over there is picking them off one by one with flawless headshots without visibly taking aim. It's only because I've been slung way the hell over to the side of the action that he hasn't seen me yet, shot me in the face, and added me to his score.

I can't get casual footage of 22, not in the sense of 28 reading comics or 08 with his skateboard, because 22 is bonded to this suborbital-dropping jackass and has no choice but to behave completely neutrally for the duration. He's just standing there like a robot, awaiting instructions.

If I go over there, I'm going to get spread across this street in an even layer. You don't make the kind of entrance new guy just made if you're planning to throw your operative buddy a tea party like whoever it was did with 38. He's going to have 22 murder anything that moves.

"Clean this up for me," new guy says, and 22 blurs into action like he's been plugged in.

In real life, therefore in the game, the SecOps operatives are blisteringly proficient not only with guns, but with hand-to-hand combat and bladed weapons as well. Their standard loadout involves a basic pistol and a vaguely katana-like sword. Here, now, 22 isn't bothering with either, just kind of plowing into fleeing knots of player characters and mowing them down empty-handed. Whatever he's actually *doing* to them is too fast for me to make out.

It might save me time, honestly. Dying and respawning is a much faster way back to my save point than walking. But I really don't want to give dipshit new guy here the satisfaction.

I flatten myself against the back of the bus-stop bench, wishing I still had my cloak. What footage I can manage of 22 is less than great. It's distant, it's obscured by smoke from the crater, and all he's doing is massacring player characters while his douche-canoe temp handler hangs back, narrating for the benefit of his audience and looting the occasional promising-looking corpse.

"Nyx," Jessa is whispering. "Get *out of there*."

There are two reasons why I don't answer. One is that 22 is going to hear any tiny sound I make and laser in on me and then I'm done.

The other is that I have a better idea.

Well. A *different* idea anyway.

I freeze and wait for 22 and new guy to work their way up the street. I don't so much as blink until they've nearly vanished down that straightaway, only 22's beacon showing where they've gone.

When it's so far off that it looks like a firefly among the long late-afternoon shadows, I peel myself off the bench and follow.

nyx. NYX. look i get what you're doing but this is suicide. just come back here and we'll go try to find somebody else with the map, we've got like an hour and change left before curfew

I have to be careful replying to this. Messaging is silent—I think and my implant translates into text—but it's something that's not concentrating utterly on not being detected, and

I need what's left of my wits sharpened to a point here if I'm going to pull this off.

an hour and change to do what? I reply, ignoring that first part. 08's despawned. 22's right here. so unless you have some kind of crystal ball that can tell us where exactly 06 or anybody else is, this is our best bet

nyx, think. i get it. i promise i do. but you have to think. you die here and that guy is going to loot all your shit and then we get to spend the next week replacing it instead of doing our fucking job. anyway, footage of you letting 22 dismember your sad ass probably isn't what she's paying us to get

but footage of the living ones is. and last i checked 22 is still alive. besides, joke's on this asshole, i have no shit to loot Up ahead, new guy checks his six, and I duck in behind a dumpster to wait it out. I reply to Jessa from my hiding spot. sooner or later somebody's going to come kill the player 22's attached to, and he's going to go wandering, and i'm going to follow him. there's nobody else left alive here so that puts me in the exact same position as last night with 28, except this time i'm fucking streaming. ok?

Unless whoever gets the top spot next picks 22 as his ally too. Unless this guy manages to hold on to him until my curfew drops me from the game. Unless whoever comes to kill him decides to take me out for fun and profit first. And so on.

For a long time Jessa doesn't answer. Then she does, whispering directly over the channel. "Be careful, Nyx."

born careful, I reply.

I step out from behind my dumpster—and right into 22.

A startled exhalation rips out of me. At the last second I catch it and form it into a word. "Hi."

22 just looks at me, head tilted fractionally like he's trying to read something written in microscopic font on my face. I get the fleeting impression people don't often try to strike up conversations with him in situations like this. "Hello."

Jessa is yelling something at me. Another two dozen people are yelling their own somethings at me. I mute them, and the whole world goes silent. 22 doesn't say anything more. He just stands there and breathes. Watching me like I'm some vaguely interesting bug.

"Hey, you found yourself a runner," new guy calls from up the street. "Good job, man. Now get rid of her and let's get the fuck out of here."

22 takes another second to size me up. As in real life, in-game 22's hallmark is this exactitude of focus. I have no idea what purpose it even serves here, he's so ridiculously high level he could one-shot me by flicking me in the forehead with two fingers. Whatever it is, it's intense. My feet are rooted to the spot, my blaster hangs at my side. Some way-back part of my brain has to be forcibly reminded that this is just a game. I want to turn and run.

Except for the part where I really, really don't. I've never been anywhere near this close to 22 before, and 22 is one of the few operatives who are still alive. I need this footage for B. I need to stand my ground and keep streaming as long as I can. I tell myself that's what I'm doing, but in reality I can no more break eye contact with 22 than I could deliberately look away from an oncoming train.

"Keep him talking," Jessa cuts in. "Get him to say something else."

I'd love to. Really I would. I want to ask him about Elena, see if I get a different answer somehow than I got from 08. I want to ask him if B was right and they were all stolen as kids and not made. Honestly, it seems unlikely. Even more so than the others, 22 makes me doubt B's story on a visceral level. Standing here in his presence, I see no reason to disbelieve the official company line, which is that the Stellaxis SecOps operatives are some kind of bleeding-edge top secret humanoid biotech, and the in-game personalities we see aren't extrapolated at all, but straight-up copy/paste, just like in the documentary.

No matter how hard I try, no matter how much B wants me to see the operatives this way, I can't picture 22 as a real person, a real kid that got nabbed from a real family or picked up out of the ruins of a dead one. Nobody's ever seen him walking around in-game reading comics about himself. Or sitting at a statue eating donuts. Or posing with a skateboard. Nothing to hint at the kind of person he'd be if he wasn't entirely busy being entirely the person that he is. Which is cold, calculating efficiency, all the way down.

He sounds boring as all hell when I put it that way.

And yet it's exactly all those things that I find so relatable.

Maybe he's just an asshole. Maybe that makes me the exact same brand of asshole as him. I don't know. What I do know is that, ever since the first time I saw him in the news, some incomprehensible part of my mind clamped on to him and hasn't let go since.

When I was a kid, I used to have these stupid daydreams of finding out 22 was my long-lost twin brother or something, and we'd go on adventures together. Even though I knew that was impossible for about sixty different excellent reasons. And why 22 and not somebody like 17 or 06 or 02 or anyone who you'd think would be more appealing to the mind of a kid, which is literally *all of them*, I couldn't even begin to tell you. That clamped-on part of my mind has always been infuriatingly immune to logic. And so here we are. I'm about to die and respawn and lose all my shit, and there's nowhere else I'd rather be.

"Jesus, Nycorix. *Say something.*"

I want to ask him who he is. What he wants. Where he'll go when new guy loses him. What the real him does when he's not busy delicately vivisecting citykiller mechs in the street.

Why I give a shit in the first place. Like he knows. Like I do. Like any of this makes any sense at all.

22 still hasn't taken me out like new guy told him to. He's just looking at me, like he's waiting to see what I'll do. In the aforementioned idiot part of my mind, this action, or lack of action, is heavily invested with arcane meaning. Like this is some kind of test.

I clear my throat, open my mouth to say *Do you know a girl named Elena?* or *Who are you really?* or *I can't tell if I feel sorry for you or if I want to be you, can you help me process that please?*

—and collapse dead on the ground behind the dumpster, 22's sword having gone through my throat and out the back of my neck, then retrieved, all too fast for me to notice until it's all over and 22 is on one knee on the sidewalk, wiping the blade on my shirt in the seconds before my corpse despawns.

The street and dumpster fade out as 22 walks away, and the empty white room of the save point fades in as I respawn. Jessa is there already, grabbing my shoulders and jumping up and down. I keep the stream muted. They're so supportive and so awesome and so great, and I really don't want to deal with it right now.

CHANGES TO CHARACTER APPEARANCE DETECTED, the game notifies me. *SAVE/DISCARD?*

I look down.

The game doesn't save death wounds. We'd all look like something out of a zombie apocalypse if it did. But you're given the choice to keep pretty much any other alteration to a character's person and clothing. A lot of people keep them. Like a record of their adventures. Never mind that most of those "adventures" involve grinding thousands or slogging through side quests or stalking NPCs for footage that hints at the secret lives of the secret molds they're cast from.

Then again, a lot of people discard them because they don't want to be reminded *that* much of the war they're living in. It's a game, not a newsfeed. If they wanted to go look at blood-splattered bodies, they could go visit a checkpoint, or a barri- cade, or subscribe to any of the drone channels that bring us news of the front, which is everywhere. Or they discard them because they want to look good. The game, like life, is perfor- mative, and evidence of damage suggests failure. Or because, like me, they don't care enough about in-game appearances one way or another, and discarding all alterations is less effort than deciding which ones to keep.

The outfit I've had on Nycorix since forever is this pitch- black, three-piece salaryman suit with the sleeves ripped off at the shoulder. There, across the waist of my shirt and the right side of my jacket and the edge of my shiny new crow-colored cape, is a long dark smear of blood from where 22 cleaned his sword.

Against the white of the shirt it looks like a Rorschach test from some movie. The pattern looks like nothing at all. I won- der what this says about me.

I consider the entire wholesale raft of shit I'd get from Jessa for doing what I'm about to do, and then I realize I don't care.

I blink at *SAVE*.

Jessa is already staring at me. Shaking her head slowly with this look of fond wonderment, like I'm a toddler showing off a dump I just took on the floor. Claps me on the shoulder. "You've got issues, my friend," she says matter-of-factly, and it is, of course, as it is of all of us, true.

THERE'S ONLY A BIT OVER AN HOUR left before power curfew at this point, and no chance whatsoever of making my thousand, and I feel like we've gotten enough footage to earn our keep with B for the day, so I log off right there at the save without remembering to say goodbye to the audience and just lie in the darkness of my blackout mask, replaying my ten-second encounter with 22 in my mind. It's gotten under my skin in some kind of way I have no idea how to begin to unpack and examine.

Have you ever felt drawn to someone for no reason that makes sense to your rational mind? I don't mean like a crush or wanting to fuck them or whatever kind of normal-person obsession. I wish it were that. That at least would make some kind of fucking sense. No, what I get to deal with is this situation where you don't want anything from the person in question at all, you just find there's something in them that speaks to something in you, and all you want in all the world is to figure out how to reply.

Jessa would say I need to get on top of the leaderboard and take 22 for some quality alone time and get this weird fixation out of my system behind closed doors. I know what she'd say because she *does* say it. Frequently. In more colorful language, and usually with some helpful instructive gesturing. But if this was a problem that orgasms could solve, I'm reasonably sure I would've figured it out by now. 22 is a deeper itch, unreachable.

Like I said. Under my skin.

Worse, it's a fixation with no origin story. I don't have an anecdote about how 22 pulled me out of the rubble of my bombed-out building, the way some younger kids on the internet do about some of the operatives, because when I was eight they were still somebody's R&D dream, solid years from being released for duty.

Whatever this is, I have no excuse for it. But I don't know how to reason it away.

That daydream I used to have about him and me being long-lost siblings, going on adventures together? I used to make up such elaborate stories about that, used to run these stories through my head when I was trying to fall asleep in the camps. I used to lie there on my cot in the dark and blink twenty-two times, carefully, firmly, like it would summon him to that shitty, sour-smelling, overcrowded tent in order to deign to befriend my sorry ass.

Is it stupid? Yes. Is it sad and hopeless and lonely and pitiable and desperate? You bet. But whatever this is, I've been waiting to outgrow it for almost a decade, and from where I'm standing, it's looking like I'll be taking it to my grave.

I'm lying there wallowing in my shitty mood when Jessa pries up my blackout mask without asking. I fight down an urge to push her off my bunk. She looks legitimately concerned.

"You didn't say the outro," she says.

"I never say the outro," I reply dully. "That's all you."

"Yeah, but you usually stick around."

"Mm."

The fact that I'm not arguing seems to throw her. There's a long pause. "You okay?" she says at last.

"Yeah. Why?"

She doesn't even bother dignifying that with a response. She's giving me this awful sympathetic look, like I'm broadcasting all my thoughts right on my face. Probably I am. I stare resolutely at the ceiling.

"You got some really sick footage today," she ventures. "B's going to *die*. I mean, everybody else sure did. Did you hear them losing their shit when you stood up and bumped right into 22? He just came out of *nowhere*, dude, it was—" At this point something in my stony silence seems to reach her. "Sorry."

"Nothing to be sorry about," I tell her loftily. "It was a good first day on the new job. I'm just tired is all."

"So I see." She reaches out with one hand, appears to realize she has no idea what she's going to do when it finds me, and ends up kind of balling it into a fist and booping me gamely on one shoulder. Then she goes.

I stare at the ceiling another few minutes, listening to the noise of the room. It's actually pretty quiet. For once I logged out well before power curfew, and it seems like most everyone else is either still online or out working various gigs. Out of the corner of my eye I see Jessa climbing back up to her own bunk, unwrapping a candy bar, casting one more furtive glance in my direction, then pulling her blackout mask back on with a sigh.

Everything's quiet. There are probably half a dozen people in this room right now, but for all intents and purposes, I'm alone.

Which reminds me.

My regulation ninety-six cubic feet of personal space looks nothing like Jessa's. No posters, no promo items, no merch of any kind. One time Jessa gave me an action figure of 22 for my birthday, and I tried to keep it on my shelf so as not to look like an asshole, but every time I looked at it, it just made me inexplicably sad, so I traded it to someone down the hall for some batteries.

My personal space contains two pillows, one blanket, one sheet, all regulation. Regulation shelf, unmodified. On that is my solar headlamp, my reusable bottles and travel cup, my dry shampoo and face wipes, my collapsible bike helmet, a few old books I hardly ever have time to read, some other assorted junk. Nothing on the walls.

Jessa would say (has said, will say again), *At least I exercise my obsession like normal people. Not . . . whatever you call* that. Her pointer finger taking aim at my regulation ninety-six. *Or are you going to tell me that* isn't *based on how you imagine 22's sense of, um, decor?*

I just like it, I tell her, not fooling anyone. *Maybe not all of us want to be merch groupies.*

At least that's healthy. You want to support their efforts, their sacrifices, you buy the memorabilia. Read a poster sometime. Watch the news. Or ask, like, literally anyone. It's common sense.

Which is why I waited until she had her mask back on before I did this.

I pull out a hardcover dust jacket from my shelf and open it. Inside isn't a book at all, just a loosely folded stack of papers. Printouts from newsfeeds. I couldn't really say why I went to the trouble and expense of printing them on actual paper in the first place, rather than just saving the relevant articles digitally *like normal people.* I guess there's no good reason. I started doing it, and I never stopped.

There are about a hundred pages here, a physical record of all the missions and engagements in which 22 has been involved. This stuff spans years. All the way back to his first major engagement, when they sent him and 06 out to zone 4, deep Greenleaf turf, to disrupt a convoy. If I flip back to that printout, I'll see him, maybe thirteen years old, bloodied gloves, smudged face, averted eyes. I don't. But I'm still thinking about what B said, so in light of that: Is this the face of a person who used to be a little kid with a favorite toy and a pet kitten and a bedtime story routine? It feels like a stretch.

My most recent printout is still in the back pocket of my jeans. It's sat there for the better part of a week while I've waited for my opportunity to take it out and put it with the others. But getting a few minutes of privacy when you live in a hotel room with eight other people is not something that happens every day.

I lift my hips to get the paper out of my pocket and unfold it.

ARMY OF TWO, the headline reads. Then under it is a picture of 06 and 22 standing in front of a pile of rubble that apparently used to be a Greenleaf weapons-development lab.

There are a lot of articles about 06 and 22 in my collection. They're the only two operatives left who were partners originally. All dozen of them were partnered up in some kind of buddy system nobody fully understands. All three surviving operatives run missions together sometimes, but 08's partner, 21, died this past autumn, killed in action like the rest.

I skim the article, like 06 and 22 would have magically gotten names attached to them when I wasn't looking. Names that aren't numbers. People names like *Elena*. But no. In the game, in real life, everywhere, they remain, unstoppably, eternally, iconically, 06 and 22.

B's out of her mind, obviously. But water's water, so I'm fine with playing along if that keeps everyone happy. I shake my head and add the paper to the hidden stack, then flop back against the pillow and pull my blackout mask back on.

Finding 08 and 22 in such quick succession seems to have been pretty popular with our viewers. Sure, there'd been hundreds of people there ogling 08 and his skateboard, but none of them were teamed with Jessa and got the rocket-fist-to-the-sternum treatment. The only decent footage of 22 that came out of that mess was mine. It doesn't really count as a sighting in the same way finding 28 did, because 22 was being piloted by that dipshit and steered directly toward the highest population density in the zone, but I don't know. I guess what happened next was amusing enough to earn us some likes and subscribes.

Are people out there making "hilarious" memes out of Nycorix getting skewered through the larynx? Almost definitely. But all my wiped inventory has already been more than replaced out of the goodness of the hearts of randos, so as far as I'm concerned, let the internet go on internetting. I'm doing the best I've done in months.

Not only do I have an impressive little pile of in-game items, but some credits and cash and water, too. And almost a hundred more fans have joined our stream. What that is is insurance. B could think better of her conspiracy theory, decide not to pay us, but if our streak holds, this will be worth doing for the subscriber swag alone.

Fifty minutes until power curfew. I pull up the footage I got of 22. I replay it all, from the suborbital drop to me bleeding out on the sidewalk. And then I replay it again. I touch the place on my throat where the sword went in. I genuinely don't know what the fuck is wrong with me.

The next time I replay the footage, I skip back just a few seconds too far. There's 08, being mobbed by three hundred dumbasses just like me. I hear my own voice saying, *Do you know a girl named Elena?* and Jessa protesting at my shoulder.

"Elena?" 08 says, and shakes his head just like before. "Sorry, can't help you."

And down comes the suborbital drop, and 08 and Jessa and three hundred dumbasses are incinerated in a bowl of fire all the colors of an oil spill.

But this time I know it's coming, and it doesn't distract me from something I didn't really notice before.

As the street beneath his boots ignites and liquefies, 08 is still talking. To me.

I freeze the replay. Skip back a second. Play.

I can't make it out. The background noise is too loud. Hell, the foreground noise is too loud. It's three hundred death cries and the sound of an eight-lane highway being blasted into fondue. I can't do anything with this.

But Jessa can.

hey. you still have all that shit you used to clean up the audio file that time we found 11 singing that weird song in the middle of that hurricane?

A couple minutes pass. I have to physically restrain myself from scrambling up to her bunk and peeling back her mask. Eventually she responds.

oh, now you want to talk to me

it's about the footage we just got

oh. yeah, that's kind of why i came up to your bunk in the first place. you looked like you needed to talk

not about that. about 08. i just went and watched the footage. he's still talking to me as the drop comes down

what's he saying??

that's the thing, it's hard to make out. i was thinking we could maybe scrub the background crap off of it a little

The pause this time is shorter. can do

I can hear her stifling a yawn from across the gap between our bunks. *Engage,* I tell myself, and message her: you fall asleep?

just a little. i was dreaming. there were some puppies but their tongues were wrong?

i'll get you some coffee Then I realize what time it is. actually there's half an hour left before curfew. i'll make us dinner while you work

is that instead of coffee?

I feel a corner of my mouth quirk. in addition to

ok deal

I leave Jessa to it and climb down to the little kitchen area. Ryan and Jackson are already in line for the microwave behind

Talya, and a quick glance at the pantry shelf informs me we're out of instant noodles.

All right. I could use the walk anyway.

gonna go grab food, I message Jessa. yell if you need me

yep yep

I speedwalk the six flights down. The hallways are more congested than usual, not only with foot traffic but with sleeping bags and yoga mats and the odd inflatable mattress shoved up against the walls. Backpacks and duffel bags and shopping bags and suitcases. Every conceivable kind of winter coat, from the smart-fabric ones that'll get stolen within days, all the way down to the ones that are threadbare to the point of nonexistence. Sleeping bodies, injured bodies, children tearing up and down the hall with more energy than all the rest of us combined.

I wonder what building's been bombed out this time. Some shitty part of my brain points out that our water rations will be cut again to make room for these new hotel residents. Some possibly shittier part of my brain responds that as long as B comes through with her payment, I don't technically have to care. But the rest of me is running calculations: either way, I just got twenty-five gallons. How much more of that can I afford to give away?

It isn't much, of course. Even the promise of five additional gallons a week isn't going to remotely take the edge off this catastrophe. And it's just going to get worse. It always does.

I get down to the company store and gather up my coffee and noodles. There are enough people here that there's an actual line backed up behind the scanners, which would explain why many of those sleeping areas I saw up in the hall were empty. I wait my turn, watching a couple of kids wander away from their group and stand in front of the display of SecOps action figures, loudly comparing which ones are in each kid's collection. I see their faces fall as it seems to hit them that their collections are probably back in the wreck of whatever building they fled from to end up living in a hallway here.

I reach over to a nearby display and grab a couple of candy bars for them, but by the time the scanner gets to me, the kids are gone.

Anyway, Jessa is messaging me.

meet me in the garden asap

I check the time. you want raw noodles for dinner?

forget the noodles just get up here

Forget the noodles is such a distinctively un-Jessa-like thing to say that it shuts me up directly. So I walk through the scanner, shoving the instant noodle packages and candy bars in my pocket with one hand, balancing the coffees in the other. Then I shoulder through the door and power across the lobby toward the stairs.

The garden is on the roof. From here that's twenty flights of stairs. It's no easy thing not spilling that coffee while I jog them. I've mostly succeeded by the time I push the door open and step out into the evening.

It's cold. Real cold. The wind is only worse up here, and the darkness doesn't help.

i'm here

by the oranges, Jessa replies. warmer in here

I head into the rows of greenhouses. Past lettuce, tomatoes, potatoes, beets. Oranges are in the same greenhouse as lemons, with some blackberry bushes let loose in the understory of the trees. I lift the flap and duck in.

It's like walking into summer. Or at least a particularly humid spring. Jessa is sitting with her back against the wall, apparently not noticing the condensation that must be soaking through her coat.

It doesn't escape my notice that she's sitting in the exact corner that's well known to be out of sight of the security cameras, now that the blackberry brambles have run sufficiently amok to hide it. I arrange myself, careful of the thorns, eyeing Jessa warily.

"What is this?"

"Just wanted to get away from the noise," she says, crooking two fingers at the coffees with so much fake casualness that her hand is shaking. "Lot of new people on our floor. Sound comes right through the walls."

"Yeah, I saw them on my way down to the store," I say, handing her the coffee.

"It's nice up here," Jessa goes on. "I just like it."

Tone and cadence and delivery, it's the exact *I just like it* that I tell her when she asks about my ninety-six regulation and she doesn't buy it for a second.

She's still looking straight at me when she takes her lenses out.

Whatever she's so worked up about, she's not exactly giving a master class in not acting suspicious. If there *was* somebody watching her, I would imagine this continuous popping-out-of-lenses would only raise attention, not dissipate it.

But B's paranoia has clearly rubbed off on her, and Jessa can be as stubborn as a bag of rocks when she gets locked on to an idea. I know this conversation isn't going to progress until I remove my lenses too, and the muggy greenhouse air is starting to lie uncomfortably on my skin.

I sigh. Then I take them out.

"Okay," I say with exaggerated patience. "*What.*"

She doesn't say anything, just hands me a pocket screen. I don't know where she's even gotten it. Nobody uses them anymore. I haven't seen one in years.

I take it out of sleep mode. There's 08, paused, standing in the crowd of player characters.

I glance up at Jessa. "This is the cleaned-up version?"

She nods jerkily. Nervous energy is pouring off her. She

looks like she's seen a ghost. Or like she's won the lottery. It's weirdly hard to say.

I unpause the file.

"Do you know a girl named Elena?" I hear me ask.

Offscreen, Jessa's voice: "Dude, *what*—"

And 08 furrows his brow at me. "Elena?" he says. Shakes his head a little. "Sorry, can't help you."

The suborbital drop crashes down, a shimmering wash of fire. But this time it's silent. The death cries are gone too. The sound of bodies dropping. It's only 08.

I blink, rewind a second. I can't have heard that right.

Jessa's eyes beam into me like headlights. I hit play.

"—can't help you," 08 says. "Elena's dead."

part two
company man

I SMASH PAUSE AND DROP THE SCREEN like it's burned my hands.

"We can't jump to conclusions," I hear myself say. "We don't know . . ."

"What don't we know?" Jessa hisses. "B was right about 05 and this is proof. What we're holding here is *proof*—"

"Keep your voice down. What we're holding is flimsy speculation at best. It doesn't mean anything definitively."

"Then why are you telling me to keep my voice down?"

"Because this paranoia is *contagious*. B gave it to you, but you're not giving it to me. It stops here."

"You know, it's no wonder you have such a thing for 22. You are *exactly alike*—"

"Okay. First? Fuck off. And second . . ." I trail off. On my lap the screen displays nothing but the jumbled rainbow of the drop. I draw in a shaking breath, swipe the file back a few frames, press play.

Elena?

Sorry, can't help you.

Elena's dead.

I look back up at Jessa. "It's weird. I'll give you that." I swallow. "It's very weird."

"Yeah." Jessa's voice has deflated. "So what the hell do we do with it?" Almost instantly she lights back up. "Oh my god. We have to show this to B. But not online. In person. Immediately."

I nod slowly. *Paranoia*, I remind myself. *Don't jump to conclusions.*

But I'm having a really hard time finding somewhere else to jump instead.

"Message her," I say at length. "Just say we have footage to show her. Don't tell her more than that. Not even if she asks. We have to meet. We have to show her something. That's all." I pick up the screen and hold it out to her. "And we need to keep this safe. Do you want to or should I?"

"I got it." Jessa pockets it. "It's easier for me to hide. I've got more stuff." She cracks a grin, which almost immediately falls away. "Should we lie low for a while? Stay off the game for a few days?"

"If I was looking for weird behavior, I'd be more interested in the person who suddenly stops doing what they do every day," I tell her. "I say we keep up business as usual, and meantime we try to get this out to B. Wherever you end up hiding it, we should both know where it is. In case . . ."

In case what? I don't know. The idea of someone coming after us because of this is like something out of a bad movie. But on the other hand . . . there's undeniably *something* here. Something we found. Something that's up to us to protect long enough to get it back to B. Then she can do what she wants with it. Anyone asks us, we're just doing our job. Taking sponsor requests. They're not about to disappear the however many million streamers who base their livelihoods on doing pretty much exactly that.

My coffee has gone cold in my hand. The noodle packages crinkle in my pocket. There's twelve minutes left before curfew.

"Let's get back," I say, putting my lenses in. "I did promise I'd make dinner."

THE NEXT MORNING I'm up early, out walking dogs again. This time it's for Mr. Assan, who commutes to his office job in the city every morning from the room he shares in a crumbling split-level ranch near the high school here in old town. I guess the place he used to live is gone, but the place he works is still there? I'm not sure, and I've never bothered asking.

I like walking his dog, though. Partly it's the dog herself, Flora, who's basically a ninety-pound puppy. But mostly it's the route I get to take when I do. His house is part of a long row of houses that backs onto some kind of abandoned nature trail. I'm not sure how far it goes. According to the only map I found online that includes it, it runs south away through woods and farmland, and north through the city. I assume it pretty much vanished when New Liberty got dropped on top of it, but I never walk it that far anyway. A mile or so at most.

The trail's so overgrown it's invisible in places, plants growing up through the pavement, but you can still find it if you know where to look. Even days like today, when it's covered with snow.

There are no footprints besides mine and Flora's, which suits me just fine. I walk and check my messages obsessively, every few minutes, like I wouldn't hear the ping of one arriving in all this snow-hushed silence. Jessa was already gone when I left. It's Wednesday, so that means she's out with Keisha collecting litter for nickel deposits out near the highway.

I check the time. 8:47. She told me she messaged B over two hours ago.

It's still early, I remind myself. *Not everybody has to get up in the freezing dark to walk other people's dogs or pick up other people's garbage.*

But we don't hear back from B today at all. Or tomorrow. Or the day after that.

By Saturday morning we're both just the tiniest bit on edge. We've kept up appearances, streaming the game like we've always done, making half-assed flailings at our thousands, trying to get the up-close footage B wanted. Our lucky streak from earlier this week doesn't continue. We catch sight of a beacon in the distance, once, and one time 17 zips past us on a hover-bike, laughing his little eternally-nine-year-old head off. That's it. There's no footage on the order of 28 alone in the field, or my bizarre staring contest with 22.

And nothing remotely like what 08 said to me.

Saturday afternoon we're up in the garden, actually working a legitimate shift this time. It's all volunteer-run, and nobody cares who takes shifts when, as long as everyone pays their watering dues and everyone pulls their weight, so it's easy enough to get in there together and talk quietly while we weed the strawberry beds shoulder to shoulder.

"She hasn't replied to you *at all*?" I whisper.

"Nothing," Jessa whispers back. "I can't raise her." She pulls out a dandelion, shaking the caught soil from the roots. How did that even get in here? "And our first week's payment was due yesterday."

My scalp tingles with sudden mild alarm. Not answering our messages is one thing. But not paying us for the job she dragged us all the way out to the middle of the city to hire us for?

"Keep trying. Tell her something else. Something that gets her attention."

"You mean you want me to actually *say* what we—"

"No. I don't know. Not that *exactly*, but—"

"I *am* trying. I've *been* trying. She's not answering." Jessa's next weed comes out at the wrong angle, pulls up a strawberry runner with it. She tucks that back into the dirt of the bed, apologizing to it under her breath like it can hear her. "I don't know what to do."

"Okay. It's been, what, three days? Almost four?" I work another minute in silence, letting the repetitive movements of my hands help get my thoughts in order.

Almost four days of silence. When we have information she'll definitely want to hear. I don't know what B does for a living, so maybe she's away for work? But her brother's account pays our water, and that was due yesterday. Could they *both* be off on business or whatever? Maybe, but it seems odd after B's extensive checking up on us before even taking us on for the job. Why go to the trouble of hiring us and then go quiet when we actually turn up something?

Did she bring someone else in to replace us? Did someone get to her, scare her into dropping her plan altogether? Did her ancient library computer finally break down? Did she decide the Elena theory wasn't worth the cost or the effort or the risk to pursue?

I can't say any of this to Jessa, of course. She'd just assume the worst.

Round and round, swirling, nothing factual to grab hold of. It's not going to coalesce until I force it to.

"I say we go out there tomorrow."

Jessa looks up sharply. "Back to the coffee shop?"

I nod. "Without actually talking to her, all we have is guesswork, and that gets us nowhere. We go out there and we sit her down and show her the file."

"And find out about our pay," Jessa adds.

"And find out about our pay. If she's not there, her sister will be, or someone will know where the sister is. It's her place. Someone has to know."

"All right." Jessa gives one decisive nod. "Let's do it."

"And who knows?" I say as we stand up to leave. "She might message you back any minute, save us the bus fare."

But I wouldn't bet on it.

WE'RE HALFWAY OUT the front door the next morning with our backpacks and coffees and energy bars when Jessa freezes like she's just walked into a field of undetonated ordnance.

"Oh," she breathes, "*shit—*"

"What is—"

"It's *Sunday*. I have to *work*. I promised Tegan I'd take over for them today at their delivery job thing because they have that other thing they just started and it overlaps? They asked me a week ago, and I promised."

I process this a second. "Can you maybe unpromise? Cover for them next time?"

"They left in the middle of the night, they're not due back until this afternoon!" Jessa's voice swoops up to this weird panicked note and stays there. "I flake out on them, they get fired. I can't do that to them!"

"Okay, calm down. When do you have to be at Tegan's job?"

A glassy-eyed pause while she checks something. "Nine thirty."

I check the time. It's 7:14. Our bus leaves at 7:30. I pull up the schedule and sigh. Buses back to old town run on the hour, which means we either somehow have to ride to the city, get to the coffee shop from the bus stop, have our dealings with B, and get *back* to the bus stop to ride back here by eight o'clock—or Jessa's going to be late. And I know without even attempting to run the numbers that option one is impossible. We'll be lucky to have cleared the checkpoint by eight.

"I wish we had suborbital drops in real life," Jessa moans, rubbing her temples.

"We do," I say absently. "Just not for civilian use . . ." I trail off. Shake my head to clear it. "Okay. You're not going to make it there and back in time. You're just not."

"I know!"

"It's fine. Give me the screen. I'll go."

Both Jessa's eyebrows shoot up. "You. By yourself."

I gesture: *Do you see anyone else around?*

"You *never* do the people parts." The idea is apparently so outrageous that it physically backs her up a step. "Not even in the game."

"Well, looks like I'm doing them today." I crook two fingers for the screen. "Give. You can process the existential horror of it on your way to work. I'm going to miss my bus."

As it is, once she hands the screen over with a dubious look that is the opposite of supportive, I still have to run, and there's not a chance in hell of a window seat.

The bus takes more or less the same route the car took the other day. The checkpoint's still there, though a second pop-up interrogation pod has joined the first, and there are more cars pulled off to the side for inspection than before. I catch a glimpse of a teenage boy on the ground between two cars, a checkpoint officer sitting on him while a woman stands over them both, screaming something too slurred with fear and fury to make out. The kid's face is bloody, one eye already swelling shut. He looks scared. He says something, and the officer lifts the kid's head and smashes it face-first into the pavement.

The bus pulls up into the scanner field, and I can't see the kid anymore, or the officer, they've been eclipsed by one of the pods. I should've been able to see the woman, though. Probably another officer tackled her, too. But even through the smart windows of the bus I can hear her screaming.

That's when I see the other kid, lying on the ground around back of the car. He looks even younger than the first one. He's not moving. Blood runs out of his mouth.

Then he's gone too, vanished behind the concrete perimeter of the scanner field.

I could have streamed that, I think, far too late. *I could have put that online. I could have done something.*

The man sitting beside me notices me trying to look out his window. "Should've complied," he says, and goes blank-faced as he returns his attention to whatever he's doing online.

"How do you know he didn't?" I ask him, but he's not listening.

We pass through the scanner field without much incident. Just twenty minutes when the driver has to pull off to the shoulder so two passengers' bags can be checked. The officers' guns stay holstered for the most part. Nobody gets dragged off into one of the pods. One of the bag-search passengers starts crying because the officers have wrecked the toy solar glider she built for her grandkids. Snapped the fuselage in half to check for contraband.

Should've complied goes rattling through my head. Except she did. I had my eyes on her the whole time, and all she did was answer questions—*I made it for my grandkids, the guidance systems are extremely delicate, please be careful*—and attempt to smile politely.

The man next to me gets off before my stop. When I let him past I trip him, just a little. Just enough to spill his coffee down the front of his suit.

"Sorry," I say. He doesn't look like he believes me. I don't think I'd believe me either.

"Stupid bitch," he says, and flounces off the bus.

Fine by me. Now I get my window seat.

I DON'T KNOW how to get to the coffee shop *precisely*. I don't even know its name. It didn't have a proper sign. Just some hole in the wall a few blocks from Prosperity Park.

I disembark and bring up the map interface I saved. It marks out my route before me in glowing blue dots that trail away down the street to my right. I follow them for five blocks, then turn left and walk another two blocks, which puts me in sight of the park. I stop there and message Jessa a snapshot of the statue. almost there

Delivery job or no delivery job, her response comes almost immediately. keep me posted

copy that

Here's the tricky part. I found the park online, but I still don't know the name of the coffee shop. We looked up "coffee shops near Prosperity Park" and got twenty results, although over half of those were company-store branches. We didn't get further than that before power curfew, and the plan was to narrow down the list on the bus, but the thing with the checkpoint was just so lodged in my head the whole way here that I never got around to it.

I pull the list back up. It's overwhelming. I put it away.

If we'd streamed the route before, I could play it back right now and follow it. If we hadn't taken out our lenses. Oh well.

Maybe my feet remember.

We followed B past the statue, I know that much. I scan the storefronts, looking for landmarks. Then I take off walking.

Half an hour of wandering and doubling back and cursing and retracing later, I'm standing in front of B's sister's coffee shop.

Except I'm not.

It's gone.

There's a Comforts of Home in its place, an exact copy/paste of the one where I buy my worldly goods every day. They may as well have portaled it out of the hotel lobby and plopped it here.

To the left of Comforts of Home is the same hair-and-nails place that had been to the left of B's sister's coffee shop. To the right, the same lens outfitters. I can even see powdery blue marks on the sidewalk where somebody stepped on a piece of the old-school chalk from B's sister's old-school chalkboard.

But no coffee shop.

Jessa's next message comes while I'm standing in front of Comforts of Home gawking like a tourist who's never seen a company store.

coffee shop eta?

I'm a moment in composing an answer to that. I can hear my heartbeat in my ears. *Something's wrong*, it's saying. *Something's very wrong.*

hit a snag, I manage eventually. i'll—

what kind of a snag?

Um.

took a wrong turn out of the park. all these streets look alike That part at least is true. should be there in a few

Then, because there's a distinct chill settling on me that has very little to do with the cold and a whole lot to do with the cheery hologram of the Stellaxis logo exactly at eye level by the door: look i gotta take my lenses out, the air is gritty as all shit here and it's getting caught in my eyes

yeah, Jessa replies. i remember. ok. poke me the second you get them back in ok?

of course

B's voice in my head: *Hey. If I suddenly disappear, at least we'll know I was right.*

Realizing I should probably have done this a while ago, I take my lenses out and put them away. Then I take a deep breath, snug my backpack against my shoulders like I'm adjusting armor, and walk into the store.

It's any Comforts of Home. It's every Comforts of Home. That's the whole marketing gimmick. You always know what to expect. The coffee machine is in a certain place. The snacks are in a certain place. The company-logo t-shirts and company-mascot plushies are near the SecOps action figures, which are near the designer lens cases and cleaning kits.

It's the same deal with the Stellaxis coffee shops, fourteen of which were cluttering up the list I pulled up in the park. And the Stellaxis fast-food restaurants. And the Stellaxis vehicle dealerships. Everything in its place. Everything sleek and shiny and utterly devoid of anything remotely resembling B's sister's coffee shop.

I go and make browsing body language in front of the display of lens cleaner. If I'm on record as having taken out gritty lenses, I may as well double down on it. Meantime I listen to the other customers. See if they have anything to say that might count as a clue.

I get a whole lot of nothing. There are eleven other customers in here, and nobody says a word to anybody else. The cashier scanners don't have the kind of small-talk AI that the screens at the company coffee shops do, so that'd be a dead end even if I wanted to openly interrogate a computer owned by the same corporation that disappeared not only B, but B's sister's *entire place of business*. Which I don't.

Don't jump to conclusions, I tell myself. But it's getting harder. It's getting a whole lot harder.

I buy a bottle of lens cleaner, a granola bar, a protein drink, and a pack of the disposable filtration masks I couldn't find in the company-store branch back home. Then I shove it all in my backpack and head out into the street. There's a bench a couple of storefronts down, outside a tiny laundromat not much bigger than a closet. I park myself there and try to look casual as I sip my protein drink and eavesdrop.

It takes a long time. A couple of hours, probably. I'd know if my lenses were in. There's something weirdly comforting about sitting here in utter anonymity, though. Nobody's messaging me. Nobody's talking to me. Nobody even knows who I am. In other circumstances it'd be pretty great.

I've gone through the entire protein drink and also the granola bar and also just kind of sat there a while doing nothing, when what I've been waiting for finally happens.

A woman walks past Comforts of Home doing a double take that almost earns her a sprained ankle. "I thought this was a coffee place," she mutters to herself or someone online.

A man on his way out of Comforts of Home with a couple of shopping bags stops when he hears this. "It was," he informs her. "The building got trashed in an accidental drone strike a few days ago. No loss if you ask me. These things are so convenient. I was hoping they'd put one on this block." Like there isn't one on both blocks sandwiching this one.

From the look on the woman's face, she wasn't actually after the free history lesson. She nods at him tightly and walks away.

I wait another few minutes, then get up and do a slow pass in front of Comforts of Home. I cross the street so I can look at it head-on from a distance. I take fifteen minutes circling around the back of the block it's in to see if that helps. Then another fifteen minutes circling around the other side to check out the rest of the block. By that point I'm moderately freaked out enough that I just kind of keep walking. Away from the park and the bus stop and Comforts of Home. Nowhere in particular. Just away.

Because here's the thing. No matter which way I look at that building, I see no evidence of damage. At all. The outer walls of

Comforts of Home and the sidewalk outside are pristine. The upper levels still look the same as they ever did. Apartments, probably, or maybe an extended-stay hotel. Lots of little windows with people's stuff in them. There's a pink plush dolphin hanging from a suction cup in a corner window, which I can't be one hundred percent sure I saw before but certainly seems familiar.

The storefronts to the left and right of Comforts: similarly untouched.

Now I don't know a *whole* lot about drone strikes, accidental or not, but this seems just the tiniest bit off.

It's past midday now, the winter sun already beginning to lower itself between the buildings, so I have to squint where the late light caroms off the glass. It's cold and I'm cold and I can't stop walking. I don't know what to do. The pocket screen and the 08 file are burning a hole through my mind. I keep having to stop myself from adjusting the backpack, like passersby can see the secret thing I'm carrying.

I have to process this—however I can, as much as I can— before I bring it to Jessa. I have to figure out how to present the facts in a way that seems the most rational. I don't want to scare her over nothing. But I'm no longer entirely sure I would be. The not-understanding is an itch in my brain that will only get worse and worse until I hammer out some kind of answer. Some way to move forward from here.

I could go home and forget about all of this. Stream the game for other sponsors, walk other people's dogs, try to grind away a daily thousand once in a while. Live my quiet little life. The loss of that five gallons a week would be a hit, of course, but we never really had it in the first place to lose. Here we are, surviving all the same. We just picked up three hundred new subscribers. We find 28 again, or do something else that grabs their eyeballs, we'll pick up more. Slow and steady. Heads down. Keep the peace.

There's a jagged edge to that plan, though, and I keep tripping over it.

Sure, B was a convicted anticorporate terrorist on a lockout. Any number of reasons she could've skipped town. Weird to do it right after taking me and Jessa on for this project, but not impossible.

But.

If B was right.

If B was right and they got rid of her because she was right.

If they got rid of B because she was right about something Stellaxis wanted hidden.

That means a couple of things.

One. It means that Stellaxis lied about the operatives. The real ones. The real ones that weren't grown in tanks in the lab at all but were actual children from actual families who were stolen from the wreckage of their lives and transplanted into some lab somewhere in Stellaxis HQ and changed and *kept*. Children, if B is right, like Elena.

The official line is that the operatives are the intellectual property of Stellaxis Innovations. That's in the small print of every backing card of every SecOps action figure in existence. It's in the end-user license agreement of the game. It's on the tags of the goddamn t-shirts. It's known. The operatives were literally *numbered* fresh out of their growth tanks. The company did everything short of stamping a logo on them. Unless they did that, too.

But how can a stolen child be corporate intellectual property? The game, sure. The copyright on the action figures, probably. But *people*?

I mean, I remember when I lost my family. I remember being taken into a big bright room full of other kids who'd been recently orphaned by the war. I remember my leg was bleeding where a piece of our building had fallen on it. I remember my head hurt from the loud noise of the transport full of cry-ing kids. I remember being asked a lot of questions, although I have no idea what they were or what I answered. And I remem-ber they gave me orange juice afterward. Orange juice and a cookie. And then they handed me off to an overseer who gave me a toothbrush and a jumpsuit and a cot in the camps, where I stayed until I was old enough to enter the housing lottery and move into the hotel on my own.

I try to imagine, if B is right, what would have happened to Elena instead when her backstory unraveled along the same route as mine. Where she got taken. Where exactly her path began to diverge from mine, or Jessa's, or everyone's. How ex-actly you go about taking an eight-year-old kid and transform-ing her, like some kind of beautiful, terrible, fucked-up butterfly, into something that can take on a mech in single combat. How exactly, among all of those kids from all of those busted build-ings and obliterated families, you choose.

Again I try to picture 22 as a kid in an apartment with par-ents, a sibling or two. Maybe a pet dog like Mr. Assan's Flora. A show he begs to stay up late to watch. A birthday cake he asks for every year. I don't get very far.

It could have been Elena in the hotel and Jessa in the field. Or me. She might have been in that bright room, right next to me. I might have been one of the last people on earth to see her—the real her—alive.

But all that, all that mess together, is only the first of the two things that are colliding in my head, raising alarms that wind up and up, louder and shriller, the longer and farther and deeper into the descent of the evening I walk.

The second is this.

If B and her sister and her sister's coffee shop are all gone because she met with me and Jessa, or because I opened my idiot mouth and asked 08 about Elena on livestream for the potential entire internet to see, or even because she lied and she's actually paying us in illegal water, poached or hacked or collected or however she got it—how long is it going to take the people who somehow erased a coffee shop and installed a company store in the span of *days* to decide to come looking for me?

It's evolving into real fear now, coiling down inside me, icy and slick. I have to get home. I have to talk to Jessa. Not online. Not where it can be traced. Somewhere quiet. Somewhere private. Somewhere like the hidden corner of the greenhouse where she showed me the cleaned-up 08 file, which feels like weeks ago.

But I'm way deeper into the city now than I ever intended. I have no idea where I am. It's less crowded here, and there's evidence of recent fighting. Scorch marks on the buildings, though whatever burned them has gone. Bullet holes. Up ahead there's the remains of a barricade, foot and bike traffic parting around it like water around a rock. A building to the diagonal of me really *has* been clipped by a drone strike or something. An entire corner of its roof has broken off and crushed a parked car that nobody has since bothered to move.

I scan the storefronts, looking for a place that's likely to have a public restroom I can use. I have to find somewhere to put my lenses back in so they can show me the route to the bus. I can't do that out here, I've walked too far and ended up in an actual no-shit war zone, there's who even knows what in the air. If I had my lenses in, they'd tell me if it was clean. At least nobody around me is wearing masks, that's probably a good—

Out of nowhere, maybe three blocks ahead of where I'm standing, a helicopter slews sideways between two buildings and cannonballs into the glass face of a third. It hangs there for a few long seconds and then drops, trailing fire. The explosion when it lands sounds like the end of the world.

People run past me, going as fast as they can back the way I

came. Away from the fireball and the panes of glass still dropping out of the broken building and the deep steady concus-
sions in the ground that at first I think are maybe aftershocks of
the explosion and then realize are something utterly and completely else.

Preceded by the blue-lit barrels of its gun-arms and a sound
like ten trillion mosquitoes, far too smoothly for something of
its size, stepping across the sun and throwing the whole street
into shadow, a citykiller mech stalks into view.

FOR LONG, LONG SECONDS I'M FROZEN TO the spot, every higher order of my brain trying to convince me that what I'm seeing isn't real. I've seen them on the newsfeeds, of course, and in the game, but not like this. Not anything *like* like this.

I have no choice now. I'm cut off without my lenses. I have to know.

I flatten myself into the recessed doorway of a vacant storefront and pop them in with shaking hands. Immediately my implant tells my lenses where I am and the alert pops up: *PHASE ORANGE—MODERATE THREAT DETECTED—PLEASE REMAIN INDOORS UNTIL FURTHER NOTICE—IF UNABLE, REPORT TO NEAREST AUTHORITY FOR FURTHER INSTRUCTION*

"Moderate," I say through chattering teeth. "Right."

Nothing about the air quality being compromised. But maybe it's different here in the actual city than in old town. Maybe a place that classifies exploding helicopters and fucking citykiller mechs as *moderate threats* doesn't bother telling people when they're breathing in necrotizing nanoparticles or hallucinogen bursts or any of the thirty-four other bioweapons on the safety announcement symptom-checker FAQ, any of which could be floating around in what I'm breathing *right the hell now.*

I unsling my backpack, grab a mask, peel back the strip, and wait while it adheres to my face. Then I creep out from my hiding place and into the street.

The crowd is rushing past me now full bore, some shrieking, some shouting, some silent. I don't know who they are or where they're going, but it's away from the monstrosity up the street, which sounds like exactly where I want to be.

If I streamed this, it'd give Jessa a heart attack, straight up. So I don't. But if I survive the next few minutes, I'm going to want to pore over the details of them later. It's like I'm in the game. It's unreal. And yet it's one of the realest things I've ever seen.

I start recording.

Where there's a gap in the onrushing of people, I slip into it and let it carry me. I blend in pretty well with my mask and backpack, but nobody's paying attention to me anyway. They're running down the street dragging their children and pets and go bags with them. A number of them are visibly freshly injured. Confusingly, others have older damage. Makeshift bandages caked in days of city grime. Like they've been out here, walking wounded, for a while. Why haven't they *reported to nearest authority,* whose *further instruction* might have involved, like, a hospital? A woman carrying two babies and a backpack twice the size of mine is hobbling next to me on a leg that looks like it's been in its splint for a while. I gesture at her to pass me something to carry—it's hard to breathe and run and talk through the mask at the same time—but she just gives me a dirty look like I'm trying to steal her backpack or maybe her babies and keeps powering forward.

A second helicopter chops the air overhead. *THIS AREA IS OFF LIMITS TO CIVILIAN ACTIVITY,* shouts a voice distorted by loudspeaker. A second, smaller version of the announcement plays directly into my head via my implant, a smaller, harmonic echo chasing the huge noise of the speaker. It also displays in a rolling banner of text across my visual field like a newsfeed chyron. *DISPERSE. DISPERSE. REPEAT: THIS AREA IS OFF-LIMITS. RETURN TO YOUR HOMES AND REMAIN INDOORS UNTIL FURTHER NOTICE.*

Well, my home is miles away. Not much chance of that.

The loudspeaker starts to say something else, but it dies in a crackle of blue fire that rips the helicopter from the sky and hurls it away over the buildings. There comes a blaring sound from somewhere behind me, deep and loud enough to rattle my molars together.

Above that, screams rise.

Despite myself, I look back.

There's a crowd of people huddled around the side of this massive fake-old building that might be some kind of museum. Dozens of them, hiding in the shadow of a gigantic pillar. They're still screaming even after the blue fireball of the helicopter has passed over them and gone. A number of them are messing with their faces, but from here I have no idea why. Something's clearly got them frozen there, together in a group. Something above and beyond the fear.

I glance from them up the street. The mech, having wrapped up its helicopter target practice, now has its hands full with a swooping murmuration of drones that arrives to lay down a peppering of suppressive fire at the level of the citykiller's pilot module.

The people by the museum thing aren't *all* that far away.

I need to get out of this. I need to get home. The smell in the air is something I can't place, but it slingshots me straight back through time until I'm a little kid in a bathtub being told jokes while I wait to die.

My hands are sweating. I wipe them on my pants. I want the sidewalk to open up and swallow me. I want to wake up and be back in my bunk. I want my vision to stop going dark around the edges like I'm about to pass out.

But at the same time, my mind has gone kind of shockingly clear. Later I'll decide I used up all my panic when I saw Comforts of Home where B's sister's coffee shop should have been. For now I turn fully back toward the museum and square my backpack on my shoulders. Deep breath.

Just like the game, I tell myself. *Just like the game.*

Pushing backward against that fleeing crowd is like walking through water up to my neck. I tuck my chin and bull forward. Within seven more iterations of the alert chyron, I'm standing in the shadow of those ridiculous pillars.

Up close, these are obviously people who are having a worse day than me, and that's saying something.

There are easily fifty of them, all crammed together. I don't know whether the injured people I saw before were all traveling together or there's just a higher concentration of them in this group, but everywhere I look are bandages and crutches and splints. Everyone's filthy and hungry looking, and I can hear at least three separate babies screaming.

Then I realize what they're reminding me of. Me. Me and the eight other survivors of my building, just after the recovery drones tasted our living-human chemical signature buried in the rubble and disinterred us. Except nobody's giving these people blankets and hot cocoa and company-logo toiletry bags. They're on their own.

At first I assume the injuries are what's slowing them down, what's making them hide by this awful building rather than getting out of the line of fire like they're supposed to.

And then I get a little closer, and I understand.

Pretty much every pair of eyes I look at is horribly bloodshot, the whites gone almost totally red like their eyeballs are hemorrhaging. Right in front of me a man cries out and scrabbles at his face with his fingers until another man stops him, and when his friend pulls his hands away, I can see where his retinas have swelled up around the edges of his lenses, which didn't pop out with the increased pressure but seem to have instead partially melted *into* the surface of his eyes somehow.

Now that I know to look for it, I see it everywhere in these people. Red, swollen eyes pushing up around lenses that won't come out. I don't know how they've been able to see enough to get here. Maybe somebody helped them this far and then ran off when the mech-helicopter-drone battle royale started bringing buildings down around their heads. Maybe whatever's in their eyes is something they picked up here. Some localized burst of something, probably not targeted at them. Collateral damage. Wrong place, wrong time. It happens.

Regardless, these people's lenses aren't interfacing with shit anymore, not in that condition. I wonder which of the bioweapons on the FAQ I'm looking at. It's like an interface scrambler admixed with some kind of hyperirritant, pepper spray or something nastier. I wonder if these people even got the *PHASE ORANGE* alert before the *MODERATE THREAT* was right on top of them.

I have a hell of a lot of questions. But no time for any of them.

Turn around, I tell myself. *Get your own ass out of here. They've made it this far. They'll be fine.*

But that's flagrant bullshit, and I know it. Maybe people who do nothing in situations like this live longer than people who stick their necks out, but I will hate my bystander ass for every day of my bystander life if I leave these people here to become collateral damage like the families of literally every single person I know.

"Follow me!" I hear myself shout. "I can get you out of here."

"Who is that?" someone calls. "That's not Emily."

"Fuck Emily," someone else replies. "Emily ditched us, and this one'll ditch us too. We stay here where it's safe."

No time to explain how where they are standing is the precise opposite of *safe*. All I have to do is hold my shit together long enough to get them out of citykiller stomping range. If I can't do that much, I'm fucked either way. "I'm not Emily and I'm not going to ditch you, but if you want to come with me, you have to fucking *move. Now.*"

They start grabbing onto each other's backpacks and coat sleeves and hands, lacing together into some kind of refugee agglomeration, like a colony of army ants or an archipelago of plastic digesters. It's pretty much how I expected them to travel, but the practiced ease of it gives me pause. How long have they been out here like this?

Three separate hands latch onto my backpack, and I have to suppress a shudder. Being touched by strangers is its own special circle of hell, and I will not be convinced otherwise. But nobody tries to take my backpack off, and nobody touches any part of my person.

I guess we're doing this.

"Everybody ready?" I call back. A drone crashes to the pavement not six feet away, drowning out my words. But when I move forward, they follow.

I travel with them for blocks and blocks. It's slow, it's painfully slow, and I haven't the faintest goddamn clue where I'm leading them, and I begin to regret my ill-advised high-mindedness almost immediately, but we make it work, staying low and tight against the buildings. Drones are still falling out of the sky, but that's mostly happening behind us now. Here the bigger problem is getting stampeded by other runners. It's like everybody in this goddamn city is fleeing on foot, and nobody knows where to go. I can hear cries behind me, but I can't stop and take account of new injuries. All I can do is keep moving.

I dare one glance backward. We're at the top of a rise in the street, and I can see way, way back over the crowd to the distant vanishing point where the mech's standing astride all eight lanes, taking potshots at something out of sight down a side avenue.

I don't look back again.

After a few more blocks, long past when my knees are wrecked from the hobbling, crouching run, and my shoulders are bruised from the backward pull on my backpack straps, and my nerves are shot to hell and back, I hear the mech take off down that side avenue, far faster than something that size should conceivably move.

But the screaming crowd is still barreling past, deafening. If I try to ask my group where they were headed or where they came from or where I should be taking them now, all it'll earn me is a squeezing tightness in my lungs from trying to yell through the filtration mask and two decades of mediocre physical fitness.

I decide to follow the main crowd. Eventually that scatters into groups, leaving me standing in open ground in the middle of a deserted street with fifty-plus people and not a solid game plan among us.

By this point I'm pretty much falling over with exhaustion and panic and relief at not being vaporized by those gun-arms or pancaked by a downed strike drone, but I can't exactly leave them here.

For lack of a better idea, I lead them into a back alley between high buildings and help them pack in. "We're safe here," I tell them, hoping this is true. "The mech is blocks away now and heading in the opposite direction." It's actually headed away at a ninety-degree angle, but I don't want to scare them more than they are already.

"Where are we?" someone asks.

Good question. I pull up a map and read off an address. As far as I'm concerned, it might as well be on the moon.

In the first piece of good news I've had all day, now that we've settled into the alley, three people immediately take charge. A woman and two men. They park themselves in the mouth of the alley, holding handguns that are going to do them a hilarious lot of good if that mech decides to double back and pay us all a visit.

Our little space backs onto a chain-link fence with a couple of dumpsters, then goes past the buildings behind and opens onto the street. If it comes to it, I wonder how many of these people are healthy enough to get over that fence. Hell, I wonder if I am. Now that we've stopped moving, the adrenaline rush of the last hour or so has run dry, dumping me entirely on my ass. We're as safe here as we're going to get, and sooner or later someone will have to help us.

I wait a few minutes. Nobody comes.

I work my way out of the packed alley and come level with the group leaders just a bit back from the street. "Do you all live in the same building? Give me the address and I can try to get you there if it's not too far."

"Address," the woman echoes, with this bitter noise that doesn't quite pass as a laugh. She's clutching that pistol like a security blanket. Would she try to fire blind against a sixty-foot-tall mech if it came to that? If she has people here to protect, her people, I know where I'd lay my money. "What *address.*"

This strikes me as overly cryptic, and I still have a bus to catch. "Whatever address. I'm saying, I can take you there. At least partway. If it's soon. I have to—"

"We're going to the hospital," someone else says. "We've been trying to get there for a couple days. It's been . . . complicated."

I can well imagine.

"I don't know where that is," I tell them. "But I can find out. Tell me the address, or the name of the hospital, and I'll pull it up. We can start making our way over to—"

Something maybe a block distant plummets and shatters, shaking the ground.

"No," the leader woman says. "We wait here until it calms down. Too risky."

I glance around. Nobody else seems in any kind of major hurry to move from this quiet space, and whatever choices they've been making have been keeping them alive so far, and I'm not about to pretend I know any better. I find myself a clearish spot against a wall and lean on it. I'm having a hard time picturing getting up and walking out there, through that, alone, in search of a bus station. Besides, I don't know who Emily is or what she did that ended with dumping fifty-plus helpless people at the feet of an honest-to-shit citykiller mech, but I'm guessing that in the grand scheme of things I probably don't want to be an Emily. Worst case, I can find somewhere to sleep tonight and grab a bus in the morning. At least I don't have any dog walking scheduled until the day after tomorrow.

Look at me, reassuring myself about job security when these might be my last minutes to live. That's pretty sad even for me.

"What happened to you," I say. "The gas attack or whatever? With your lenses? Is it water soluble?"

"How would I know?" the man says. "Do we look like we have any water to try with?"

"Well, what I'm saying is I do." I pull the bottle out of my backpack and hand it over. "It's not a lot, but it might clean up a few of you. Your lenses are probably toast, but if you can calm down the reaction enough to get them out, you might at least be able to see where you're going."

That is, if your lenses aren't completely melded to your eye-balls, I don't say. I imagine they're pretty well aware of the depth of the shit they're in without me spelling it out for them.

There's a pause. Even at this distance I can hear the city-killer mech clearly: the holding-pattern hum of its gun-arms, punctuated by a periodic dark blare as one discharges, then the sound of something imploding into blue fire.

I'd know that string of sounds anywhere. I just didn't fully appreciate until now how accurately they rendered it in-game.

Other sounds join it. Machine-gun fire pocking into con-crete, the whirring chop of another helicopter. An unseen shriek of metal, followed by two seconds of perfect silence and then a concussion that blows out so many windows I can still hear glass tinkling to the street a full minute later. Another drone array dopplers past us with a whine that hurts my teeth.

From the alley behind me comes a collective moan. Some-where a child starts crying.

"We lie low here," the leader woman says in a tone of quiet command. "When it dies down out there, we move out."

"It's going to be okay," the second man adds, voice pitched to carry. "Plan hasn't changed. We're still going to the hospital. We just have to wait a little, that's all. Just until it's safe."

That seems to be a long time coming. Plenty of time for me to sit against the wall and watch them splash the last of my water into their eyes and have a good long think about what exact type of hell I've wandered into and what my odds are of wandering back out of it anytime soon.

I can just hear the woman, speaking under her breath: "I told you, the hospital's full."

"You got a better idea?" the man says back. Not even angry. Just tired. "Sixty-some chemical attack victims? Bunch of kids? They'll have to let us in."

They start whispering to each other furiously, heading out to the mouth of the alley, just out of my hearing range.

After a few minutes the other man works his way back along the wall, holding out the now-empty bottle.

"Did it help?" I ask him, meeting him halfway to take it off his hands. Though I can guess the answer from how he's squinting and flinching like he's got all his eyelashes stuck in his eyes all at once.

"It's better than it was," he says, though every inch of his body language says different. "Appreciate it."

I glance over toward the other man and woman. Whatever happened to their argument, they now have their pistols out and are making some kind of squinty attempt at covering the street outside. They must have been given a turn at my water bottle, because at least now they're aiming the right way.

"Sure. Where'd you guys come from anyway? Somebody said you'd been out here for a while."

He snorts, then waves in the general direction of the mech, invisible but for the plumes of smoke thrown upward by its destruction. "One of those goddamn things took out our building in the middle of the night. You're looking at the last survivors of Hawk Watch Gardens."

I nod my sympathies. "Sunset Vista."

"Who names these places anyway? You ever even *seen* a hawk?"

"Sure. Few months ago. On a calendar."

He shakes his head. "Wait. Shit. Sunset Vista. I remember when your place came down. That was, what, ten, eleven years ago?"

"Going on twelve." I lift my chin at the packed alley. "At least they dragged me out of it."

"Yeah. Well. We were *asleep*, man. It was three in the morning. Do you see all those kids?"

"I see them."

"No way to prepare. Nobody came for us. And absolutely the fuck nowhere to go."

"Thought you were headed for the hospital."

"Hospital's closed," he says. "It's all over the news. They've been out of beds since last week. We've been figuring we'll run into a field clinic somewhere, but it hasn't happened yet. And now our lenses are all fucked, so they'll probably finally decide to make an announcement about the hospital opening back up, now that we won't—"

He cuts off, whirling, as the two guarding the mouth of the alley start to shout. They're losing their minds at something up the street I can't see from back here. The man I was talking to staggers out of the alley to join them, gun ready.

I swing my backpack around front and fumble for my taser. For all the good it'll do against whatever's coming down that road.

Whatever it is, it's not firing on us as it approaches. It's talking.

It's talking, and I almost drop my taser and my backpack when I hear it.

"Hold tight, we're gonna get you out of there," it says, and even with the speaker out of sight I know that voice, I've known it for years, game update by game update to keep it sounding as old as it should.

It's 06.

She glides into the alley, all in black, weapons in her belt. She stands with easy confidence, the kind of predatory grace I can't even compare to anything else except the in-game versions of the operatives, or maybe a tiger or something, if those extinct-wildlife minidocumentaries are true.

Jessa isn't going to believe it. *I* barely believe it. I check to make sure I'm still recording.

"Stellaxis StelTech SecOps operative 06 reporting," 06 says. "Who's in charge here?"

The woman with the gun steps forward amid a general background wash of exactly the kind of chatter you'd expect from several dozen people being paid a personal visit by a real-life SecOps operative, specifically the one who's pretty much universally lauded as a real-life fucking folk hero, fucked circumstances or no. Of course, they only show up when the circumstances are fucked. They're held in reserve for precisely that. The problems nobody else can or wants to fix. They're the shitshow brigade.

"Nobody really," the woman says. "I was leading them for a while because I knew the way to the hospital, but then . . ." She trails off, gesturing at her face. "We tried putting water on it."

06's brow furrows. She takes the woman's face in one gloved hand and tilts it into the light. She's obviously trying to be gentle, but the woman's expression makes it very clear this is not 06's strong suit. "Can you see?"

The woman shrugs, a little twitchily. She's got fifty-plus sort-of witnesses of 06 physically touching her. That's a story she's going to be telling for a while. "The water helped some. I'm at, I want to say, maybe sixty percent."

"I don't think this is one of ours," 06 says. "If I treat it wrong, it could just make it worse."

"We don't know what it was," one of the men says. "Some kind of blue mist. Kind of . . . sticky, almost? We were hiding under an overpass. I don't think it was meant for us. It just kinda slid the whole way up the street like fog."

"No," 06 says, her face clouding over. "I don't think it was meant for you." She sighs and lets go of the woman's face. "Well, I'm seeing plenty of busted legs and things. That at least we can do something about."

We?

Then I realize who's standing behind 06, facing out into the street, watching for trouble.

No, I think. *No fucking way.*

Though I've seen enough newsfeeds, read enough articles, to know the likelihood is high—they're partnered, they work together, 06 is known to help civilians more than the rest of them combined, and where she goes he goes, intellectually I *know* this—it still hits me like a slap.

As if he can feel the force of my stare on the back of his head, 22 breaks focus just enough to glance over a shoulder. His gaze slides off mine like rain down a window. He goes back to watching the street.

All my plans of bus-finding and home-going vaporize.

06, meanwhile, has taken some kind of little black device out of a pocket. She checks something on it while gesturing one-handed at the crowd. "Whose vision is the least compromised right now?"

I freeze.

The woman hooks a thumb over a shoulder toward me. "Hers."

Before I can so much as throw my hands up in protest—I don't know what I'm doing, I'm nobody useful, wrong place wrong time, I don't even know where I am, et cetera—06's gesture turns into a two-fingered beckon. "I need to borrow you a sec."

I don't feel myself move forward. I'm not aware of so much as peeling myself off the wall before I'm standing in front of her. I resist the urge to do something unfathomably pathetic, like copy the SecOps salute they're constantly doing in-game when you recruit them or fulfill a mission with them or just do something they're programmed to respect.

"Sure," I croak. "Happy to help." At least that's what I mean to say. Let the footage be the judge of whether any voice comes out.

"Want to bring me some injured people?" 06 asks. "The worse off the better."

I nod and scurry off, feeling somehow both uplifted and diminished by 06's presence. The way she moves, the way she carries herself, she's like an alien trying to pass as human by crushing herself down in our miserable mold.

I bring 06 a woman with a splinted leg, another woman with a dislocated shoulder, a teenage boy with a horrifically busted kneecap, a man with his hand wrapped in a huge mitt of bloody gauze. That's just the first batch. Lots more where they came from.

I gather them and lead them back to 06, each holding on to the other.

"Perfect," 06 says. She kneels down, resting on her bootheels in the middle of this filthy alley, and gestures at the empty space in front of her. I lead the splint-leg woman forward first and drag over a crate for her to sit on. She sucks in air through her teeth as 06 and I work together to get her leg unwrapped.

It takes some doing because the splint isn't any kind of proper medical equipment, just a piece of a plastic toy running down the inside of her leg and what looks like most of a hoverbike bumper running down the outside. The whole thing is strapped together with the better part of a roll of duct tape.

06 pulls out some kind of fancy utility knife and makes a long careful cut the whole way down, then tugs the duct tape cast away and opens up the jeans leg to get at the injury.

Underneath, the woman's ankle is swollen, puffy, and green, practically double the size of the other.

"Hang on," 06 says, and the gentle medbot tone coming out of her is like hearing a lullaby from a shark. "You're doing great. That's the awkward part done."

She takes the little black device and presses the pad of her thumb to one side. It lights up with a little trill as it powers on. Whatever this thing is, I've never seen it before. They haven't even added it into the game. I don't know if that's because it's too new or too classified, but I realize I'm staring at it in open fascination.

The injured woman, about to have rather a more intimate relationship with whatever this thing turns out to be, is squinting toward it doubtfully. "What is that? Is it going to hurt?"

"Less than walking on that mess," 06 says. "I promise. Try to stay still."

She presses the other side of the device to the most trashed-looking part of the joint. It chirps twice and starts humming, a sound like the way a robotic cat would purr. The woman winces, bites her lip, and visibly rides out a wave of pain, then another.

It's maybe twenty seconds of this before 06 lifts the device away, and the woman rotates her foot experimentally. "It feels different."

06 is grinning like she invented the thing. "That's the idea."

I help the woman get up and the next person—bloody-hand guy—gets into position. I try not to sneak too many glances at 22, though it's hard, it's very hard, and Jessa will cackle herself stupid when she sees this footage later. He just stands there, so still I'm not entirely sure he's breathing. He might as well be a statue. Except that even from here you can feel the coiled tension radiating off him. He's not standing still because he's bored or powered down or whatever. He's standing still because he's on high alert. He's three hundred percent business. He's like a bomb that hasn't yet been set off, waiting for a reason.

Then I realize how he's positioned himself to keep watch. He's occupying the exact slot of space that specifically covers 06's back most precisely. Not the civilians. Not even the babies and little kids. 06.

I wonder if he knows there's an echo of him wandering around somewhere in a game right now. Being made to follow dipshit players around like a heavily armed dog on an invisible leash. I almost want to tell him, to have the excuse of running my idiot mouth at him, maybe to prove to myself that he's real. *You came down on a suborbital drop right onto 08's head,*

I could tell him. *Took out three hundred people. Just a few days ago you stabbed me in the throat, and now here we both are. What are the odds, huh?*

I want to talk to him. I don't care what about. I want to stand there in companionable silence and help him watch the street. I want to drag him out of here and get him drunk and make him tell me stories.

I get it. It's weird to want to be best friends with a piece of biotech, a robot or clone or monster or whatever it is he's supposed to be. Now ask me how many fucks I give about that.

Bloody-hand guy gets fixed, and I bring over busted-kneecap kid. That one takes a little longer because 06 has to pop the kneecap back into place in two pieces before she closes the wound with her piece of classified hardware or "it'll go all weird," quote. Looking at it makes me feel like I'm going to hork up my protein drink and granola bar all over 06, and if that happens, I'm heading right out there to feed myself to a mech because it's either that or die slowly of shame.

The kid submits to the hydraulic strength and unearthly delicacy of 06's gloved fingers with, to his credit, just one scream. He passes out at the end of it, but still.

While the device hums, 06 appraises me. Looking down the barrel of that gaze is like nothing I've ever had to do. It's like she's running calculations on me, hundreds of calculations all at once, based on data I can't see.

Machine consciousness, I think. But there's something undeniably human about her. Like human dialed up to eleven. I try to weigh that against my other impressions of her and get nowhere. Maybe she's not human at all, and the uncanny valley is messing with my head.

I mean, they do say the operatives are essentially superheroes, just not the fake kind from movies who can turn invisible and shoot lasers out of their eyes and move things with their brains. You'd expect a superhero to act, well, superhuman. Regardless, standing in front of one, it's a lot to take in.

"You're not from this group," 06 says.

My attention startles back to her. "I joined up with them a little while back. They were taking cover by some kind of museum or something when the citykiller mech started chucking helicopters around."

06 looks amused, but not at-my-expense amused, and I begin to see why she, personally, has a fanbase of several million who would happily follow her through hell. "The what?"

"Citykiller mech? Giant robot suit the size of a building with a person in it?"

"Oh," 06 says. "The Greenleaf TacSystems X10."

I'm about ready for the street to open up and swallow me. *Citykiller* is the in-game name for it. I guess it was too confusing or boring to have everything called Stellaxis this and Greenleaf that, so the game devs got creative. I *know* it's a goddamn X10. The things show up in the newsfeeds often enough that a toddler would know what they're called. This all—the day, the mechs, 06, 22—has got me dangerously flustered.

"Not from around here," 06 observes.

"Old town," I admit. "You guys, um. You don't come out there much. Well. Ever, really. It's, uh, that way." At least with my lenses in I can point accurately. Then, because I am a catastrophe of a person who should be put out of the misery of everyone within a mile radius, I paste on a smile that probably looks more like I'm about to be sick. "You guys should come by sometime. I'll buy you a drink."

I expect 06 to laugh. Roll her eyes. Stab me in the throat. I don't know. Instead she just looks sad. Sad, but, like, with this weird backlighting of something else. I can't explain it. Like she sees something in the distance that she knows she'll never reach. Probably the face I make when I think about 22.

"I ever get out of here," she says softly, "I might just take you up on that."

I blink. I want to say something witty, something charming, something that keeps her talking, helps me make sense of what she just said.

I come up empty-handed, and we all—06, the broken-knee kid, the two men, and the woman—all watch as the wound on the kid's leg finally begins to seal shut.

The man I talked with earlier edges into the conversation, recycling the same story he told me. "One of those goddamn things took out our complex," he tells 06. I don't know if he's trying to rescue me from myself or he just wants 06's attention, and right now I don't care. I shut up gratefully and usher over a new batch of wounded. I tell the rest to get in line so I can get them to 06 more efficiently, and they do their best to cooperate.

When I come back, the man's gesturing toward the crowd. "We're what's left."

06 gives the crowd a once-over. "Sixty?"

"Sixty-two," says the woman, joining in. "Eighty to start. It's been a rough few days."

06 makes a face and opens her mouth to say something, and the device in her hand gives three little dead-battery beeps and powers down. "Oh what in the shitting hell now," she mutters at it, and reaches upward without looking to pluck from the air an identical device tossed to her by 22.

I swear I didn't even see him move.

"If you can walk, get out of line and bring me somebody who can't," 06 calls back into the alley. "Fast. Then get ready to get the hell out of here."

The medbot-like bedside manner and the neighborly friendliness are both vanished from her voice. *Unsheathed* is the word that comes to mind. She's unsheathed her true self from the self she put on to keep us from devolving into panic.

But why would we? It's been calm here. The fighting's moved off, like a storm, leaving us behind.

Although if I strain my ears, I can just start to make out the beginnings of a new sound developing out there, somewhere in the unseen maze of streets. There's a string of explosions like immense firecrackers, a slurry of gunfire, and shouting. Then something else that can only be the weighty, monstrous, elegant stride of the citykiller mech—the Greenleaf TacSystems X10—patrolling.

Except now—and I can only hope it's just a trick of the distance—it sounds like there's more than one.

No sign of surprise from either 06 or 22.

If the stories are true, they've been listening to it this entire time, keeping tabs on it as it shifted in intensity and tone, not mentioning it because why worry the puny humans with danger they can't even hear?

06 drops her voice. Her quiet intensity is more commanding than a shout.

"You're in the wrong place at the wrong time, and things are about to get pretty hot where you're sitting, believe me," she says. "And you need medical attention." The two men and woman all nod. "More than we can give," 06 admits. "But we can clear a path. Hospital's still standing, last I knew."

Something complicated and silent now occurs between 06 and 22, something conveyed entirely in over-the-shoulder looks. Eventually 22 nods. It looks like he's lost an argument, but they didn't say anything. Fleetingly, stupidly, knowing full well they have implants like everybody else, I wonder if one of their superpowers is reading minds. If so, 22 is probably wondering which one of these sixty-two-plus-me people is broadcasting such a tangle of thoughts at such high volume in his direction.

"Food and blankets," 06 continues, pulling that false good cheer back around her like a cloak. "Worst soup you ever ate, but plenty of it."

The two men and one woman all exchange a glance, inasmuch as this is possible. *This* one I can read. It's *we thought the hospital was full* and *but she might not know that* and *if we tell her, she might not try to take us there* and *if we show up with a SecOps escort, they'll have to let us in.*

The woman opens her mouth to speak and is drowned out. The sound outside has changed. It's closer.

It's a lot closer.

22 draws his sword. "You just ran out of time."

06 pockets the device and stands, brushing off her legs. "How many?"

"Enough."

The crowd starts agitating. Guns drawn, kids and people with babies guided to the back. I want to help them, I do—they can't see, someone's gonna get trampled—but this is a tiny thought that reaches me from the back of my mind, because ninety-nine percent of me is straight-up blaring *danger.*

I could leave now. I could head out, on foot, in the opposite direction from the approaching mechs. 06 and 22 are here, these people are in no danger now, there's no need in the world for me to be here, no help in the world I can provide that they can't.

But—apart from all the obvious stuff about how I'm safer here with them than I am out there on my own, and how the concept of me deciding to *leave* 22's presence is laughable—06 asked for my help. And when someone like 06 asks for your help—someone who puts her neck out for strangers like these ones every goddamn day she sets foot on the unworthy earth— you put your shit aside and do the thing.

I'm not going anywhere.

06 stations herself between the crowd and the street. 22 is already out there somewhere. 06 stands with her hand on her hilt, warning us with her eyes. "Heads down," she says. "No heroes. I mean it."

She turns to leave, and one of the men calls after her. "Thank god they sent you in for us," he says. "We never hoped—"

06 shoots him a look like she just bit into something foul. "They didn't," she says, and is gone.

"Stay put," I tell everyone, because a few of them are starting to look like they might just make a break for it instead. "They'll come back."

"They're fighting?" someone asks.

"I'll check." As if I need an excuse.

I plaster myself to the alley opening and peer out up the street to the left. 06 and 22 are standing there facing down not one but *three* citykiller mechs, barreling down the street in our direction in V formation, their gun-arms lit with blue fire.

Facing them down—with swords.

"Yes," I say weakly. "They're about to be."

"Tell us what you see," someone else shouts.

What I see. Of course.

"They're—"

One of the gun-arms discharges and blows out the street right in front of 06 and 22. For a second they're silhouetted against a wave of searing blue fire like something out of a goddamn movie.

06 doesn't miss a beat. She picks up a chunk of the rubble and hurls it like a snowball, a hundred feet if it's an inch, and lands it in the barrel of the first mech's second gun-arm just as it readies to fire. There's a low detonation, then a louder one, and the point mech drops to its knees, burning.

I try to narrate this, but it's hard. Everything moves so fast.

Specifically, 06 and 22 move so fast. When they open up to top speed, they literally blur. Especially what with the street now being on fire, it's a little hard to make out. I tell the crowd what I can.

"I think 06 just jumped off the downed mech and swung herself up onto the gun-arm of another one and it shot off the gun-arm trying to aim at her?" I say, but that's just based on movement patterns and the fact that I can't see 06 on the ground anymore, and the fact that something obviously drags that gun-arm down and then it gets shot off and tumbles to the street.

"22 just got up onto the third mech and took out the pilot module," I say, but I don't catch the process between *standing on the street a hundred feet from the mech* and *someone in the pilot module choking off a scream as 22 withdraws his sword.*

One mech left, something visibly wrong with its gun-arms— the cannons are having a hard time spinning up, or there's something else lodged in the barrel, I don't know—and 06 darts sideways toward an object she's spotted at the side of the street, near the remains of a barricade.

That's when I hear the helicopter.

It's coming in from the other direction, fast and low from the sound of it, slaloming between the buildings. A few people burst past me and out into the street, firing into the sky.

They're just wasting ammo. The helicopter isn't within range yet. It's not even in sight. They don't care. They're just dying to feel useful. I can certainly appreciate the sentiment.

Thing is, I'm having the same problem. If these people get themselves killed, I'm going to feel like I personally let 06 and 22 down, and that is not even remotely an option.

"Get the fuck back in here," I stage-whisper at them, for all the good it does. "You're not going to hit it."

But 06 has already noticed them. Of course she has. She tears back toward the alley, shouting, dropping whatever it was she found by the barricade.

22 picks it back up. It's a looped length of steel cable.

I want to help 06 corral these reckless idiots back into the alley, but I can't. I'm physically incapable of taking my eyes off 22. Partly because it's 22. Partly because I have no idea what the hell he's doing.

What he's doing is unlooping the cable, tying something onto one end of it, listening a second, and then flinging the end of the cable up into the air, straight into the path of the helicopter as it appears between two buildings, strafing the street on its approach. The cable tangles in the tail rotors and whips the helicopter into a one-eighty, and he gets a grip on his end of the cable and rips the helicopter from the air. It whirls around and slams into the third mech.

The impact seems to knock something free in the gun-arm, and the cannon discharges. A ball of blue fire slips past 22 like a whisper and wipes out the front half of a building down the street.

22 comes back to the alley at what I can only describe as a leisurely stroll. Behind him, the entwined mech and helicopter explode together, blowing out windows on both sides of the street.

"I was just going to try to tangle its legs," 06 informs him when he gets here. Apart from a bullet hole in 06's shoulder where the helicopter's fire must have caught her when she came back to deal with these people who were my goddamn responsibility, they both look pretty much pristine. She nods up at the blaze. "But that works too."

I feel awful. 06 is having her shoulder bound right now by one of the men because of me. I mean, nobody *told* me to babysit these people. But I also didn't expect them to *run out into the street.*

"There'll be more," 22 says. "Soon."

06 nods. She doesn't look tired as much as she looks like she's *trying* to look tired, so the rest of us don't feel like such shit about our weak human bodies and weak human minds. Or maybe I'm just projecting.

"No rest for the wicked," 06 says, levering herself up. "Okay, everybody, on your feet. We'll have a roof over your heads by sundown, but you have to do *exactly* as we say."

It's getting on for evening. I remind myself that, 06 or no 06, 22 or no 22, I really do need to figure out my bus situation eventually. If there are buses even still running. I don't know. There are thirty-five messages from Jessa piled up in the corner unread. As I glance at the notification, the thirty-sixth lands.

i'm ok, I send. running late. talk later. don't be worried i'm fine

Something touches my shoulder. "Hey."

I turn. It's 06.

"I know you don't need the hospital," she says, "but every one of these people does. I can't fix their eyes in the field. And it's going to be dark in an hour." She's rolled her sleeve up at some point, so when she runs a hand through her cropped hair, I catch a glimpse of the number tattooed on the inside of her forearm, just below the crease of her elbow. "We don't usually do this. But you're here. They trust you." She raises her eyebrows at me like this last part's a question.

I shrug. "I guess? I mean, maybe? I kind of just met them and—"

"Would you be willing to help us escort them to the hospital? Just keep them together while we worry about keeping them safe? And then I'll personally make sure you get where you're going."

"That's against regulations and you know it," 22 says. I didn't even know he was listening.

"Next you'll probably tell me I look like I care," 06 responds. She leans in to keep her voice from carrying. I'm standing in a genuine strategic huddle with 06 and 22, and I can barely hear her over the pounding of my heart in my ears. "You want to walk two miles through this shit with all those people getting lost or hurt? Don't you think they've been through enough already without hanging on to *your* sleeves the whole way? We need her."

"I don't recall receiving orders to come out here in the first place," 22 replies evenly.

"We went over this," 06 said. "I felt like taking a walk. Get some fresh air. You decided to come with me."

"We are under orders to accompany each other outside the building," 22 says. "As you *well* know."

"Exactly! So if they ask: I took a walk. Accompanied by you."

"In a restricted area."

06 grins. "Restricted to civilians. Not to me." And then she angles her head a few degrees and winks at me. 06, hero of engagements, savior of thousands, turner of tides, real-life motherfucking superhero *winks*. At me.

22 opts to ignore this. "Nor do I recall receiving orders to escort anyone anywhere." He sets his gaze on me like a weight, holds it for a second, sweeps it back to 06 while the rest of him stays motionless. "That said," he continues slowly. "However we got here, we're here. And we're headed more or less back that way anyway. And you didn't abandon these people when you were given ample opportunity."

It takes me a second of fumbling to realize he's talking to me. I shake my head. "Their lenses are all fu— They can't see. I couldn't just leave them."

06 is losing patience. She bounces on her toes a little. "So we're good?"

22 is looking at me like he's reading secrets etched on the folds of my brain through the backs of my eyeballs. What a ter-

rifying concept. After a moment he gives me a little half nod. "We're good."

"Then let's get the fuck out of here." 06 steps out of the huddle, raising her voice to the crowd as 22 glides away from me and out to the street. "Okay, everybody. Sorry about that. Just working out the details. Hospital time. You are all going to follow—"

06 looks at me quizzically. "Mal," I say.

"Mal. Do just like you did to get here. Stick to her like glue. 22 and I will take point and rear guard with you all in the middle. Got it?"

Nods and *got it*s and a couple of *yes, sir*s.

"All right." 06 nods back. "Let's get this done."

0 0 1 0

OUR WEIRD-ASS PARADE GOES 22, THEN ME, then sixty-two civilians hanging on to my backpack, then 06. We walk through the sunset, and nothing stops us. The streets have gone quiet like somebody's hit pause on the war. There aren't even any more wounded to pick up. Nobody around to comment on us. No drones arrive to stream this gold mine of SecOps footage online, or if there are, I can't see them in the gathering dark. Everyone's inside, and this place is as dead as a freshly cleared playfield. I lead my group around busted barricades, seas of broken glass and machine oil, the smoking junk-metal twist of a helicopter. Most of the fires we pass have already gone out.

With a group of this size, it's an obstacle course. We walk single file, and when someone behind me trips or slows, the pull travels up the line and ends with a backward jerk on my backpack. Not that I for one second hold it against them. If the wind had blown slightly differently, it'd be me hanging on to someone else's backpack, and I know it. This mess has room for all of us.

Still, I'm dragging ass, falling over with exhaustion. I've done more walking today than I have in a month. All my nervous energy has burned out, and I'm running on stubbornness and fumes and the desire to not look like a fuckup in front of 06 and 22.

22 must hear me stifling curses, because he periodically throws back to me what he seems to think are words of encouragement.

At least we can breathe this air. If that changes, you'll be the first to know.

Snipers are usually pretty quiet through here. In any case, they'd be aiming at me.

If you hear a resonance grenade activating, drop to the ground faster than it can imprint and you'll probably survive. Pause. *And we're en route to a hospital anyway.*

If 06 sounds like an alien who's learned how to pass as a human, 22 sounds like an alien who skipped class on small-talk day. Try as I might, though, and walking this maze of wreckage is giving me ample time to think, I can't square this 22 with the one who sized me up like a specimen and then stabbed me in the throat. My random sampling of his dialogue and mannerisms and bizarre, awkward, stone-dry humor is lamentably small, but still. Maybe the SecOps NPCs aren't as copy/paste as BestLife's marketing claims.

The hospital is surrounded by barricades. Their searchlights are visible before the hospital complex itself is, beams of grainy brightness cutting through the orangey purple of the sky above the setting sun.

22 calls a halt before we hit the barricade. It's a twenty-foot wall of wrecked vehicles and corrugated metal, topped with razor wire. A guard hails us from somewhere. "Hospital's full," she calls out into the dark. "Move along."

22 steps into the light. He says nothing. He does nothing. He just stands there like he's wearing a giant lit-up sign that reads DO YOU KNOW WHO I AM.

"What's happening?" voices ask behind me. "What's going

on? Is that the hospital? I think I can make out the searchlights."
Et cetera. Drowning out any chance I had of hearing what 22
ends up saying to the guard. Which probably wasn't much of
one to start with.

"I don't know," I tell them. "We'll get an answer in a minute."

Whatever the guard tells 22, it takes a few minutes of back-
and-forth, and then 22 switches out with 06, who's shouldered
up to the front, muttering something about people skills, to see
what she can see. 22 sweeps back down toward the tail of the
crowd to take up 06's abandoned rearguard, and 06 resumes the
argument or whatever with the people at the barricade. I still
can't hear a thing over all the questions coming in thick and fast
from behind me.

"Is it full?"

"I told you it was full."

"You said no such thing. *I* told *you* it was full."

"Well *now* what do we do?"

"Listen," I tell them. "06 and 22 are taking care of it. The second I know, you'll know."

I'm trying to keep it together, but I'm tired and I'm hungry
and I gave away all my water and my arms have gone dead from
the constant pressure on my backpack and Jessa must be losing
her mind wondering where the fuck I am.

While we're stopped, I take the opportunity to message her
again real quick, just enough to let her know I'm okay. Then I
check the bus schedule. Not that it tells me anything I didn't
suspect. Today's last bus ran over an hour ago.

I pull in a long breath, hold it for a ten-count, then exhale.
It doesn't help.

It's fine, I tell myself. I'll rent a hotel pod. I'll sleep in an alley.
Plus, 06 said she'd—

As if on cue, 06 comes stalking back, her mouth mashed
into a line. She gives the street a once-over, nods the all clear,

and signals to 22. He appears almost immediately, and the two fall into whispered conference at the head of the crowd.

This I can hear. At least one word in every maybe six. I strain my ears and catch *choice* and *days* and *protocol* and *reprimand* and *shit*.

All at once the whispering breaks off, and they turn back to us like parents in a movie about to announce a divorce. 06 has her gloved fists pressed knuckle to knuckle in front of her like she's trying to physically hold this situation both together and off the ground by force alone.

Then she takes a half step forward and collars me with her eyes. "You good to get these folks a little farther?" she asks me quietly.

The hell else can I do? I'm dead on my feet and my arms are falling off and I nod.

06 nods back. "Glad to hear it," she says, and claps me on one shoulder. It feels like being walloped with a sledgehammer.

"New plan," she says loudly. "I promised you food and beds and medical attention, and you're going to get it." Behind her, 22 is keeping his face studiously blank, like he really wants to argue but knows this is really not the time. 06 plows on, oblivious or uninterested. "Sorry, but you're gonna have to walk a little farther than we thought."

06 starts walking back to resume her rearguard position, and before I can think better of it, I reach out and touch her sleeve. She stops and raises an eyebrow at me.

"I promised I'd tell them where we're going," I say.

"Stellaxis Innovations," she says. Then, with an ironic twist to her mouth, she adds, "Home."

I blink. "Wait. What? We can't go there. They don't let civilians—"

06 silences me with a gesture. "We are escorting a party of civilian *casualties*. They will not turn us away." Something

sparks in her eyes, something dangerous and sleeping. "I won't let them."

"But I'm not injured," I protest. "I could be arrested, they'll think I'm an infiltrator, that literally just happened on the news, someone was there trying to sneak in with a protest sign and—"

"Very well. I hereby temporarily requisition your services under the 2109 Stellaxis/Greenleaf Neutralities Accord, section eighteen-point-three-five-C: Temporary Requisition of Civilian Services. This is not an honor bestowed lightly. Congratulations." 06 salutes me. "Now let's get out of here."

"You just made that up," 22 hisses. "There is no section—"

"Well, yeah, but." 06 shrugs one shoulder in my direction. "She didn't know that."

06 executes a swift ninety-degree pivot and takes up the rear guard. We move on.

It's not all that much farther from the hospital to Stellaxis HQ. Either that, or I've passed into some kind of walking haze where I lose all track of time and exist only in a kind of bubble of diffuse discomfort.

It's getting dark now, though, real, true dark. Which scares me a little. I can increase the brightness on my lenses, but that's not going to be much help in this landscape with sixty-plus people relying on me to place each footstep perfectly. No more mechs appear, nothing that dramatic, but there's glass and rusted metal and burned-out lumps of who knows what all around. I'd know an in-game resonance grenade by the sound it makes as it wakes up, but was that rendered accurately from life? How the hell would I know?

We step around a string of downed breakaway drones that's spewing something orange and noxious into the air. 22 kicks them out of the way, and we file past, coughing, breathing through our sleeves. Next we have to make a detour because the entire top of some building has sheared off and is lying in the street. Then we walk unimpeded for a few minutes while in my head I run the loop of questions I wish I had the guts to ask 22. After a while they condense down to one question, which becomes the metronome of my footsteps: *who are you who are you who are you.*

Eventually we break out of the skyscraper landscape of the city and into a tidy park, a weird blob of green in a sea of glass and steel and concrete. We approach a checkpoint, but this one is unmanned, just AI with ginormous fuckoff guns. It takes one look at 06 and 22, and we file through without incident.

On the Stellaxis lawns there's a decorative pond or two, and some trees that are winter bare, but I know from photos will be covered with tiny pink flowers in the spring. There's a sunken concrete area with benches and a softly lit fountain with a statue in it. Fish dart in the basin, flickering like flames. There are weeks' worth of water rations just spewing out of the top of the fountain like nothing, and I want to climb up there and shove my face into the spray and drink forever. It's like we stepped through a portal into another place entirely, some other city that hasn't completely gone to shit.

In the middle of all this the black glass dagger of Stellaxis Innovations HQ rears up before us, blocking out the moon.

Not even in BestLife have I gotten this close to this place. It's crawling with disgustingly high-level players, racking up points on a robust constant spawn of disgustingly high-level mobs. We tried once and got sniped off our bike from eight hundred yards. But even from a distance it looks exactly like its in-game echo.

I wasn't sure I'd spoken aloud. If I did, it was under my breath at most. But 22 hears me, stops crisply, half turns to address me over a shoulder. "What *game.*"

For ages I've wondered how much the operatives were told about the game they star in. I guess now I have my answer. I feel weirdly dirty, like 22's just discovered I have a body pillow of him the way Jessa used to have that one of 08.

"Um. It's a . . . it's not important."

22 gives a little *hmm* in response to that and leads on.

We stop by the fountain. I can smell the water. It's pulling me forward like the smell of blood pulls a zombie. I set my feet and my jaw and ride it out.

06 stalks past us, her whole face and stance loaded for bear.

"Stay here," 22 tells me. "It's safe. If the perimeter was going to vaporize us, it would've done it already."

Like the crack about the resonance grenades, I guess I'm supposed to read that as reassurance. If his sense of humor was any drier, it'd crumble to ash and blow away.

22 follows 06 up to the building without another word, leaving sixty-three unchaperoned civilians loose on the grounds of Stellaxis Innovations HQ.

"We're here," I tell them, because doing them that courtesy seems to have slipped 06's mind and probably never crossed 22's. "Company HQ. Don't wander too far. There are probably—" I bite back the word *snipers.* "Stairs. There are stairs right in front of us going down to a fountain. Come on, let's go sit in the grass."

So we go and we sit in the grass and it's really very nice grass. Hideously well watered. It's like grass from a movie, more grass than I've ever seen all at once in one place in my life.

It's even softer than it looks. How is it alive this time of year? I just kind of sit there and swish my hands through the blades of it while everyone else does whatever. It's hypnotic, really. All this time I've been assuming, from the game and the documentary and all the ads and whatever else, that it was fake. Who has this much *real grass*? Where are they getting the water?

I don't even notice 06 and 22 have returned until I look up and 22 is standing right over me, hands clasped behind his back, looking down at my grass-swishing with bland scholarly interest.

"I, uh." I scramble to my feet. Clear my throat. Nod at the building. "What's the word?"

But 06 is already rounding up the *civilian casualties* and leading them in through the front door, and 22 is giving me a *well-let's-go* look, and I'm almost glad the last bus has come and gone, because there could be a whole fleet of buses right here, parked and waiting for me, and I'd still walk into that building with 22, and that would be a lot harder to explain to Jessa and right now I don't much care.

The smell of that fountain follows me the whole way inside.

THE LOBBY OF the building is exactly like it is in the documentary. Your basic huge cave of a room with gentle archways and a sleek desk or two and *another fucking fountain*, this one a weird eight-foot-high wall thing with the stars-and-arrow Stellaxis logo carved into it and this endless sheet of water running down the face.

A security guard comes out from behind one of the desks to greet us. Or stop us. At first it's not real clear.

"You're late," he says. "The Director was about to have drones sent out to bring you in."

Inexplicably, this seems to amuse 22. "Was she."

06 doesn't bother responding. "I'm taking these people to Medical," she says. "Write me up if you need to."

The guard volleys his gaze between 06 and 22. "You didn't say anything about Medical a minute ago. You said aboveground floors only. You know I can't authorize—"

22 runs over him. "Under the 2109 Stellaxis/Greenleaf Neutralities Accord, denying medical care to civilian casualties in a combat zone is a war crime. Section—"

"All right, all right." The guard backs off. "Just be quick about it." He consults something on his lenses. "Dr. Kessler is on duty until the hour. I'll let them know you're headed down."

"Dr. Kessler is getting paid overtime tonight," 06 replies, brushing past him.

The guard calls after her. "You know I have to report this to the Director."

06 gives a little shake of her head, like there's a mosquito by her ear. "Of course you do," she says under her breath, leading the group over to a bank of elevators. As she passes 22, she raises an eyebrow at him. "A war crime?"

This earns her a minimalist shrug from 22. "It could be."

"Wait." Not quite ready to give up, the guard jogs over from his desk. "I have to run them through security."

06 doubles back on him, planting herself between the guard and the crowd. "Already done." She gestures at three extra pistols shoved into her belt. When did she collect those?

He pans a suspicious gaze over the crowd. "They're not recording?"

Reflexively I almost hit stop on mine and delete it entirely.

But 06 and 22 are faster. 06 makes this big exasperated *what-a-question* gesture, while 22 slides a few centimeters to the left, blocking me from the guard's line of sight.

I freeze. What the hell are they doing?

"Do these people *look* like they're recording?" 06 demands, flinging out one arm in the direction of all those melted lenses fused to eyes. I cast my own eyes downward, thankful that it's not outwardly obvious in real life when a person is recording, the way that it is in-game. For some reason, nobody in this whole crowd narcs on me.

No response from the guard, so 06 cranks up the volume. *"Well?"*

This has the desired effect. The guard practically evaporates.

We split the group into batches and ferry them, one elevator run at a time, toward Medical. 06 goes down with the first batch to handle any trouble they might encounter downstairs, while 22 stays up here to help load the elevator and keep the security bots calm. I ride with each batch and press the button.

Why didn't anyone rat me out? A few batches in, observing the sheer exhaustion of these people, it starts to make sense. They've been in the trenches for days. Trenches the company dug, practically pushed them into, and then did jack shit to help them climb back out of. If it were me, right now I'd be thinking Stellaxis could go take a flying fuck off a short pier for all I cared.

As for why 06 and 22 covered for me in the first place, those answers are taking a little longer to arrive. It feels like a question that'll chew on me for a while.

It takes eight awkward runs in the elevator, but we get them there. 22 gets in with the last batch, and we all ride down together, me crammed shoulder to shoulder with 22 like old pals, and now we're all pretty much vacuum-packed into this basementy-looking, white cinder-block hallway.

It's a lot less high-tech down here than I expected. It smells familiar, like a hospital. 06 leads the way to Medical, letting the front people in the crowd touch her shoulders for guidance. I follow with 22.

Medical turns out to be a big window-fronted room with MEDICAL BAY stenciled onto the white brick above a heavy automatic door. Two more security bots stand sentry. "At ease," 06 tells them, and their posture changes fractionally.

It isn't a hospital, what this place smells like. It's . . . I'm not sure. It's reminding me of something I can't place.

06 ushers the crowd in, then pokes her head back out. "I'm going to stay with them in case anybody shows up with questions," she tells 22. "Dr. K has enough on their plate right now without getting hit with my paperwork."

Then she seems to notice me there. "I really appreciated your help today. I didn't forget about getting you home. Can it wait a little? Unless . . ." She trails off, glancing at 22. "You want to help her find a bus or something?" Then, without waiting for an answer, back to me: "Is that okay?"

I try to give her a nonchalant one-shouldered shrug, but my shoulders and my mind and my entire state of being are in such a state right now it comes out as this weird twitch. "Sure," I try to say. "That'd be fine."

06's gaze zeroes in. "You're sure you don't need a doctor? Not even a little? I won't let them charge you, if that's the problem."

"I'm okay," I tell her. "Just thirsty."

She gives me a puzzled look. "There's a water fountain right over there." Then she straightens up, probably receiving some kind of message over her lenses. "Ah, shit. Okay. I'm out. Thanks again!" The automatic door seals shut over her voice as she pulls her head back inside.

Whatever happens next, I need that water fountain *yesterday*. I practically hurl myself at the thing.

Only to find that it's got some kind of really cutting-edge reader that I can't even locate. I'm torn between staying thirsty and admitting I'm an ignorant old-town idiot in front of 22.

I'm standing there in the middle of this crisis when he reaches in and floats his hand near an edge of the fountain. Water arcs out of it, wasteful and beautiful. He pulls away and it stops.

There must be an invisible reader built into the fountain that only interfaces with company employees. Typical.

Now that the fountain's keyed itself to 22's account, I put my hand where his was, and water shoots out. There must be a sensor built into the reader. *That* I've seen before. I drink and drink until I have to stop myself forcibly. It tastes better than hotel bathroom sink water. Better than company-store water.

It tastes how the water in ads looks like it tastes, all clear and sparkling and too perfect to be real.

I dig my empty bottle out of my backpack and fill that. Then I take three more measured sips from the stream. Then I wipe my mouth on my sleeve and try to retrieve what little remains of my dignity.

"Thanks," I tell 22 in this voice like *sure, I drink water this perfect every day no problem.* "You didn't have to pay for me. I can cover it. I just—this reader is different than I'm used to is all." Then, because he's staring at me like I'm speaking a foreign language they never taught him in supersoldier school, I add: "I'll get you back, just tell me how much I owe you."

22 treats me to a long, slow, considering blink. "Owe me for what, exactly?"

"Um." I wave feebly at the fountain. "The water?"

In response, 22 gives me this unfathomable look. Then he removes one glove and, still holding my gaze, waves that in front of the reader. The fountain activates, the water arcing just as high and full as before.

The answer is obvious enough but hits hard all the same.

It's not a reader. It's a motion sensor. The water here is free.

22 tugs the glove back on. He's not looking at me anymore, which I'm guessing has something to do with the awful roil of emotion I'm sure is showing on my face. Two fountains. Free water. All that lush green grass.

That glove goes back on with every bit of the efficiency I expect of him, but not before I catch sight of the bare hand beneath. There's something not quite right about it. It's human enough, but something's been done to the tendons and bones of it. There aren't scars *exactly,* or wounds *exactly,* but . . .

And then it's gone, back under the glove, and I don't know what I saw. But it makes me remember the awful strength of 06's hand, clapping me on the shoulder, and 22's hands, fishing for helicopters. The old photo of 05—Elena—flashes through my mind. What exactly do you do to a child to turn them into this?

"I'm afraid you're going to have to walk me through the process of helping you find a bus," 22 says. "It is not what you might call my area of expertise."

"I believe it," I say.

22 tilts his head half a degree, like he's receiving a message from the mothership. "What's that?"

"A joke. I was joking." I swallow. What the hell is the smell of this place reminding me of? "Badly."

The silence and my composure slowly unravel.

"Let me check the bus schedule," I blurt out. Like it will have changed from when I checked it half a dozen times before. I make a show of letting my eyes focus on a display that isn't there. "Oh no. Looks like the last bus already went a while ago."

"Hmm." 22 looks to be at something of a loss. I take a few absent sips from the water bottle I'm still holding, waiting for him to push back through the door to Medical and drag 06 out here to rescue him from civilian-babysitting detail.

But what I get is very different.

I'm getting used to his mannerisms, his and 06's, their real-life ones. There's startlingly little overlap between them, and the echoes of both exist accurately enough in-game that the meanings of some are easy enough to decipher, although some remain mysterious. 06, for instance, has more sadness in her eyes than I expected, and a way of angling her whole person toward you when you talk, like she's sizing you up as prey. In contrast, 22 hoards movement like water. Like he's doing brain surgery 24/7, every motion is that measured. He'll stay perfectly still until he blurs into action. He'll shift his eyes from target to target without moving the rest of his head. That's all exactly like in-game. What's different is that in real life it turns out he has a sense of humor, like I saw earlier on our march to Stellaxis HQ.

It's weird, and it's subtle, and mostly has to do with the timing of horrifying statements delivered utterly deadpan—*we're en route to a hospital anyway*—but it's there.

One thing that definitely did not make it into the game is how they both have a way of talking that makes me feel like they're trying to tell me something they're not allowed to say. Keeping me around, bringing me here, protecting me and my lenses from a security check—it makes me feel like they're lobbing messages in bottles, over and over, mistaking me for an ocean when I'm generally more of a puddle.

What 22 does now is more in-game standard. He raises an eyebrow one millimeter and nods to a depth of maybe two.

What he says is not.

"So. I could escort you back to the front desk and have whoever is on duty find you some manner of public transport that is still running at whatever time this is." He holds up one gloved finger to forestall me telling him what time it is, as if he doesn't know. "Or. Option two. I thought you might be hungry."

22 TAKES ME to a cafeteria-looking room signposted DINING FACILITY. There's nobody else here. Just the softly blue-lit serving bots, dormant along their wall. There's another security bot posted at the door, just like at most of the doors in this place as I am learning, but 22's presence is enough to make it lose interest in me fast.

"Take a seat," 22 says. "It's late, but I'll see what I can do."

I find a chair and watch 22 hassle the bots out of hibernation. This is beyond surreal at this point. I could believe that the on-duty 22—the one who ignored sixty-three civilians in the alley because only 06's safety was deserving of his notice—is what the in-game version is copy/pasted from, absolutely faithful to the source material. But the off-duty one—the one that took over as soon as we began that long march to the hospital and then here, who told me horrific sort-of-jokes and smuggled me through security and pretended he had no idea what time it even is, of all things, like he doesn't have an implant and a superpowered brain—the one who's about to serve me dinner, personally, in a building I never should have seen the inside of? I don't know what this is. It's something new.

After a few minutes 22 arrives with a tray in each hand. "I did warn you," he informs me, setting them down. A wave of food smell hits me palpably.

I mean, I don't know what they eat at a pseudomilitary-corporate-army mess hall at a reasonable time of day, but it turns out that even after hours they still get a hell of a lot better than instant noodles and peanut butter sandwiches.

This is some kind of stir-fry thing out of a food blog photo, with decidedly-not-instant noodles and tofu and more fresh vegetables in it than I see in a week.

"They had to reheat it," 22 clarifies, apologetically. "But calories are calories."

He vanishes again and returns with a pitcher of water and two glasses. There's ice in the water. Ice and lemon slices. He pours me a glass. I drink it slower than I want to, faster than I mean to. 22 absorbs this in silence. Then he pulls up a seat across the little table from me.

I try not to inspect him too blatantly, which is one of the hardest things I've maybe ever done. I justify it by reminding myself I'm still recording, and this kind of intel gathering is the exact thing B tasked me to do. The exact thing, presumably, that 22 and 06 wanted me to *keep* doing when they covered for me upstairs.

But that's all rationalization. I'm sitting across a table from 22. Any other situation in the universe, I could feign apathy. Here, though, it's not happening.

Up close he looks too precisely calibrated to be real. Like

something grown in a vat. Like an idea. Mentally I hold up the words *proprietary biotech*, the words *machine consciousness*, and try to take 22's measure against them. But I can't get them to stick.

If B is right, I'm looking at the product of alteration, not creation. Intense alteration, with years of combat training and brainwashing and supersoldier drugs and mystery procedures I can't even conceptualize outside of shit I've seen in movies. How would the end result differ? How could my sorry civilian ass so much as pretend to know?

Get him talking, that's what I've got to do. If you were the Stellaxis labs, and you were programming a machine intelligence to pilot a superweapon, why bother to give it conversational skills? From what I've seen of the public-facing side of the SecOps program, it'd be a waste of resources at best.

I think back to 22 and 06 out there in the streets this afternoon. Talking to each other, to the civilians, to the HQ security guy, to me. Speech patterns, inflection, word choices, vocabulary: all as different from each other's as either's is from mine. As anyone's is from anyone else's.

He's sitting there, hands flat on the table, watching me fail to appreciate his hospitality. Get your shit together, Mal. Say something.

I am about four thousand percent too nervous to eat at this table in this building in this company, let alone strike up conversation. It isn't the biggest or most pressing of my questions by far, but I say: "What if they find me here? I thought the Director was coming?"

"The Director isn't here tonight. She's at a meeting in Shanghai." He catches sight of my confusion. "Ah. You thought she was going to head the search fleet herself?"

"I don't know. Maybe."

"No." 22 draws the word out an extra half syllable, investing it with some layer of meaning I can't read. "She doesn't do that.

She's kept quite busy otherwise." Unconsciously he brushes his thumb against the back of his other hand.

"Still. If they find me here. Won't I get arrested or something?"

"No."

"Why? This place is supposed to be locked down like a prison, *nobody*—"

"Because I won't allow it."

It's almost exactly what 06 said before. Now as then, it sounds like bluffing. Which, considering who these people are, what they are capable of, is ridiculous.

I can't help it. I have to ask.

"You, um. How exactly does that work? You're—" *intellectual property*, my brain supplies helpfully—"don't your orders, um—" I grope for vocabulary—"supersede—"

For a long moment 22 just watches me. I fill this silence by pouring myself some water. At least a little of the shaking of my hand has to do with the wreckage of my shoulder muscles.

"My orders are nonspecific in this particular regard," 22 says, with so much stilted precision that it reads for all the world like irony. Like he's parodying himself, or at least the side of him Stellaxis shows us. A trivia tidbit pops into my head from somewhere: there is only one face of the moon we ever see. "As there is very little precedent."

"You don't usually feed leftovers to civilians."

"No."

"Not even temporarily requisitioned ones, section eighteen-point-whatever-C."

22's mouth quirks, there and gone. "We do not encounter those as a general rule."

"Wrong place, wrong time?"

"Perhaps for you. But sixty-two civilian casualties arrived safe with your assistance." He makes a vague gesture at the trays. I notice he hasn't removed his gloves. "This is the least we can do."

We, he says. But he and 06 have done nothing but grate against this building since the second we set foot on the lawn.

The question is a scab I can't stop picking. What am I doing here?

"You could've called in a medical transport."

22's everything goes guarded. "We could have. And painted those people with a twenty-ton target."

"Or called in 08."

"08 is lately indisposed."

This seems almost to trip him up. Like he was about to say something else instead of *08.* Like maybe a name. An actual human person name he's not allowed to say in front of some dumbfuck civilian like me who entirely lacks the clearance for that kind of information. And maybe it only almost caught him up because this, whatever's going on right here at this table, does not tend to happen, and his guard is down.

All of which is quite probably a pile of nonsense. The idea of 22 with his guard down is laughable. But there's something. I don't know what it is, but I can see its presence clearly. I can see all the ways he's dodging around it. Whatever it is, he's uneasy with it, and that's enough to put me very much on edge.

Why I can read 22 better than I can read normal human people is a mystery for another day. Jessa would laugh her entire ass off as a certainty.

Moreover: What does *indisposed* mean for a lab-grown weapon? Malfunctioning? Broken? In for repairs? If B is right, I'd read it as *sick,* maybe *wounded.* Either way: odd. It'd be the first I've heard of that happening, but then again, it doesn't really seem like the kind of thing they'd announce on the news.

"I'm sorry to hear that," I say carefully. "I hope he recovers soon."

"Occupational hazard," 22 says evenly. This seems to amuse

him, but darkly. Little green shoots of anger poking up through an endless field of calm and being crushed back into place. I'm beyond lost trying to parse this.

I haven't heard anything about 08 taking fire. Or being in the field at all. For months. What other occupational hazards do they have? The newsfeeds have been reporting that 08's been away, doing some kind of diplomatic something or other in another country somewhere. Jessa would know.

But 22 didn't say *busy* or *unavailable* or *away*. He said *indisposed*. With the same downplayed deadpan he'd used to joke about being mangled by resonance grenades, being vaporized by the HQ grounds perimeter.

In his understated, on-brand, 22 way, he is saying something he's not actually saying. To me, or to whoever it is he thinks I'm recording for.

What in the comprehensive fuck did I walk into?

Whatever it is, I'm not sure how much deeper I can go and still find my way back out. Just shut up, Mal. Stop talking. Stop recording. Delete the whole thing. He'll never know. You're going to get yourself arrested. They're going to write essays on you: How Not to Be a Spy.

"Was he wounded?" I ask. "At the front?"

"The front," 22 echoes. "No, he won't be—" Deliberately he pauses, resets. "No."

I make *oh-right-of-course* body language. "Because he's still away on that mission. That diplomacy thing."

There is a look Jessa will give you if you try to debate her when she knows she's right. Flat, open, do-go-on-enlighten-me. There is statistically significant overlap in the Venn diagram between that look and the look 22 brings to bear on me now.

His looks a lot less passive-aggressive, though, and a lot more flat-out fucking confused. Inasmuch as he allows this to signal on his face, which is not very.

"Diplomacy thing," he says with studied calm. Smooth and serene and fragile as glass. "Is that what—"

Something passes over his face, vanishes like a rock into a lake. Pause. Reset.

Programming or brainwashing? Which wall is he coming up against? Hell, people can be programmed too. Look at me, happily paying a dollar an ounce for my company-store water while this place sits here on its watered lawn with its pond and its fountains and its—

"08 is unfortunately feeling a bit under the weather," he says. Softly, so softly, and his whole self is braced like the saying of it causes him some kind of unseen pain. There comes a sound, which I realize is his hands, gripping the stainless steel table edge. He lets go and makes an unconscious smoothing motion over the surface, but the dents remain.

He looks at me, and his eyes are asking me something his voice, for whatever reason, cannot say. I can't make out the detail of its outline, but its general shape looks, horrifyingly, like *please*.

"That isn't really what you meant to say," I whisper before I can stop myself. "Is it?"

Something in 22's face wrenches hard, once, then almost instantly shuts down. The hesitation before he speaks is infinitesimal.

"Eat," he says. "Then I'll see what I can do about getting you home."

I push some food around on my plate, buying time. This is a dead end. They can't tell me anything. I've seen that much already. But can't as in *not allowed to* or can't as in *goes against their programming*?

The longer I see them, the actual, real-life them, the more convinced I am that they're human. If pressed, I'm not even sure I could tell you why. Neither robots nor people are fields of study in which I am what anyone would call competent.

Before B brought it up, I wouldn't even be questioning what the operatives were. But now that I've spent some time with them, what 22 and 06 seem like . . . Have you ever seen one of those big old houses they used to have in movies, with those trees that rich people have cut into the shapes of other things? The Stellaxis CEO had some of those in his yard in the documentary. He had one shaped like a bird in flight, one shaped like a bear on its hind legs, one shaped like some kind of fish. Really detailed shaping, really intricate, the positioning of the limbs and wings suggesting naturalistic movement. But for all of that? Still trees. That's what they remind me of.

All that aside, I can't see some lump of hyperrealistic biotech doing what 06 and 22 have done in just the time in which I've barely known them. Why would they, for example, help those people against orders if they were robots? Why would they hide me from the security check? What benefit would it be to an AI to keep me around? Feed me dinner? Attempt, however awkwardly, to engage me in conversation?

But the same question applies if they're human. Why do any of this? It's like I'm being tested, and I don't know what for.

All the obvious answers point one way. I'm not being paranoid. They *are* hoping I'm recording. They don't want Stellaxis to know. There's something they want me to carry out of here for them. Some information. Whatever's really going on with 08, maybe. I don't know.

If they're acting against orders, though, why hasn't anyone come to chew them out? 06 is just sitting there in Medical, and 22 is here eating stir-fry with an intruder. I don't get it. I don't get the first goddamn thing about it.

Was B right? I don't know. I wish I could just open up my mouth and ask. Obliquely is the only way I can bring myself to arrive at this. I have a sneaking suspicion that coming straight out with a *so hey, they say you're a machine, what's your take* is going to sour this implausible moment of hospitality that I am currently enjoying. I am finding that I need, on a gut-deep level, not to wreck this. Whatever it is.

Do you know a girl named Elena? I want to ask, but my mind is at war with itself because asking the wrong question is going to catapult me straight out of 22's limited supply of good graces, and I am not a saint.

I can't give up, though. Not when I'm in this deep already. Whatever he is, he's my age, and he's lived in this building for at least the better part of, and maybe all of, his life. I don't make the mistake of assuming that means he wants conversation for conversation's sake—I like to think I've assessed 22 a *little* more accurately than that—but there is no question there is *something* he's trying to tell me. He is drilling it into my head with the force of his attention. I just have no idea what it is.

It reminds me powerfully of how his in-game version regarded me in those few seconds before it killed me. I set that thought aside.

It's the hardest thing in the world not to just ask him straight out. *So. Funny question. What are you really?* But I just manage to talk myself out of it. First off, an AI designed to pass as human probably wouldn't know the truth. Second, that would almost definitely qualify as *asking the wrong question*, and then it's game over, the end, thanks for playing.

"22," I say, fake-casual. "06. 08. 17. 33. Why not consecutive numbers? Or, you know, *names*? Doesn't that get confusing?"

"No. It doesn't." Each syllable neatly bitten off. Then, just when I'm certain I've fucked this up categorically, he seems to reach a decision. His whole posture tightens even further, like he's bracing for something. Raises his gaze from the table and locks on. "Not anymore."

This throws me. "Because . . ." I falter. I am walking a minefield. I just can't see it. "Because there are only the three of you left."

Another silence. But this one feels different. He's not stone-walling me. He's watching me expectantly.

Sometimes back home we play charades after power cur-few. Well, usually *I* don't—performative is not my flavor of choice—but a few of the others do. What this reminds me of is watching them play. Like 22 is waiting for me to say something he can't.

What does he think I am? What does he want from me? What does he mistake me for being capable of? I feel like an actor in a drama, missing my lines over and over. If you asked me this morning how I thought I'd be spending my day, *being tragically overestimated by 22* would not have topped that list. The whole situation is drifting slowly away from what passed for my control. Irreparable.

For the first time in my life, the conscious thought: *I wish I were smarter.*

"It must have been a lot harder with all twelve of you," I say slowly. "Especially when you were so young."

This is the bait I am hoping he'll rise to. An artificial intel-ligence will not have at any point been *young.* At least not in a way that would make remembering a dozen two-digit numbers a challenge.

But no.

"By that point it was easy," he says quietly.

And flinches like he's been stung. Hard enough to drop the fork he wasn't really using anyway. Then it's gone, like it never happened, and he's already on his feet and gesturing me to mine. Every motion has gone clipped all of a sudden, and in a way I recognize. It's the way you carry yourself around pain.

I look at the dented table. I look at how 22 holds himself, always holds himself, like the world is a trip wire he'll set off if he breathes wrong. That razor-edge precision. That balance.

Something in my mind shifts a little, makes me think of the

videos I've seen of icebergs, the way they were supposed to have been. The surface fractions. The mass beneath.

Sudden unshakeable feeling that I've been staring at him all evening but I haven't seen him, really seen him, up till now.

"You wanted to get home, yes?" he says. "I won't keep you waiting."

If I had a coherent protest formulated, I'd have to shout it at him, because he's already cleared the room and is making his way out the double doors.

But I don't, so I don't. Besides, I've seen the SecOps documentary. He could hear me if I whispered it across a city block during rush hour. I swallow all my questions and walk after.

On the way back to the front desk, the halls are still pretty much deserted. Sentry bots, the odd soldier or scientist or salaryman, but that's all. It's only nine p.m. It's not *that* late. Then again, it's a big building. For all I know there are thousands of people here.

I follow 22 to the elevators and ride up to the ground floor in silence. He's just standing there now, hands clasped behind his back, elegantly glowering. Neat if I had the faintest inkling how I'd managed to disappoint him, foregone conclusion though that certainly the fuck was. We have the elevator to ourselves.

It's now or never. Whatever *it* is.

The doors whish open, and I mash the button to shut them again.

This gets 22's attention. He whirls on me, hand on sword hilt, faster than anything.

"Wait," I choke out. "Wait."

I stop the recording and palm my lenses. Nowhere to put them. Doesn't matter. I hold both hands up, palm out, trying to keep my lenses in place with a thumb.

"I can help you," I whisper. I have no idea what I mean by it, how I'll make good on it, why this lie is falling out of my mouth.

But if B is right about the operatives, then Stellaxis has told a lot worse lies than that. If B is right, then the superweapon menacing me with a goddamn *sword* right now is a human person pretty much exactly my age, who lost a family just like me, and might be living in old town with me and Jessa and the rest of us if this place hadn't gotten its hooks in him first.

"Do I give the impression," he breathes at me, "that I am in need of your help."

Maybe I have him all wrong. Maybe I have his life all wrong. Maybe B is full of shit, and I'm about to paint an elevator with my insides on somebody else's misguided assumption. And there's no save point waiting to respawn me.

But I've been watching some buried conflict go at it with itself all across his face for an hour now, and I know better. Or I hope to holy hell I do.

A test, I think.

Slowly, looking straight at him, I nod.

22 rears back a couple inches like a slow-motion snake. "Is that right."

"I know," I say, and my voice gives out.

He watches me in level silence. His patience is the patience of the sea.

"I know that the company has been lying about you and 06 and all the others all along," I say, forcing the words out, even though my voice is cracking. "I know that they tell people you were grown in a tank and given computers for brains, and I know that's not true. I know they're doing something to you when you say things they don't like. *And* I know this," I continue, searching his face. It's a gamble, but I think of the way he never takes his gloves off, the way he touched the back of one hand when he mentioned the Director, the way he brought me here in the hope that I could see between the lines to everything he's been trying to tell me, and I go all in. "Kidnapping children to torture them into becoming weapons *is* a war crime. Or it fucking well should be."

Minutes of silence, or so it feels. It's probably seconds at most. Whatever conflict he's been suppressing escalates from periodic skirmish to full-on brawl. He's wound so tight it's like someone has tasked him to keep all the world's secrets. If he so much as twitches at such close quarters, I could die.

"Forty-eight," he says at last. It's the barest whisper, and I have to strain to hear it. There's no footage to replay this time. "There were forty-eight."

0 0 1 1

THE DOORS WHISH OPEN, AND I MASH *the button to shut them again.*

This gets 22's attention. He whirls on me, hand on sword hilt, faster than anything.

"Wait," I choke out. "Wait."

The recording ends on a freeze-frame of 22 looking like somebody just flipped his murder switch. A replay icon pops up in the middle of the screen.

Jessa nearly throws the pocket screen across the room. "You *stopped recording*?" She's too worked up to wait for an answer. "*Why?*"

She definitely wants an answer to that part, but I'm not sure I have one she's going to like. I've been kicking it around in my head since I left the Stellaxis building, mentally replaying that conversation over and over, as if by so doing I'll etch it indelibly into my brain.

"I think he knew I was recording," I say slowly.

"He *what*—"

"I needed him to trust me." I pause, remembering. The words come to me slowly, one by one, feeling my way through a maze in the dark. "I needed him to know that whatever he said, it was

safe with me. That I wouldn't go rat him out to the company."
The Director, I think. I have no idea who that is. Bad news, I
imagine, anycase. I find I'm picturing her like something far
worse than, but not unlike, a mean teacher. 06 and 22 passing
notes under the desks. Until one of them found its way to this
hopeless dumbass right here.

"Rat him out to the company? Mal, he *is* the company."

"I know," I say. "But I don't think he wants to be."

"Tell them to come live with us," Jessa says, like this hasn't
occurred to me, like it hasn't been occurring to me at full blast
for seven solid hours at this point. "We'd make room."

"Make room," I say. "Where? Under the bottom bunks?" *Monsters under the bed* skims across the surface of my thoughts, but
here's what's really got me. Here in old town, we're free. A whole
lot more free than 22 and 06 and 08 and all the SecOps dead back
at company HQ. As long as you don't look too closely at the part
where Stellaxis owns our water. Our power. Our privacy. Even
if we could somehow rescue them, fuckwit fangirl daydream
though it is, what do we have to offer them?

What, for that matter, do we have to offer ourselves?

Jessa gives up on getting any further response out of me and
goes back to staring at the screen. "22. Shit. The real one. 06
also, because of *course* you'd run into both of them when I'm
not there. I'll have you know I am *insanely* jealous right now."
She shakes her head, holds the screen up to scrutinize 22 at eye
level. "He looks like he's about to kill you."

"I think that was a reflex. He had no idea what I was doing."

Jessa side-eyes me. "Did *you*?"

It's a question I've been asking myself for hours.

When we got out of the elevator, 22 brought me back to the
front desk, where the security guard eyed me suspiciously and
caused a sleek black car to materialize out front of the building,
leaving me to wonder all over again what I was doing eating

dinner in the cafeteria if summoning company cars had been an option all along.

22 walked me out through the grassy-smelling night to the car, opened the door for me, and said absolutely nothing. *I'm going to try to help you*, I wanted to say, but the car was probably listening, and I had no concrete plan to back it up anyway. So I just gave him a little nod and tried to project my intentions with my eyes and said, "See you," like an idiot, and he watched me for a second, not visibly disappointed but not visibly *not*-disappointed, either, and then turned on his heel and stalked away.

The car was about a million times nicer than the one we'd taken to the coffee shop. It slid out of company grounds and into the city, slicing silently through the dark while I sat staring out the window at nothing, my thoughts a tangle of razor wire.

After a while I put my lenses back in. Jessa's messages were still there sitting in the corner. No new ones for hours. Not surprising. Power curfew would have been in effect since early evening, taking her internet access with it, and it was going on ten p.m. Apparently, along with water accounts, they don't have power curfew on Stellaxis property either. Fantastic.

I skimmed the messages but saw nothing I didn't expect to see. Worry and anger and more worry taking turns in the driver's seat.

The last few were a little different.

dude. where the exact fuck are you? they're saying on the news that zone 15 is total chaos, there's some greenleaf mech shooting the news drones out of the air, nobody knows what's going on

desperately sorry to keep pestering you in the middle of WHATEVER THE ACTUAL SHIT YOU'RE DOING but we have no idea what's going on, all the footage coming out is garbage and we're all super worried about you

At one point she attached a grainy image from a newsfeed. From the angle, it must've been taken by a drone, hovering at a high diagonal beyond the reach or notice of the mech. It showed the same trashed street we all had fled down initially. I could make out the wreckage of the thrown helicopter, the pillars of the ugly building all those people had tried to take cover behind. In the background was the mech, its glossy finish streaked by the long chemical burns of the drone swarm's fléchettes. Memory slammed me with the smell of that street. Blood and burning. I swallowed.

please tell me you're in a different part of the city and it's at least 200% safer than this

Then another image: 06 and 22 battling the three mechs. This one looked like someone might have taken it with their lenses from a window a block or so away.

you will not believe this, 06 and 22 are out there protecting a ton of wounded civilians from THREE greenleaf mechs and it's the most on-brand 06 thing i've literally ever seen, someone posted this shot earlier and people are losing their absolute minds

In hindsight I don't really know why I did what I did next. Maybe some useless part of my brain thought it was still in the game and there were no real stakes involved in sticking my neck out. Maybe I was still pissed about what I had seen earlier at the checkpoint, about Comforts of Home where B's sister's coffee shop should have been, about all that green grass and those ponds and fountains at Stellaxis HQ. About 22's hands and B's photo and the dents in that table and how the man in the alley said *Thank god they sent you in for us* and 06 said *They didn't*, in this tone like they were more likely to be rescued by the tooth fairy than by the company. About the note in both their voices when they talked about the Director or Stellaxis. What was it 06 said? *I ever get out of here, I might just take you up on that.* About 22 and 06 covering for me when I was recording, and how I was too stunned or too stupid to figure out why. About 22 looking the closest to scared I'd ever seen him when he dropped eye contact and said *Forty-eight. There were forty-eight.*

Or maybe it's just that my footage sucks a whole lot less than this one blurry photo, and if 06 and 22 are out there putting their asses on the line to help a bunch of *civilian casualties*, then people should know the truth.

Right there in the car, I pulled up my recording. My connection was still solid, but by now the car had taken me out of the city limits—I'd passed the trash-fire constellation of the mall camps a minute ago—so I had to be fast. And I had to decide what I did next alone. I had no way to confer with Jessa, who'd be under power curfew until morning, just like I would be as soon as the car dropped me off. Whatever happened would be on me.

I saved my footage as two separate files: one for everything before we left the alley for the hospital, one for everything after. Not perfect, but the easiest way I could figure out how to divide the footage, keeping aside anything that seemed likely to get 06 and 22 in trouble.

I swiped the second file over to the drive in Jessa's pocket screen, along with the in-game footage of 08. I logged in to our streaming account and posted the first file online. Then, as an afterthought, I backed up that one too. Whatever happened next, there was a lot that had happened already. I wanted all this evidence somewhere I could keep it.

Now, back at home, Jessa hits the replay button on the second file. I've already told her almost everything. I left out the part with B's sister's coffee shop for right now because she's already so keyed up with worry she's practically vibrating. She hasn't even asked about my meeting with B, so I guess I'll leave that for the morning, or when she brings it up, whichever comes first. I told her the rest, though, from the first appearance of the mech on down, but she keeps poking and swiping the screen to skip around, seemingly at random. Shaking her head in disbelief pretty much everywhere she lands. She's been doing this for the past fifteen minutes or so, just jumping back and forth between both files, eating through all the remaining battery on the screen. Before that she watched them in their entirety. It's past four in the morning, and we're tucked up together on my bunk, whispering. It was way too cold in the garden, and the hallways are full.

When she gets to the last few minutes of the second file, she lets it play through. I watch it with her. It feels like it happened a million years ago. It feels like it's still happening now. I rub one hand across my throat. He could have killed me. I could be a corpse abandoned in an elevator right now. I might have never come home.

Instead of . . . I'm not entirely sure. I'm alive, anyway. Alive and confused. My whole body aches. My eyeballs feel like they've been exfoliated. I'm too tired to sleep.

Onscreen 22 opens his mouth to say *You wanted to get home, yes?* and the battery finally dies. We both stare at the blank screen some seconds longer.

"Okay, but," Jessa says. "What happened after the elevator?"

I force a shrug. My mind feels like a buzzsaw. *Do I give the impression,* 22 whispers in my head, *that I am in need of your help.* "They sent me home in a company car."

"And I'm supposed to believe you really think that's what I mean?"

"I posted the footage."

"You *know what I'm talking about.* You had a real-life operative about to real-life mess you up and you talked him down. In what reality is that actually a thing you can *do.*"

"I—" My voice catches. To my horror, the backs of my eyes start prickling.

It's the stress of the day catching up with me, that's all. Nervous energy releasing. I walked through an active war zone all afternoon. No fucking way am I about to do something as ridiculous as start fucking *crying* because I'm pretty sure I failed whatever test 06 and 22 were trying to administer.

Beside me, Jessa pretends not to notice, badly. For one awful second I'm convinced she's going to try to hug me. But she busies herself dusting the panel screen with her sleeve.

I know she just wants answers, and she deserves them. The account I posted the footage on is half hers, after all. We've been a team for years. I don't know why it's so hard to tell her. I mean, for whatever incomprehensible 22 reason, he entrusted me with a secret. A dangerous secret. What if whatever happened to B happens to Jessa? It's one thing to put myself at risk. I've done that already. It's bad enough I had to use our shared account to post the footage. But I was careful not to post the stuff that could get anyone in trouble. Wasn't I?

Jessa, paragon of mercy, rescues me again. "Let's talk about it in the morning," she says in an elaborately sleepy voice she didn't have a minute ago. "You work tomorrow?"

"Day after."

"I do but not until afternoon. Breakfast? My turn for it."

"Yeah. Sure."

"You care if I stay here? I'll wake everybody climbing over to mine."

We're packed in here tight enough she can probably feel my shrug in the dark. She rolls over and is out almost immediately.

I wish I could fall asleep that easily. Instead I stare at the ceiling, reviewing.

I wonder what happened to B and her family. I hope she sensed trouble and got the fuck out before they came for her.

Which leads me to: if it's actually true that Stellaxis is faking the deaths of children in order to steal and torture them, and then claiming them as *intellectual property* and making them fight in their corporate war, they nabbed those kids over a decade ago. Someone else must have figured it out by now. B can't have been the first.

Which leads me to: What happened to *those* people? Did they get disappeared? Did they have businesses to straight-up erase and replace as well? It makes you think about the eighty zillion company stores you see every day in a slightly more ominous light.

Forty-eight. There were forty-eight.

But we only ever knew about twelve. 02, 05, 06, 08, 11, 17, 21, 22, 28, 33, 38, 42. They're the ones who got sent on missions, were reported in the news, made into NPCs in-game. The ones who got turned into celebrities, dead or alive.

Unless I've monstrously misinterpreted what 22 said in the elevator, there are three dozen others nobody's making action figures out of, because they died before they got that far. Four dozen little kids in total, vanished off the face of the earth, returning—some of them—unrecognizable. Especially if nobody knows where to look for them. Or that they're anywhere to be found.

Why not consecutive numbers? Doesn't that get confusing?

Which leads me to: I am a goddamn idiot.

What *should* I have said? What could I have done smarter? Was there some kind of clever one-liner I could have dropped that would have translated into some kind of much more chill version of *you have to trust me, I will do literally anything within my power to help you, I am loyal as fuck to the few things I genuinely care about and for some reason one of those things is you?*

I don't know. I mean, it's unlikely. But that doesn't keep me from sinking into the quicksand of that thought and staying there until the sun is peeking through the curtains.

I must fall asleep sometime after that because when I wake up, it's not Jessa beside me, it's 22, and he's here because I rescued him, and we get up and drink coffee and make breakfast, and I take him down to the company store and we start to get him outfitted with the shit he'll need for his new life in the hotel, the reusable bottle and headlamp and peanut butter and batteries, but then I start taking all that stuff back out of our shopping basket and put it back on the shelves, and I take 22 outside the company store, outside the hotel, out into the abandoned fields outside old town, and I point into the distance away from the city and I say, *Go, I'll cover for you*, and I have no idea how to cover for him but he goes all the same, and it's both the best and the worst day of my life.

Then Jessa starts shaking me, and I wake up again. I know it's for real this time, because I feel like I've been hit by a truck. Repeatedly. The light through the window has not visibly changed. Why is it that a tiny bit of sleep makes you feel worse than no sleep at all?

My alarm hasn't gone off yet. From the morning sounds of the room, it's a few minutes, max, since power curfew lifted for the day.

I try to roll away from Jessa and bury my face in the wall, but she's not having it. She pulls me bodily over onto my back. I drag the blanket over my face, but she yanks that away too. I open my eyes, ready to shove her off my bunk.

I freeze when I see her face. My whole yesterday comes flooding back. I've fucked us. Whoever came for B is here for Jessa and me. It's too late.

"Wake the others," I say. "We can go out the window. Down the fire escape."

Jessa blinks. "What? Dude, you're dreaming. Get up. You're not going to believe this shit."

"Okay. Okay. Just . . . coffee first, all right?"

"No. Most emphatically not coffee first." She fiddles with something online. "Holy shit," she whispers, not to me. "Holy *shit*. Are your lenses in?"

Now that I'm awake, her body language isn't projecting danger at all. She's just really, really keyed up over something. I nod.

"You are, like, almost admirably oblivious. Are you not seeing your messages?"

I hadn't, no. I take a look.

Twenty-six thousand three hundred eighty-six new messages.

When the shock subsides, I skim through a few. They're all the same. *Faelynne has subscribed to your stream! Say hello! MyNameIsName has subscribed to your stream! Say hello! Lone-Wolf14 has subscribed to your stream! Say hello! SummerKnight has subscribed to your stream! Say hello! NOOBCRUSHR69 has subscribed to your stream! Say hello! 08sGrl has subscribed to your stream! Say hello!*

And they're still coming in. They must have been arriving all night, throughout power curfew, and I didn't hear them land this morning because my notifications are muted until my alarm goes off.

"Is this . . . ," I say slowly, then stop and start again. It can't be. It sounds absurd to even say it. But I don't have another explanation. "Is this because of—"

Jessa nods frantically. Her eyes are actually sparkling. "You got the only clear footage of what actually happened out there. All the news sites picked it up. It's *massive.*"

She has to be exaggerating. I pull up a newsfeed. She's not.

I scroll past headlines like 62 WOUNDED IN GREENLEAF INDUSTRIES CHEMICAL ATTACK and 2 STELLAXIS OPERATIVES VS 3 GIANT MECHS: WHO WILL WIN? [VIDEO] and MAJORITY OF 62 CIVILIANS BLINDED IN CHEMICAL ATTACK EXPECTED TO REGAIN SIGHT THANKS TO QUICK ACTION BY STELLAXIS OPERATIVES 06 AND 22 and YOU WON'T BELIEVE HOW 06 AND 22 JUST RESCUED THE HELL OUT OF MORE THAN SIXTY CIVILIANS AT THE FRONT.

"Holy shit," I whisper. I realize Jessa just said the same thing a minute ago. It seems a proper enough sentiment for what I'm looking at.

"Right?" Jessa whispers back. "Check out our page."

I open the main page of our channel because I'm still having the tiniest bit of trouble believing this is real.

Yesterday, Jessa and I had a little over twenty-four hundred subscribers.

Right this minute we have just under twenty-nine *thousand.*

Then I see the view counter on the video I posted from the company car, and I can feel the blood drop out of my head. It has over six million views, and the counter is climbing even as I stare at it in disbelief.

"You see the tip jar?" Jessa asks.

I open it. There's more money in there than I make in two months walking dogs. It's all small amounts, of course, but it's a *lot* of small amounts. I scroll down the list of recent payments for a few seconds, and I still haven't reached the end. I mean, it's not like we're overnight millionaires, or anything like it, but we're doing a lot better than we were twenty-four hours ago.

For a minute Jessa and I just sit there and look at each other. Then we both bust out laughing, trying to muffle it so we don't wake everyone up.

I don't even know why. It's not that it's funny. It's just such a hell of a sideways goddamn thing to happen. It's like, I stayed in one piece all day yesterday, company store to company war to company building to company car, and this is finally the last straw that crumples my rational mind like paper. Here we are, a couple of nobodies, slapped upside the head by fame. In our sleep. For reasons we wouldn't have seen coming in a million years. For ages I've been chasing the analogue shadow of 22 in a world that's the analogue shadow of this one, only to get blindsided by the real one in the real world out of nowhere.

I shouldn't even have been there, out in the city. I would never have been there if I hadn't been trying to find B.

What's left of my nervous laughter shrivels up and dies. Jessa's stops too, fast, when she catches sight of me.

"What is it?"

"You still haven't heard from B," I say.

Jessa shakes her head slowly. "I guess she backed out on us. It sucks, but I mean . . ." She shrugs. "We keep even a tenth of these new subscribers, we'll probably do okay without her."

"Yeah. Um. Jessa, about that—"

Rustling from the bunk below. "Oh my god." My bunk gives a violent shake as Suresh sits up fast. "Oh my *god*." His head pokes out, angled up at my bunk. "Mal. This video that's all over the news. This is *yours*?"

"*Yeah*, it is," Jessa says.

"I, um. I kind of had something of a day."

"No shit. Wait. Is that *06*?"

I nod.

"The real one?"

"Yeah."

"Give it a second," Jessa says. "You know 06 doesn't work alone."

Suresh's playthrough of the footage seems to have reached that point already. "Oh no. Oh *no*. No fucking way. You got *both of them*?"

"Correction," Jessa says. "She *worked with* both of them. Watch on, my friend. All will be made clear in the fullness of time."

The others are waking up now, whether from their alarms or the general increased noise level of the room. Within a few minutes they all know. I get mobbed, congratulated, fussed over. Tegan sits me down in the only chair while Talya starts a full pot of coffee with Jessa's water account, and everybody grills me for details while they get ready for work. Was I scared?

What made me go back for those people? What are 06 and 22 like in real life? Was 08 there? Et cetera.

I answer as best as I can, which is probably not very. Yes, I was scared. I don't know what made me go back for them, except that I had time to and nobody else was and they reminded me of when my building came down when I was a kid. (They all nod at that part, knowingly.) No, 08 was not there. 06 and 22 are . . .

This one gives me pause. "A lot like how they are in-game, really," I lie. It's simpler than trying to explain all the things they said and did that I don't even understand, and I've been replaying it all in my head pretty much nonstop since it happened, turning each moment over and over like a puzzle piece I can't figure out what fits to.

It comes to me that I'm not thinking of 06 and 22 as biotech anymore. That I haven't done that in a while.

Jessa, actual saint, does not breathe a word about the second video file. I glance at the charging station, where she's got the panel hooked up already. I reach over, remove the drive, and pocket it. Beyond what's on my implant, the only physical copy of that second file is on that drive. I'm not letting it out of my sight.

Gradually, one by one, the others start to clear out for work, chores, errands, and so on. I have three back-to-back dog-walking days starting tomorrow, but today my schedule is pretty empty.

Jessa doesn't work until the afternoon, so we grab breakfast real quick and head up to the gardens. Today's my turn to pick up produce rations for the room, and I don't think for an instant I'm done being questioned. Anyway, we have things to discuss. Details to hammer out. I check our page again right before we leave, and my video's logged another eleven million views since I woke up. We've taken on another twenty-six hundred subscribers. More than we had, in total, yesterday. This is certifiably outrageous.

"What do we even do with this?" Jessa asks, like I have given her any reason to think I have enough experience with sudden internet fame to know the answer.

"Keep doing what we're doing, I guess. Play the game."

"But what about B? We just overhauled our whole strategy because she was paying us to. You haven't seriously gone after the boards in like a week. And now she drops us. Do we keep doing the work she's supposedly paying us for or don't we?"

I sigh. I have to tell her. We're partway up the next-to-last stairwell to the roof, so when we make the next landing, I pull her aside.

"I don't think we're seeing any more payments from B," I say.

"Yeah, I pretty much figured it was too good to be—"

"No. I think she . . ." I trail off, unsure anymore what's safe to say. Then I realize my footage has gone viral, and whatever comes out of my mouth now is going to be the tiniest drop in the bucket of trouble I may well have just landed myself in.

I take out my lenses, for all the good it's going to do if they've already decided to come after me. Jessa blinks up at me, then does the same.

"Sit down a second," I say, and then I tell her. Everything. All the missing time that bookends the two files. I tell her about Comforts of Home and the so-called drone strike and how the coffee shop had been straight-up deleted from the world within the span of *days*, and how I went walking because it was too big for me to process sitting still. She already knows this part, but I find myself telling her about Stellaxis HQ and its grass and its fountains, about 06 and 22 sneaking me in past the security guard, about all those people being brought to Medical against apparent orders. I tell her about 22 sitting me down and feeding me stir-fry and talking weird awkward circles around something, like he was under some kind of fairy-tale curse not to speak of it. I tell her about his hands under the gloves, about the way he speaks of the Director, about the look on his face when I asked if the operatives' numbers were confusing. How much it looked like it hurt—something they're doing to him via his implant, probably—for him to act against the company, even in such minor ways as that.

Then, even though it feels like some kind of betrayal to do so, I tell her what happened in the elevator after I took my lenses out. Because whatever I've landed in, she's in it now too. She deserves the whole truth, at least the wholest one I can access.

It doesn't take as long as I thought it would. It felt bigger, holding it in my mind.

She sits and soaks it in, then sits with it a little longer.

"Forty-eight what?" she asks at last, although her eyes know the answer. Forty-eight kids like Elena. Like whoever 22 and 06 and all the others used to be. Would have continued to be. Forty-eight kids orphaned by this endless corporate war, just like me and Jessa and pretty much everyone we know.

"Fuck," she says, realizing she doesn't need me to spell it out for her. *"Fuck."*

I nod. I don't know what else to do.

"When your building came down," I say at last, and pause so she can steady herself before following me down that particular traumatic rabbit hole, "did the rescue people take you to a big room somewhere? Bright lights? Full of kids?"

"Yeah. There was this woman asking me questions. Then she gave me a cookie. Why?"

"I think they all went there. When their buildings came down."

Her face creases. "You lost me. All who?"

"The operatives. Elena and all of them. Back when they were still kids." She opens her mouth, probably to tell me I've lost my fucking mind, but I steamroll over her. "When I was in the sub-levels at HQ, it kept reminding me of something."

"Mal. I don't know where you went, but where they took me back then was an empty room. There was nothing there. I don't even mean, like, nothing *distinctive*. Just empty."

"Empty and white, with bright lights, and a ton of kids running around. No adults, except the ones asking questions. Right?"

She nods.

"Me too. Probably everyone else our age in old town, if we ask around. Why not the SecOps kids?"

"So they were kids now? You've decided?"

"I don't know for sure. I'm starting to think so."

"Where is this coming from all of a sudden?"

"That's what I'm trying to tell you. When I was in the sublevels with 22 and 06, there was a smell in the air. You know, like a hospital smell or a library smell, you'd know it anywhere? The smell of that basement was like nothing I've ever smelled anywhere else. Except once. It was reminding me of something, the whole time I was there. I didn't place it until later, while I was trying to fall asleep. But then I did, and the memories all came flooding back. It was like I was there again."

She's gone quiet, wide-eyed, waiting for me to finish.

"I think those forty-eight missing kids got picked, and we didn't make the cut. But we all started out in that room."

If she was quiet before, it was nothing to this. It's a full minute before she speaks. "I've never been glad about being rejected for something before," she says, her lighten-the-mood tone falling utterly flat. "Can you imagine if we—"

Of course I can. A few days ago, the possibility would have been intriguing. But I'm rapidly being made aware that there's nothing glamorous here. Just shit and lies the whole way to the horizon. "Yeah," I say. "We'd be dead."

"Yeah," Jessa says. "I guess we would." She stares at nothing for a moment, shakes it off. "So it wasn't us. Then who was it? The other thirty-six."

"I don't know," I say. "But what we *do* know is that they *did* number the operatives consecutively. Or the kids who would have been operatives, I guess, if all of them had survived."

"But that makes no sense." Jessa is almost visibly squirming, chafing hard against this abrupt rearrangement of her whole heart's mythology. "Okay. Look. So they announce the SecOps program and the creation of the operatives on January 1, '26 under the New Year's Initiative, and they send them to the front. The media has been all over them ever since. We're talking *eight years.* Where have these other three dozen kids been hiding? Why don't we know about them? The media coverage just ignored them for some reason?"

She pauses like she's done, but no. If there's a topic Jessa will keep on warming to until she's practically incandescent, it is this. "Besides, the company makes millions of dollars off SecOps merchandise." She lifts the front of her 02 t-shirt away from her body in illustration. "You're telling me they had the opportunity to make *four times the profit,* and they just, what? Chose not to?"

I shake my head. "I don't think it's that. I mean, think about B's picture. Elena was, what, seven or eight when she lost her family? And the operatives don't appear in the field until they're twelve or thirteen?"

"17," Jessa reminds me.

It takes me a second to realize she's not talking about their age. "17 is an outlier whichever way you cut it," I reply. "He didn't die in the field. He didn't survive long enough to be deployed. Nobody ever saw him in person. Hardly anybody even *knew* about him until they put them all in the game, and then he got added to the next wave of marketing."

"So they'd have one that younger kids could relate to," Jessa says impatiently. "Expand their marketing base. 17 was a 'tragedy that forged the path for the project's optimization.'" This with actual air quotes. "You forget who you're talking to."

"Now the first to actually be killed in action was—"

"38," Jessa says. "I've done my homework, Mal. You can't tell me anything I—"

"She was, what, thirteen? Fourteen?"

"Thirteen."

"And how long between general deployment and 38's death?"

Jessa visibly runs the numbers. It doesn't take long. "Almost a year and a half. Sixteen months and a few days."

"Okay, so. Bear with me here. They take kids Elena's age. Our age, when the company pulled us out of our buildings and put us in that room. Sevenish, eightish. These kids get their ink—01 through 48—and disappear into the Stellaxis labs for about five years. Something happens to most of them in there. Whatever got 17 gets them, too, maybe. With me so far?"

Jessa gives a kind of diagonal nod, like she'd really rather be shaking her head no instead. "I'm listening."

"Okay. They get their forty-eight kids, they do whatever to them to turn them into what they are. But only eleven of them end up living long enough to send to the front. Nobody tells us about the rest. Who they are, how they died, nothing. I mean, this is a giant corporation we're talking about. They probably get written off as *nonviable materials* or something. And then the others, the ones who lived long enough to get sent out into the field, they get announced in the New Year's Initiative, they show up in their little uniforms with their swords and guns, and they unleash all hell on the Greenleaf army." I fold my arms. My hands are shaking. "I mean. I don't know how much of that is *right*, but you have to at least admit it would explain a lot. You know?"

"Well, I mean. This all is assuming that B was right."

"B for-real disappeared," I say. "You weren't there. That coffee shop was like *erased from the fabric of reality*. There was no trace of it. And there was no trace of any drone strike either.

That building was *pristine*, okay? And then the way 06 and 22 were acting . . ."

I ever get out of here, 06 whispers sadly in my head, *I might just take you up on that.*

"There's something going on," I say. "I think B was right. I think they took Elena and they took the rest of these kids and they did something to them to turn them into what they are now. If they were just made like that in the first place, grown in some tank with a computer for a brain, 22's hands wouldn't look like they do."

"Which is how exactly?"

"It's hard to explain. I only saw it for a second." Then I realize. "It's in the video. Take a look yourself if you don't believe me."

"It's not that I don't *believe* you. When B met with us, *you* were the skeptical one, remember? You thought it was conspiracy theory bullshit. But I mean. I saw your video. There's something about that place." She sighs. "I wish you'd been recording at the coffee shop. What used to be the coffee shop. Whatever."

"Maybe someday we take a bus out there and you see it for yourself. But it's just another copy/paste of the one downstairs."

"Maybe I'll go check out the company HQ while I'm at it," Jessa adds. "See if they have any hospitality left over for me. I could do with getting in on all this mythical *free water* and *actual food*."

"Yeah, well, unless the planets magically align and give us another day where 06 and 22 are in a position to actually ask for our help *while* their boss is out of town, we're not getting back in there in this lifetime," I say. "But yeah. There's something about that place. 06 and 22 pretty obviously want out. But I think they're stuck there."

The phrase *intellectual property* throatpunches me all over again. You can't go where you want if you don't have rights. Which you don't if you're not human.

Or if someone has convinced the rest of the world that you aren't.

Jessa chews all this over. She gets up and starts pacing back and forth on the landing, running her hands through her hair. Then whirls on me. "Okay. Say B's right. Say you're right. Say it's all true. What do we *do*? Lie low until this blows over?" She gestures frustration. "Whatever *this* even is? I don't want to get disappeared!"

"No," I say slowly, realizing the answer aloud. "We do the opposite. We stay visible. We keep as many eyes on us as possible. B kept her head down, and look at what happened to her. We have a lot of attention right now because of the video. Millions of views. Thousands of new subscribers. But that probably means we have other attention too. The kind we don't want. All the security cameras at company HQ will have picked me up. I don't get the impression the operatives usually bring in random people off the street for dinner."

"You really think they're going to try to . . ." Jessa knots her fists in her hair. "To do to us what they did to B?"

"I have no idea. But I think we need to do whatever we can to make that really, really awkward for them."

"We go big," Jessa says, nodding thoughtfully. "I can do big."

"We go big," I agree. "We double down. We don't drop our guard. And we don't stop until we get the fuck to the bottom of this."

"Sure, but. This is some random viral video we're hanging all this on. Nobody's going to remember it in ten seconds. Half these new subscribers are probably going to bail when they see that our regular content is, um . . . less exciting. Unless you're planning to document more war zone field trips."

We both know that's beyond unlikely. Yes, the circumstances aligned to land me with the only footage of that operative/mech showdown, but that was the kind of luck you run into maybe once in all your days. Next time it'd probably be me getting my lenses gassed and brought to a hospital. Or killed. Or disappeared.

"No," I say. "I think we go back to what we know. Except this time we do it better."

"The game?"

I look at her.

"But if B's not—"

"I'm not talking about B. I'm talking about going legit. I'm talking about—"

"The boards," Jessa finishes for me. "That's nuts. We can't bring it to those people, they'll paste us. We've tried it before. It ended how it's always gonna end."

"It's millions of subscribers if we can pull this off," I say. "Millions and millions of views. Not just once but consistently." I start counting on my fingers. "Consistent visibility. Consistent *pay*. We drop all our other jobs and focus on this. Bring in a few of the others, I don't know. Put together an actual team."

"There are definitely a few people in our room who'd be happy to help out with that," Jessa says. "Especially if this turns out to be an actual conspiracy. Oh my god, they'd *shit*."

At once we both realize what we're saying. I'm watching it dawn on Jessa's face. We can't put that kind of target on the others. It's bad enough I put one on Jessa. We have to go this alone.

Which reminds me.

"You can back out," I tell Jessa. "You didn't sign up for this. I can, I don't know, make a new account that's not attached to—"

I trail off when I see her face. She's grinning.

"As much as I'd love to see you attempt that," she says, "I've witnessed your flailings at human interaction, and I can't in good conscience wish that experience on your audience."

"Fuck off."

"See?" she says brightly. Then her expression sobers. "Seriously, though, I'm all in. We're a team. Live and die as one and all that junk. Besides, no way am I letting you walk off with all that sweet, sweet sponsorship, so back up." She reaches in, gives my shoulder a quick squeeze, lets go.

I nod. It's all I can think at the moment to do. Gratitude has me in a choke hold, and the words won't come out.

Jessa seems to get it all the same. "So no more of that shit, understand? I don't know what you and B have dug up here, but it's . . . it's something. What kind of asshole would I be if I went around wearing this stuff—" another flap of the t-shirt—"and then sat around going *well it sucks, but it's not my problem* when these for-real people are in for-real trouble? If they're *actual people* who were *actually kidnapped* and nobody's helping because nobody knows the truth? I mean, it's bad enough I— Oh god."

Jessa freezes. I raise an eyebrow. Though I already know where this is headed.

"I mean. Not everyone's intentions have always been as wholesome as yours. If it turns out these were *real people* this *whole time*, that's—" Jessa stops short, shudders a little, tries again. "Virtual or no. That's skeevy as shit." She goes still, a look on her face like she's remembering something she'd rather forget. "No, really. That's disgusting. If they really . . ." She trails off for a moment, then shakes her head to clear it of whatever memory has lodged there. "Yeah, no. We have to tell people the truth. We have to shut this down."

"Shut it down. Stellaxis. Me and you. A second ago we were just trying to make it harder for them to shut *us* down."

"Well, *something.*"

"And end up like B? Maybe they get us on a terrorism charge and lock out our lenses. Maybe they gas us and we wake up in an interrogation cell. Maybe they manage to precision strike us. Maybe they blow a giant hole in the side of this hotel and kill a few hundred people who were just minding their own goddamn business. We have to do this smart. Play the long game."

"Which is what exactly? Go get our faces kicked in at a protest? Boycott Stellaxis and Greenleaf and then die of thirst and starvation, in that order, when we remember the part where they own *absolutely everything*? And what's that about anyway? No power curfew at HQ, you said. As much free water as you can drink. Why there and not here? Why am I looking at spending two months' pay at a rehydration clinic if my account runs out of water when I can just roll some barrels over to the company drinking fountain and fill those motherfuckers up? The operatives aren't the only thing they have to answer for. Your video is proof of that, too."

"I *know*. But we're not going to do anybody any good if we're dead. If we do this, we're going to have one chance to do it right, because as soon as we make our move, we'll have their attention, and that's only gonna end one way."

"So you want to just sit on this. This new intel."

"Until we know how best to use it effectively," I say. "Yes."

Jessa resumes pacing for a minute or so, messing with her hair. "I don't like it," she says at last.

"Neither do I," I say. *22 across the table, trying to tell me something I didn't know how to hear.* "Not even a little."

Everything I'm trying my feeble best to suppress, Jessa reads it in my face. "No," she says. "I don't imagine you do."

There's a little moment of silence. We're a couple of dipshits with fifteen seconds of internet fame. We can't change the world. We can't bring free water and jobs and power and food to old town. We sure as fuck can't stop a war. We can't even rescue the three people who happened to survive the ongoing train wreck of the other forty-five.

We have no proof. We have no allies. We're conspiracy theorists at best.

And yet. If we're wrong, we have nothing to lose.

But if we're right?

Jessa shakes out of it first.

"All right. Now that that's all cleared up. Here's the actual problem. Why is this going to work this time? It never worked before. We got our asses handed to us. We never made it up the boards."

"We've also never had—" I pop my lenses back in and wait the three-count for them to interface, then nearly choke when I see what they're showing me—"two hundred and fifty-six thousand subscribers before."

Jessa stares at me, stunned. I can see her mouth begin to shape the words *two hundred and fifty-six thousand* and then give up, like saying it out loud would make it disappear.

"So," I say, "let's take a look at what they gave us."

part three
hearts & minds

NINE HUNDRED FIFTY-THREE. NINE HUNDRED FIFTY-FOUR. Nine hundred fifty-five.

I slide the hoverbike up the long drive through those grassy lawns to Stellaxis HQ like a boat powering upriver. A gunner in a Greenleaf exosuit rushes us from near the fountain. Jessa takes him down with a clean ninety-yard headshot through the faceplate from the moving bike. Nine hundred fifty-six.

"Oh my god, you guys," she shouts, "I am *loving* this new blaster."

Exosuit gunner guy seems to have radioed his buddies before charging the bike, or else we've tripped some kind of alarm just by setting voxelated foot on the property. Out comes a swarm of breakaway nanodrones from the building, taking point for a full squad of these exosuit gunner dudes who pour out of the front door like pissed-off wasps whose nest got bopped by a stick.

Lucky for us, we've been able to acquire some upgrades.

I flip up the bike's reflector field and check its stats: 89.4 percent remaining. That starts to drop as enemy fire pings off it, but some of it ricochets back and lands lucky hits on the exosuits. A couple of health bars diminish marginally.

One hand on the bike controls, I pull up a string of resonance grenades from inventory. Two weeks ago, before posting that video, I'd hoard these things like treasure. They only drop from high-level mobs or sell for thousands of credits a pop on the market. Now I pull the pins on half a dozen and chuck them at oncoming enemy clusters. A few bodies drop and are trampled. Even from inside their exosuits we can hear the snapping of their bones, though that's probably more from the resonance charges than the stampede. Those suits are no joke.

My kill counter whirs up as the resonance killing field winds down. Nine hundred eighty-eight.

Some blaster fire is clearing our shields, but it doesn't bother us overmuch today. We're kitted out to the eyeballs in Think-Fluid smart armor, which spikes and smooths around us like living oil, absorbing fire with ease. It's what Stellaxis's elite soldiers use, the ones who get brought in more and more to do what the operatives would be doing if they weren't mostly busy being dead, and as armor goes, I have to say it gets the job done. We're driving through a rain of blaster fire and sustaining barely enough damage for our health bars to visibly register. Part of that is the reflector shields doing their thing, but still.

The glint in a high window comes at the same time as Jessa's shout behind me. "Snipers!" she yells, and switches out the blaster pistol for a rifle of her own. As it appears from her inventory she's already swinging it around to twelve o'clock and resting the barrel on my shoulder to take aim.

Her first shot shatters a neighboring window. Her second tags the sniper but doesn't finish it off, just drops that distant health bar by a hair shy of half. She doesn't get a chance for a third.

The sniper's round hits its palm-size target dead on. The bike's field projector shorts out, and the shielding system fizzles down to nothing, ripping us wide open as the exosuits converge. The proprietary nanofiber shields stand no chance against plasma cannon fire. The bike shudders beneath us, hard, crapping a breadcrumb trail of shielding scales the whole way up the road.

Not that we're particularly difficult to find on our own. A solid dozen exosuits have their arm cannons locked onto our position, and the commotion is drawing players from across the lawns. One blue fireball wings the edge of our armored skirting, upsetting the dregs of the hover calibrations royally. Another slams into my shoulder, biting a chunk out of my health bar. A third passes between Jessa's head and mine, crackling gently. It melts the side of my helmet back to its constituent particles and whites out Jessa's whole visual field. I know this not just because of her thumbnail feed display in the corner of mine, but also from the collective groan of our momentarily light-blinded audience.

The fourth fireball slags the road to hell just feet in front of us, giving me a split second to choose between dumping the bike in this mess of blue-fire lava or cutting our losses and facing down this exosuit army on foot.

I try to yank the bike sideways, but all that gets us is caught on an upthrust slab of road junk and flipped into the air. More shots pepper the bike's undercarriage. When this thing lands, it's going to be in pieces.

"Over my dead body am I losing this bike," Jessa yells.

I know what that means. I lift my hands off the now-useless controls and lace them behind my head, another layer of smart armor that might just keep my skull from smashing when I hit the ground.

Not a second too soon. Jessa flashes the bike back to inventory with a couple millimeters of blinking red remaining on its bar, and we land tumbling, ass over teakettle, singeing our knees and boots and elbows on what's left of the road. The smart armor soaks up as much slack as it can, which it turns out is enough. We come up shooting. Some nonplayer mobs, some player characters out of their depth. Nine hundred ninety-four, nine hundred ninety-five, nine hundred ninety-six.

Funny how we've been high enough *level* for this place the whole time. Endless grinding will get you there easy. It's not a matter of skill. It's a matter of ass-in-chair clock-punching. What we'd been missing was the *stuff*. All the high-level equipment and heals and general inventory we were too poor to buy, too fragile to loot off high-level mobs or top-tier players.

Now, two weeks or so after I posted that video, we're optimized. Our armor is top-of-the-line. Our blasters and plasma guns, top-of-the-line. Our bike has been modded into oblivion. And all it took to get us off the ground was that initial wave of sponsorship. A few nice pieces of armor, a couple of gun upgrades, enough credits to buy some decent heals for once, and from there the work carried us. We quit our other jobs and put in the time here instead. We make enough credits to buy the in-game items we need, and sometimes audience sponsors will drop stuff in our inventories just so they can watch us use it and then comment on the feed: *Hey, that was me.* I'm not going to lie: after the fruitless, mind-numbing grind the process has been in years past, this new way is . . . refreshing.

Not to mention how we can make our thousand a whole lot faster as a team than I ever did as my little side project, on my own time, alone.

Today's one thousandth kill is a drone that Jessa hauls out of the sky on the end of a magnetic harpoon. It smashes to the ground and fades into a tidy heap of tradeskill items, the little twenty-four-hour countdown ticker starts up in the upper right-hand corner of my view, and just like that, we're on the boards.

Again.

These days this part is surprisingly easy. Getting on the boards is easy. Climbing most way up the boards, almost as easy. Hitting that top spot is harder, but we've done it a couple of times. Briefly. Okay, really briefly. Basically, one time Jessa got hold of 05 for about two minutes, and the three of us had this epic throwdown against a pair of six-player teams out by the Monument, and another time I lost the top spot while I was still on the NPC selection screen for the nanosecond it would have taken me to pick 22.

So that part hasn't been great. And we've definitely lost some of that initial batch of subscribers. But we've kept plenty too, and more trickle in day by day. Jessa says the contrast in our personalities is entertainment enough. I'm not that optimistic. I figure it's more that it amuses them to see us fail. And that we throw ourselves into unwinnable fights, taking on unkillable enemies, calling out famous players by name on a pretty much daily basis, doing top-speed balls-to-the-wall hoverbike chase-downs of whoever's got that number one spot. Keeping on *doing that crazy shit*, as Jessa would say.

Staying visible.

Here comes the tricky part.

"Just—gotta get—to the—building," Jessa grits out for the audience's benefit as she backs her way across the molten road, using downed exosuits as stepping stones. "Real—party starts—in there."

By *real party* she means *monumental clusterfuck.* We came here because the company HQ interior has just been flagged as a PvP zone. These last precisely one hour and draw pretty much everyone. You want to pick yourself a fight you probably can't win and go down in a blaze of—*glory* is much too strong a word for what we're about to experience, *schadenfreude-providing amusement* is probably closer. Anyway, this is the kind of thing you go after.

"Heads up," someone says from the audience. "Just heard there's a full team camping the lobby, taking people out as they zone in."

"Perfect," I mutter. "Thanks for the warning."

We smash in reloads, perform a half-assed armor recharge, and slap some heal patches on.

Jessa adds an extra patch to my shot-up shoulder. "You want to stand and bang with these people, or . . . ?"

"I actually want to live a little longer than if I'd just climbed up this thing and jumped," I reply, nodding up at the vanishing point of the spire. "I say we make a mess and run like hell."

I pull out another string of resonance grenades and raise my eyebrows at Jessa. She nods and calls up a projection field.

We zone into the building just as a blue fireball from a re-spawned exosuit clips the upper corner of the doorway, shower-ing us with droplets of flash-melted black glass.

Straight into the shit as expected. Someone's taking potshots at my head even before I've fully faded into the building. They hit Jessa's projection field like snowballs against superheated metal, and I start slinging grenades.

Thanks to my little adventure with 06 and 22, I know the layout of this lobby well enough. I space out my throws accord-ingly and make sure to include one toward the wide desk that somebody is almost definitely hiding behind, waiting to am-bush players going for the elevators.

We don't wait to loot, or exchange fire, or see if our points spike. We reallocate smart armor to thicken over head and neck and center mass, and we tear ass for the elevators while the field spits and crackles around us like hot oil on a pan and our points accrue as the grenades go to work. If the leaderboard is a giant ladder, we're up maybe the bottom few rungs. But we're also not dead, so we're doing better than usual.

There's more to the ground floor than the lobby, of course, but we're not looking to camp out here. That's boring. According to the touchscreen panel in this elevator, there are seventy-six floors above us and four sublevels below. Plenty of room to explore.

Jessa reaches to press her thumb on the *76*, but I'm faster, and I take us in the opposite direction, down one floor to sub-level A.

Call it nostalgia, I guess, or unfinished business, or obnoxiously unbridled fascination. Believe me, I wish I was over it. All of it. And yet here we are, our elevator descending toward the virtual approximation of the floor where 06 sat with those people in Medical while 22 pestered the serving bots into reheating my stir-fry and hinted dark things at me cryptically. I wonder what it looks like in-game. Probably nothing like it does in real life. The lobby is close enough to the reality—it's in the documentary, people expect it to look a certain way—but I'm guessing the rest of the floors tend more toward generic corporate in design.

Meanwhile, Jessa furrows her brow at me so hard she's liable to hurt herself.

"High-level players go *up*," she says. "There's going to be one hell of a fight on the roof, and forty-one minutes left before this zone reverts. What are you doing?"

What I'm doing is . . . I don't know. At least not intellectually. Which is the part I hate. I can't rationalize why I hit that button, and my inability to make logical sense of my own motivations makes my brain itch.

"I thought—" I say, and then realize I have no idea how to finish that sentence accurately. I reach up and hit the top-floor button instead.

We ascend in silence, double-checking our armor and inventory. Or I do. Jessa is busy presenting.

"Gonna be a fun one, guys. I have a good feeling about this. Oh shit! Nyx! We gotta do rock-paper-scissors. Guys, in case you missed when I explained this before, the game tracks individual kills as well as team kills, in case a team breaks up or whatever after bringing a SecOps dude on board, just to be sure that the person who earned said dude gets the keepsies. So instead of being assholes and fighting it out, Nyx and I decided the fairest way to choose, in the event that our next kill puts one of us in first place on the boards, you know, we do rock-paper-scissors, and whoever loses stands down on that last kill so the winner can grab it."

"The probability of which happening is, like, *vanishingly* small," I add.

"It's good to be prepared," Jessa says. "Best of three."

So we rock-paper-scissors the whole way up to 76. The tie breaks to my paper just as the elevator stops. "Maybe today we stream *Nycorix and 22: Drinking Buddies*," Jessa says, drilling an elbow into my smart armor. "I'd watch that."

Thus ensues some supportive commentary from part of the audience—drowned out by wildly predictable commentary from the rest of it. Jessa starts scolding them. "Gonna need you to keep that shit clean, guys. Nyx isn't into it. Our house, our rules."

I don't hear what witty rejoinder they come up with because I've already muted their stereotypical asses. I stroll out of the elevator blasting.

The top floor of company HQ is exactly the mess we expect. Pretty much everyone I see is level-capped, but most are in full six-person squads. It's explosions and shoot-outs and corpse looting and general mayhem as far as the eye can see. Jessa dials her field projector to *electromagnetic pulse*, and we storm in, disabling power armor and wide-beam wrist cannons and auto-targeting systems in a traveling ten-foot radius.

Behind it, we lay down as much fire as my two blasters and Jessa's two plasma guns can muster. We wipe out one team, then another, and are making a decentish dent on a third when someone overhand pitches a nullity charge over the top edge of our field. It lands at our feet, and instantly our EMP shield wisps away like smoke.

"*Fuck*," Jessa breathes, and slams her back up against mine as we fire in four directions, a gun in each fist, spinning a slow circle as we try to work our way toward the stairs to the roof.

Some kills, some points. Not enough. More teams are coming up from the bank of elevators, and while of course they're not all targeting us, enough of them are that this situation is swiftly deteriorating.

We have to get to the roof. That's where the main fight is, but also the game counts it as an outdoor area, which means we have a way out with the SecOps NPC we hope to leave with: a portal evac/suborbital drop combo that Jessa bought on the market this morning for the occasion.

First we have to dig ourselves out of this. Our smart armor is steadily snowing off of us in oil-slick-colored nanoparticulate, faster than we can reallocate effectively. I try to recharge mine, but it's too slow, and I'm eating concentrated fire from all directions.

I switch my blasters to auto and strafe the full one-eighty, left to right. It buys a couple seconds. I stow one blaster to free up the hand. I jab myself, then Jessa, with heal syringes, then open my inventory to pull out more resonance grenades.

No dice. All that's left in there is a few heals, some ammo, and something I was saving for the fight on the roof, but we're not going to get there if we don't live through this first, so.

I pull the tab out of the hallucinogen grenade and chuck it into the crowd. "Mask up," I tell Jessa, and we both make swiping motions in front of our faces, chin to eyes, nudging some of the smart armor material into its new assigned position.

Not a second too soon. The hallucinogen grenade bounces off somebody's helmet, drops to the floor, and vanishes in the crowd, invisibly vomiting its bioweapon load.

Out of the corner of my eye I see someone notice it, dive for it—presumably to throw it back in my direction or out the window—and get trampled underfoot. The airborne hallucinogen is laced with propellant nanoparticles and engineered to soak into mucus membranes like water into a sponge. The real-life one is, anyway, so the in-game one, lacking these things in the virtual, makes do with a real-time approximation. It's not long before they're all freighted to the eyeballs with Stellaxis Innovations' finest distillation of bewildered-to-shit murderousness and slaughtering each other where they stand.

Nifty bit of programming, really, a BestLife hallucinogen grenade. Picture this. Your character is minding its own business, racking up points, looting a corpse, whatever. Suddenly you can't do a goddamn thing with it. You can't walk. You can't get things out of inventory. You can't loot your corpse. Your character's been hijacked, and it's going to stay that way until the effect wears off. For the duration it's going to do one thing and one thing only, and that's killing, or trying to kill, anything in your visual field. Enemy, teammate, best friend, grenade doesn't care. Your best shot is logging off and coming back in when the zone you left is likely to be empty, because the game remembers the grenade effect was still in play, and you're going to do your time sooner or later.

Here on the seventy-sixth floor, player characters are dropping like flies. Up and down the hall they fall in piles, enemy and teammate alike. Chaos spreads down the halls and out of sight around corners. The nano-propelled hallucinogen reaches into the unloading elevators and grabs another batch of guys by the lungs, then travels down in the elevator airspace to whatever floor they're headed to next.

We inch our way along the corridors, mincing over corpses, staying out of sight, meeting token resistance from the few players who had the good sense to mask up when they saw what was going down. We reach the rooftop stairwell and yank open the door.

At first I assume the gas will dissipate in the open air, but this is an old-school bioweapon, one they've discontinued from the game because it was too overpowered. It only exists anymore on the market, and rarely.

The replacement version goes inert after sixty seconds. The one I've deployed runs for five full minutes before it dies.

The hallucinogen gas ascends before us. We follow it up and step out onto the roof into a massacre. There must be five hundred people up here, all busily obliterating one another as the gas takes hold. We stand in the doorway and watch as the little red hostile-player blips on our minimaps wink out in a rolling wave, like town lights at power curfew. We throw up our shields and shoot the stragglers fast, before they figure out we're not infected. Then we get to looting, one eye on the door in case somebody else makes it up here alive. Just grabbing stuff at random, no time to pick and choose in the seconds before these corpses despawn.

Our points go up and up—and then keep going up, even after everyone on the roof is dead and warped back to their respective save points.

"The elevators," Jessa whispers. "The gas is traveling in the elevators. Holy crap, you guys, this stuff is *cleaning this place up.*"

Our points keep climbing. We hit the top hundred on the leaderboard. Then the top fifty. Then the top ten. While we stand here staring at the numbers. It's thoroughly ridiculous. How the hell many people were in this building?

When we're in fourth place (Jessa) and third place (me), the door to the roof slams open. Out comes a five-person team in full riot gear, of all things, with filter masks under their visors. The one taking point out the door has a rocket launcher, and she's aiming it between my eyes.

"Fucking get *down*," I shout, and drag Jessa with me by a handful of smart armor, which helpfully generates enough slack for me to get hold.

We drop, throwing up a shield and firing through it, and the rocket sails over us and plows into some kind of transmitter thing near one edge of the roof. I'm already skimming my inventory to see if anything we've looted off these guys might save us now, grabbing and hurling any kind of grenade I can find.

Beside me, Jessa is doing the same. We throw particle grenades and stun grenades and plasma grenades, double-fisting them out of inventory and hurling them at the doorway like a couple of panicky noobs, and this brilliant tactical maneuver by some miracle concludes with the other team shouting and scrambling and firing over their shoulders at us as they retreat down the stairs, where of course our grenades follow. There's some audible bouncing and rolling, and then quite a series of explosions, and then four colors of smoke and two colors of fire erupt from the open doorway, along with a sound like air leaking out of a tire and another sound like popcorn popping.

CONGRATULATIONS, the game says when the dust has settled, throwing up the NPC selection screen and raining virtual confetti around us both. *YOU'RE #1! SELECT AN ALLY.*

Except it's not showing it to me. I'm seeing it in my thumbnail of Jessa's feed. I guess her grenades racked up enough damage to scoot her past me on the board.

Jessa stares at that for a second. They're muted now, but I know from past experience that the audience is shouting suggestions at her. My guess is she'll take 05 again like she did a couple weeks ago, as some kind of remembrance. It's 05 who got us into this, who got B disappeared. Jessa has also taken to wearing her old 05 t-shirt a lot more than she used to. I guess if I were to put a name to what she's doing, I'd call it an act of resistance.

But she doesn't. She picks 22.

She picks 22, and then she stops the stream, reaches into her inventory for the escape route stuff—the portal evac and sub-

orbital drop summons—and pushes them into my hands just as he pops into existence between us and executes the world's crispest salute in Jessa's direction. "Awaiting orders."

"Go with her," Jessa instructs him. Then she gives me a little shove, but she's smiling when she does it. "Fuck off out of here. Go get your weird-ass fangirl friendcrush closure or whatever. I'll hold this place while the evac spins up. 22, eyes on that door until she's ready."

"Acknowledged," 22 says, drawing his sword.

Deploying the portal evac is easy. It's just a matter of waiting the twenty seconds it takes to ready itself. It's the game's way of making it slightly less overpowered an item than it is already. While its progress bar ticks down to zero, I clear both blasters and help guard the door. There's something racketing around down there, on the lower levels, working its way up toward the roof. A whole lot of something.

"You don't have to do this," I tell Jessa.

"Oh, and here I was thinking I did," she replies dryly. "If you waste that portal, I'm going to kick your ass, so get moving. Oh—almost forgot." She rummages in her inventory and comes out with a bottle. She flip-tosses it, catches it, holds it out with a wink. "Drinking buddies, right? Hey. Pour one out for me." The noise below gets louder. "All right, enough of that. Get gone."

The portal is ready, a slowly spinning silver ring filmed with a slight sheen, a bubble not yet blown from its wand. "That's your cue, soldier," Jessa tells 22, and he sheathes his sword and returns to my side.

About to step through the portal, I yell over a shoulder, "What're you going to do?"

"Keep my lead as long as I can hold it, obviously, and cross my fingers I make good use of it." Then she turns her side of the stream back on. "Check this out, you guys, I have *always* wanted to try this."

Next thing I know she's inside a fucking Callisto Deadshot, the three-part summon for which she must have looted off these corpses, then assembled in inventory. The Deadshot's gun-arms activate with a *chunk-chunk* noise I mostly feel in the pit of my stomach and start whirring up. She whacks her heels together to activate the thrusters and white fire ignites out of the soles of the mech's feet, levitating her half a foot off the roof. She belts out some kind of movie supervillain laugh and launches herself down the stairwell.

Leaving me on the roof with 22.

I look at the doorway. Then I look at him.

"I have been tasked to stay with you," he says.

"Yeah." Even on-duty 22, the real one, was more human than this. "All right. Come on."

The portal vanishes behind us as we step through.

We emerge in a blank gray hallway, decorated only with glowing spots on the floor at regular intervals. The spot I select expands when it realizes it has two pairs of boots in it, and I punch in the coordinates, and the floor drops out from under us.

We land at the exact coords I've selected, which is nowhere in particular. I didn't exactly have time to plan this out, but I'd be lying if I said I haven't put at least a little subconscious consideration into it *generally*. The suborbital drop sets us down just on the edge of the game map, some little stretch of forest full of absolutely nobody and nothing but silence and trees.

22 starts scanning the middle distance, alert for trouble.

"Stand down," I tell him. "Um, at ease. There's nothing here."

In-game 22's idea of *at ease* is maybe different on a microscopic level from whatever he was doing a second ago, but I can't detect any change at all. *You brought me noodles*, I think at him. *You joked about being vaporized. You invented a war crime to cover for me. You'd hate this. All of it. Everything they've done to you that you don't even know about. That we do. That I am doing now.* "What is the objective?" he asks. "In this place. Were the coordinates erroneous? I can call in transport."

"No, that won't be . . ." I open Jessa's bottle and sit down on a rock. "Sit with me. I mean, if you want to." The label says it's rum, but this is a virtual reality. It's weighted like liquid, it sloshes around. It'll debuff my acuity and dexterity and raise my constitution, briefly, before dropping it to lower than before. Nevertheless it's easy to see that *Nycorix and 22: Drinking Buddies* is going to be a far sad cry from whatever ends up happening here.

I pass the bottle up to 22, who still hasn't sat down. When he just stares at it, I wave it around a little, lamely. "Here."

22 takes the bottle without expression, raises it to his mouth, puts his head back, swallows. Then he hands it to me.

Erroneous, I think. This is what I spent years chasing the boards to get at? This 22 is some kind of other thing, some uncanny-valley bodysnatcher bad translation of the person I followed through a war zone to the basement of Stellaxis HQ. It hurts to look at him. He's like a taxidermy replica of himself. Like a pirated copy. I think of where I am, what this would have meant to me even a few weeks ago, and it just makes me sad.

I should be continuing the conversation from the elevator. Getting those answers. Doing something, anything, to prove to him I'm on his side. But this isn't 22, and this 22 wasn't there. It'd be like shouting down a well, mistaking echo for reply. *Message in a bottle*, I think.

I toss back a gulp of my own, then pour one out for Jessa on the mossy ground. 22 observes this in quizzical silence. "My friend," I explain. "On the roof. She sent us here."

"To what purpose, I wonder."

I shrug. "Whatever purpose we want."

This seems to strike him as inadequate. He *hmm*s a little.

They got that part right, at least, as well as the exactitude and economy of his movements as he parks himself on the rock beside me.

He's close. So close. There's a faint chemical smell to him, like he's dragged it the whole way out here to this half-assed scrap of forest from the antiseptic white halls of whatever sub-basement of the Stellaxis building they stash him in.

An idea strikes me.

I pour out another. It splashes to the moss between our boots. "For Elena," I say clearly.

As shots fired go, this one smashes into 22's glacial demeanor like a bird into a window. There's a long few seconds of silence. You can almost see the virtual gears turning in his virtual head: *make conversation, do as ordered, fulfill directive.*

"Is that your friend?" he says at last. "Who sent us here?"

This sets me back. "No, it's—it's 05. Elena?"

Nothing. Just the blank wall of his regard. What has happened between my footage of 08 and this?

Suddenly I feel very, very tired.

"To the dead, then," I say.

He nods a little. This at least he understands. "To the dead."

The bottle shakes a little as I pour. "To 17." Another. "To 38." Another. "To—"

22 vanishes. Doesn't atomize to pixels, doesn't shimmer back out of existence like a mirage. No fanfare, no preamble, no warning from the game when somebody else nabs that top spot and claims him out from under me. Just straight-up disappears, like a projection that's been switched off. Leaving me to stare at the impression in the moss the game has so carefully rendered, indicating where his boots had just been.

sorry, Jessa messages. bit off a little more than i could chew there. it go ok?

fine, I reply because it's easier than honesty. thanks again well come on back—we got loot to divvy

on my way

First, though, I sit there a while longer with my bottle, pouring shots out into 22's boot prints—*to 28, to 33, to 42, to 02, to my parents and Jessa's and Suresh's and Keisha's and Allie's and Tegan and Talya's and everyone's*—until the bottle is empty. Then I smash it on the rock and walk away.

THAT NIGHT, AFTER POWER CURFEW, I HEAD up to the roof alone. These days the weather is turning, winter's slow fade into spring. Still cold, but not abrasively so. Scents are clearer, less muffled. I can smell thawed mud and garbage and rain and the faintest possible perfume, like distant waking trees blossoming.

It's just about warm enough that I'm not taking refuge in the greenhouses. I'm standing at the edge of the roof, leaning against the parapet, staring out toward the distant skyscrapers of the city.

Cycling through my head on infinite loop is in-game 22: *To what purpose, I wonder.*

All I can think is: they got to him. Even though there's no *him* there to get to. 08's response before was some kind of glitch, something overlooked when they fine-tuned the dialogue parameters on the SecOps analogues. Something they weren't supposed to know, or show they knew, the way 06 and 22 referred to each other in front of us civilians by their numbers, not their names. 08 should in no way have responded to *Elena.* They must have ironed out the glitch the way they ironed out the glitch of B digging too deep into their business.

I'm the glitch that's left.

I'm under surveillance, and I don't know it. They've got me on a list. They're watching my every move. They have to be. The remaining untouched eye of the storm of this is me. Me and Jessa. And whoever else gets in the—

The light hits before the sound. Against the dark it's scouring. An air strike? Something out over the city buildings, something that rises in a swift tight parabola, whistling. A ground strike. Surface-to-air.

Then it explodes into scatterings of white light, and my blood runs ice. There's only one thing it can be.

I never chanced upon one live before. Typically I see them in newsfeeds, repeated over and over from different angles with various commentary.

It's a remembrance flare.

I don't know whose idea it was, somewhere in Stellaxis's probably labyrinthine marketing department, to send one of these up whenever an operative dies. It's a weirdly touching tribute, the modern-day equivalent of the last centuries' gun salute and half-mast flag. I stare at it, white-knuckle on the parapet, my breath a blade in my throat.

There were three operatives left alive this morning. 06, 08, and 22.

Now there are two.

I have never grabbed for a newsfeed as fast in my life as I do now. But of course there's no newsfeed to be found. Not until morning, when power curfew lifts.

I don't remember turning from the parapet, or crossing the rooftop gardens, or descending the stairs. I fumble my sensor reading twice before I a) remember it's past power curfew and b) realize someone's left the door ajar. When I burst into the room all I have to show for my haste is a twisted ankle and a panicked tightness in my chest.

"Who was it?" I rasp out as the door clicks shut behind me. The words are like a solid weight I have to squeeze through the constriction in my throat. Even as I stand there like a person who has some reason to expect a response, I know it's hopeless. They don't know any better than I do.

Allie sits up, rubbing sleep from her eyes. Was I up there that long? "Who was what?"

Ryan looks up from the chair, where he's been reading a comic book by headlamp. "Christ, Mal, where's the fire?" But he puts the book down. They're not used to seeing me this worked up. I'm the levelheaded one. The one who doesn't get riled by drama. Joke's on me, I guess. "What's wrong?"

I point at the window. "Flare. Just now."

Allie goes gray. "Oh. Oh no." She flings herself out of her bunk and skids to a halt at the window. Then she seems to realize it's over and done and she missed it. She turns around, still clutching the curtain like it's holding her bodily upright. "When?"

"However long it took me to run down here."

"Shit." Ryan joins Allie at the window. They stare out over the night together like there's ever been a second flare. "You're sure?"

My teeth are chattering. Adrenaline. Jerkily, I nod. "I have to find out whose."

"You and everyone." Allie is climbing back into bed. "Got six hours left before power comes back on. Goes faster if you sleep."

I look around, helpless. Everyone else is either asleep or out somewhere. It's just me and Ryan, and he gives me this *what-can-you-do?* shrug and goes back to reading.

"It'll be all of them eventually," he says, not looking up. "Does it really matter which one it was tonight? It's shitty news regardless. Honestly, I'd rather not even know."

It's like he's speaking a language I don't understand. I turn and push back out of the room and run straight into Suresh, standing in the hall in the classic power-curfew stance: fist raised to knock on a door his lenses won't open. "Flare just now," he says. "You heard?"

"I fucking *saw*," I hiss at him. "Who was it?"

He shakes his head. "That's what I came up here to find out. Nobody downstairs knows."

Of course they don't. We're all in the same awful dark until curfew lifts. But sometimes people have their ways. When 02's flare went up a couple of years ago, somebody rode through old town on a hoverbike yelling at the top of his lungs, presumably having come the whole way from someplace on a different curfew cycle. Sometimes flares go up after they've announced the loss of an operative, because they always wait until dark to set them off. Usually, though, we get to settle in and wait.

I wish Jessa were here, but she's off babysitting for a friend a few streets over. I need someone to help me hold this in my mind, this thing that's spinning its wheels so furiously, gaining no traction.

Three operatives left this morning. Now two. Every flare I've ever seen, I've wished the same wish on it, like it was some kind of birthday candle and anyone was listening.

One in three odds that was 06's flare. Or 22's. Did I do this? Would they vanish an operative the way they did B? They'd lose the war for sure if they started eating their own.

Wouldn't they?

I shoulder past Suresh and out into the hall. People line both sides of the space, on foot and in sleeping bags and sitting against the wall, doing whatever evening things by the light of solar lamps. I hear plenty of chatter about the flare, but no number attached to it.

I double back for my headlamp and go downstairs. Same deal as in the hall: people talking, no answers. Just your regular battery of rumors, which I make myself ignore. Something about

22 being assassinated by Greenleaf Industries drone fléchettes. Something about 06 throwing herself on a grenade to save some civilians. Something about 08 taking a hallucinogen blast to the face and jumping off the roof of the Stellaxis building. Something about none of them actually being dead and it all being a marketing hoax to sell funeral memorabilia. I tell myself it's all bullshit and power walk across the lobby toward Comforts of Home. Being a company store, it runs on its own generator, even when the whole rest of the hotel has gone dark.

I go straight to the back, where the coffee machines are, and the touchscreen to project the TV on the wall while you wait for your coffee to dispense. A crowd has gathered around it, but there's nothing on the news any of us didn't know already. Just the remembrance flare playing over and over in slow motion and regular speed and from five different angles, but nothing about whose it *was*.

Typical. They did this last time, when 21 died, and the time before that with 11. I don't know why they don't just get it over with. It's like they enjoy leaving us wondering. People more entrepreneurial than myself will be using this window of time to buy up as much SecOps stuff as they can get their hands on, knowing an operative's merch will skyrocket in collector value posthumously, and Stellaxis gets to sell three times as much crap this way. I don't know. Some back channel of my brain is babbling nonsense like this. It's like it's trying to distract me from thinking too hard about how I will never have a chance to use the information 22 gave me to help him. How I left him there to die while I dicked around in-game for half a month because I didn't have a solid plan of action. How the in-game version of him, that sad, flat, hollow approximation, may well be all that's left of him forever.

I wheel back around and take inventory of my options. I'm about to go outside and start shaking people down in the street, as if they're likely to know something the news isn't saying, when I'm struck by a truly terrible idea.

The water distribution people are long gone for the night, but the standard armed guard is stationed by the supply closet where the barrels and the tap on the ration main are locked away. I march straight up to him, semiautomatic rifle and all. From the look on his face, this does not happen often. I am in no mood to care. This is a Stellaxis employee. He might have answers the rest of us aren't authorized to deserve.

"Excuse me," I say in my nicest no-trouble customer-citizen voice. "The flare a few minutes ago. I was hoping you could tell me who they sent that up for."

The guard looks me up and down before settling his gaze on mine expectantly.

"I don't have much money," I tell him.

"Then I don't have much info."

"Okay. Okay." I go to check my account, then remember that's shut off for the night too. "I'll give you what I can. You just have to come with me to the company store so I can access—"

"We're done here," he says. One finger reaches down lazily, switches off the safety on the gun. "Get lost."

"You don't understand," I hear myself say. I need to stop talking. Right now. But I can't. "I need—"

"You *need*," the guard says, sharper now, "to get the fuck out of my sight before I report you for attempting to bribe a security officer."

I don't even know what's gotten hold of me. Something stupid and desperate. Something that shut down my higher functions the second I saw that white light scattering.

I take a step forward. Something grabs me from behind and spins me around.

"Oh hey, *there* you are," says the something. Jessa. She's dialed the loud-and-bright up to eleven. People glance over. This is probably the point. She starts marching me toward the door to the street, still hollering. "Been looking *allll* over!"

She gets me outside and backs me straight into the wall. "The fuck? Are you actually *trying* to die."

I shake her off, miserable. "There was a flare—"

Jessa flinches like I've slapped her. "When?"

"I don't know. Ten minutes ago?"

She runs her hands over her face. "Fuck."

"Guessing you don't know whose it was either."

"Obviously. I didn't even know it happened. I must've just missed it before I left for home." She looks up at the sky, like she can will the sun to rise faster. "Fucking curfew."

Then she catches sight of me, staring off into the distance and blinking hard, willing my face to stop crumpling ominously. I don't want to fucking cry. I want to go and smash things. My biology is betraying me.

Jessa swoops on me, all concern. "Hey—"

"Allie said to sleep," I manage. "How the fuck am I supposed to—"

"Easy," Jessa says. "You're not. You're coming with me."

"I don't want to go anywhere."

"Nobody asked you, you giant baby. This is me as your roommate and your teammate and your business partner making an executive decision. The same teammate who tanked a whole building full of assholes so you could have a picnic in the woods with *my booze*. I think you'll find you owe me."

"Virtual booze," I mutter, because it's either banter back or lose my shit entirely, and once I uncork the panic in my head, it's not getting put back in.

"Fine," Jessa says, like she's acquiescing to something I never asked for. "Then let's go find some that'll get you good and drunk for real."

I don't have much counterargument. So Jessa drags me the long way around back to Comforts of Home, out of view of the guard, and she buys us a bottle of dirt-cheap vodka and we work our way through the crowd, which has only gotten larger. They're seated all around the screen with their drinks and snacks, and the AI says nothing, because the longer they hang around, the more chips and beer and shit they'll buy. Jessa sits me down on the floor and sits herself across from me, and we pass the bottle back and forth for what feels like a million years. It's like some weird mirror-world inverse of my few minutes in the virtual woods, pouring shots out for the dead. Except now we're pouring shots into ourselves, keeping vigil for the not-yet dead, like we're holding up our end of a bargain nobody else agreed to.

My sodden brain informs me if I don't leave this spot, if I don't let my guard down, it can't have been 22 they set that flare for. If I get up, if I fall asleep, if I pass out, all bets are off. So we sit, and we drink, and we wait. Around us the crowd dilates, contracts. People give up, go to sleep. A few stick around. Nobody talks to anybody else. The newsfeed cycles through stories about some pop star's outfit, spiking costs of suntouch paint and solar batteries, a hot new game module on BestLife, yesterday's death toll from an ongoing protest on the Greenleaf Industries side of the city, drone recovery efforts of the wreck of some free-trade gunship being delayed by Superstorm Emmeline, and so on.

No security guards show up to kick us out. The AI, having flagged us as paying customers, leaves us alone. So we keep holding up our end of this batshit unspoken agreement with the universe until at one point Jessa stretches out one leg and jabs me in the hip with her toe. "Look."

I look. The newsfeed has cut back to the remembrance flare story, but this time the report has changed. Now, overlaid on the footage of the flare, there's a picture of 08 looking dutiful and dignified, gazing out of the screen with his eyes on some unseen horizon. From down here it looks like he's making wistful eyes at the soda machine.

Killed in action, the newsfeed says. Some engagement out by the Monument. Details emerging.

I gape at the screen, too drunk or stunned or both to process this at first. I'm startled out of this glue-brained stupor by a sound, a loud harsh exhalation that I then realize came from me.

"That—" I say at the same time Jessa says, "It was 08."

I don't hear much past that. The blood is too loud in my ears. For a second I think I might faint. I feel like I've dodged a bullet. A barrage of bullets. It's not too late to help them, 22 and 06, and live up to whatever the hell it was they expected of me. I won't see them again, not up close and personal like before, but that's almost okay, because I didn't bring this down on them, they're still alive, 22 is still alive, it wasn't—

Jessa is staring into the bottle. She looks every bit as wretched as I felt up until a second ago. She swishes the last two inches or so in the bottom, then pours a little out on the tile floor of Comforts of Home and pounds the rest. Then she wings the bottle at the recycling bin near the coffee dispenser and misses spectacularly.

"I didn't want it to be any of them," she says softly. "I was hoping maybe they'd say it was a mistake. Somebody fired it by accident. Or maybe, like, to fuck with Greenleaf's intel? Or to sell funeral merch? I don't know. It's stupid." She gets up abruptly and nearly falls back over. She steadies herself against a muffin display. Shoppers glance over from the front of the store. "I'm happy for you, though. Honestly. I am."

We stagger against each other the whole way back up six flights of stairs and into our room. Maybe we brush our teeth? Probably not. Time skips and I'm in my bunk and Jessa's beside me again and the shelf is digging into my back and I can't get her to move because she's already asleep and if I try to push her over, she'll fall.

My mental state just now, for any number of reasons, is not maximally displaying its best self. My mind feels like it needs to puke, and not even because of the vodka. The vodka isn't helping, though. The room is spinning. I close my eyes to make it stop, and instead it speeds up, wobbling on an axis I wasn't aware it had.

The last thought that flits through my head before I pass out isn't even a thought at all, it's a disembodied voice, a memory.

08 is lately indisposed.

Occupational hazard.

A bit under the weather.

Actually, that's not entirely accurate. The *last* thought that flits through my head before I pass out is: *That was two weeks ago, and now 08 is dead.*

WHEN I WAKE up the next morning the entire push-pull of emotions that was having its way with me the whole day and night before—starting with my little misadventure with in-game 22 and ending practically blackout drunk on the company-store floor, grieving for something that I thought I'd lost my chance to save—has distilled itself into a pure clean flame of rage.

I know what I have to do. It's not much, and in all honesty I could've done it before, and it probably won't make any more difference now than it would have made then, but if I sit around and wait for the next flare, I'm—I don't even know what. I don't know what that makes me. Nothing I can live with.

"Morning, sunshine," Jessa says. She's still there in my bunk, doing something on her lenses. "How're you feeling? I feel like somebody stuffed me in a barrel and rolled me off the top of the building." She stretches and winces. "Hangover breakfast? You're buying."

"I'm going to post the video," I say.

"I'm thinking we go get a pile of really greasy— Did you just say post the video? What video? You already posted the video."

"Not that one," I say.

I watch it dawn on her face.

"22 trusted me to do *something* with that information," I whisper. She'd pulled the privacy curtain at some point, but you can't be too careful. Which is hilarious, given how I'm planning to spend my day. "I don't know what, exactly, but I'm pretty sure keeping it secret isn't going to help matters any."

"Hold up. My blood sugar's too low for this. Back it up a little. You're going to, what? Put the whole second half of that video online? The part that's full of all the incriminating information that we deliberately did not sign our names to on the *entire internet* before? I thought we were trying to *not* end up like B?"

"I don't want to. But I also don't want 22 and 06 to end up like 08, and 17 and 11 and 28 and 02 and the rest of them. I don't want to wait for the next flare. I want to *stop it from happening.*"

I watch this strike her, watch her absorb the blow and keep on coming. "And what do you think this is going to accomplish? If they're actually trying to communicate with you against orders, what does that mean for them when it gets back to the company? This Director person 22 mentioned in the video? This is going to fuck all of us. Us and them."

"This is why I said before I'd go it alone. Okay? That's fine. I stand by it. But we've been sitting around for two weeks waiting for a definitive plan to fall in our laps and it hasn't. They've left us alone, but that's only because we're playing along. Not making any noise. Still being loyal customer-citizens who don't suspect anything about the operatives, who just accept the fact of *all that water* at HQ while we're out here paying our dollar an ounce and scrambling to stay out of the company rehydration clinics. Who don't put this shit together: If they're lying about these things, what else? I have to do *something* with this, Jessa. Make some kind of move. While I still can."

"What *move*? We *have no move*."

I ignore the fact she said *we*. That's a fight for later. "I have the video. 22 *says* 08 is unwell. I have that on record. That's during the same time 08 was supposedly off doing some demonstration in wherever it was—"

"Moscow," Jessa supplies.

"Right. Exactly. Which, when I mentioned it to 22, he gave me this look like I have no idea what the fuck I'm blathering about. So wherever 08 was, it sure wasn't there. And now he's killed in action? With no mention in the news of him even *seeing* action since, what? Last fall? It doesn't add up."

I stare at the ceiling a minute. This is coming out all wrong. Supposition, not motivation. I don't know how to make her understand. I don't know how to make her see how it's personal. I could say, *It could have been us they kept and changed.* I could say, *When the last flare goes up, who will they take next?* She knows all that already. I have to dig deeper.

Personal isn't exactly my area of expertise.

But I have to try.

"The next flare is either 06 or 22," I say. "They trusted me, Jessa. *22 trusted me.* Ever since I was a kid, that's, like, all I've ever wanted. I don't even know why. I know it doesn't make sense to you." A little laugh coughs out of me. "If it's any consolation, it doesn't make sense to me, either. It's—"

"It's love, dumbass," Jessa says gently. "I know you don't want to hear that, but that's what it is."

"Definitely not in whatever kind of fucking way you're thinking," I tell her, "but if that's what makes you understand why I have to do this, then sure. Fine. Whatever. Look. I'm not asking you to help me. I started this. I'm the one who has to see it through. I guess what I'm saying is that if something happens to me, I'm sorry."

Jessa blows a long breath out the corner of her mouth. She's exasperated. That's fair. I'd be pissed at me too.

But when she speaks, it reminds me all over again of what I already know: I don't for one second deserve her.

"What if we, like, post it, but with added commentary? Like the director's cut, except maybe we do the talking after the video so they can hear 22 really clearly? Point out that thing you just said, about 08 being sick or whatever. Really underline it. He's *not feeling well* and now he's *dead.* After not being seen in engagements for *weeks.* After being *away* from engagements *specifically*, off doing that demonstration in Moscow. And how is he not feeling well if he's what they say he is? None of what they're saying adds up. And that thing 22 said about how there used to be more operatives in the program?"

"Yeah," I say, half sure I can't be hearing all this correctly. "He did. But I didn't record that part."

"And the thing with B and the coffee shop." Then her face falls a little. "You didn't get any of that in the video either, I don't think. No proof."

"But we do have what 08 said when I asked him about Elena. We can explain why we asked him about her in the first place, and talk about how the coffee shop disappeared right after we took that video. I mean, it's *gone.* That has to mean something. All this together *has to mean something.*"

Unless it doesn't. Unless we put it out there and nothing happens at all. That would certainly be the safest option, anyway. For me, that is. Not so much for 06 and 22.

And the alternative? *Hey. If I suddenly disappear, at least we'll know I was right.*

"Well," Jessa says, echoing my thoughts, "it's staying visible anyway." She sighs, then sits up abruptly, rubs her palms together, cracks her knuckles. Nervous energy. "People better watch this one. A *lot* of people. This thing better go septuple platinum viral or whatever the fuck. I've never really seen the appeal of martyrdom, personally."

"No. No way. I told you, this is my—"

"Oh fuck you. My god, Mal. I told you before. I'm in."

We go quiet for a moment. There will be no remembrance flare for us if they get us. Nothing to mark our passing. Only the assurance that we were on the right path and the hope that someone might pick up where we left off when we are gone. Not only for 22 and 06, but for all of the others, and for the children they take next when these are gone. And for all the rest of us who might have ended up in the Stellaxis labs with numbers tattooed on our forearms instead of being given toothbrushes and blankets and sent to the camps. If we'd made the team.

Either path, either way, same ending. One's faster and more glamorous. One's slower and involves more kidney failure. We're all Stellaxis property.

But property can be stolen. Maybe it can steal itself back.

"I wonder if 22 has any idea how lucky he was, running into you that day," Jessa says at length, softer now. "Someone who'd actually go so far as to do this. I mean. It could have been anyone. Instead he gets you. Looking out for him. Keeping an eye on his six, you know?"

"I'm trying," I say, but my voice isn't working so great right now. It comes out all brittle, whispery, and cracked.

Jessa's nodding anyway. "And for the record," she adds with satisfaction, "that's exactly the way I was thinking."

THE FINAL VIDEO RUNS ALMOST FIVE HOURS.

It's the whole thing, uninterrupted, uncut. From me hunched in the doorway of that building fumbling my lenses in while the citykiller mech bears down, all the way through to the elevator with 22. We go back and forth on this for a while but then decide it looks better if the second half is seamlessly attached to the part everybody's seen. It looks less like a fake, less like I saw the video on the news, took it, and altered it. That's the hope, anyway.

"My name is Mallory," the commentary says before the video starts. We nix a faceless voice-over and just have me speak directly to the viewer. Visibility is our new motto. No matter how much I hate talking into a camera, how much I hate the idea of having my face plastered all over the news. We're way past trivial shit like my comfort level.

"I was born on July 20, 2113. I live in old town, on the sixth floor of the hotel by the movie theater." Then, realizing that the target audience for this video is *everyone, everywhere*, I specify: "Outside New Liberty City. On March 14, 2134, I took the 7:30 bus to the 63rd Street stop near Prosperity Park. I was trying to meet with a woman I only ever knew as B. She used to babysit a little girl named Elena, before Elena's whole family died when their apartment building came down in the war. B had reason to believe that Elena did not die with her family but was taken by Stellaxis Innovations, taken and raised and *changed* into Stellaxis StelTech SecOps operative 05. She hired me to gather intel on the in-game versions of the operatives, and when I did—" cut to the footage of me asking 08 about Elena—"B, and her sister's coffee shop where we'd met, and very probably B's sister as well, disappeared. It's now a Comforts of Home company store, location number 8943, and it appeared there almost literally overnight, despite that location appearing nowhere on the Upcoming Branches page of the Comforts of Home website."

This was Jessa's idea. Cut to a screenshot of that, with my speaking face thumbnailed in the corner. "As you can see, they never listed it there, and it isn't with the existing branches. It didn't even appear in online searches for locations of the store by address until a few days ago." Further timestamped screenshots: before, after.

"That coffee shop was established almost a decade ago. For it to vanish without a trace, directly after I received information that could help make B's case against Stellaxis, with no word about it from the family who owned it? Well. It's interesting to consider."

And so on. I avoid words like *suspicious* and *conspiracy* and *lies*. I simply present the information as I have it. I keep this up throughout the video, pointing out key moments. 22's painfully weird behavior every time he so much as approached the topic of 08, yes, but also the pond. The decorative fountains. The lushly well-cared-for grass. The free drinking water.

It's a lot, all at once. But spreading it out, handing bits of it off for all these potential viewers to help me carry, is a weight I can feel diminishing every second the video ticks on.

Then, once the footage is over, it's back to my full-screen face again.

"I have reason to believe that Stellaxis Innovations did not create a dozen operatives in their labs but rather stole *four* dozen children and attempted to turn them into weapons without their consent. I believe these children were tortured in the sublevels of the Stellaxis building, and some of them were damaged irreparably."

I replay the section of my conversation with 22: *It must have been a lot harder with all twelve of you. Especially when you were so young.*

I replay the close-up of his hand without the glove.

By that point, 22 says, *it was easy.*

I talk about 08 last. 08, who was *lately indisposed, under the weather,* and nowhere Stellaxis said he was. 08, who is now dead. I point out that in the news the same day 22 said *occupational hazard* and not *off at work,* 08 was reported to have been in Moscow, giving a demonstration. How the last time 08 was known to be involved in combat was almost three months ago. How the story behind the remembrance flare was *killed in action.* How none of these pieces even begin to fit together.

"'If I suddenly disappear, at least we'll know I was right,'" I say. "That's what B told me. Right before she *did* disappear. Here, now, I say the same to you. This video is my insurance policy. I stream BestLife every day. My avatar is called Nycorix. If nothing happens to me, I'll show up there every day, alive and well. You can check in on my stream anytime. Come say hi." (That last bit was Jessa's idea.)

"BestLife is my job. I'm not going anywhere. If I stop streaming, if my character suddenly gets deleted, if one day I out of nowhere decide to quit? Then something's happened to me. Something bad. They locked out my implant, or they arrested me, or I'm lying in a ditch somewhere with a bullet in the back of my head. I don't know. Maybe I'm being melodramatic. I hope I am. If I'm wrong about the operatives, I have nothing to hide, and no reason to fear for my safety. Nobody will come to shut me up, and everything will go on exactly as it did before. But if I'm right, then the operatives aren't what we've been told they are. They're not intellectual property. They're not even soldiers who signed up to fight in this war. They were human children. Systematically kidnapped, and tortured, and used until they died. And it's time for Stellaxis Innovations to answer for what they've done."

Having thrown down that gauntlet, I pause for effect. "17 is dead. 28 is dead. 33 is dead. 42 and 38 are dead. 11, 21, 02: all dead. 05, Elena, is dead. And now 08 is dead too. Along with whoever used to be 01. And 03, and 04, and all the numbers in between the ones we see on the news and in the stores and in BestLife every day. Children like the one I used to be, like most of the people here in old town used to be or are today, with bombed-out homes and dead families. Children who died twice over. Children like Elena, who we're too late to save."

The video ends on a shot of 06 and 22 in the mouth of the alley, 06 healing civilians while 22 keeps eyes on the street outside. My face is gone from the screen now entirely, leaving only my voice: "It's not too late to save the last of them."

I'D BE LYING if I said I didn't sit there for the whole rest of the day, watching the view counter climb. Checking the newsfeeds obsessively until the video gets picked up and broadcast. The Stellaxis-owned feeds won't touch it, of course, but the Greenleaf-owned ones snap it up, and a bunch of indie feeds and blogs take it up from there, and people spread it around. Jessa informs me it's popped up on "the three best-known conspiracy sites," whichever those are, but I don't even care, because the view counter climbs through the thousands, the tens of thousands, the hundred thousands, and on into the millions by early afternoon.

It helps that I had the other video, before. It helps that this is about the operatives, pretty much universally adored as heroes and celebrities, even on the Greenleaf side of the city, where there's apparently a thriving black market in SecOps merch. It helps that the whole entire dragon's hoard of water at Stellaxis—and maybe elsewhere in the city, where the *important* people live—makes thirsty people really, really angry. It helps that this war has gone on so long that so many can effortlessly relate to the concept of a collapsed building, a dead family, a missing child.

I wonder how many of the thirty million viewers and counting can remember that big bright empty room full of kids. I should have mentioned that.

I don't budge from my bunk until evening. Some of my roommates—Suresh, Keisha, Tegan, of course Jessa—bring me coffee and snacks and encouragement. I think the others are pissed at me. Talya in particular is going around making comments under her breath about how I'm going to get them all killed and I should have said something, we should have decided together, as a group. Instead of me clawing after another fifteen seconds of internet fame at everyone else's expense.

I don't even know how to respond to that last part, but as for the rest? Maybe she's right. Maybe I should buy a tent and sleep up on the roof so if someone tracks me by my implant and calls in a middle-of-the-night precision strike, I won't take anyone down with me. Maybe I should go into hiding. But where? I don't have anyplace to go.

When I finally gather the nerve to read the comment threads, though, I start to wonder if I was worried about nothing.

I get to learn all about every random person's expert opinion of how ugly and stupid I look in the video, or how annoying my voice sounds, or how much I suck at the game so of course I'm attention-whoring here instead. The word *traitor* makes repeat appearances, and *ingrate*, and *insane*. And if I had an ounce of water for every time I scrolled past *bitch* and *cunt*, I could probably drown them all.

"This was a stupid idea," I tell Jessa. "Nobody's taking it seriously. Or they are but they don't care."

"It's the internet," Keisha says. Of course they're all listening in. I'm the fuckup of the hour. "It's a petri dish for loud obnoxious assholes. It doesn't mean nobody else is paying attention."

"What was even the goal here?" Talya asks. "You thought, what? People were going to march up on the Stellaxis building and demand 06's and 22's release? They're not prisoners, Mal. They're *weapons*. At worst they're *employees*. Besides, there are entire sites dedicated to the kind of conspiracy theory bullshit you're slinging here. It's called *conspiracy theory bullshit* for a reason."

"Right, because it's better if she just sits on this legitimate exposé of company lies," Keisha tells her. "Yeah, that makes all kinds of sense."

"If it's conspiracy theory bullshit, what are you worried about?" This from Suresh. "Everyone forgets about it in five minutes and life goes on."

"You think that's the part that worries me?" Talya says. "That's cute. What you just described, that's the *best-case scenario*. I'm thinking more about the part where we come back from work one night and the hotel's a pile of rubble because somebody high up in that corporate tower needed to make this go away." She shakes her head, trails off, then reignites. "Or, even better, maybe we're here when it happens. I've already had one home fucking explode around me, and so have you—" pointing to Suresh—"and you—" Keisha—"and both of you." This last is a dismissive gesture in my and Jessa's direction. "I would've thought you'd know better."

"How can you not get that's *why* we're doing it?" Jessa shouts at her. "I know you saw the video. B tried to keep her end of things on the down low, and she has *vanished* off the face of the earth. Spreading that video around is the best way to protect all of us. Anyway, please. You've been an 02 fan as long as I've known you. Where's your loyalty?"

"*Brand* loyalty. That's like telling me that just because I like some artist's music or some designer's lip gloss or some gamer's fucking limited-edition lens case that I should be willing to put my ass on the line for them. Well, I'm not."

"You don't think that," Jessa says, taken aback. "These people weren't given a choice to be what they are. They got buildings dropped on their heads too, you know. Just like me—" Jessa's pointer finger is doing a deliberate echo of Talya's, making the rounds between us—"and Mal—and every one of you."

"Besides," Talya continues, like she hasn't heard a word of this, "02's dead. She's been dead for years. No stupid conspiracy video is gonna change that."

I don't need this shit. Not right now. I get up and put on my coat and backpack and leave. I go and find an empty stairwell, and I sit in it and wait for something to happen.

What that is I don't know. I'm not a leader. I don't have the first faintest fucking idea how to gather people to a cause. I wish life were like a movie, where some antisocial nobody like me could get up in front of a crowd, have a token moment of shyness, and then magically belt out this huge amazing speech about how the revolution starts right the fuck now, before leading my massive crowd all the way to Stellaxis HQ, breaking down every checkpoint and barricade in our way, and parking ourselves on that green green grass and refusing to budge until 06 and 22 are freed and the CEO himself has admitted to the systematic kidnapping and torture of forty-eight children, the murder of forty-six and counting, and any other lies they've been feeding us all this time.

Instead what I get is my one halfway-decent idea being sidetracked into a series of really long comment threads about my looks and my lack of gaming skills and how I should just shut up and be grateful that Stellaxis is fighting to protect our rights to water rations and safe housing and conveniently located company stores. Here and there I'll see something supportive, something along the lines of *Holy shit this is insane. Somebody has to do something* or *This war has gone on forever, enough is enough*, but it gets buried in the background radiation of assholery.

It must be bad, because even Jessa is steering clear of me.

I sit here, alone, for hours. Until my ass goes numb, until my back is in agony, until my bladder threatens to explode. Periodically blinking at *LOAD NEW COMMENTS*, periodically checking newsfeeds, reading those comment sections too for some godforsaken reason. Waiting for someone to get more productively angry than I know how to get. Someone to gather people and storm the building. Someone to break the locks on the water supply room and tell Stellaxis to shove their fabricated ration system straight up their ass. Someone in a position of power to believe me and be galvanized into action. Something, anything, to sprout up out of the trashfire of this.

Time passes. The heating in the stairwells has always been middling at best, but right now it feels like I'm sitting in a refrigerator. At least I have my coat.

I'm sorry, I think at 22, wherever he is. *I'm sorry I couldn't think of a better way.* I hope he and 06 didn't get in too much trouble for what I did. At least I wasn't still recording when he told me there used to be forty-eight kids. That probably wouldn't've gone well for him. Then I almost wish I had been so

I had his testimony to add to my little pile of evidence. For all the good it'd do. These jackasses wouldn't believe that, either. Or wouldn't care, which is worse.

At some point a message comes in from Jessa. hey, gonna hit the water line, you want me to save your place?

Water line. Guess I *have* been here a while.

I want to say no. Fuck the rations. I'm boycotting them. How can they be anything but bullshit, having seen what I've seen? How can I stand up against Stellaxis Innovations if I'm busy drinking from their cupped hand?

But I remember thirst, real thirst, like the time when my account got hacked and I got locked out of the water line for two weeks until it was resolved. If Jessa and the others hadn't shared their rations with me, I'd be paying back the clinic bills for the rest of my natural life.

sure, I message back. yeah. there in a minute

i'll grab your bottle for you

appreciate it

I close the chat. Immediately self-loathing settles on my shoulders, a familiar coat. I open it back up.

never mind. i'm not coming

what

i'll buy water with the stream credits. i'm not taking any company handout. not anymore. i'm taking a fucking stand

There's a pause, so long I assume she's given up on my bullshit. While I'm waiting, I hear something going on downstairs.

I swipe away the feeds, pry myself up out of the corner of the stairwell where I've so ill-advisedly wedged myself, and stagger down the stairs, wincing as the blood returns to my legs.

As soon as I get to the ground floor, something's obviously wrong. At first I think the several hundred people packed into the lobby are freaking out for the same reason Talya was, that Stellaxis has sent in some corporate muscle to do to this place what they did to B's sister's coffee shop. It wouldn't take much down here, everyone crowded together and murmuring ominously about something as they are. A fleet of drones would do it. A few security bots with their wrist guns set to strafe.

But I don't see anything like that. I don't see anything *at all.* Just a crowd where this time of day there's usually an orderly line. Some idiot daydreaming part of me wonders whether they've gathered here to set out on the march to Stellaxis HQ. That part of me pictures us striding across the city, gathering people to us until our crowd has snowballed into something big enough and angry enough to knock the whole place down.

But nobody notices me, and nobody else takes charge. They're agitated about something, though. I see a man pick up a chair like he's going to throw it through the glass front of the hotel, but someone talks him down. It doesn't look like it'll hold for long. A few other people start pushing one another, but their friends break it up before it escalates. Again, this looks like a temporary fix. A bandage on an open vein.

where are you

lobby, I reply. something's going on

where, I'll come to you

by the stairs

Jessa spots me and hurries over. "The fuck is this?"

I shake my head. "No idea."

Some residual paranoia keeps me from drawing attention to myself by asking around. Jessa seems to have caught a bit of the same malady. We hang back and observe.

After a minute I realize how many of them are carrying their bottles and cups, just like the one Jessa's holding. But they're not in line.

All at once I realize what I'm looking at. Or what I'm not looking at. I *should* be looking at the rations cart. Huge plastic drums of water, wheeled around by armed guards. But I'm not.

I double-check the time, which is wildly optimistic. All these people know what time it is. What should be here and isn't.

Then one of the armed guards comes down the hall from the direction of the water-storage room. I don't know if it's the same one from last night, because he's in full carapace with the visor down. Whoever he is, he's got his rifle held at the ready. It flashes through my mind that I don't know whether they use live rounds or riot-dispersal shot or lockout identification tags or what. From the way he's leading with it, like it's a flashlight he's carrying into a dark room, we might be about to find out.

DISPERSE, comes the voice through the helmet, made louder and deeper by the built-in modulators. He flicks the safety off the gun and brings it to bear. *YOU ARE IN VIOLATION OF CUSTOMER-CITIZEN CODE OF CONDUCT REGULATION ELEVEN: UNAUTHORIZED ASSEMBLY. RETURN TO YOUR HOMES.*

"This is our home!" somebody shouts.

VACATE THE PREMISES OR RETURN TO YOUR INDIVIDUAL ASSIGNED QUARTERS UNTIL FURTHER NOTICE. THIS AREA IS OFF LIMITS TO CIVILIAN ACTIVITY.

A few more shouts rise up.

"We're just here for the water!"

"It's water line. We come here every day! Every day at six! Where's the water?"

"My children are thirsty. I'm nursing two babies. We need this water!"

THIS WATER DISTRIBUTION STATION HAS BEEN DISCONTINUED. DISPERSE.

"Discontinued? Did he say discontinued?"

"You can't just turn off our water supply. What are we supposed to drink?"

*WATER CAN BE PURCHASED AT YOUR LOCAL COM-
FORTS OF HOME BRANCH. FRIENDLY NEIGHBORHOOD
24-HOUR SERVICE, SEVEN DAYS A WEEK.*

"Yeah, for eight dollars a bottle!"

"A *tiny* bottle! Water line gives us a quart each for free!"

DISPERSE. THIS IS YOUR FINAL WARNING.

In illustration, the guard lets loose a volley of shots into the ceiling. It's like hitting pause on the room. We all look up at the two dozen holes punched in the plaster. They don't look like lockout identification tags or riot-dispersal shot.

From somewhere beyond the ceiling, the sound of something heavy toppling. A few people, presumably ones with residences on the second floor, bolt for the stairs.

And the room unpauses.

Someone hurls a garbage can through the glass of the double doors. A few other people take advantage of the commotion to dash for the water-storage room, or Comforts of Home, it's hard to tell which. The guard whips around and strafes low, aiming for their legs, but someone else grabs the gun and the shots fly wide, chewing up a wall.

Then all hell breaks loose.

"Come on!" Jessa shouts in my face. People are storming into the street, trying to push their way into other buildings, presumably to get into those water lines instead. We squeeze out through the remains of the hotel door with them.

We didn't even notice from inside, but the street out here is full. Crowds pouring out of buildings up and down the street. The elementary school, the movie theater, the bookstore. Anywhere that's been repurposed as housing. People rush out of them and into the street, waving their bottles and buckets and cups. They're all yelling.

More specifically: they're all yelling about water.

From these same buildings, armed guards follow. One starts firing straight up into the air, but this crowd's momentum is well beyond the stopping power of intimidation tactics. Another is bashing skulls with the butt of his gun. The guard from the hotel tears ass out the door past me and Jessa and does a flying tackle on a woman who was making a beeline for the old toy store. They go down in a tangle of limbs, and then the guard gets up off her and starts kicking. Two other women try to come to her aid, but another guard gets between them and the scene on the ground. There's a crackle of electricity, and both women drop to the pavement, writhing.

"What the *fuck*—" Jessa breathes.

I grab her and fling us both back against a wall as a security bot lands in the middle of the street and starts nanotagging people indiscriminately. I don't know if these tags are the lockout kind or the neurotoxin kind or some other kind I haven't seen, and I don't want to stick around to find out. I don't even know where this fucking thing deployed from. It just dropped out of the sky to land in this action-movie stance, one hand one knee, stood smoothly, and started firing.

We hustle into the little nook between the hotel and the old office building next door and hide behind the mailboxes, staring out at the street. Jackson's back here, and some girl I vaguely recognize from a different floor of the hotel, and about a half dozen people I don't know at all.

"No, seriously," Jessa whisper-shouts. "What the *fuck*?"

I still don't have an answer to that, so she turns to Jackson, who shrugs, wide-eyed.

"Nobody said anything," says one of the others, a guy about our age. "We went down to get water. They said no water." He shows us an empty soda bottle with the label peeled off. It's been reused so many times that his name, permanent-markered onto the side, is faded to illegibility.

"Yeah, they cut off the whole hotel," Jackson tells him. "We were there too."

Soda bottle guy looks confused. He jerks his head sideways toward something up the road. "I'm at the school."

Something's wrong. Something's very wrong. No way can *all* the water lines be out. Not with all that green grass, those fountains, that ornamental pond still in evidence. All the eight-dollar bottled water stacked in their neat six-foot-high pyramids at Comforts of Home. This is something else.

I have to stream this. I have to show people what's happening here.

But I can't. My lenses won't interface. It's like power curfew came early today.

They threw us into blackout deliberately. Just in time for whatever's about to happen here.

In comes a helicopter, whipping in low and fast from the direction of the city proper. This one's got the typical loudspeaker but also simulcasts the same lines on a holoscreen projected above the rotors. Which makes sense, really. The noise on the street is beyond deafening. It's a wall of sound you could practically reach out and touch.

"What's he saying?" Jessa shouts next to my ear.

I shake my head. "There's a holoscreen—" I point up. The projection ring hovers over the rotors like a halo, words slowly marching around its outer edge. Just too far away to make out.

There's a pause while Jessa peers upward, shading her eyes, zooming in on the slowly marching caps-lock. Or tries to. "Are your lenses working?" she yells. "Mine are dead."

"Power curfew's early today," I say, lifting my chin at the helicopter.

Jessa freezes. "They didn't."

"Somebody sure did."

Whatever's going on, there must be two thousand people out

here. It's like some giant hand picked up each one of these buildings and shook all its inhabitants out onto the street. I've never seen anything like it. Even the crowd at the annual Valued Customer Appreciation Day parade is probably smaller than this, and today I don't exactly see any reps dressed up like the company mascot throwing free samples and water coupons to the crowd.

Then the holoscreen drifts close enough to make out if I squint. The words hit the pit of my stomach like rocks.

DISPERSE. DISPERSE. THE STELLAXIS INNOVATIONS WELLSPRING™ WATER DISTRIBUTION PROGRAM HAS BEEN DISCONTINUED IN YOUR LOCALITY. RETURN TO YOUR HOMES IMMEDIATELY. FAILURE TO COMPLY WILL BE ADDRESSED WITH FORCE. THIS IS YOUR FINAL WARNING. DISPERSE.

"Our *locality*?" Jessa's voice cracks with panic. "The hell does that even . . ."

She trails off, taking in the magnitude of the situation. We can't see a whole lot from back here, but what we can see doesn't look good. The security bot is marching slowly up the street, one step and spray, one step and spray. People run past, carrying their water containers, carrying their children, even carrying protest signs, some of them, that they must have gone back into their rooms to draw with markers on whatever they had to hand. Pizza boxes. Paper plates. Old t-shirts.

Riot cops are dropping down out of the helicopter, activating their wrist-mounted shield projectors as their boots hit street. A man tries to dodge past one, but the cop pivots at the last second so the man slams full force into the shield. He's flung back maybe eight feet by the force field, smashing backward through what's left of the glass front of the movie theater.

Somewhere, someone tries to start up a chant, and their voice is joined by a few others before they all stop abruptly for some reason I can't see.

A teenager runs past and hurls her empty red plastic cup at one of the riot cops. It melts on contact with the shield. Another cop tackles her, landing on her hard enough to bounce her head off the street. I don't see her get back up.

"Guys," Jackson is saying. "Guys, come look at this."

He's climbed up the back of the mailboxes and is staring out at something above the buildings. I'm closest, so I scramble up after. It's a measure of the weirdness of this day that I let him reach down and grab my wrist to help me. I get up there and almost fall right back off my perch when I see what he was looking at.

The buildings are pretty low in old town. Nothing like the city proper, where probably ninety percent of the buildings top thirty stories. The hotel and the office buildings, fifteen-twenty stories apiece, are the tallest we have. Most of those are behind or beside us, giving me a clear view over the movie theater, the toy store, and so on.

There's not just one helicopter. There are four. And lots more where those came from, probably, beyond my narrowed field of vision as it is. But the ones I can see are disgorging their security bots and riot cops and drone fleets, not only here in our street, but in the next one, and the next, and the next.

It's not just the hotel that's been cut off. It's not just this street. It's old town. All of it.

And I've got a growing suspicion it's all because of me.

"Come on." Jessa is tugging at my pant leg. "We gotta go. We gotta go right now."

I jump down, and someone else climbs up into the vacated space. "Go where?" I shout. I can barely hear myself. "This place is—" I don't know what it is. It's too one-sided to be a war zone. It's being quashed too effectively to get traction as a riot, or even a protest. It's too tidy to be a bloodbath. "We go out there, we end up like that." I point at the twitching body of a man who looks to have recently gotten up close and personal with the business end of an implant-delinker beam. If somebody doesn't drag him out of the way, he's going to get trampled before he remembers how to use his legs.

But I can't seem to remember how to use mine, either. It's like a lag spike, but I'm not in the game. Just like that man won't respawn when he dies, and I don't have any ten-second cloaks, and I can't go out there sticking heal patches on protesters as the riot cops batter at their heads.

"—go back in," Jessa is saying.

I look at her blearily.

"Snap out of it. Where's the Mal who led all those people to safety when there was a goddamn citykiller mech on her ass?"

I don't know. Whatever that was, it was a one-time power-up, and I don't have another.

Jessa pulls harder. "We gotta get the fuck out of here before one of those riot cops decides to look back here."

"Not happening. I'm not going out there."

"No shit. Listen. We go back *in* and lie low until this blows over. We—"

A fireball erupts at the doorstep of the hotel beside us.

Blue. The fireball is blue.

"Oh *fuck*," I hear myself whisper, at the same time our entire hiding place falls into deep shadow.

We look up and up and up until we're staring into the armor-plated face of what at least in-game is called a shadowstrider mech. I didn't even know Stellaxis had these. Big-ass mechs have never really been their style. They must have copied the Greenleaf design. Which is: smaller than the citykiller, the same approximate height but more slender. It's built for stealth, inasmuch as a mech can be. Certainly it's come here out of apparently nowhere. It may as well have spawned here on the street.

We're all standing here gawping up at it like a bunch of morons when it turns its colossal head with colossal slowness, rightward and downward, and its visored gaze alights on me.

This is not eye contact. Intellectually I know that. The domed roof of the pilot module starts a solid six feet below the faceplate. Still, that giant head stares at me, then turns a few degrees to give the inferno of the hotel sidewalk a pointed look, then back to me.

It's two seconds, maybe three. Then the shadowstrider turns and stalks away eastward up the street. It doesn't deploy any more weaponry. It doesn't engage. The one shot it did take didn't even do any damage. A couple of degrees higher and the plasma-cannon shot would have turned the lobby into a firestorm. But it didn't. The mech just tossed it directly on my doorstep like a paper bag full of dog shit on fire. And made sure I was watching. And only then walked away.

"Did—" Jessa falters, tries again. "Did it just—"

"I, um." Whatever's gotten hold of Jessa's voice has mine, too. I swallow. It doesn't seem to take. "I think it did."

"Subtle." For some godforsaken reason, Jessa's *grinning.* "Got you, you fucker."

I open my mouth to ask her what she means, but that's a stupid question. It's Jessa. I know exactly what it means. I glance down, and she's got that ancient pocket screen cupped in her palm, angled to catch the mech while being at least mostly hidden from view.

"That's a threat," she continues. "That was one million percent a threat." She grabs me by the coat front, eyes shining. It's like her fear of the riot cops has been eclipsed for these few seconds while she beams into my face. "They are *trying to shut you up.* And I have *proof.* Say hi to Mal, everybody! Now go blow this up. They took our water. Now we *burn them down.* They can't—"

Directly behind us something metallic clangs, startling us into an about-face. There's Jackson, standing on top of the mailboxes, both hands on the fire escape ladder. "Not to interrupt whatever the fuck you're doing, but we really, truly have to go. Now." He's not even looking at us. He's looking over our heads at something. Riot cops, security bots, it doesn't matter. Whatever it is, it's coming.

Jessa's already halfway up the ladder. She looks back down at me. "Mal, come *on.*"

"One sec." I glance back out into the street. The unconscious man is gone, hopefully somewhere safe. I don't see a bloody drag trail leading off from where he'd been lying, and that's something, I guess.

I turn to the others hiding here with us. There are four left, a few of them apparently having run off somewhere. They look back at me blankly. Shock, I figure. If they had somewhere to go, they'd be there. If they were trouble, they'd've shoved past me and climbed up into the hotel without waiting on anything as flimsy as my say-so.

I slap the ladder. "Go," I tell them. I don't need to say it twice.

I wait until everyone else is up before I climb.

0 0 1 5

THEY DON'T LOCK OUT MY IMPLANT THE way Jessa expects them to, like they did to B when she went up on her initial terrorism charge. It doesn't surprise me. They came, they sent their message, they left. We watched out the hotel window once we were safely in our room, and the stealth mech leaving seemed to be some kind of signal for the rest to disengage and follow. The helicopters dipped down and retrieved their riot cops and sentry bots and drone armies, like the whole ordeal was being played in reverse. Then they lifted off the street and were gone, pelted by water cups and empty soda bottles that hit the projection shields and fell as melted-plastic rain as the helicopters ascended. All that was left was the damage to our streets and buildings, and a tripling of the guard by our water-storage room. Everyone else's too, presumably.

Later we'll learn that apart from the burns people got from turning their faces up into this shower, there were surprisingly few injuries. Some broken bones, a lot of bruises and lacerations. Three deaths. Being out there, it felt like there'd be more.

"The more of us they kill, the more customers they lose," Keisha points out darkly. It's late, the evening of the incident, and we're still huddled in our room, living off the combined pool of our individual food hoards. Dry cereal, peanut butter, soy jerky, candy bars. No one dares go up to the roof to fetch our vegetable share. We sit on bunks facing each other, on the floor, in the one chair, by the light of our headlamps, for hours. Dissecting the situation.

"If I were them and I was trying to suppress your video, this is exactly what I'd do," Keisha continues. "Turn people against you. Make them think this is all your fault."

"It *is* all her fault," Talya says, eating a candy bar. "I still think we should—"

"We're not kicking anybody out," Tegan tells her. "Like we even own this place. Enough."

"You study them," Jessa says to Keisha. "How do we get out of this? What's our play?"

"Turn yourselves in," Talya says. "Maybe they'll start the water lines back up."

We all go quiet at this. Most of us agreed to share our water, preloading it into the sink reader from our individual accounts as soon as the power comes back on, an even pool and split. Talya, of course, is resisting, and she's convinced Tegan to do the same. Ryan argued with them both at first but got nowhere. Anyway, nobody's preloading anything until the curfew lifts. Which could be in the morning, or it could be never. We're in uncharted territory here.

Between the remaining seven of us, we have about forty-five gallons. It sounds like more than it is.

"Fuck that," Jessa says, leveling a finger at Talya. "This is a standoff. They came in here to bully us."

"Yeah, well, you ever consider it's working?"

"Only if we let it," Keisha says.

"There are three hundred thousand people in old town," Suresh adds, pitching his voice low. Power curfew or no, we've taken out our lenses for this conversation, but all it would take is one of those nanodrones to have stayed behind and gone into hiding, gathering intel on me and mine. "Every building with a water line has a water-storage room. If those mains were shut off, they wouldn't still be behind locked doors and crawling with armed guards."

"There are *six* of those assholes down there now," Allie says. "Jackson took a picture."

"Somehow I doubt they're here for the air-conditioning," Jackson says. "There's still water behind that door. A lot of it."

"I've seen in through the door one time when it was open," Ryan says. "That room is bigger than four of this one. Water barrels stacked to the ceiling the whole way back."

Talya stares, horrified. "Are you out of your *fucking minds*. Is this really what we're doing now? Sitting around discussing water terrorism and eating candy bars?" She rounds on Tegan. "Are you really okay with—"

"You know this is what they want, right?" Tegan says to her. "Keisha's right. They want us to turn against Mallory. Because she called them out on their bullshit. They want us to shut up and say we're sorry and go back to being—"

Talya pulls a face. "We?"

"—good little happy customers who don't make too much noise." Tegan shakes their head, then stares off into space a second, thinking. "But they wouldn't have come out here if Mal wasn't onto something. Which means it's time to make as much fucking noise as we can."

"Tegan—"

"There's about four and a half gallons on my account," Tegan says. "When the power comes back on, I'm going to preload it to the room."

"Noted," says Keisha. "And I agree. If there's a time to make noise, it's now. Not just us right here. Not just the hotel. I'm talking about all of old town. Everyone who's been hit by this. Because if this is how Stellaxis deals with people airing out their dirty laundry for them, you kind of have to wonder how much of it they still have hidden away. If she wasn't onto something— something big—they never would have responded like this. This is a show of force. To keep the rest of us in line."

"So we, what?" Talya says. "Have some kind of protest, and the company magically gives us back our water because they see how much we really, really want it?"

"Yes," Tegan says. "That's exactly what we do. And we get online and we tell everyone what happened here. Stellaxis just cut off our water because we hurt their delicate corporate feelings. No way can that be legal."

"Legal's what they say it is," Allie replies. "You know that."

"Well, it's fucked up."

Allie raises both hands in mock surrender. "No argument here."

"Do you know what a firebreak is?" Keisha asks out of nowhere, and we all turn to look at her. This country averages three hundred and fifty thousand wildfires per annum. Of course we know. It's how you stop something too big to handle, or at least slow it down, when all else fails.

"That's what we're doing," she continues. "What we have to do. We're the firebreak. They want to run over us and keep on going. If they shut Mal up, if they shut us up, they're going to do the same thing to the next person and the next town, and the next one, and the next. We draw the line and we hold it."

Talya makes a face. "By . . . burning down old town before they can? They never said they were going to do anything like—"

"Don't be so literal," Tegan tells her. "This is serious. They're going to do *something*. What we have to do is get ahead of it and set the terms of how it's going to go."

"What does that even—"

"It means we hold that protest," Keisha says, "and we all record it. We get everyone to record it. We stream that entire fucker live from five thousand different angles, and we show the world what Stellaxis does when they get backed into a corner. Not just New Liberty. Not just the supercities. Not just Stellaxis territory. *Everywhere.* It's a company. They have to care what they look like to their customer base in the rest of the world. We just need to get proof out past their reach and hope it runs. See how they innovate their way out of *that.*"

Jessa, uncharacteristically quiet until now, finally speaks up. "I got video. Of the mech. When it threatened Mal. It was looking right at us. It wanted us to see."

"I hope you streamed that," Suresh says.

Jessa shakes her head. "They'd already cut the power." She taps the pocket screen she still has not let go of. "Saved it, though."

"So post it! Even if we don't get power back tomorrow, we'll put you on a bus to the city and you can post it there. I'll buy your ticket."

"I'll go half," Keisha says.

"I'm in too," says Tegan.

"Oh, I'll post it," Jessa says, but there's something strange in her voice. "I just gotta figure out how to frame it as a piece. Like we did with Mal's."

"The one that started all this," Talya mutters, but nobody replies.

"I'll go talk to some people I know in the school," Ryan says. "They'll be all over this. They've pretty much been waiting for an excuse."

"I'll tell my friends upstairs," says Jackson. He gets up, then sits back down. "Wait. Tell them what exactly?"

Nobody answers. It comes to me that they're waiting for me to speak. I'm the one who set this rolling, after all. I'm the nail that the company is trying to hammer back down into place.

Whatever happens next, they'll find a way to revisit it on me. That much is terrifyingly obvious.

"Tell them why this happened," I say at last. "All of it. Tell them how Stellaxis has been lying about the operatives and the water scarcity and who knows what else, and how I tried to make people know the truth, and how Stellaxis retaliated when I made it hard for them to quietly make me disappear. And tell them I'm not backing down. I'm going to make more videos. I'm going to find a way to get them out past where the company can shut them down, like Keisha said. I'm going to tell people all over the world what happened here today. I'm going to make as much fucking noise as I can—" I nod to Tegan, who nods back—"until they come here themselves and stop me."

It sounds insane. I'm listening to myself, and I sound like a person with a death wish. But I'm over the shock and the fear now, or mostly. It's been pushed back to—if not the background, at least the middle distance. In the foreground, I'm pissed.

"I'm never going to be able to organize a protest," I admit. "That is a much higher ratio of people-to-idea than I will ever know what to do with. It'll fall apart before it gets off the ground."

"We got that part," Tegan says. "Keisha, I know you're with me."

Keisha nods. Then Suresh and Allie and Jackson and Ryan do too.

"We're in," Jackson says. "All in. You guys didn't see that mech. It was *right there.* They might as well have stabbed a note into our door that said *OBEY OR DIE.*"

"I think you mean *DISPERSE,*" Allie says, grinning.

"Or *COMPLY,*" Ryan adds.

"Should've complied," I murmur.

"What's that?" Jessa asks.

I shake my head. "Nothing."

"I didn't even know Stellaxis *had* those now," Suresh said. "That's a Greenleaf design."

"They're running low on SecOps," Ryan says. "Guess they're diversifying."

"You want your water line back?" Tegan asks Talya. "This is how you get it back. They can't hear you pouting from way over there." They gesture at the window in the vague direction of the city. "You're pissed at Mal. I get it. But all of *this*—" a slow up-down sweep of Talya, fidgeting with her candy bar wrapper—"is misplaced. They cut our water off because of Mal's video. They'll cut it off next time one of us steps out of line. Or maybe the next shot won't aim for the sidewalk. You're smart enough to know that."

There's a long silence while Talya's face undergoes at least three costume changes that I can discern. It's like we're watching her dig down through all the slapped-on layers of anger and bitterness to the glowing reactor core of whatever lies beneath.

"I thought," she says at last, "that when we came here, it was over. We were safe. Nobody else was going to come for us. I thought old town was different. Its buildings stay up, you know?" Tegan opens their mouth, but Talya forestalls them with a gesture. "And don't tell me no buildings came down today. That's not the point. This was just a warning. It's only going to escalate from here."

"So help us," Tegan says. "The more eyes we put on this, the harder it is for them to keep it quiet." Without looking away from Talya's face, Tegan says, "How many views on Mal's videos?"

"About a hundred and fourteen million on the big one," Jessa says, "last I saw before the company had it taken down."

"When did that happen?" I ask.

"I checked on it right before the water line went out, and it was gone. Sorry I didn't tell you. A riot in the hotel lobby's pretty distracting, turns out."

"There are reshares circulating on tons of other sites," Allie says.

Jessa nods. "Greenleaf newsfeeds."

"Weirdly, no. Indies mostly. Blogs, social media."

"Outside the city?"

"Some. And people keep reposting the original. At least they were when I checked before curfew." Allie jabs a thumb into her own sternum, adding: "I can vouch for at least one person who's gonna share the hell out of it in the morning."

"And that right there," Tegan says, "is what they don't like. They want to come in here and try to scare us? Cut the problem off at the source? Fine. Let them come. We'll make sure the whole fucking world is watching when they do."

"All because Mal wanted to help a couple of operatives who're probably going to die anyway," Talya mutters, but softer now. I don't know if the edges are ground off her anger, and maybe I don't want them to be.

I realize I don't even care if she hates me. She also hates what this corporate war did to her family and her home, and that's good enough for me.

"It's bigger than that now," I tell her. "Yes, I did, and I do, and I'd make that same video again and again forever if I thought it would save them, but right now it's bigger than 06 and 22 and the other ten or forty-six or however many others that are already dead because nobody did anything to stop it. Here, today, Stellaxis made it bigger."

"It was already bigger," Keisha says. "They made us part of this when they smashed our homes and killed our families and sent us here. And now they take our water, just like that, to punish us. They own us as much as they own the operatives. Them coming here today was to remind us of that fact."

This hits the mark I failed to. I don't know how people like Keisha and Jessa can do this, say the right thing at the right time, so effortlessly. I shut up and let her take over.

"It was always all of us," Keisha continues. "All of us together. The difference is that now we know it."

"There are water lines in every town and camp and city in the country," Jackson adds. "People will listen to us when they see what happened here today. Because they'll know they could be next."

Tegan takes Talya's face in both hands. "I miss them as much as you do," they say, and I know they're not talking about anything the rest of us are privy to. Tegan's a few minutes older than Talya, but both were old enough to remember when the war chewed up their family and spat them out alone. Whatever wreckage of whatever life they walked out of, they walked out of it together. "What would Mom say if she saw you giving up when things got shitty?"

Whatever Talya replies, she mumbles it too low for me to hear. Not my business anyway. I decide to leave them to it. Besides, I can feel Keisha staring at the side of my head, waiting for me to turn. *Video*, she mouths at Jessa and me, and Jessa gives her a totally made-up salute that's at odds with the weird unease in her face.

"Come on," I tell her, tilting my head toward Talya and Tegan, who've retreated to the back of the room to sit in a corner together and talk in hushed voices about something that keeps making Talya sound like she's about to cry.

We go sit in our stairwell instead. "I'll post it," I say. "Give me the file and I'll post it first thing in the morning. I don't need the next mech trying to figure out which one of us to aim at." Then, because I don't know what I should say to the naked relief on her face, I lie: "You'd just fuck up the narration anyway."

IN THE MORNING, the power's back on. Maybe they figure we've learned our lesson. Maybe they've just realized we can't very well contribute to the economy if they shut us off. Doesn't matter. We all preload our water to the room (even Talya, astonishingly, though she doesn't look too happy about it), and then I post Jessa's video. Turns out she started recording even before the mech showed up. There's footage of the riot cops with their forcefield projectors, security bots tagging people, that one guy getting flung backward into the front of the movie theater across the street. The works.

A preliminary search has shown us that a few other people found low-tech workarounds like Jessa did and posted footage of their own. I hope it spreads like hell, faster even than the speed of corporate suppression.

My voice-over for Jessa's video goes like this:

"Within six hours of my exposé going live, Stellaxis Innovations sent what amounts to a strike force to shut off my building's water line. Not just my water line but every water line in old town outside New Liberty City. Because they felt threatened. Because they wanted to bully me into backing down. They'd already taken down my video, but enough people had saved and shared it that they felt they had to take more drastic measures. What does this look like to you?"

Footage of the mech blasting a crater in the sidewalk at my front door. Looking directly at me. Making sure I'm paying attention. "This thing might as well have drawn a finger across its throat and pointed at me. Threatening a free customer-citizen because a megacorporation doesn't like her little internet video is not a good look. They want my attention? They've got it. Fully."

Dimly I wonder at what point I'll have crossed the line that galvanizes them to stop messing around trying to hammer that irritating nail back down and send some SecOps pliers instead to remove it permanently. I wonder if 06 and 22 will remember me. Whether they'll refuse the order and side with me against their oppressors. It's a nice daydream anyway.

"This is old town." I'm walking out the hotel door now and into the street, streaming. I posted Jessa's mech video half an hour ago with instructions to stay tuned to our channel and a reminder that if no new content appears by noon, something's happened. I can only hope that the company is taking me seriously enough to worry about martyring me to an exposé of their practices. If people didn't believe me before, they probably will then. Enough of them, anyway.

"I live here," I narrate quietly. Jessa and a few of the others walk with me for protection, and I've got a scarf pulled up over my lower face so you can't from a distance see that I'm talking. My taser's living in my pocket now. I don't see that changing soon. "Maybe you didn't believe me when I posted that video yesterday. Well, Stellaxis clearly did." Footage of the cratered sidewalk outside the hotel. Footage of the smashed-in movie theater. Footage of bloodstains in the street, of the scattering of plastic cups and bottles, of the multicolored splatter on the street where they hit the shields and liquefied. "I wonder what they're so afraid of. All I did was make an honest video. Do they have something to hide?"

I narrate everything I look at. I give as much detail as I can. I encourage people to go find those other videos and share those, too. Make it obvious this isn't just some pet delusion of mine, some kind of ploy for attention. It's real. And it could be anybody else's town next.

I post that video and pace up and down the stairs to keep a drain on my nervous energy. Then I remember I haven't gotten a chance to check out the stuff our sponsors have given us for yesterday's video, so I sit in the stairwell to take a real quick look at that before I start moving again.

There's a *lot*. A few hundred dollars in combined cash and company-store credits, almost five gallons of water, and a massive pile of game items that I can sell on the market for cash, which I can use to buy water. Overpriced company-store water, from a corporation I'm much more inclined to boycott entirely, but I don't exactly have the luxury of being picky. I can't very well fight them if my kidneys give out.

I swipe the water and money to their respective accounts and breathe a sigh of relief. It's funny, really. Jessa and I used to dream of streaming game sessions full-time, making enough to live off. But that'd put us in the top maybe zero-point-zero-zero-one percent of gamers at a generous estimate. Rarified air for sure. And now here we are. Finally able to live off our streaming income. At least for a while. And for all the wrong reasons.

I get fidgety, so I go downstairs thinking I'll buy some water, but Comforts of Home is like a war zone itself. Where there used to be a giant pyramidal display of water bottles, there's now the smashed remains of several on the floor and armed guards breaking up brawls when people try to grab water bottles out of each other's hands and shopping baskets. There are people filling their ration cups and bottles with soda instead, as, compared to water, it's practically free. People swiping thumb interfaces at each other in the middle of the store, buying water off each other's accounts, haggling loudly.

Not ten seconds after I start streaming, a full-on display-crashing fight starts in the checkout line, complete with people physically throwing their bodies on the bottles as they roll away across the floor.

I keep my distance. At least I have that extra water in my account. Those five gallons will keep the nine of us healthy for another couple of days or so. As awkward and shitty as it feels to just stand here and watch this play out, I hang back and run the stream.

One time I saw a newsfeed where some immaculately made-up reporter went to the aftermath of Hurricane Astrid and cabled down from a helicopter to talk to some people stranded on the roof of their drowned house and baking in the sun. They'd been there for four days, out of water for two, and at least one of these people was visibly dying. The reporter might've offered them water after the segment was filmed, I don't know. All I know is that she shoved a drone camera into their faces and asked when they hoped to be rescued. And that when she left, it wasn't with any of them in her helicopter. Or any of the people on any of the other rooftops either.

I wonder if someone made her do that. Document and flee. Leave no trace. I remember thinking at the time I could never do what she did. That I could never be that callous. I'm trying to convince myself that what I'm doing now is different. There's nothing I can do for these people. Not in the short term. Even if I had enough money to buy water for everyone in this store right now, there's no water left to buy. Even if I split up my water account between them, they'd each get a few ounces at most, and the borrowed time I add to their tallies is borrowed time I take from the eight people for whom I'm directly the fuck co-responsible.

Stellaxis did this, I remind myself.

But right on the heels of that is: *Stellaxis did this because of me.*

Still, if it wasn't me, it would've been somebody else eventually. Somebody who exposed something the company didn't want seen. I didn't do anything special. There's nothing about me that's particularly threatening to their status quo. I was in the right place at the right time. That's all.

And because they decided to bring this fight to me, I'm in the right place at the right time now, too. All I can do is make the most of it. Make sure people see and understand. Here but for the grace of corporate goodwill goes every one of you.

I stand there and stream until a guard sees me loitering and shoos me away. At the last second she seems to realize who she's yelling at—I'm sure they all know damn well who I am— but then a couple of women pelt past her holding a shopping bag full of someone else's bottles, and she backpedals out of my face fast to pursue them.

Stupid to push my luck further here. Still, on my way out I risk a glance up the hall toward the water-storage room, still streaming. Allie was right, there are six guards there. Holding the guns like the safeties aren't going back on again until all this is quashed. Panning over all of us with their eyes. I don't doubt for a second that they're sending surveillance footage back to HQ. I imagine someone in a business suit sitting in a room full of screens, parsing this, writing up a progress report. *Intimidation tactics met with widespread success.*

Still, the guards themselves are quietly watchful. Like this whole place has been doused with gasoline and they're biding their time until one of us shows up with a match.

They've projected a shield over the door. No way to know what kind it is until someone touches it. I have a feeling it's set to something stronger than *repel*.

I hurry off before they take note of me. Which I realize is stupid: of course they have. This whole thing has been staged for my benefit. Mine, and anyone else's who gets similar ideas.

Someone runs out of Comforts of Home, sobbing. The guards twitch to attention, and I use the distraction to cross the hall out of their line of sight. In the lobby I notice Suresh and Tegan talking quietly to three or four people over in a corner. They're all holding massive sodas and leaning against the walls fake-casual, like they're gossiping about some celebrity or discussing something that happened in a game, but I know it's an act. Tegan and Suresh are putting into action what we all decided on last night after Jessa and I returned from the stairwell. Elsewhere, Keisha and Jackson and Allie and Ryan and Jessa are too.

They're spreading the word about the protest. This Saturday, the tenth of April, we all take to the streets together. Us and anyone who'll join us. In old town and elsewhere. We stand together and we stream together and we ram the entire internet down Stellaxis's throat.

Tell everyone, they'll be saying. *Online and in person. Make flyers. Whatever. But remember: no violence.* This part I was very clear on. It doesn't make much sense to try to free 06 and 22 from systematic cruelty, and avenge the deaths of the others, if we're just going to add more dead to the heap. Any violence that occurs, I want it to be company violence, not ours. Company violence that we can broadcast to the world. We so much as break a window, that's the way the story gets spun. We've seen enough newsfeeds to know that.

Not for the first time the thought strikes me: Okay, what then? The rest of the world might have enough consumer clout and corporate regulations and whatever to bring Stellaxis down, but . . . what does that mean for us? Best-case scenario, Stellaxis is done. Would we be better off under Greenleaf?

Say 06 and 22 get released from company control. Say the war ends and they walk out of those glass doors free. Are they going to move into old town just to work four jobs and live in a room with eight people and end up in the rehydration clinics with the rest of us?

Is there an answer here? Or has this, all of this, gone on too long for anyone to even be able to conceptualize an alternative?

Tegan catches my eye and knows better than to nod, just lets their gaze slide off mine and laughs too loudly at something that even from my distance looks cued.

One of the strangers turns and leaves in one direction. Then another leaves going a different way. Followed by the other two. One goes for the elevator, one for the stairs, two out into the street through separate doors with a half-minute delay between them.

Them gone, I glance back and notice what was obscured before. Or who. Talya is there with them, hanging back mostly behind Tegan, looking deeply conflicted, but *there*.

It's more than I expected.

dude. did you look at the video you just posted

no, I send. been trying to avoid it actually

well stop avoiding it

Jessa wouldn't fuck with me. Not about this, anyway. I climb the stairs to our room.

She's already there, beside herself with what looks like at least three separate emotions at once. "Post another one," she says. "About the protest. Right now."

I dodge around her toward the coffeepot. I can't afford to use much water, obviously, but I have a feeling I'm going to need caffeine to help me get through whatever she wants me to see. "Everybody's downstairs right now spreading the word," I say, scooping grounds. "It's gone beyond *me* now. Water-line cutoffs, that's what'll get people's attention. Numbers. Reach. Widespread awareness."

"Nonono. You don't understand. *Look.*"

She's got the video up on the pocket screen. She holds it in my face and starts slowly scrolling through the comments. There's the usual trolling garbage, of course, but this time it's practically drowned out by this tidal wave of . . . support.

They took your water? That's fucked up.

your whole town's water lines got cut off because of some video?

that fucking mech looked right at you, no way is that not a threat, you've got them dead to rights

share this everywhere, people, they can't get away with this, blow it up

Anybody know what we can do about this?

"Okay," I say slowly. "Okay." I take the screen from her, heft it thoughtfully in my hands like I'm going to uptake inspiration directly through my anxious-sweating palms.

That's when I see something else. A kind of comment I've never seen before.

Solidarity from Mexico City.
Love from Cairo.
Auckland stands with you.

Then I put it down. I pull up our streaming account and send out a notification to our subscribers that I'll be starting a new stream in five minutes.

There are millions of them these days and more subscribing by the tens of thousands every time I check. Whether they believed my videos or not, apparently they were at least entertaining enough for the audience to want to keep me around. Right now that's fine by me.

It doesn't take long for them to start showing up. The active-viewers icon climbs. When it's nearly been five minutes, there are one-point-one million of them gathered.

That's when I start to lose my nerve.

"Jessa, I can't even present a game stream to our regular audience without a script. I can't, what, *rally* people to—"

"Just tell them," Jessa says gently. "This coming Saturday. April tenth. The same stuff we agreed on for everyone else. Hell, it might even be better if it doesn't sound super polished. Let it look like we're hurting here. It's not like we'd be lying. We have water for a few more days, max. We need backup. Badly." She shrugs. "Just be honest."

I think for a minute. Then I turn on all the lights, stand in front of the bathroom mirror, and start streaming.

"They took our water," I say without preamble. "There are nine of us living in this room, and we pooled together what little we have left. It won't last much longer. Other rooms, other buildings probably have even less. Some might have already run out. We were at least lucky enough that our housing lottery landed us in a building with a roof. The camps are probably way worse off than this. They say we can buy water at the company store, but it's a dollar an ounce, and nobody in old town can afford to live on that. They know this, of course. This is a power play. It's time to show them that they're not holding all the cards. They can't push us over if we all stand together. Join us this Saturday, April tenth, and do whatever you can, wherever you can, to show them that they can't keep hiding. They hid what they did to the operatives. They're trying to hide what they did here. Stand with us and say with us: *We see you.* We—"

The feed cuts out. Not just the feed but my lenses. Not just the lenses but my implant. I can't even pull up the time and temperature, the safety alert dashboard. Nothing.

The fuckers locked me out.

Not just from our channel. Not just from the game. From everything. My cash. My company credit. My gallons I never got a chance to preload to the room. My pile of game items to sell. My entire actual *water account.* All of it.

It's gone.

"Oh hell no," Jessa says. Her eyes are like spotlights. "They didn't just—"

I take my lenses out, top up their interface fluid, put them back in. To predictable effect. Whatever shock I feel is distant, dulled, a detonation heard from far off. It's been a long time coming.

"This is stupid, though. You disappear, then everybody *knows* the company's trying to shut you up. They could've thrown you into jail and sent the same message. Or killed you!" Jessa's pacing now, shaking her head like she can dislodge the calamity that's landed on her. "Well, fuck that." She stops and stares at the wall, obviously pulling something up on her lenses. "I was too scared to do this yesterday, but that ship has fucking sailed. I'm going to share this into *oblivion.* I'm going to make so much fucking noise that they're going to have to cut me into pieces and mail each piece to an *individual soundproofed room* on *separate continents* to shut me up. They're—"

She stops like someone's pulled her plug. At first I think they locked her out too. But no. She's staring at something. Staring at something that's turned her face the approximate color of wet cement. She staggers back until the insides of her knees hit the nearest bunk, then sits. One hand comes up to cover her mouth.

"Dude," I say, because I have an immediate sinking feeling that somehow, whatever she's looking at is the latest landmark blown past by the runaway train that is our week, and I have to say something stupid to keep from careening off the tracks entirely, "you look like you're reading your own obituary."

With visible effort she draws me into focus. Her panicked stare isn't exactly less unsettling when it's aimed right at my face. If she's ever looked this shaken, I haven't seen it.

"I think," she says slowly, "I'm watching yours."

SHE GESTURES WHATEVER IT IS OVER TO the wall screen, then points at me with shaking hands. "Sit," she says, her voice cracking. "Sit down."

I sit, and I face the screen.

What's on it is—me.

Or something *like* me. Something close enough to *pass* as me. Something that is to me what the in-game version of 22 is to the real one.

It's a video.

"Restart," Jessa tells the wall screen. "Pause." Looks at me. Waits for me to nod the go-ahead. Seconds tick by before I can. Whatever this is, it's really, really bad.

"Play," I whisper.

It takes a moment to realize why the screen ignores me. I'm locked out. At literally any other time, this would be enough to make me comprehensively lose my shit. But right now I've got bigger problems.

"Play," Jessa tells the screen, and it does.

"My name is Mallory," says the not-me thing on the wall. "You may know me as my BestLife avatar Nycorix, or from videos like this." Cut to a clip of 06 and 22 fighting the mech in my first video, which cuts in turn to a clip of a girl throwing a soda bottle at an armed guard in the one Jessa took. "Gaming and protesting's been fun, guys, but I'm over that now. Wait until you see what I have in store for you next."

"Pause," I croak. It feels like someone's throat-punched me. Hard to catch my breath. Jessa pauses. I stare at the thing with my face, now in freeze-frame, smiling coyly. "The *fuck is this*."

"I think it's like . . ." Jessa trails off, fishing for words. "A composite video? Some kind of actor-dies-while-they're-still-filming-the-movie deepfake shit?"

"Do I look like a fucking dead actor to you?"

We're both still staring at the wall screen in profound horror. Like the not-Mal might crawl out of it and wear me like a glove.

Giving Jessa the go-ahead to play the rest of whatever's on this video is, at the moment, a bridge just the tiniest bit too far. "I don't even talk like that! *In store for you?* When have I said that?" I can't shake the thought that if I touched the not-me thing on the arm, its skin would feel like picking up a half-dead earthworm off the sidewalk.

"They must've used footage from your video, the one you're in, but . . ." Jessa messes her hands through her hair. "But that wouldn't be enough. They must have mined surveillance feeds from the hotel. Something. I don't know. I don't *know*."

I look at her. Then I look back at the screen. The desire to dig it out of the wall and pitch it out the window is a physical itch in the muscles of my shoulders and the backs of my hands. But I have to know. "Okay," I tell her. "Play the rest."

The not-me beams out from within. It's weirdly backlit, like a halo dialed up too high. "I've been in negotiations with Stellaxis Innovations, and I can't even tell you how super excited I am to share this with you. Introducing the newest addition to the upcoming summer '34 line of exclusive Stellaxis StelTech SecOps merchandise . . . *me!*"

Cut to a CG animation of an action figure that looks like Nycorix in some kind of pseudomilitary pseudopunk poser getup: cargo pants, combat boots, weird distressed t-shirt with the sleeves ripped off that reads RESIST in stencil font. The shirt is torn down the front to show my cleavage, because of course it is.

This cuts to a reenactment of the mech fight scene from my first video, except with 06 and 22 action figures subbed in for the real thing, and the Nycorix action figure standing back waving a no-shit anti-Stellaxis *protest sign.* Then she throws that down, rips off the RESIST shirt to reveal a black tank top, draws a pistol from fuck knows where, and runs to join the battle.

At the last second she turns to address the audience over one shoulder. "Come fight the good fight with me."

"Turn it off."

Jessa pauses it. Nycorix looks, sickeningly, like somewhere inside the next ten frames of animation she's going to wink.

"No. Off."

Jessa gestures, and the screen goes dark.

We stare at it for long seconds past when the image has faded to nothing. When Stellaxis finally made their move, whatever I expected it to be, it wasn't this.

"That—can they *do* that?"

I shake my head. "They're doing it." The shock isn't wearing off. More like it's turning transparent, and I can see my thought processes beneath. "They couldn't make me disappear because that would be essentially proving I've been right about them all along. So they sidestepped my insurance policy."

"They *stole you.* They can't just . . ." Jessa trails off, outraged. Her fists clench and unclench at her sides. "They *added you to the brand.*"

Intellectual property, I think. A nervous laugh rips out of me. *You're like 22 now. Isn't that what you always wanted?*

It's too surreal. I can't parse it. I need time.

But I don't have time. The realization takes me like a brick upside the head. Time is exactly what I'm out of.

"I have to get out of here," I say. "I have to hide. People are going to believe that shit. That I sold out. That I lost them their water line to make a fucking profit."

"They can't believe that. They know you."

"Who? Who knows me? *You* know me. The people *in this room* know me." I fling one hand toward the window. "You saw the crowd out there yesterday. What happens when they realize they have a much softer target to aim at than Stellaxis? That's what they want," I continue, understanding even as I say it. At the very least they discredit me. Utterly. If they're lucky, I go away for real, forever. "They want old town to eat me alive and save them the trouble. Where did you see this?"

Jessa's eyes flicker as she scrolls. "It was a news alert. One of Stellaxis's special announcements."

"Then everyone got it," I whisper. "Everyone saw."

"Jesus." Jessa's hand is over her mouth again. The mannerism seems to have suddenly appeared on her, the way in a movie you wake up from a shock and find your hair has turned white. "You need a disguise."

She rummages in her swag stash and emerges with a pair of oversize sunglasses. Little cartoon 21s decorating chunky black frames. I recognize them as the limited ones they released when 21 died a few months ago. Her date of death is on there too: October 26, 2133. Killed in action, like they always say. But now I can't help but wonder whether 21 did some time meeting with mysterious *occupational hazards* before her flare went up too.

Jessa fits them onto my face, then steps back. "It's not enough. Put on a hat. Borrow somebody else's coat. I'll talk to them. Then get out of here and go someplace quiet while I find the others and spread the word, make sure everyone knows that video is fake as shit and you would never."

Most of the coats are out of the room with their owners, but Jessa rummages in the back of the storage closet and comes out with an old camo-print jacket. She sniffs it, makes a face. "I don't even know whose this was. Here." She shoves it at me, releasing an incongruous lavender scent.

The irony of the camouflage is not lost on me, but it looks a lot different from my usual coat. I shrug it on, then freeze, one hand reaching out habitually for my backpack.

"Leave it," Jessa says. "You'll be back soon. Just go."

I fish the taser out of my coat anyway and pocket it in the borrowed one.

"Go up to the garden," Jessa says. "I'll meet you in a few hours. Actually. Wait."

I turn. Jessa's holding one of Allie's lipsticks. I raise an eyebrow. "Seriously?"

"You want to not look like you? Come here."

She lipsticks me, then does something with my hair that hurts my scalp. Then she finds somebody's knit winter hat and pulls it down onto my head. "All right, total stranger," she says, giving me a sad little shake. "I'll see you soon."

The door bangs open, and Talya comes in, Tegan on her heels. "You sellout fuck," Talya says. "I knew you were full of shit. But this is like a *whole other level*."

My hand slides into my taser pocket, but Jessa is already stepping between Talya and me. She's several inches shorter than Talya, but at this moment I'm pretty sure she's keyed up enough to face down a tank. She stares up into Talya's face with angelic calm. "Relax," she breathes.

"Relax. Fucking *relax*? That fucking asshole cost me my water! And now she's *working* with them?"

"It's a fake," I say. "That's not me. They locked out my implant and put this video up instead."

"Oh come *on*. You expect us to believe—"

"Because they couldn't just lock you up," Tegan says, cutting her off.

"Or kill me."

"Or kill you. Holy shit. They're trying to erase you instead."

"Erase and replace," Jessa adds. "Just like the coffee shop."

Tegan levels their gaze at me. "You *swear* you weren't part of this?"

"I swear. I didn't know they were going to take the water lines either. I thought if anything, they'd kill my game account, lock out my lenses. Worst-case scenario, grab me off the street." I shake my head. "Not this."

Tegan eyes me calculatingly, then nods. "Shit. I believe you."

"Thanks."

"You must have really pissed them off."

I essay a lopsided grin. "I hope so."

Talya looks me up and down. "You're getting my water back."

"We're going to get everyone's water back," I say, investing my voice with a confidence I don't quite feel. "Together."

Then Talya notices the outfit. "What are you doing in all that?"

"Protection," Jessa says. "You're not the only ones who won't believe her at first."

"Or ever," I say.

"It's some elaborate fuckery," Jessa says. "People are going to fall hard for this. And they're not going to be happy."

"Of course they won't be happy," Talya says. "We're all going to die if we don't get—"

"Our water back," Jessa says. "We know. But you have to understand we *have to* hold this protest. We can't back down. W
have to stand with Mal. If they see her there with us, they'
know she's not playing for the company team, no matter ho

many commercials they run. I mean. You saw it. Having her throw away her protest sign and the world's most on-the-nose shirt? How fucking unsubtle can you *be*?"

Talya chews this over. "I don't like it," she says eventually.

"There's nothing to fucking like about it," Jessa replies. "But if we—"

"So hold up." Tegan is eyeing me differently now. "What's trying to disappear going to solve? If you want people to see you're still here, still resisting, they have to *see you* here. Resisting. Not hiding somewhere buried under whatever the fuck that all is."

"They're going to kill her," Jessa says. "They're going to see that video and they're going to come here and they're going to—"

"No," Tegan says. "They're not. I just put out a call to the others, told them what happened. What really happened. They're coming up here. We're going to walk downstairs together. All of us."

"No," I say.

Tegan looks at me. "What?"

"I can't do that. I can't put other people at risk because of me." *No worse than I have already.* "The water line— I never meant—"

"Dude," Jessa says. "We know."

Tegan nods. Talya at least doesn't disagree.

"I—" I begin, and then the door opens again, and in come Allie and Jackson and Keisha and Ryan and Suresh. As well as a solid dozen people I don't know. They're carrying something. Signs. Protest signs. One of them has a giant water droplet drawn on it in blue marker. I can't make out the words. They cram in and in until we're all stepping on one another's feet.

"These guys came to help," Jackson says, hooking a thumb over a shoulder in explanation. "They've seen you stream the game, and they know you wouldn't do, like, a *tenth* of that shit."

"I saw Nycorix start grinning like that," one of them pipes up, "I knew they got to you. I thought they had you locked up somewhere with a camera in your face. Under duress, you know?"

"Bullshit," Keisha says. "That was some bottom-shelf trash CGI." It's a blatant lie, but one that's meant to cheer me up. I try to let it. "Can't a company that owns half of everything come up with better animation?"

"Okay, but." Allie loops her pointer finger in my direction, a midair figure eight that starts at my feet and cups the top of my head. "I have to ask."

Right. I shuck off the jacket and stuff onto my bunk and wipe the lipstick off on my sleeve. Then I remember the taser and retrieve it. I put it in the pocket of my own coat, then put that on, followed by my backpack. Someone pushes a sign into my hands. A marker drawing of a water line, except in reverse, and weird: the people in line are filling the ration barrels through IVs in their arms. The tubes going into the barrel run red with blood, but what the barrel is packed with is dollar signs painted in gold.

It's all a little too cluttered for a decent protest sign, but it illustrates which side I'm on, and really that's all I need.

"Hard to make the case that you're a corporate sellout when you're down there with a sign telling Stellaxis to go fuck themselves," Keisha says. "Everybody recording?"

Everybody is. Everybody but me.

Jessa nudges me. "Ready?"

As much as I'm going to be. I follow them out of the room and into the hall.

THEY ARRANGE THEMSELVES around me with extras in front and behind, and we walk down all six flights of stairs together. Our hall is practically empty. Whether they've all gone to Comforts of Home to beg for water or they've just cleared out so nobody thinks to associate them with me, I don't know. But only a few people yell at us, and that seems to be mostly because we're taking up the entire hall.

Keisha walks backward in front of me, recording. She doesn't stream the game or even play it as far as I'm aware. The only time I ever hear her discuss it is in the context of how the module Jessa and I play is "thinly veiled war propaganda." But apparently this whole time she's secretly been a mod of one of the indie news blogs that helped blow up my videos, and she opens up a live feed there.

Or, I realize, maybe it's never been secret at all. Maybe I was just keeping to myself too much to know. It's not like I go around asking people about their day.

Four years I've lived with these people, and I know virtually nothing about them. We've been background extras in one another's lives at best. Side-quest NPCs. And yet here they are, walking shoulder to shoulder with me. Putting their asses on the line for me.

Or no. That's not even right. Not *for* me. *With* me. It's so strange I can't even fully process it. It strikes my mind and glances off. Would I have done the same for them? I'd like to think so. But after all these years of being a good little customer-citizen, it's honestly anybody's guess.

"Here's the *real* Mallory," Keisha's yelling. "The *real* Nycorix. She posted a video about the SecOps program, and Stellaxis didn't like that. They didn't like it at *all*. So they tried to shut her up. They killed our water lines, every building in old town, *gone*, to get her to stop, to make sure none of us got the same idea. She said fine, you want to bring other people into this? Let's bring other people into this. She planned a protest so everybody would know about the corruption and greed and lies we're living with every day. So they locked out her implant and invented a version of her they could control. That puppet shit you saw? Remember whose channel you saw that on! Are you really going to believe the same people who cut off our water? Believe us instead—believe that Mal would never sell out to these greedy fucks—and you hit them where it hurts. There's some shady shit going on here, no question, but remember: you want the real Nycorix, the real Mal, the real truth, you follow the feeds coming out of old town, live, unedited, untouched, and you see for yourself what's what."

She goes on like this the whole way down all six flights of stairs to the lobby. Or she would have, except they catch on and lock her out too before she hits the fourth-floor landing. So Tegan takes over, streaming on the same site. I mean, I knew they didn't like the company, but I didn't know about *this*.

"These people control everything," they say, their gaze panning from me to Jessa to the crowd around us, holding protest signs. When I glance around, there seem to be more people now than we left with. Our little crowd isn't so little now. It stretches back down the hall, trailing behind us like a banner. "Stellaxis and Greenleaf, owning our food and our water, our power and our communications. What next? Our air? What does that leave for us? What do we get to control? Nothing! Nothing except what we take back for ourselves. Thanks to the Neutralities Accord, we can't grow our own food unless it's Greenleaf Industries seeds and Stellaxis Innovations water. They don't let us drink unless we're begging for their rations or we're paying a dollar an ounce at the company stores. Every single person in old town is clinically dehydrated, and you better believe we're not taking as many showers and doing as much laundry and flushing the toilets as often as we should. Poor hygiene spreads disease, but do they care? I say to you they do the fuck not. They love it because then we have to pay four hundred dollars to so much as show our faces at a walk-in clinic! A *company clinic*! Is that any kind of fucking way to live?"

"I thought the protest was Saturday," Talya mutters behind me.

But Tegan hears her. "The protest *is* Saturday," they shout. "And every day before that, and every day after, until we get our *goddamn fucking human rights. And then—*"

That's when they cut Tegan off too. Suresh steps in, but then the whole crowd stops moving. We're at the landing between the lobby and the second floor, and whoever's in front stops dead on the stairs near the door, backing all of us up behind them. All kinds of thoughts race through my head, none of them good. Guards blocking the exit to the lobby so they can shoot us when they let us through. Guards blocking the exit to the lobby because they've already chucked something into the stairwell, and my part of the crowd hasn't happened on it yet. Resonance grenades. Hallucinogen bursts. Drones. I listen for the telltale sounds of each of these but can't make them out over the crowd.

Which has only gotten bigger. I'm on the landing, and it's solid-packed people the whole way down the flight of stairs between me and the door. It's loud and uncomfortable and smells like the sour laundry and sweat and breath of many dozens of borderline-malnourished and chronically dehydrated humans.

We must have gathered bystanders from each hall, a few here, a few there, the whole way down. I can't really blame them. It's probably not too clear at a glance what the fuck is going on here, and they're sticking around until they figure it out. Certainly they seem more curious to check out the drama than fired up to join any kind of half-assed cause. Already Keisha's and Tegan's speeches have sent some of them scurrying back up the stairs at top speed. Covering themselves from the inevitable facial recognition sweep that's going to get us all flagged and tagged if this escalates much further, and very possibly even if it doesn't.

"No matter what, everybody keep recording," Tegan yells. "What's going on down there?"

There are windows in each stairwell just in front of the door. Whatever's transfixing the people in front, it's out one of these windows. Others are pushing down the stairs to see, but before this ends in full-on disaster, somebody yells up, in a tone almost like awe, "It's raining."

For a second we all look at one another, and in that silence I hear it. It's the first rain after long months of sleet and filthy snow, and it's battering the fire escapes and pounding on the roof and sizzling to the street in sheets upon sheets of water.

Water.

For a second we're all held there, tense and undecided, while the rain hammers down. It sounds like all the barrels in all the storage rooms in all the buildings in every street in old town being emptied out at once. We all stand and look at one another, listening. Waiting for someone to make the first move.

Then somebody below us shoves that downstairs door open, and we pour out into the lobby. "Keep recording," Tegan shouts as we get swept down the stairs, jostled by a few more people as they detach from the group and push their way back up the stairs. Their voice is lost in the commotion. "Keep recording and watch the guards!"

By the time I get out into the lobby, the guards have abandoned their post at the water-storage room in order to cover the stairwell with their guns. "We're not doing anything," a man shouts at them. He holds up his protest sign. "Just exercising our free speech rights. Last I checked, we still have those. And we're all streaming this."

One of the guards grabs him and slams him to the floor with one hand. The other hand waves the protest sign in his face. "This is libel and defamation against Stellaxis Innovations, subject to prosecution. Stream that."

"That's not prosecution—that's assault," a woman yells back, and rifles swing around to bear on her. She kneels, hands in the air, sign held up above her head. It reads WATER-FOR-ALL™ MEANS WATER FOR ALL. Another guard rips it out of her hands, sets one booted foot to her shoulder, and pushes her over sideways. "Stay down or get put down!" he screams at her.

"We are being assaulted and demeaned by Stellaxis's sec forces," Suresh is yelling, sweeping his head back and forth to get a nice clear panning shot of the action. He points down the hall toward the water-storage room. "There are thousands of gallons of water locked up in there while *people are dying—*"

I crash to my knees. *They recognized me*, I think. *It's over.* But it's just the crowd that knocked me sideways. Jessa hauls me back up.

"Disperse!" another guard is shouting at us in a tinny monotone through the bug helmet. "Disperse. Disperse."

"You heard him," Keisha shouts. She's holding the outside door open. The crowd disperses into the street. The guards chase after, shouting, having abandoned the man and woman on the floor, so a few of us help them up, and then we all run out together.

It's funny how you forget how hard it can rain. It drenches us immediately, and it's cold as hell, and it melts my protest sign to sludge in my hands, and I turn my face up to it and open my mouth, and it's delicious. They always try to scare you out of drinking rainwater. It's a crime, of course, but they always hit up the disease angle for good measure. *There are at least twenty-five commonly known waterborne pathogens in everyday rainwater. That's why we at Stellaxis Innovations spare no expense in running every drop of our water through state-of-the-art filtration systems.* We see that safety alert every time there's so much as a drizzle. And at the moment we don't care. It's colder than what comes out of the ration barrels or the hotel sinks and it tastes completely different and it's free and it's water and it's ours.

"Disperse," the guards are shouting. "Return to your homes." Some people lose their nerve, break, and run, but a surprising number of them stay. It's hard to hear threats over this kind of rain. Besides, we've all seen the news clips of protests being disbanded before. They don't open fire into a crowd, not with live rounds anyway, not when so many people are watching. And there are hundreds of us out here. Thousands, maybe. People are walking and running and biking in from other streets. Some of them are flying drones before them, getting footage from a bird's-eye view. There are countless eyes on these guards. Countless eyes broadcasting to the world. Whatever these guards' orders are, for now they're stopping right at the threshold of what they'd clearly rather be doing, which is beating our faces in. Lucky for us, the last thing the company needs to top off their week is a bunch of trigger-happy security guards doing target practice on unarmed civilians exercising their free speech rights all over the internet.

I've been so caught up staring at whatever is unfolding here that I've lost sight of Jessa. And now I can't find her. It's chaos out here. Total chaos. I don't know where anybody is. Jessa, Tegan, Suresh, Keisha—the rain has drenched us all, rendered us all practically unrecognizable from a distance. The guards are yelling and firing their guns above our heads and people are yelling back and waving the sodden mess of their signs and more people run out of the hotel, maybe having seen us from the windows, and a little group of them comes out with giant packages of company-store plastic cups under each arm and they rip them open and people take stacks of cups and dash around handing them out and everyone holds them up above their heads and the rain falls and falls. People are *pouring* out of other buildings now too, people and guards, and some of the people bypass the guards by filing down the fire escapes, and some of them just stay put but start holding their own cups and bottles and bowls and even plastic baggies out the windows, throwing more plastic cups and baggies down to us in the street.

There's a sound that starts to grow, a soft, low rattling that swells louder and louder and eventually reveals itself to be the sound of rain falling into red plastic cups held in dozens and then hundreds of hands raised to the sky.

I have no idea how this happened. I guess somebody posted the idea and it spread fast. Or maybe it's a thing that just occurred. We're thirsty, after all.

It's a nothing little symbol of a protest or a resistance movement or a riot or a revolution or whatever this turns out to be, but at the moment it strikes me as oddly beautiful. Red plastic cups full of rain.

Still the guards don't make a move. Which is strange. People are overtly poaching water right under their noses. But they're just hanging back by the buildings, yelling at us to go home. They're not even firing taggers. It's almost like they're waiting for something.

Then it happens.

All at once, almost everyone around me stops like someone's hit pause. At first I think it's something the guards are doing, but it's not. It's their lenses. Stellaxis shut off the power again.

And then comes a new sound. From the left and the right of us, all up and down the sidewalks lining the street, back where the guards were standing. It's a sound like water being sprayed into a fire and sizzling into nothing.

I turn, already knowing what I'll see. The sound is rain vaporizing against the guards' repulsor shields, which they've activated at some point in the five seconds since the power shutdown.

From each side of the street, the guards advance. Not one by one. In lockstep. Together.

Something very close to panic seizes me by the spine. "Jessa!" I scream, but my voice is swallowed by the sound of the shields and the rain and the yelling of everyone else around me when they notice what's going on.

The guards take another step. Steam pours off the glowing orange wall of the collective shield projections. The rain that falls before them doesn't get a chance to hit the ground.

"Jessa!" I can't see her anywhere. I squelch the reflex to try to message her. The people around me are getting agitated. The crowd is rocking back and forth, fighting to keep clear of the repulsors. People are pitching their cups at the oncoming shield wall. It's like throwing mosquitoes onto a bug zapper. At least three separate groups start chanting some kind of protest thing, which breaks up immediately into screams. "Jessa, where are you!"

A rushing, shouting sound from up the street toward the school, and *more* people start stampeding down toward us from somewhere. It's getting too crowded to move.

"They're herding us!" somebody is shouting, hoarse and strange. Gas? Or did they just blow their voice out trying to project? "Stop moving! This is organized assault! They can't chase you if you don't run!" I catch a glimpse of the speaker—a waterlogged person that might have been Jackson, standing in the stirrups of somebody else's hands, shouting through a crappy makeshift megaphone made out of a red plastic cup—before he's toppled from his perch by the jostling crowd.

Herding us where? Away from the school puts us down toward the old highway to the city, where the checkpoints are.

I remember the interrogation pods, the boy on his face on the pavement. But there are too many of us. It makes no sense.

I whirl back around as something bright catches my eye. Brighter than the shields. A teenage girl runs down the street from the direction of the school, holding something burning in her hand. She pitches it in a high overhead arc above the shield wall, forcing the guards beneath it to break the wall and raise their shields over their heads like umbrellas.

The object—a bottle?—smashes against those horizontal shields, and burning oil slips and skitters off the edge, dripping globs of fire onto the guards. They're maybe ten feet up the line from me, and I can hear the burning oil hit the wet ground. It smells like a new-paved street after a summer storm.

The opening in the wall does not go unnoticed. People are pelting the few exposed guards with anything to hand. Cups and bottles, but also broken pieces of sidewalk and glass frontage that have lain in the street since the helicopters arrived. Someone throws a water-credit reader exactly like the one above our sink. Someone else lobs a brick, and it takes a guard square in the face. Bug helmet and all, he staggers.

That's all the invitation needed. People rush the weakness in the line, trying to break back through and flee. I try to run after them, but I'm wedged in place by bodies on all sides, and I can't get any traction on the street. My worn-out shoes slip against the wet pavement, and I get nowhere.

They push and push, and the line almost breaks. And then the guards swing their shields back down into position. Straight down into that tight-packed mass of bodies.

And the bodies go flying.

As far as they can. There isn't much room. They're repelled back against the crowd as the crowd is still pushing forward, and four people—five?—get caught between the press of the crowd and the repulsor field.

And then the real screaming starts.

"Get back!" I try to yell at them, but my voice is for shit in all of this. I shoulder forward and try to haul people backward away from the ones crushed against the shields, but there's nowhere for them to go either. Nowhere for any of us to go. The screaming is only rising in pitch and volume both, joined now by a frying sound and a smell to match. And now it's starting on the other side of the street as the space grows too small to contain the people being chased down from the school.

They're not going to herd us down toward the checkpoint. They're not going to take us anywhere. They're going to pin us down here with their repulsor shields until a helicopter or drone fleet comes in from the city and gasses us. At which point maybe we wake up in jail or maybe we wake up dead.

I try to tell myself that this has nothing to do with me, nothing at all to do with that video I took of 06 and 22 that day. Not really. If I hadn't scared the company into cutting water rations, it would've been someone else eventually.

But this time it was me.

"I need to get up higher," I say. Then I say it louder. "Somebody help me get up higher!" Like they did with Jackson, or whoever that was. Nobody hears me, or nobody cares.

I cup my hands to my mouth and shout, as loud as I can, "I'm Mallory Parker and I give up, I surrender, I turn myself in, just fucking *stop*—"

The crowd is surging behind me now, shoving in every direction at once. I get worked some paces away from the place where the shield wall almost broke, and then the tide turns again, and I get shoved back around toward the movie theater across the street. I step on something that is not pavement. It *gives* underfoot, and I stumble sideways and am steadied by the pushing bodies. I'm bobbing in this fucked-up panic ocean, and I can't turn around.

And then the wall of people behind me starts to break and scatter, inasmuch as they can in the press, leaving a gap just big enough for me to lose my footing and pitch into sidelong.

For one blissful second I don't know what happened, why there's now this space. Then I see the orange glow of the shields. Somehow the crowd's movement has inched me from the center the whole way over to the sidewalk, where the guards are waiting.

"Hey," I yell at them. My voice is fucked, and it comes out as more of a shriek. "I'm Mallory Parker. This all started because of me. Just arrest me and leave them out of this."

Now, I fucking well know the bug helmets amplify sound. Not to the extent that the operatives can hear with their actual ears, but still I'm upwards of ninety-eight percent sure these guards hear me. They just don't give a shit. My window of opportunity for turning myself in was narrow and fleeting and closed up shop days ago, and they probably would've just tossed me in the plastic digesters anyway, maybe even doing me the kindness of shooting me first.

As it is, the bug helmets stare me down impassively while the crowd to all sides pitches and I trip over something else lying in the street and I look down to make sure it isn't what I hope to shit it's not and it is—of course it is. I'm standing on a fucking person, and she's not moving, and there's blood coming out of her ear. "*Move!*" I scream, and nobody moves, and I'm trying to clear space and haul this girl up by her shoulders when the crowd senses the tiny open space around me and moves to fill it. They heave up behind me, and I'm thrown bodily forward onto the shield wall.

It should be flinging me backward, I have a few seconds to think before I black out. *It's a repulsor. I should be being repulsed.*

But there's nowhere for me to be repulsed *to*. My feet aren't even touching the ground anymore. I'm pinned to the orange glow of the forcefield projection like a fly on a windshield. My teeth are vibrating in my head. It feels like my eyeballs are going to shiver into warm jelly and run down my face. Like every part of me that's touching the shield is trying to dissolve into its constituent atoms and scatter.

Disperse is the last thought I can grab hold of, and then I drop down into the dark.

part four

NPC

"—THAT IF I WERE YOU."

Bright light. White. Smells like a hospital. I try to stand up, and something stops me. A tugging sensation in my arm. But something else besides. I can't lift my head. A helmet? I reach up to touch it, can't. Neither arm will move. I try to turn my head, and some injury to my face I wasn't aware I had rockets up out of nowhere to brush a solid eight on the pain scale.

"Like I said. I wouldn't do that if I were you."

I blink and blink. It's like I've been in a dark room for ages and walked out into the full beam of a spotlight. Shapes blur and resolve. A white room. Small. There's a table and mirror. Someone sitting across from me: business suit, slick hair, patient hands folded. Heavy door. Keypad, no handle. The light isn't as bright as I thought, just overhead fluorescents.

I strain my gaze downward. My eyes feel like someone took them out, rolled them in an ashtray, and put them back in, but they work fine.

My clothes are gone. I'm wearing some kind of hospital gown, but I'm not in a hospital bed. I'm sitting in a hardback chair. There's an IV line in the crook of my right elbow. My wrists are attached to the arms of the chair. Nanofilament cuffs. They've always looked so flimsy in news clips of arrests. They're not.

I try to move my legs. Something around my ankles says no. The chair is bolted to the floor.

It comes back to me: the crowd, the shield, the repulsor shivering hotly against my face like something alive. And then—

"Where am I?"

Though the answer can't be anything good. White room, bright light, two-way mirror, restraints. I've seen enough movies to know where this is going.

"Pleased to finally meet you in person, Ms. Parker. We'd like to ask you a few questions."

"Am I under arrest? On what charge? Where are the people who were with me?" *Where are Jessa and my roommates,* I want to ask, but then I remember something that stops me cold. Something 22 said to me. *We could have. And painted those people with a twenty-ton target.* I grit my teeth. If by some miracle they don't have Jessa and the others, they're sure as shit not going to get them from me.

He sips from his dispenser coffee, says nothing.

"I know my rights. I demand to know where I'm being held, and by whom, and why."

Silence.

The phrase *intimidation tactics* floats up from the murk of my brain. I picture the white room broadcast on all news channels. My reaction. My groveling. My fear. I thought they wouldn't risk martyring me. Now I'm not so sure. This looks to be skewing alarmingly in the direction of *make an example.*

That's when I recognize the hospital smell of this place. The white walls. Even the pattern of the tile floor is familiar. I'm back in Stellaxis HQ.

I think of 06 and 22 and B and Elena and whoever I stepped on in the street. Of everyone in old town assuming I sold them out. Of fake Nycorix's t-shirt: RESIST. There's a joke here, but I'm too fucked up on adrenaline and shock and fear and rage and pain to bring it fully into mind.

"I can help you," I whisper to a 22 who's not here. A noise comes out of me, half laugh, half cough, when I realize I've whispered aloud. Or at least I think I did. My mind is full of dulled echoes, a layer of soundproofing between my thoughts and me.

Maybe I'm still unconscious. Maybe I'm dreaming. Maybe it's me being trampled in the street. I hope 22 never believed me. I hope he had a good laugh with 06 about the sadsack fangirl after sending me home in that company car. Help you indeed. Because I'm so good at that. Helping.

"I was hoping you'd say that," says the suit at the table.

I wasn't talking to you, I think, and swallow another nervous laugh.

"This will be simpler for all of us if you cooperate."

"Oh good." I'm rapidly passing into the overwrought-babbling phase of things, I note. "That was definitely my top concern here. Simplicity."

"Who hired you to incite the riot on the sixth of April?"

This does wonders to clear my head. Anticorporate agitation is a terrorism charge, even heavier than water poaching. If they can land that on me, I'm done. "I didn't incite any riot. I called for a legal, peaceful protest. It hasn't even happened yet. What happened on April sixth was that we were attacked."

"There is extensive surveillance footage that puts you in the middle of the riot of the sixth of April. It began as you exited the hotel, and followed directly on the heels of a little speech posted online from inside the building." Suit guy holds a fist out and opens it. A holoscreen projection floats up from the implant in his palm. There's my face, wearing the stupid dazed expression I get when there's too much shit going on around me and it jams the signals from my brain. In the video, Keisha is walking backward down the stairs, declaiming, *That puppet shit you saw? Remember whose channel you saw that on! Are you really going to believe the same people who cut off our water?*

"Yeah," I say. "They were thirsty. It was raining. It wasn't any riot. Their water had been cut off, which by the way none of them deserved. They were trying to keep their fucking kidneys from failing."

"Prior to this you had been posting inflammatory videos defaming Stellaxis Innovations. Videos that serve no conceivable purpose but to foment paranoia and unrest. You were caught on camera entering Stellaxis Innovations HQ on the evening of the fourteenth of March in the company of SecOps operatives 06 and 22. I'll ask again. Who hired you?"

"Stellaxis Innovations HQ, by which you mean where we are right now?"

I hoped to unbalance him, but suit guy just smiles blandly. "I'm asking the questions today, Ms. Parker."

"So go ask 06 and 22. I was helping them escort some refugees to the hospital. They'll corroborate my story."

"You did not bring refugees to the hospital. You brought them to Stellaxis HQ."

"Because the hospital wouldn't let—"

"Where you took footage of company property—private property, Ms. Parker—and shared it publicly. Do I need to spell out how illegal that is?"

Something flickered across his face when I told him to ask 06 and 22. Annoyance? I decide to test this. I arrange my body language into the best possible analogue of stubbornly folded arms that I can manage with my arms, well, restrained. "Like I said. Don't believe me? Ask 06 and 22."

There it is again. He's burying his reaction admirably, but something about what I said is visibly pissing him off.

I walk it back a little, see if I can gain some breathing space. If I can put this jackass more at ease, I might be able to get him talking. More than this anyway.

"I'm sorry," I make myself say. "I make my living streaming live broadcasts of video games. I guess recording is a habit. I started taking video that day so I could show my friend, and then that mech started attacking and I was running with all those people and there was all this *screaming . . .*" I trail off, let myself go glassy-eyed. *I've seen some shit,* I try to project at him. *I was not my absolute best self that day.* "They said we were going to the hospital, but the hospital was full. Then they asked me to keep walking, so I kept walking. I was so tired. We were all so, so tired. It's so second nature, what with my job and all, I guess I just . . . forgot to stop recording."

"You forgot," suit guy says, and his tone is the tone Jessa gives me when I say I forgot to unmute the subscriber audience on a stream.

I try to shrug helplessly. On several levels, this proves difficult.

He looks at me. I look back at him.

"SecOps operatives 06 and 22 were providing an escort to wounded civilians," he says. "A situation of which you took advantage. What you are here to tell me is what you were doing there in the first place."

"Like I said in one of the videos you just said you knew about, I took a bus to the city to go to the coffee shop. Which is now gone. I was understandably a little confused to see the place had been *completely erased*, so I took a walk to think. I ran into some fighting. You saw the rest."

"And you were going to the coffee shop to meet with this woman, I believe?"

The holoscreen shows a mug shot of B. Her hair is different in it. It's not a new picture. Possibly from when she was arrested on her water terrorism charge?

"Yeah."

"For what reason?"

"It's in the video."

"Indulge me."

"She hired me. Payment never came through. I couldn't get hold of her online. I didn't want to keep working for free, so I went looking for her."

"I wonder how you thought you'd *get hold of her online*," suit guy says. "She was serving a five-year penalty. Her lenses were inoperable."

"Her sister set up the one meeting we had. But you know that. She disappeared too."

"Is this who you mean?"

Photo of a woman. If it's the same one I caught a glimpse of behind the coffee shop counter, I'm not sure.

This one's not a mug shot. She's dead.

The fact that I've just apologized to this smug fuck, whether or not I meant it, is burning in the back of my throat like bile. I just stop myself from asking what happened to B's sister. I know what happened to her. She had an accident. She tripped and fell onto some company bullets.

"I'll ask again," suit guy says. "Who hired you to record footage of the interior of the Stellaxis building?"

"Nobody." My voice cracks. "I told you. It was my idea."

"No, Ms. Parker," he says gently. "You told me you forgot."

"I meant it was my idea to record *initially*," I say. Struggling to sound calm. Like a person who hasn't just been caught out contradicting her own story. B's sister's dead face stares out of the holoscreen at me. Of course he hasn't taken the photo down. I wonder if there's another photo he's waiting to show me, this one of Jessa. I push the thought away. "In the street. With the mech. Then when we got to Stellaxis HQ, I guess I just—"

"Forgot? Yes, you said."

"There was kind of a lot going on. You have to understand. I come from old town. Not the city. Where I live, mechs trashing buildings in the street isn't exactly an everyday occurrence. It scared the shit out of me."

"Did it?" Suit guy's brow furrows. Up comes a clip from my second video. He gestures at it with his other hand until it gets to the part he's after.

There's the front-desk guard at the company building, looking at our wounded-civilian crowd suspiciously. "They're not recording?"

And 06 telegraphs massive annoyance and shouts, "Do these people *look* like they're recording?" I glance down fast to hide the fact that I *absolutely am*, so we just get 06's voice for the rest, overlaid over the image of the tiled lobby floor and the tops of my sneakers. *"Well?"*

The holoscreen freezes.

"She didn't know," I say. "She never asked me if I was."

Even leaving my mouth it sounds unlikely, though at least the second part is technically true. Still, it doesn't explain 22. There he is in the playback, faster even than my downswept gaze, having moved ever so subtly to block me from clear view while 06 keeps the guard's attention on her.

Suit guy says nothing, just gestures at the video to replay those last couple of seconds. It's unmistakable. I looked down to hide my uninjured eyes from the guard. The only eyes in that crowd apart from 06's and 22's that *could* possibly be recording. But that's not the worst of it.

22 is not given to aimless fidgeting. His movements are calculated, meticulous, efficient, precise. And he moved to cover me, and suit guy has the footage to prove it.

Footage that I took.

Fuck.

Suit guy eyes me. Maybe he's waiting for me to sell out 06

and 22, like I haven't already accidentally done that by posting the second video. As far as I'm concerned, he can wait until the heat death of the goddamn universe. They covered for me. Least I can do is return the favor.

"Do by all means take your time, Ms. Parker," suit guy says. "Sometimes in a stressful situation such as you describe, it takes some while for the details to return fully to memory. I understand completely. Please do not rush to force recall on my account. You will find over the coming days that I am in no hurry at all."

He unfolds to his feet and crosses the room to the door. It's all I can do to keep myself from saying *No, stop, don't leave me here, I'll tell you whatever you want to know.*

And then that window of opportunity closes too.

TIME PASSES. I'M not sure how much. The lights are always on. Always the same brightness. No windows on the outside world. Suit guy's presence gave shape to my fear, transformed it into something that felt more like anger. Anger at least is a motivator. Now he's gone, and it's just the drip of the IV and the faintly audible buzz as one of the lights in the ceiling slowly dies. The chair digs into my back. I desperately have to pee.

I try not to think of Jessa and the others. Of 06 and 22. If I'm in trouble here, where are they? I can't really picture what *trouble* would look like for them. I can't imagine them cuffed to chairs in interrogation rooms. What's suit guy even trying to get me to say? Greenleaf Industries hired me to, what? Post intel on Stellaxis HQ to the entire internet? Wouldn't I just, like, *sell* the footage to the Greenleaf newscasts if I actually stood to gain?

Only in my head, probably, does the truth make more sense. Somehow I doubt the whole *the object of my lifelong fangirl friendcrush trusted me to do something, I had to at least try* angle is going to play well to this crowd.

For a while I expect some muscle to show up and torture me until I talk. I think of the screams I heard coming out of the interrogation pod by the checkpoint, and cold sweat runs down my back. But nobody appears.

The idea strikes me that they don't want to torture me in a way that leaves visible marks. They could kick the shit out of me right here, just like they could kill me when they're done with me, but that would look too much like martyrdom.

For now, at least, they must be planning to let me go.

Eventually.

Maybe.

I keep trying to check the time on my lenses. But my lenses don't work. They're still there, still in my eyes, they just don't interface. I'm still locked out. It's almost funny how little sense of time I have without them. Or maybe it's this room fucking with me. Days and nights could pass, and the light wouldn't change.

After an interval a doctor-looking person comes in to check on me. White coat, handheld screen, syringes. They could have sent a medbot. I guess they want me to know how seriously they're taking my residency here.

She changes out the bag on my drip. "Fluids," she explains. "You were dehydrated."

No shit.

Takes my vitals. Does something to whatever's wrong with my face. She peels something away that I can't see—smart bandages, at a guess—and the air-conditioning hits my exposed skin like a blowtorch.

I'm tempted to ask for a mirror. Then I think better of it. I don't want to give them the satisfaction of refusing my requests. Or of seeing the expression on my face when I see how bad the damage is.

"Do you need anything?" she asks, once she's replaced the smart bandages. A lot of smart bandages, from the look of the pile of wrappers on the table.

Get me out of this fucking chair for starters, I'm tempted to reply, but very soon I'm going to have to choose between swallowing my pride and pissing on the floor. "I need to use the bathroom."

She produces a bedpan. *Not happening*, I want to say. Instead I shut my eyes and nod.

The doctor comes back later to disconnect the IV. Takes a few vials of blood. Sticks me with a syringe of something. I don't ask, and she doesn't say. Then she leaves.

Pain meds. There were pain meds in the syringe. Probably. I'm not asking them that, either. But whatever it is, it's not enough. It barely takes the edge off. I've got bruises on bruises, and every muscle in my body is sore from fighting to keep my footing in that crowd. But the worst of it is where I was crushed against the shield. The side of my face and neck, the arm I tried and failed to wedge in between and push off the shield, that shoulder and hand, all feel like someone's pressing them to a stove top and gradually turning up the heat one degree at a time.

No. The pain meds weren't in the syringe. They were in the IV. And now it's gone.

They're trying to grind me down. Well, fuck them.

Slowly, agonizingly, one millimeter at a time, against the restraints and the pain and the voice in my head telling me to stop before I damage something worse, I force my head to turn.

That has to be a two-way mirror. Who's behind it? Suit guy with his coffee? Somebody worse? Distantly I wonder if somebody just watched me pee.

More time passes. The ceiling of this room is divided into one hundred twenty-eight squares. There are forty-nine floor tiles that I can see, only eighteen of which are not broken up by the lines of the table and suit guy's abandoned chair. There are sixteen whole white-painted cinder blocks reflected in the two-way mirror, and if I add the fractions of the partially reflected ones together, I get another ten. I can hold my breath for thirty-nine seconds before my vision starts to sparkle. I should really work on that.

At some point they bring me food. Water. A big cold glass of it. Ice and lemon. Condensation beaded down the sides. The fact that it looks exactly like the glass of water 22 poured me a lifetime ago is almost definitely no accident.

A bot comes in and sets it all down on the table and then leaves. Nobody uncuffs my wrists. They just leave me here with it. Who knows how long. My stomach went beyond growling some while ago and is now trying to chew off its own leg. The water in that glass is the most beautiful thing I've ever seen.

I sit there long enough for the food to congeal, the ice in the glass to melt. Then suit guy comes back in. He doesn't undo the restraints either.

"Who do you work for?"

"I'm a game streamer. I work for my subscribers. Like the one you people killed."

"Who sent you to take footage of the Stellaxis Innovations sublevels?"

The sublevels specifically. Interesting. He watches this register in my face and flushes with anger.

"Look. Whoever it is, they're not coming for you. I am trying to treat you civilly here."

"By tying me to a chair?"

"By not doing worse. I'm willing to buy that you're a dumb kid who got in over her head. But for that to happen, I need you to tell me who put you up to it."

"Nobody put me up to anything."

"Right." He reaches across the table, slides the glass of water back across toward him, takes a sip. "You forgot."

"No." *You unmitigated douche.* "I didn't. But there's no way I could possibly make somebody like you understand."

"I'm afraid you're going to have to try."

"Have you ever been to old town?"

He nearly spit-takes my water. Asshole. "I can't say I've had the pleasure."

"In old town, that glass of water is half a day's ration. That's for eating, bathing, laundry, cooking, making coffee, brushing your teeth, flushing your toilet, whatever. You want more water, you're buying it. A dollar an ounce at the company store. Almost nobody has jobs, not full-time city jobs. All the abandoned stores and restaurants and stuff have people living in them. I live in a hotel room with eight other people. One hundred percent of my income for the past couple of weeks has been from the internet. Before that, in case you were wondering, I used to walk dogs." Very glamorous. Very spylike.

"Elaborate, please."

"On the dogs? Well, there's this—"

"No."

I fail to shrug. "I stream a video game. I post videos. People pay me tips. A few dollars here, an ounce of water there. The more interesting the stream, the more tips. The more time I can borrow before I'm in a fucking rehydration clinic getting new kidneys printed. Okay?"

For a long, long moment he watches me. "You can't possibly be trying to convince me that you posted that video for *tips.*"

"Really? Look, I don't know how much people get paid to walk dogs where you come from, but—"

He tilts his head to one side, like he's just heard some fascinating distant sound. "Then why not post it immediately? You sat on the second half of the footage for days. Why?"

"I wanted to post the first half first," I say. "Give people a taste. Like a cliffhanger in a TV show?"

Suit guy smiles like a shark. "Do you want to know what I think?"

I don't trust my mouth to answer this, so I just sit back and wait.

"I think something happened to your contact and left you holding the bag. I don't know why you posted that video eventually, and honestly I don't care. I want to know who you were reporting to in the first place."

He wants me to say *Greenleaf Industries*, or drop the name of some kind of mole or double agent or I don't even know what. The only person from the Greenleaf side I could even name-drop if I wanted to is the CEO, and that's only because she shows up on the news.

"I'm not a spy," I say tiredly. "I'm telling you. Up until last month, I used to walk dogs. Streaming pays better. Believe me—I wish I had a shiny glamorous secret job. I probably wouldn't be so thirsty all the fucking time."

He sets both palms flat against the table and leans forward conspiratorially. "If only that explained the later videos you posted," he says. "Or the riot you incited." He swipes the still from the HQ video down to the smart surface of the table. 22's back and shoulder shielding me from view. 06 in the background, up in the guard's face. "Or whatever I'm looking at here."

"We were taking those people to the doctor, the medical bay, whatever you call it here. Their lenses had melted to their *actual eyeballs*. That's what you're looking at. That's all that happened. Watch the video again. Does it look like I'm trying to sneak around taking secret footage? We go to the medical bay and then to the cafeteria. Then I go home."

"Oh, but you're leaving out one of the most interesting parts." Suit guy swipes the video forward and forward, the whole way to the end. 22 stares up from the table at me. Suit guy unpauses the video, and my voice drifts up tinnily from the smart surface: *Wait. Wait.* "You stop recording here. In the elevator. Why?"

I open my mouth, then close it. *I wanted 22 to trust me* isn't going to get me very far here. Or, for that matter, *why* I needed him to. What I was about to say to him next. *I can help you.*

Sure I can.

I'm trying, man. I'm really, really trying. But I'm useless at this. You should have been in that elevator with someone else. Someone who can make good on the shit that falls out of their mouth.

"I panicked," I say. "I thought he was going to kill me."

"One would think you might have attempted to *exit* the elevator in that case, Ms. Parker. Not lock yourself in with him."

"Like I said. I panicked."

Suit guy gives a disappointed little head shake. "Well. This *is* confusing. Up until that point in the video, the overwhelming impression one gets is that the two of you were getting along rather well."

"I was in the right place at the right time," I say stiffly. This part is, at least, true. "I helped them with those people. They got me some food and gave me a free ride home. Benefited everyone."

"You like to help people, don't you." The image on the table changes. Surveillance footage. Me giving up my spot in water line. Me swiping water to the people in line behind me. Me buying those candy bars for those sad kids. How did they even know I did that? Watched me and made an educated guess, based on the rest of it?

Because there's a *lot* of it. Going back years. How the fuck much homework have they done on me? "Then help us. Tell us what we need to know."

"About *what*?"

For a moment he seems to weigh something in his mind. "About this."

The image on the table changes. It's newsfeed footage. Blurry, drone-taken, distant. A figure in dark clothes stands in the middle of a city intersection, a ring of bodies around its feet. All the bodies are in uniform. Stellaxis army uniform.

The image zooms in slightly, sharpens. It's 06.

I suck in a breath.

"What am I looking at?" Suit guy says nothing. I look up to find him scrutinizing my face. "That can't be 06—those are your guys on the ground—" Reflexively I go to shake my head, then realize that doesn't work here. "When did this happen?"

"Yesterday." Not that this means anything to me, really. I couldn't have told him what day it is now, not if I had a gun to my head. Is this still the day of the supposed riot? It feels like days later, but I can't say for sure. This white room eats time. "SecOps operatives 06 and 22 smuggling you into Stellaxis headquarters, your amateurish exposé, the riot in old town, and now this? These things are obviously connected. We need your help to figure out how."

I bark a laugh. "*My* help? I didn't know anything about this. She—" I can't stop staring at the footage. Are all those people dead? I blink, and 22 is in the ring of bodies with 06. A glitch in the footage? Or are they really that fast? He's holding 06 up two-handed by her jacket front. He looks epically pissed.

The drone cam doesn't pick up whatever he says to her or what she replies, but he puts her down. They talk for a few more seconds. Then 06 takes off running, and 22 lets her go.

It's a moment before I find my voice. Pride be damned, stoicism be damned, I have to know. "What is this?"

"Treason," suit guy says, "is what it is."

"But what exactly did she—"

"You ask a lot of questions for someone who refuses to answer any. The details are a bit above your pay grade, I'm afraid." He chuckles. "Or are they? For all I know, you know more than we do." Abruptly he switches gears on me. "I don't want to have to send you to questioning."

"What's this, then? The waiting room?"

"Something like that. I'm what you might call the first line of defense. The gentler, more civilized line of defense." He holds one hand out over the table and makes a crumpling gesture. 22 and the ring of bodies vanish. "Someone got to 06. Put ideas in her head. I am thinking you were the courier of said ideas. That your meeting with them on the fourteenth of March was arranged for the purpose of *delivering* said ideas. That you delivered them at some point after you stopped recording that video. And that the riot you incited was a ploy to distract attention from 06's sabotage of a hostage transfer."

This perks me up. He'd said that was yesterday. Does that mean the so-called riot was somehow yesterday too? Fuck, it feels like ten times that long ago.

Wait.

"Hostage transfer?"

Suit guy draws himself up and glares at the sudden brightening of my expression. He's said too much. "The only piece I am missing," he hisses, "is the name of the person or persons who hired you to do so. That is what you are here to provide, and you will remain here until you provide it. Is that clear?"

I turn my face away, inasmuch as the restraints allow. Suit guy literally *tsk*s. Gets up. Crosses over to my side of the table. Cups my face in one hand. Jams his thumb in under the smart bandage.

I can't help it. I scream.

"Take your time," he whispers. And then he's gone.

ALL MY FEEDING and hydration gets done through the IV. My toilet is the pink plastic bedpan. My bed is the chair. Occasionally they bring in food and water, as before, to try to break me. But what they don't seem to understand is that old town people are used to being hungry and thirsty, used to food scents blowing over from city restaurants when the wind is right, used to seeing ads for delicious things we can't afford to eat. They're not breaking shit.

Nobody lets me wash. My mouth tastes like something died in it. The lights stay on.

My face is healing, though. Bit by bit. The pain has receded to a dull wash of background noise. When did that happen?

I can't feel my legs anymore. It's a goddamn miracle I haven't died of a blood clot, sitting here this long. Maybe the doctor shot me up with something to prevent that from happening. How considerate.

They bring the food at odd times. Sometimes it seems like one meal has just grown cold on the table before the next one comes. Sometimes it seems like a plate will sit for days. It's hard to say for sure. I can't picture anything rotting in the aggressive air-conditioning of this place. No flies or ants appear. Anyway, I can't judge time from the level of my thirst or hunger. They do not lessen.

At one point something slams the wall to my left, hard, once. I think of calling out to whatever made that noise, then think better of it. The sound doesn't come again. Nothing else of note occurs.

Suit guy comes with questions. Leaves with the same answers as before. He seems harried now, distracted, like I'm an after-thought, a sideshow to some main event happening elsewhere.

I have a long, long time to think about what suit guy said to me. What 06 and 22 said two—three? more?—weeks ago. What they didn't say. What they were speaking careful circles around.

They wanted out. I could tell that much from two hours in HQ. I don't know what 06 was doing in that clip, I don't know what hostage transfer she's supposed to have sabotaged, but I don't think she switched sides or whatever it is they're accusing her of. I think she was looking for the exit.

I wonder where they are. 06 and 22. I hope to whatever the fuck is listening that they got away, and the company is sitting on me like an egg because the answer they're trying to hatch is *where the hell they've gone.*

"Go," I whisper to the white room airily. "Run. I told you I could help."

I'm probably losing my mind.

Whatever else happens, Jessa's not here. That much I'm sure of. If she was, they would've used her against me. Or me against her. They would have tortured one of us in front of the other. They would have at least threatened it.

Which means either she's still in old town or she's dead.

"Did you ever consider," I say to suit guy at one point, "that maybe 06 wasn't working for anyone? That nobody *got to* her? That maybe she just wanted out of the war? Out of this place? And she decided to do something about it?"

He stares holes through me in silence. He looks almost as tired as I feel. Then he leaves.

The white room lines up hours and chain-smokes them, one by one.

I have a lot of time to think about everything 22 said to me in that cafeteria. And everything he didn't say. But I try not to. For all I know, they're reading my thoughts through my implant, lenses or no. Who knows what kind of nefarious-shit tech they have here.

I have an equal amount of time to think about how stupid we've all been, all this time. Believing everything the company told us, whether it made sense or not, just because it had a full-scale media/marketing juggernaut to back it up. And what were our suspicions in the face of that? *I'm sorry,* I think at all ten dead operatives in turn. *We were all too fucking dumb to save you.*

For a while I dare to hope suit guy's forgotten to follow through on his threat of having me tortured.

He hasn't.

He comes in empty-eyed, hands in pockets. His jacket is gone, and the rest of his suit looks like he slept in it, and not for very long. His shirtsleeves are rolled up. There's dried blood on them. "Who sent you to the Stellaxis building?" he asks. "Who paid you to incite the riot on April sixth? What message did they have you deliver to SecOps operatives 06 and 22 on March fourteenth?"

A litany I know by heart. But the syringe he's pulling out of his pocket is new.

"Do you know what this is?"

I try to come up with some snarky response, but what's on his face sobers me. He looks like someone who's about to have to do something he really rather wouldn't. I shake my head. In the restraints it comes out as more of a quiver.

"I don't like blood," he informs me.

"Really? You got some on your shirt."

He grimaces faintly. "Yes, well. It's been a trying few days. You're not the most interesting puzzle down here this week. Or the hardest to crack."

06, I realize. He means 06. The blood on his sleeve. The most interesting puzzle. They didn't get out after all.

Which makes no sense. I saw that video. 22 and 06 in that ring of bodies. He let her *go*.

I scramble to throw a mask of defiance over the alarm on my face. "I don't know," I say weakly. "I think I'm doing okay so far."

He doesn't deign to reply to that, just stalks over and jabs me in the muscle of my shoulder, right through the hospital gown. "The *fuck*—" I gasp, but he ignores me. Takes a step back, as if to admire his handiwork, and throws up an image on the tabletop. It takes me a moment to recognize it as a person.

It's curled up unnaturally, like someone who's been imprinted upon by a resonance grenade, but the bones don't look to have snapped. It looks more like it's been mummified. Like something dug out of a desert cave. And yet the color of its skin is weirdly mottled. It's hard to tell through all the desiccation, but it looks bruised.

It's obviously dead. Long dead.

Then it moves.

"As I said, I don't like blood, and as you've noticed, I've seen more of it this week than I'd prefer. This way is much cleaner, wouldn't you say?" His eyes do the classic dart-to-the-corner of a person checking the time on their lenses. "Within about twenty minutes, you'll start to feel very thirsty. You will want to be talking by then." He taps the table. "This is you in about five hours. By that point you will have passed the point of no return. You will be experiencing the onset of cascading organ failure two hours before that. At some point your airways will become so dehydrated that the mucous membranes in your throat and lungs will rupture and bleed. Ditto the mucous membranes in your mouth and nose, your intestines, et cetera. Ditto the walls of your blood vessels. By that point it will really be in your *very* best interest to have already answered all my questions in *as* much detail as you feel inspired so to do. Now." He pulls a case out of a pocket. In it is a second syringe. "This will deactivate the nanobots that are currently swimming around in your bloodstream. And it's all yours. As soon as you tell me what I want to know. At which point—"

He breaks off as a look I remember all too well comes over his face. Something happening on his lenses. Something big.

At first he looks almost relieved he doesn't have to stick around and watch this nightmare scenario play out on my body. Over the next few seconds the enormity of whatever he has to do instead visibly sinks in.

The condescending dickhead demeanor falls away. Under it he's pale and scared. His eyes flick back and forth, scrolling through something. "Shit," he whispers. Then, in a very different voice from any of the ones he's used on me in however long I've been here: "I'll be right back." He whirls around, one hand held out to the keypad. It's shaking so hard the reader is having a hard time recognizing him.

"Wait!" I start yelling. "You can't fucking leave me here with that stuff in me. I'll talk. Okay? I'll tell you everything. Don't—"

I'm still yelling as he steps out into the hall without looking back. As the door whispers shut behind him. As I hear his footsteps hurry away.

The tabletop catches my eye. Overlaid on the image of the dying person, there's an alert banner flashing red. It's still interfacing with his implant, and he's not yet out of range. *ATTENTION. EMERGENCY ON SUBLEVEL A. ALL SECURITY PERSONNEL REPORT.*

There's more, but I don't have time to read it before his implant finally passes out of range and the whole smart surface goes dark.

It's all I can do to slow the pulse hammering at my ears. I'm locked in a room, cuffed to a chair, shot up full of slow-acting murder. While fuck knows what goes on out there in the hall.

Sublevel A. That's where I was before, with 06 and 22. Where Medical is. Am I on sublevel A *now*?

If I break my thumbs, I might be able to get out of these cuffs. It works in the movies anyway. But that's with old-timey metal handcuffs, which are not my problem here. All that's going to accomplish is losing me the use of my hands. If I ever have use of them again before I turn into that thing on the table. Which looks unlikely.

I'm thirsty. Am I thirstier than usual? I'm not sure. My eyes and mouth are dry. But they've been dry. The air-conditioning is cranked to somewhere just above freezing, and I haven't been drinking anything. There's bruising on my wrists, but that's from struggling against the cuffs for days. At least . . . I think it is? Suit guy hasn't been gone that long. Or has he? How would I know?

I scream at the door for a while. Nobody comes. I'm definitely thirstier now, and there's a headache blossoming behind my eyes. Part of that could be from the screaming. What does twenty minutes look like in the white room? What about an hour? What about two? The bruises on my wrists aren't any worse. I run my tongue along my gum line, tasting for blood.

Noise outside, somewhere out there down the hall. Crashing. Shouting. Gunshots. Some crazy fucking notion lodges in my head that Jessa and Keisha and Tegan and the others have led some kind of rescue army in here after me. The white room's wicking my rational mind away. I start shrieking, *help, let me out, I'm in here,* and a sudden hush falls on whatever shitshow is underway down the hall. Then another burst of gunfire, the loudest crash yet, the panicked screams of several people all at once—then silence.

I don't hear footsteps approach the white-room door. I don't hear the distinctive beep of the keypad reader. There comes a paint-peeling screech of metal tearing, and suddenly there's a hole in the wall where the door used to be.

Standing in the middle of it is 22.

He's got more blood on him than suit guy did. A lot more. His expression is a total blank. He grips his sword—blood on that, too, lots of blood—and stalks into the room.

With sudden, perfect clarity I realize the following four facts:

All the crashes I heard previously were other locked doors elsewhere in the building being ripped out and flung across the hall. All the screams were from the people behind them. I'm looking at the emergency that summoned suit guy from the white room. And the next casualty of it is going to be me.

22 stands above me, flat annihilation in his eyes. I'm not sure he's even seeing me. Just something in the way. No, not even that. Like he's pattern seeking, and I'm a person-shaped object.

This is something worse than on-duty 22. This is off-the-rails 22. It's not that his switch has flipped. It's that his switch has *broken*. I never should have drawn his attention. Slowly, casually, almost languidly, he raises the sword.

I try and fail to throw my arms up between my body and the blade. *Wait*, I try to say. *It's me, I'm not one of them, they locked me up in here, I'm on your side, I promise, don't fucking kill me.* But my mouth won't work to make words. After all this, I'm going to die here in this fucking chair. At least it'll be faster than the syringe.

The blade flashes down—and stops, a millimeter at most from my head.

Behind it, 22 has drawn me into focus. He zeroes in on my face. He's examining me.

"It's me," I croak. "Mal. From before. Remember?"

He looks at me a second longer. Then, with a speed and accuracy and delicacy that will break my brain if I stop to think about it, the sword moves, and the nanofilament bindings at my wrists and ankles fall away. Then he slings the blood off his blade, sheathes it, reaches toward my head with both gloved hands. *He wouldn't cut you free and then crush your skull*, I just have time to think, when I feel a pressure lift from around my head, a pressure I'd gotten so accustomed to I'd almost forgotten it was there. 22's hands return to my field of vision with a kind of metal band held between them. I have no idea what purpose it even served, except to maximize my discomfort. At which task it performed admirably.

22 nods at me once, like he's just satisfactorily completed a transaction. Then turns on his literal heel and stalks back out.

"Wait," I yell after him. "I need to find—"

I scramble to my feet and fall over. My legs have forgotten how to work. By the time I stumble out into the hall, he's gone.

Knowing what I'm going to see out here isn't nearly enough to prepare me for it. Every door has been ripped off and flung hard enough to crater cinder-block walls. There's blood everywhere. Bodies everywhere. Heavily armed bodies. Security officers. Walking arsenals. All dead. It's so over the top that I'm staring around me in a kind of numbed awe.

I have no idea what happened to provoke the massacre I'm looking at, but I don't see suit guy, and I don't see his antidote syringe, and at the moment that's enough to narrow my focus to a laser point. I pick up a gun from the floor, hoping to all the gods of handheld weaponry that it works enough like an in-game blaster that I can figure it out, and I start walking.

I'm starting to feel like reheated shit now, and it's slow going. My throat feels like someone took a belt sander to it. My head is pounding hard enough to make my vision pulse white. If someone takes a shot at me, I'm going to absolutely die.

Nobody does. This wing of whatever sublevel I'm on is dead, figuratively and literally. Whatever sent 22 on this rampage, he's executed it with characteristic meticulousness. I can hear more screams and gunfire in the distance, but it's moving off. Nobody's paying any attention to me.

I go from body to body, looking for suit guy and his syringe. He's not here. I zigzag up the hallway, checking each room. No suit guy there, either. I find a map on the wall near a water fountain. It's not a holoscreen, just old-school printed plastic with a YOU ARE HERE star on a branch of blue-coded hall. I bend my head to the water fountain and drink and drink. Then I force my attention to the map. The white room is labeled, predictably, INTERROGATION. There are six of these rooms in total. Why the fuck they need a half dozen interrogation cells is beyond me. The rest are empty, but one looks to have been recently used.

There's a coffee ring on the table nobody got around to cleaning, and a faint smell of cigarettes. Also, this room's version of my chair has been ripped partially out of the floor. Blood spatter on the tile. The same blood I saw on suit guy's sleeves? 06's blood? I don't stick around.

Halfway up the hall I double over coughing. I spit out phlegm, which turns out to be a blood clot the size of my fingertip. I stare at it for a second. Then I hurry on.

The hall ends in a T junction. I go left. Gun first, I slip into each room. No suit guy. No syringe. No 22.

One room is obviously empty of these things, but I linger anyway. There's a bank of holoscreens displaying what I assume to be surveillance footage. One screen is frozen in place, flickering, like the security camera that informs it has been damaged and this was the last image fed back to this room. It's timestamped, but after the white room, that tells me almost nothing. From the carnage in the halls, I'm guessing it wasn't all that long ago.

It shows a room I don't recognize. It's big and dark and full of dead bodies. Easily twenty of them, scattered around the floor like they've been dropped there from a height.

A little ways away from them there's one that doesn't match. All the others are wearing security uniforms or lab whites. This one's wearing a jumpsuit with two bullet holes punched through it, belly and chest. It's lying there, and 22 is kneeling beside it, fists knotted in the front of the jumpsuit like he's trying to shake this dead person awake.

Since the image is frozen in such a way that 22's shaking has angled the body's face toward the camera, I can make it out. Although, given 22's reaction, I could have figured.

I guess I know now where 06 went, when her own white room was done with her.

Another coughing fit doubles me over. My mouth tastes like rusty nails.

I lose track of how long I walk. I have no idea how it measures against the time I have left. *Cascading organ failure*, I think. *Point of no return.* I stagger past more bodies than I can count. I can't tell how much blood smell is coming from them and how much is coming from inside me. The next left takes me to the cafeteria where I sat with 22 a million years ago. That door doesn't have a keypad lock, so it admits me. I poke the gun in first. But nobody's there.

I'm running out of time.

I try to retrace my steps to the medical bay where we brought the civilian casualties. It's a last-ditch effort. Even if there are preloaded syringes there, they'll be locked up, and besides I won't know which one I'm looking for, but I have to try. When I eventually find the room, though, the door's locked, and I have no way of opening it. Outstanding.

Strange, though. Medical isn't trashed. It's pristine. Then again, so was the cafeteria. And every room I passed since that last left-hand turn that took me there. I wasn't paying full attention because I was so bent on reaching the medical bay. But I'm paying attention now.

I pause to drink from the water fountain here—the same one 06 pointed out to me two weeks ago, and by no means is this getting less surreal—then start retracing my steps again. If suit guy is dead somewhere, he isn't in this hall. I go back to where the bodies were. I'm falling over my own feet at this point, and I'm pretty sure my tongue is actually leaking blood. My gums and my nose and the beds of my fingernails definitely are. One foot in front of the other, I drag ass down that endless hall, and then the next, and then the next.

And then I find him. Suit guy, lying across what used to be a doorway, his bottom half in a room marked OBSERVATION CELL 26 and his top half in the hall. I recognized him from a distance by the dried blood on his sleeves.

I rush over, my whole chest heaving like it badly wants to vomit up my lungs. I fall to my knees painfully and dig around in his pockets.

The case is there. Even better, it's intact. I open it with shaking hands. It's padded on the inside. The syringe is fine. I uncap it and slam the needle into the meat of my thigh. *Please be on time*, I think at the needle. At the fluid I pump into the big muscle of my leg. At the feeling of not-quite-freezing, not-quite-burning, that spreads from the injection site. *Just let this one fucking thing go right for fucking once and be the fuck on time.*

When it's done, I still feel like I've been steamrolled. But with luck I'll have stopped the damage from worsening. After a lifetime in old town, I'm no stranger to dehydration. It'll slow me down, but I'll bounce back. Stellaxis itself inured me to this shit long ago. "Should've done better research on me, asshole," I say to suit guy's corpse.

Then I make myself get up, though every part of me creaks in protest. I have to get out of here. Get home. Make sure Jessa's okay. But I'm not going to get far in a hospital gown.

I strip suit guy of his pants, shirt, shoes. He has one of those early-wave ID chips implanted at his temple, and for a second I consider removing it. But I don't have a knife, and I don't really want to stick around here looking for one.

Suit guy's shirt isn't quite dark enough to hide the blood, or the bullet hole that punctured his sternum, and I need something to cover it. There's a bunch more clothing lying around to choose from, but none of these other people have personally tried to kill me, so I'm a little queasy at the prospect of looting their corpses. Still, if I don't get out of here, I'm just going to join them, and besides, they won't miss this stuff anymore.

I consider a white lab coat that somehow has managed to stay relatively clean, but I don't want to get stopped by survivors looking for medical attention. Every other jacket in this part of the hall is utterly unusable. I scurry up a little farther and find an honest-to-shit treasure: a dark blue suit jacket draped over the back of a hastily vacated chair. I shove my way into it and do a real quick go-through of this person's desk drawers. There're some random devices I'll never be able to log in to, some folders full of paper, office supplies, et cetera. The real prize is in the bottom drawer. Apparently whoever this desk belonged to was a snacker. I cram my new pockets full of candy bars and soy jerky and trail mix, shove a protein bar into my mouth, button the jacket over the bloodstains, and whisper *thanks* to the previous owner of this stuff, like whoever it was can hear me.

Then I lurch back to the second water fountain, the one by the medical bay, and drink until I feel like I'm going to slosh when I walk.

Still nobody. The distant sounds have stopped entirely. It comes to me that it's been quiet for a while.

I squint down each hall that I can see. I take a few tentative steps in each direction to make sure of what I earlier surmised. The theory holds.

22 didn't destroy everything in this place. Just what got in his way. He was cutting a path. To or from what, I don't know exactly, but I would bet everything I have ever owned that it had something to do with 06 dead in that room.

This path doesn't extend down to the medical bay or the cafeteria, or the length of a couple other halls I glance down. It came up from one direction and only detoured for the interrogation cells when my yelling drew his attention. It's a clearly marked trail, made of broken doors and dead bodies and bloody boot prints.

It ends at the elevators. I ride them up to the lobby. Similar scene up there. I can hear voices farther back down the hall. They don't sound like security officers, and they don't sound panicked. Whatever danger was here has passed. In its aftermath, people are pacing around, talking into their implants, going in and out through the front doors. Paramedics dash back and forth. The place is a kicked ants' nest. Everybody scurrying. I guess they're sending everyone home for the day. Clear the way for emergency personnel to do their thing.

I catch up with two women walking side by side in front of me, on their way out of the building. I use them as cover. I put my head down, mutter like I'm talking about something extremely important to someone over my implant, and head for the doors.

Really what I'm doing is watching the floor. The red boot prints are fainter here, tile carrying the blood away one step at a time, but it's unmistakable. 22 has already left the building. Alive, and on his own steam. Not that I have the first fucking clue where he's gone.

The state this place is in, I probably could've walked out in the hospital gown after all. There are ambulances parked the whole way around the front driveway and out on that lush green lawn. Bodies being shuttled out on stretchers. I doubt there are enough ambulances in the state for what went down in this building. If any of the bodies are still moving, I don't spot them.

It's a beautiful spring morning. The air smells like flowers and blood. I put my hands in my pockets and start walking.

ONE TIME, BACK IN MY DOG-WALKING DAYS, I looked up a map of that trail where I used to like to walk Flora. I remember thinking how strange it was that if you just took the time to walk far enough, you could go from old town to the edge of the city proper, on foot, avoiding all the checkpoints and barricades and security bots and tolls and bullshit. But, of course, I never got around to trying. And I only have the vaguest sense of where it is now.

I know it runs along somewhere near the west edge of the city, though, which puts it nearish Stellaxis HQ.

If only my fucking lenses still worked, I could look up that map right now.

Then it hits me.

I get away from the edge of the company property and onto a crowded street. Then I keep walking until I find an information kiosk. "Library," I tell it.

The nearest library turns out to be a solid twenty blocks away. I've lost my backpack and my coat and all my cash, and I can't swipe a reader to buy anything to drink, and with those nanobots freshly neutralized in my system after merrily wreaking havoc for however long, each block feels like a mile. But once I drag my carcass up the shallow steps and into the building, there's a water fountain. It's not free, like the ones in the Stellaxis building, but I guess I look pitiful enough that a librarian comes out and swipes me a couple ounces from her account, which very nearly makes me cry. Even better, there's a bike-borrowing station right outside, and best of all, that *is* free. I drink my water, and then I go into the restroom. I thought I'd have to pee, but I can't. Still too dried out. I walk past the sinks I can't pay for and stop as I catch sight of my reflection.

Much of the left side of which is swaddled in bright blue smart bandages. Noticeable from a block away, if anybody's looking. Carefully I peel them back.

What's underneath isn't too pretty, but smart bandages work fast, and honestly, I was expecting worse. And at least it isn't *blue*.

There's the tiniest puddle of water on the sink counter. I soak it up with a paper towel. I'm not putting standing water anywhere near those half-open wounds, but I wet the back of my neck and I start to feel a little better.

Then I go to find myself a computer.

IT'S BEEN THE better part of a decade since I've touched an actual keyboard. It's been nearly half that long since I had to remember a password. They've locked me out of Jessa's and my streaming account, my water account, my bank account, everything that was currently in use on my implant when they got me.

But Jessa and I go way back. And lucky for me, I used to use the same goddamn password for everything.

I log in to the oldest email account I possess. It's so ancient I'm surprised it hasn't timed out by now and been deactivated. I use that to sign up as a subscriber to our stream. Jessa's not live now, and I wince at the way my mind phrases this, but she's Jessa, and if she is physically capable of checking messages when they come in, she will.

I should be thinking of something clever to say. Something only she and I will know. Something she can recognize me by, leaving any eavesdroppers in the dark. But this isn't a fucking movie, and I need to know she's okay.

jessa?

A minute passes. Two. While I wait, I pull up the trail map and print it. Still no reply. I sit and study my map and tap my fingers and glance over my shoulder like any second a pile of company sec goons is going to bust down the door and black-bag me. Something about the map looks familiar, but I don't have anything like the attention span to put my finger on it now. "Come on," I whisper at the ancient screen. "Come *on.*"

Just when I'm finally convinced she's either dead or arrested, or has finally done something to get her implant put on lock-down, she responds.

mal??

tell me you're ok

holy shit. it can't be you, they took you. wait. where are you?

i'm coming home. i just needed to know you were ok. what about the others?

bruised. pissed off. thirsty. couple of fractures. guards in the street now. we'll live A pause. wait. how do i know you're you? quick, tell me something only the real mal would say

fuck off, you first

. . . ok, good enough

I have to shove part of one fist in my mouth or I'm going to start laughing my head off. They're okay. They're all okay.

No time to ask Jessa any of my billion questions. What happened after I passed out against the riot shields? How long ago was that? Did 06 and 22 make the news? The footage suit guy showed me of 06 standing in that intersection. What was that about? Is 06 really dead? Given what 22 did to the building, signs point to yes. But why would they kill her? They were the only two operatives left. What does Stellaxis's play look like without them?

What happened to 22 after he left that building? Did they bring him back? Shoot him down where he stood? I never heard a flare for either of them. And wouldn't Jessa have *mentioned* it if—

No. No time.

i gotta go i'll see you soon stay safe

And then I disconnect.

THE QUICKEST ROUTE to the trail involves retracing my steps from the library to Stellaxis HQ, but it's a million times faster on a bike. I give the company property a wide berth of several city blocks and pedal past it quickly. Eventually they're going to realize their prisoner is gone. I can only hope they assume I'm somewhere among the bodies and leave it at that. It might buy me some time anyway. They kind of have a lot on their plate right now. Either way, I'm leaning pretty hard on the hope that most people don't even know about this trail, this overgrown path connecting New Liberty and old town. *Safer than the checkpoints*, goes the rhythm of my pedaling. *Safer than the checkpoints.*

What will I do when I get back to old town? I'm not honestly sure. Pack a bag, I guess. Get gone. No matter how well Jessa and the others try to hide me, eventually a surveillance feed will pick me up. A guard will recognize my face. Mr. Assan or the Carvalho family might turn me in for a reward. What kind of punishment gets doled out to people who harbor an ex-guest of the white rooms of Stellaxis HQ? If this works, Jessa and the others will never find out.

I can't stay in old town long-term, not after that escape. They'll have me on camera, being deliberately spared the blood-bath in the subbasements. Far as they're concerned, I probably just got a whole lot more interesting.

All I need is a breathing space to knock a game plan together. One more night of sleep in my own bed. One more hot meal in me while I can. Get some supplies in order. Give everyone a proper goodbye.

But first I have to get there.

Every so often I stop to consult my map. It's still reminding me of something. Maybe if I'd slept properly within the last however many days, or had something more in my system than a protein bar and some IV fluids, it'd come to me. For now I just follow the map out of the city and toward the fields and woods beyond.

The supercities aren't like the cities of the old world, with a couple of centuries to accrue suburbs around their messy borders. At least this one isn't. New Liberty is bounded on two sides by the river that divides it from old town and feeds the reservoir to the southwest, but the other sides are clean-cut. Like they dropped the city in one preassembled piece out of the sky. I follow the map out from between two apartment buildings, and that's it—the pavement is just gone beneath me, and I'm pedaling on dirt, dead plant matter whipping at my legs.

There are no signposts, no streets, no nothing. It's a field. Maybe it used to be farmland, but it's overgrown with last year's dead grass and the beginning of this year's new shoots. Trusting to the map, I head leftward, which is approximately south.

I pedal for what feels like hours, but my sense of time has been put through the blender of the white room and can no longer be trusted. When I get hungry, I stop and eat snacks from my pockets. When I get thirsty, I pedal faster. Eventually

I hit the woods and work my way around the tree line until I find the remains of the wooden trail sign, posted there over a century ago. It's rotten and overgrown, and the trail behind it is almost unrecognizable, but I made it. I'm here.

I head in under the trees.

It's theoretically a straight shot of a few miles from here to old town, but it's starting to get dark. In a way I'm almost glad to see it. It anchors my sense of time.

The grass is too tall to bike here. Walking is difficult enough. Suit guy's shoes don't fit me right, and by this point I've got blisters on my blisters, but I try to ignore them. I wish I had my backpack. Then I'd have my headlamp, my warm hat, a water bottle I could've filled at the fountain back at HQ. My taser. Are there bears out here? I read once that this used to be black bear country, and sometimes somebody still spots one. It's rare enough that it makes the local news, but still. If I were a bear, and they'd dropped a couple dozen million tons of steel and glass and concrete on the land my parents' parents used to walk, this untouched stretch of trees would look like paradise.

I squint at the printout in the dying light. Looks like if I just follow this, eventually I'll hit the part of the trail that will be familiar from my dog-walking days, and I can find my way out from there. I can't march straight back into old town with my face all messed up, probably covered in nanobot bruises, wearing the clothes of the Stellaxis HQ dead, so I'll have to be careful not to draw attention to myself. That thing Jessa said about guards in the street. I wish to all that's holy I still had my fucking taser.

Every sound in the woods stops me dead in my tracks, my heart trying to headbutt me in the throat. Squirrels, probably, or chipmunks, or whatever's in these woods anymore, but I'm convinced I hear something louder. Something rhythmic. It doesn't sound *exactly* like footsteps. It's more of a *shhh, shhh*. With a few seconds in between each one.

Deer, maybe. Bears would be louder still. Who am I kidding, I have no fucking idea how loud a bear is. In a fair world, I'm hearing deer. Or hallucinating, thanks to the nanobots' damage of my system. How bad was it? I haven't seen much of my own skin since putting on the jacket, but if the bruising looks anything like how it feels, that's probably for the best. All I've gotten a good look at is my hands, and the glimpse I got of my face beneath the bandages in the library bathroom. I don't *feel* any blood leaking out of any orifices. Would I be aware of internal bleeding before I collapse of a massive hemorrhage? Nobody knows I'm here, and I have no lenses to call an ambulance and no money to pay for one, and the ambulances all looked pretty busy last I saw and couldn't drive this trail even if they weren't toting all the Stellaxis dead to some hospital morgue. I'd be bear shit in these woods inside a day.

I'm in this wonderful mental state of quietly crawling out of my skin when I hear the sound again. It's different now. I don't know how. Maybe I'm just picking up on more levels of it because it's closer. It doesn't sound like animals scurrying in the undergrowth. It sounds purposeful. Like someone out here doing something. Which makes no sense. Who the hell is out here? Whatever's making this sound, it's not far. Or it doesn't *seem* far. Sound carries weird out here. It's off to the right for sure. Another ten big steps forward might bring me level with it. From there, it's maybe twenty-thirty feet back off the path.

I stand there, looking into the woods off the side of the trail. Maybe a minute, maybe ten. The sound stops after a while. I wait. It doesn't start back up.

Now I have a real vague memory from some story my mom read to me as a kid that one thing you do *not* want to do in strange woods is step off paths. You pretty much up your risk of getting ganked by monsters or fairies or whatever by, like, several orders of magnitude. And believe me, I plan to stay on this path. Walk a little faster, in fact. Get away from whatever mystery thing is out there in the rapidly darkening woods.

But then a thing that's been bothering the back of my brain for a while now snaps into sudden clarity.

I know what this map reminds me of.

The crowdsourced maps we used to use in the game. The way each operative had his or her own color-coded line to show their most-traveled paths.

Jessa's voice in my head: *They're all over the place. I mean, look at 06, she's taken up, I don't know,* hiking *or something—*

Hiking. In the woods. Doing laps around the virtual city.

If there was a flare for 06, I didn't see it. I never saw her actual corpse. She was shot, yes. But this is 06. It has to be harder to stop her than that. I think of that classified device she used to heal those civilians in that alley. How fucking poetic would it be for her to have faked her death to get away from a company that faked her death to steal her?

If she's out here, that means she finally ran. That means we have a common goal. She might know of a safe place. Someplace that might have room for one more.

Carefully I lean the bike against a tree and tiptoe farther up the path until I come level with the sound. Or my best guess of where the sound was. Sometime over the past minute or so, it's stopped.

I don't want to spook her. If that surveillance footage was true, even if she managed to heal herself partway, she's badly hurt. She might not recognize me at a distance. She's going to interpret me as a threat. Company muscle come to bring her back to the fold. And there is zero doubt in my mind that even grievously injured she's still a hell of a lot faster than me.

To the right there's the faint suggestion of a rudimentary path, a place where someone has cut their way through the undergrowth. Recently. And without too much care toward staying hidden. The sliced-off branches lie where they've fallen. Beyond is silence.

This gives me pause. I would have thought a person on the run would have been more discreet. Do murderers dispose of their victims in these woods? Wouldn't they also try not to be so obvious about it?

I could go on past. I could get on my bike and speed off to old town.

But I'm thinking of 06's in-game map, and how perfectly it lines up to *where I'm standing now*, and how if anyone could successfully fake their death to get away from Stellaxis, it's her.

As quietly and calmly and unobtrusively as I can, I follow this new path. It's all wintering thornbushes of some kind back here, some just beginning to sprout new growth but densely packed enough that even without leaves, my visibility is reduced to nil. New grass pads my footsteps, for all the help that's going to be if that's actually 06 back there. She could've heard me coming a mile off.

I'm going to feel like a big old fucking idiot if this turns out to be a bear.

I step through into a kind of grassy overgrown clearing. I think it used to be somebody's yard. There's the ruins of a house back there, half digested by thornbushes, the roof fallen in. There's a sunroom, or what used to be one. All its glass is shattered, and there's a tree growing up through the rusted framework of the ceiling. A little ways away from that is the dark shape of a tree stump, maybe, or a rock. Sitting in the middle of a sea of tall grass, all alone.

It's brighter here, out from under the trees. It's a shock to see the gray glare of the sky, the faint orange wash of the lowering sun. I don't see 06. I don't see anyone. Maybe she's gone into the house? It looks structurally unsound as shit, but it's cover. Not totally drone-proof cover, but better than out here.

As I push my way through the tall grass toward the busted house, my scalp prickles. It's not movement that's caught my attention, but a *lack* of movement. Something that my brain registers as *should be moving* but isn't.

I turn and shade my eyes toward that sea of dead grass where I saw that blackened tree-stump shape.

It's not a tree stump at all. Or a rock. Or 06, for that matter, which is my next thought. The darkness of her uniform and hair might have, from behind and at a distance and to my glare-blind dried-out fucked-up eyes, made her look like either of those things.

But it's not 06, although I'm getting warmer.

It's 22.

There is no feasible way he doesn't know I'm here. He probably heard me laboring up the trail from the moment I hit it, crinkling my printout and cursing my wrong-sized shoes and my unrideable bike and the too-tall grass and breathing like a person whose blood is lousy with the flotsam corpses of a slaughtered nanobot battalion.

He doesn't attack. He doesn't retreat. He doesn't so much as glance up as I approach. If the idea of getting caught out here by Stellaxis drones bothers him, it is not apparent. Do they think their escape plan is that watertight? Was this house their midway point to freedom all along? 06 is in the house, I decide, getting stuff together for the road. Why isn't he in there helping? He's not standing any kind of guard at all. He's just sitting there.

Then I get closer, and I see what he's been out here doing, and all the air goes out of me at once.

He's been digging a grave.

I don't ask. I don't need to. There is only one person on this godsfucked planet that 22 would be digging a grave for. He's sitting in the dirt, boots just touching the edge of the mound, his forearms resting loosely on his knees. There are two swords stabbed into the ground beside him. One of them I recognize as his. The other is a short sword I haven't seen before. He's cleaned the blood off them somehow, probably on the grass.

Those swords are the only things he has with him out here. No shovel, no nothing. He must have dug this hole and filled it back in with his bare hands.

I didn't see a flare, my brain protests weakly. The rest of me just stops moving. Whatever momentum has carried me this far will carry me no farther.

I'm not aware of sitting down beside 22, only that time skips and I'm there. He's covered in dirt and dried blood. A garden smell reaches me. Fresh-turned soil. I could sit here until the earth spins into the sun and still have no idea what to say. The idea that 06 is in the ground because I was never anybody powerful enough to help her, laughably self-centered though it is, is still a wire tightening around my throat.

I tried. That's the fuckedest part. I told them I could help them, and I tried my level utter best. I made noise. I uncovered secrets. I outlasted the white room. I escaped Stellaxis HQ. And for what? Old town slowly dying of thirst and 06 about to be worm food in somebody's yard.

"You could see this place from the roof of the building," 22 says at last. I don't need to ask what building. There's only one building he knows. "The woods. She always wanted to go."

I think again of the game maps, 06 pacing her circuit beyond the city limits. Out where they couldn't reach her. I swallow.

"What happened?" I ask before I can come to my senses and stop myself. 22 glances at me sharply. But he doesn't look pissed. He looks—I'm not sure I've ever used the word *bereft* in my life before, but it comes to mind now. He looks like a person who's had literally everything he ever cared about ripped out of the death grip he thought he had on it.

Which, of course, he is.

"Sorry," I mutter. I feel like the worst kind of asshole. "Forget I said anything."

"This was a long time coming," he says, ignoring my apology. "She'd been trying to end this war for years. But she had no idea how. Eventually she just—" his hands lift in an incomprehensible, vague sketch of a gesture, like he's opening two fistfuls of ash for the wind to blow away—"pushed too hard. This time they pushed back."

I want to ask what exactly she did. Why she did it. Why she let them take her in. Why, for that matter, 22 allowed it either. I don't for one second imagine that 06, that either of them, could have been overpowered by anything Stellaxis had to throw at them, short of each other. But I remember the footage suit guy showed me. 22 had her in that ring, and he let her go.

I think of those bodies fallen in the street, a still frame from some long game I can't begin to guess at. But I'm looking at 22 and I realize I can't do that to him. It's bad enough having to relive my own mistakes, and none of those got me killed.

And maybe in the end it doesn't matter what she did. Just like it doesn't matter what I do. We're ants trying to take on a colossus. It's only ever going to end one way.

"She was brave as hell," I say instead, forcing myself to meet 22's gaze fully. "Fighting her way out of that place."

A sound comes out of him at this. It's almost a laugh, but also very, very much not. "Yes," he says. "Well."

I decide not to insult him with another dumbass apology. I shut up, waiting for the earth to swallow me.

"It's what she should have done," he says after a moment. "It's what I told her to do. I told her to get out. I told her to run. It would have been easy. But no. She waited just a little too long."

He doesn't clarify, and I don't ask. The question burns a slow hole in my mind for what feels like full minutes before he speaks again. "For me. To stop being an idiot and decide to go with her. And fight our way out of that place together."

"You wanted out," I say. "You both wanted out." Captain Obvious over here, wasting breath stating this out loud. I guess what I mean to say is: *I'm here, I hear you, I'm listening.*

Then I realize what he's saying, and my breath catches in such a way it's several seconds before I figure out how to draw one again.

22 glances over.

"This is on me," I say, helpless. "I took too long. Everything you tried to tell me about that place. You trusted me to get that information out. Of course she lost patience with me. I'm sorry. I'm sorry I fucked up. I'm sorry I wasn't someone . . . better."

He hasn't even bothered to kill me. It's anyone's guess as to why. I'd want to kill me, if I were him.

It isn't exactly getting easier to breathe. I will myself not to have a panic attack on top of 06's grave. You stupid fucking fuck, Mal, this isn't about *you.*

22 says something that I definitely mishear.

"What?"

"I said." 22 shifts a little. It is the second time that I have ever seen him fidget. "She didn't know."

"*What?*"

"I couldn't tell her. They were listening." Something passes over him, almost like a shiver. "They were always listening."

"No."

Silence.

"You're telling me. When you took me to the cafeteria. And told me all that stuff. You're telling me 06—"

"Thought I had sent you home. Yes." Here he hits some unseen wall, recovers less smoothly than he probably thinks.

"Safer. For them to think. That I was." He sucks in a sharp breath between his teeth. Seems to freeze in place a second, riding out some unseen assault. "That it was only her." He sets his whole self like he's walking into hurricane wind. "That I was. Still. Theirs."

"You were covering for her." I can't even believe what I'm hearing myself say. "The rebellious one, the obedient one. That was an *act*? For the Director, the company, sure. But. You're telling me *06 didn't even know*?"

He doesn't reply. He doesn't need to. Every atom of him answers.

Too easy to imagine: he went all in and kept it up until he saw the best play at his disposal. Someone who could get the truth out. Who could throw that message in a bottle overboard on his behalf. At which point Stellaxis must have learned what he was up to. I guess I know the rest.

"Then what kept you there? Why not run? If that's what you both wanted?"

I don't expect an answer. He doesn't owe me shit. I wouldn't answer me either.

However.

"I think," he says, "I always doubted it was possible. Getting free of that place."

"But not 06?"

He shakes his head so subtly I'm not sure it actually moves. "No. But she didn't just want to escape. She wanted for there to be no Stellaxis left to escape from. No facility left for more children to vanish into. No more operatives. No more numbers. She was trying to stop it. The SecOps program that fed the war. The war that fed the program. All of it."

"They told me she sabotaged a hostage transfer."

The nod is very similar in character to the head shake, and followed by long silence.

"Stellaxis and Greenleaf have been in stalemate for years," he says. "She was trying to upset the balance."

"She . . . switched sides?"

"That's not how she'd put it."

"And how is that?"

He thinks that over a second. "That she was trying to break through to a place where there were no sides." Sharp glance in my direction: *Keeping up?* I nod. As goals go, it sounds familiar. "She was getting desperate. She had some dangerous ideas. But that was how she was. She *tried.* While I—"

Again I wait. Less long.

"She let them take her. She could have run, she could have killed them all, but she let them take her." His voice catches, is forcibly smoothed. "To protect me. She sat there and let them torture her because they knew what she'd done, and she wanted to make sure they didn't think I was in on it too. So that I would still have a home there. In that *place.*" He spits the word. It comes to me that he is sitting here in this field because he wants them to find him. He's looking to die. "If I decided, *finally decided*, that was what I wanted."

Waves of pain visibly crest and break on his face, minimally signaled. How much is Stellaxis and how much is guilt? Does it matter?

They were protecting each other. Both of them, each in their own dumbass way, protecting each other.

Which is worse: To take your shot and miss, like 06 did? Or to hesitate too long, like 22, and miss your chance to take the shot at all?

I open my mouth, close it. I don't know how to respond to any of this, how to keep him talking, how to keep him from deciding he's done monologuing at me and walk away. Or worse. It's not that I'm afraid of him hurting me. I'm afraid of him hurting himself. So I sit, and I listen, like I'm feeding out a line to a drowning person, inch by inch, and I hope to all fuck it's enough, because I don't know what else to do.

"Yes, I wanted out. As you say. At least I thought I did. But when it came to it—" Another shiver briefly overwrites that studied calm. He picks up a rock in one fist, squeezes. It falls as powder. I swallow. "Leave and go *where*. Everything we had left in the world was in that building. I don't even know how long it's been."

"Twelve years," I try to say, and my voice cuts out. I clear my throat. "It's been about twelve years. Since they took you."

Another rock. If he were to wring his hands, every bone in both would shatter. "Twelve years."

"You were eight when you went into that building?"

He's watching me steadily, sidelong, like he can't quite believe what he's hearing. "I think so," he says. "That sounds right."

"They took me, too," I add, and he turns to regard me full on at that. He doesn't look like a person waiting for a punchline, but I've got one chambered anyway. "Guess I wasn't special enough to keep."

No reaction. Just that look, like he's x-raying the folds of my brain. Who knows. Maybe he is.

"I wish," I say, and pause because my voice is doing something ominous, and by god I *will* keep my shit together in the face of this, "I wish I could have helped you both find somewhere to go."

In response to that, he pulls one of the swords out of the ground, uses it to tap the grave mound lightly. "No need," he says in this voice like he's putting out cigarettes on his arms. "She found it on her own."

I think of that other interrogation cell. The blood on suit guy's sleeve. The chair ripped out of the floor. I think of the short work 06 would have made of nanofilament cuffs. Of the strength of will required to sit and let a person torture you if you could just get up and walk away at any time. If you'd only been willing to leave alone.

If the long game your partner was running hadn't run just a little too long.

"They shot her," I hear myself say. "I saw."

The silence at that goes on for so long that the sky darkens several shades. A star comes out. Another.

"I came to get her out," he says. "Once I realized what they were doing to her, I . . ." Another silence. "I killed them all. Everyone in that room. They were shooting at me, but . . ."

I look at him. Hard to tell if he's injured. At a glance, I'm not sure any of the blood on him is his. "They didn't hit you?"

How is that possible? He must have, I don't even know what. Moved too fast for *bullets*?

"I don't know if they meant to shoot her, too. She was cuffed to a chair. She ripped the cuffs free and stood up and." The sword's tapping the dirt again. How long has he been doing that? "Fell."

I don't have anything intelligent to say to that, either. 06 dead. It's unbelievable. My mind is glancing off the fact of her there in the ground. The grave. I can't make it sink in. 06, who helped those people against orders. 06, who has *always* stuck her neck out for civilians. Heading up evac teams from strike zones. Accompanying emergency response teams when the evacs don't take. Hand-delivering masks and water when a zone gets pinned down. Just last year she and 22 pretty much single-handedly rescued twelve hundred people when the New Liberty Mall ate the cluster-bombing meant for that transport hangar. The company always took credit, but now I'm not so sure it was orders that sent her there. I think she sent herself.

06 was pretty much everyone's favorite operative. Hell, even her fucking NPC would go out of its way to help player characters in trouble, spawning out of nowhere to back them up and resupply and heal them. And all we ever did for her was use her.

She was the closest thing to a real-life superhero that I for one am ever going to see. And now for the same reason she was so universally beloved, she's dead.

Because she stuck her neck out. Because she planted herself in the path of something bigger than herself and said *no*.

"Come back to old town with me," I say all in a rush. "I can hide you from them. Get you some normal clothes. Someplace to clean up. Some smart bandages. A place to sleep. Until you figure out what to do next. How much of that blood is yours?"

"I'm not going anywhere. I'm staying here."

"They'll find you. They'll—"

"Then let them."

"They're not going to kill you. You're the last one left. They can't afford to lose you. They're going to bring you back there. To Stellaxis."

"They are welcome," he says in a voice like desolation, "to try."

At that moment something flashes high above the trees. Something white. A remembrance flare. We both turn to regard it over our shoulders as it screams upward and blossoms, then falls, scattering.

I wait a ten-count, breath held, for a second one. *Please*, I think at that empty space of sky. *Please.*

It doesn't come.

"They won't give up," I say at last. "You know that."

Silence. His face is the thinnest possible sheet of ice over the deepest, darkest lake. He is going to sit here in this field until he drops his guard and they feed him a fucking drone strike. It's infuriating. All the more so because there's fuckall I can do to stop it.

"I'm going in there," I say, pointing at the house. Now that I'm really looking at the roof, it hasn't fallen in at all, it's been blasted in. Somebody's smart bomb missed. It happens. "See if there's anything left we can use." I pause, knowing the answer before I ask. "You coming?"

But he surprises me. In one fluid motion he gets to his feet and pulls the second sword from the dirt. "Lead on," he says, and follows.

WHOEVER USED TO live here either evacuated before the strike hit or their bodies have long since been taken care of by local wildlife. There's no sign of anyone. I make a quick sweep before the daylight dies. 22 isn't much help. He stands sentry by the big living room window, staring out at the backyard and 06's grave.

I don't press matters. I wasn't expecting to get him through the door.

The house turns out to be fully stocked, as long as you're okay with ignoring expiration dates. There's food in the kitchen and clothes in the closets. The water doesn't run, of course, but I find a sealed package of baby wipes, use a few to clean up sparingly, and give the rest to 22. He needs them more than I do. Along with those I hand him a change of clothes I found that looks to maybe fit him. Jeans, a long-sleeved shirt, a hoodie. It's cold as shit in here. In a different bedroom I dig up a similar outfit for myself. It doesn't fit perfectly, but it's a hell of a lot better than a dead man's suit.

Dressed, I realize I still have no idea whether 22's been wounded. I double back to the bathroom. Smart bandages and antibiotic cream in the medicine cabinet. Score. But he's not in the living room where I left him.

Shit.

It's not a vigil I'm keeping precisely, but after the day he's had, I'm finding it difficult to let him out of my sight for long. But there he is, standing with his armload of clothes and baby wipes in some teenager's bedroom that's been practically wallpapered with SecOps posters. The door's open, so I walk in to find him studying them, like a Martian anthropologist just landed here

on what remains of Earth. From the look on his face, he's finding its relics bewildering. Dead kids on a dead kid's wall.

"Didn't you know?" I say. "You're famous."

22 doesn't turn. He's staring at a picture of himself. He looks a lot more dangerous in the poster. "For what?" he asks. "For following orders? For being good at war?" He doesn't wait for a response, which is good for me because I doubt I have one that's adequate. *Because you're pure*, I want to say. *Because everything else is corruption and fuckery to the horizon, and you and poor goddamn assassinated 06 are the rock around which it passes.* But that's not any kind of answer. It's my answer, maybe. They're famous because a corporation that controls everything wanted to sell its customer-citizens a war. Even the swords, I realize belatedly. They weren't taught to fight with blades because it's efficient. They were taught to fight with blades because it looks appallingly fucking cool.

Weird kind of strategy to win a war, but goddamn if the image hasn't moved billions worth of merchandise.

22 lifts his chin at the poster array. The motion hitches partway as he hits that invisible limiter again. He's pushing past it better now. Given what he told me outside, he's got years of practice in so doing. I can't even begin to imagine what that took to overcome. Is taking now. "All these people are dead."

"Not all of them."

He doesn't respond.

"I found smart bandages and antibiotic ointment," I say in my best subject-changing voice. "They're old, but that stuff keeps."

"I'm fine," he says.

"You're bleeding on the floor."

22 glances down. There's blood running out his left sleeve, down his wrist and hand, dripping from his fingertips. He looks back up at the poster. His expression doesn't change.

"What about that thing you had, that you healed those people with in the alley?" I ask. "Can't you use that?"

Something snags in his face now, snags and is ironed back out almost immediately. This one looks less like pain and more like anger, but I don't think it's at me. "That won't be an option."

I want to press the question. Something inane about how it might be worth at least a *try*. But this is 22, and I know better.

Then I realize why he doesn't have it. Who he tried to use it on and failed.

I make a double handful of smart bandages and ointment and shove them at him. "Here."

He looks at the bandages, then at me. He takes them wordlessly and vanishes into the bathroom.

While 22 is off getting cleaned up and changed, I check out the kitchen. Field mice have gotten to it long before and stripped it of any food in packages they could gnaw through. And I'm not touching some rancid fridge. I manage to excavate a sealed jar of peanut butter, a few cans of beans and vegetables, some soup. On top of the freezer is a bottle of something with no label, but is definitely home-brew booze of some description. It takes the tossing of four drawers to find a can opener.

I take the peanut butter and cans and bottle and put it all on the coffee table in the living room. I take the remaining snacks out of my pockets and add them to the pile. I throw a couple of dusty couch cushions on the floor as seats.

When 22 comes back out to the front of the house, I almost start laughing. I can't help it. It's not that he looks *funny*. It's that he looks *normal*. He looks like a human person my age. Which, of course, he is. If he wasn't—if he were anything like what Stellaxis has been trying to convince us he was all along—neither of us would be here.

It's an interesting thought.

Even harder than getting him to bother bandaging his wounds is getting him to eat. I've eaten practically nothing since before the white room, so this is not a problem for me. He mostly sits and stares out the window while I shovel beans into my face. I notice he's brought the two swords over at some point and has stabbed them into the moldering carpet beside him.

It isn't that one sword is shorter, I see now. It's that one of them has been broken in half. Not too hard to guess whose it was.

The only liquid in this entire house is the contents of that bottle. I take a couple of sips and immediately hit pause on that endeavor. Whatever it is, it's a whole lot stronger than the stuff I used to make, and probably going to do more harm than help in the hydration department. I put the bottle down and watch 22 not eat for another minute or so.

"Hey," I say eventually. "Calories are calories."

He blows a little air out his nose at that. It's not exactly a laugh, but I'll take it. I slide a candy bar across the table to him. He looks at it. "What is that?"

"Calories," I say. "Lots of them." *You absolute fucking alien.* "Eat it, it's good. It's fuel. Anyway I still owe you a meal, so . . ." I gesture expansively. "You *are* the one who didn't want to go back to old town. This is kind of on you."

He unwraps the candy bar, sniffs it, takes a bite. Chews thoughtfully, swallows. "Hmm."

"They didn't let you out much, did they?"

22 gazes at me for a long moment. Then he reaches over and swipes my bottle. Gives that the sniff test also. Takes a drink. Treats the bottle to the same scholarly regard he did the candy bar. Takes another drink. "What did you do?"

I blink. "Sorry?"

"You were in an interrogation cell. You must've done something they didn't like."

He has no idea what I've been through these past weeks. Nothing since what I told him in the elevator. I suppose it's a reflection of how desperate he and 06 were to find a way out of that place that he's trusted me this far.

Not desperate enough, apparently, some asshole part of my mind chimes in. Or else 06 would be here with us, or none of us would be here at all.

I wonder, in 22's position, how hard it would've been for me to leave the facility and try to make my way out in a world I never got the chance to know. If I would have hesitated. If 06 would be in the ground right now because I waited too long to get up the nerve.

I'd like to say I know what I would've done. But I don't. I've never left old town to look for something better. I've never even tried. All my life I've gone through the motions of survival. Kept my head down. Done what I'm told. Because of this war. Because of Stellaxis. It's twelve solid years since either of us has been free.

So I tell him. I tell him everything. The game. B. The coffee shop. The day I met him and 06. And everything that came after.

"You showed people the footage you took," 22 says. "Of the facility. The Director made sure we knew." He seems to realize what he's saying. "That's why they had you in the cell. I'm sorry. I brought you into this. I didn't mean—" He breaks off, tries again. "I didn't know."

The same almost-laugh again, and this time I recognize it. He's furious with himself. "That's two people I managed to land in those cells. Trying to help me."

I would do it again, I think. *And so would she.*

Instead of that I say, "Did I get you in trouble?"

He shrugs a little. "No more than usual." Another drink.

"Nobody knew what Stellaxis did to you. I wanted people to know. I wanted to make them pay. It wasn't enough. I didn't *do* enough. All I did was make things—" My voice fails. I try again. "Looks like we put each other at risk."

"We were already at risk," he says. "Every day. All Kit ever wanted was to finish it. Shut down the Director's project. End the war. It's what she died trying to do."

"Kit?"

"Kit. Catherine." He pulls the broken sword out of the floor, stabs it back in. "06."

Catherine.

"Broadcasting that footage is exactly what she would have done in your position, if she'd had the means and opportunity. I guess I saw how that worked out for you."

The white room. The chair. The burns on my face. I nod.

"And yet," he says, "you did it anyway."

"I guess we have a common enemy," I say.

22 looks at me. His eyes are bottomless. He looks away. "Yes," he says. "I think we do."

I reach a hand out and crook two fingers at the bottle. He passes it over. I sip and hand it back. *Nycorix and 22: Drinking Buddies.* If only Jessa were here to see this. If only 06 were sitting here on this disgusting carpet with us, on her way to anonymity and freedom instead of lying out there under six cold feet of somebody's bombed-out yard. If only I hadn't managed to screw old town out of its water supply. If only someone else could have exposed the company's lies before me. Someone who would have done it better. Smarter. Gotten fewer people hurt. Actually made some kind of fucking difference.

22 drinks and passes the bottle to me. *To Catherine,* I almost say, because *Kit* seems like an inner-circle thing that is light-years from my business, but then I realize: it's an inner-circle thing, but the fact I even know it is because 22 let me in.

"To Kit," I say, and pour a shot out on the carpet, then drink and hand the bottle back, wiping my mouth angrily on my sleeve.

Only the slightest possible hesitation before 22 follows suit. "To Kit."

I don't know how to say the next thing gently, and I'm just drunk enough to say it anyway.

"It fucking sucks that they got her. I mean. It's horrible. I can't imagine what you must be feeling. But, I mean, I didn't know her well at all, obviously, but the impression I got is that she wouldn't want you to do anything stupid. She'd want you to get the fuck out of here. She'd want you to live. For all the rest of the operatives—the stolen kids—who never got the chance. And for her."

"Is that what you think I'm planning to do?" he says. "Sit around and mourn her? Kill the soldiers who shot her? They're all dead. It doesn't matter. No," he continues, drawing it out that same extra half syllable as he did when he spoke of the Director back in the Stellaxis basement. "She was my partner. I am going to finish what she started."

"Then come back with me." Aware that I'm repeating myself. Aware that I sound like I'm pleading. Maybe I am. I'm straight out of fucks left to give. "Come back to old town. Tell your story. The truth about Stellaxis. We'll broadcast it to the world. The videos I posted are getting global support. That means *beyond* Stellaxis. This could lead to worldwide boycotts. Protests. Something. Their stock will fall. They'll lose credibility. They'll go out of business. No more war. No more stolen children. They'll disappear."

But even as I speak, I'm thinking, *Is Greenleaf Industries any better? If the city goes to them, what difference will it make? A different logo on our water kegs, our company stores. And there are no stolen children left to save.*

I wish to fuck there were a third option I could give him. Or myself. Or all of old town. Right now I'm looking at this house and thinking: What else is out there to be reclaimed, beyond the supercities? We old-town people are resourceful. We know how to purify rainwater. We know how to sprout greens. We know how to cobble together a living out of anything. What else might we learn, given time?

He doesn't say yes, but he doesn't say no. Either way, I can't think of anything new or useful to add. I consider giving him some cheesy line about redemption, but I bite it back. That's not a useful angle here. Maybe after we sleep on it, I'll find a way to convince him.

We pass the remainder of the bottle back and forth in silence, gazing out the window. The moon paints us silver-blue and luminous, like something put on ice and preserved outside of time forever. Its light is the only light we have.

I WAKE UP ON THE COUCH. THE cushions that were on the floor are under me. There's a blanket on me I didn't put there. It smells of mildew. It's patterned with flying birds. I vaguely recognize it from one of the bedrooms farther back in the house.

It's still dark. The empty bottle has fallen over on the table. Moonlight shines through it. 22 is nowhere to be seen.

Panic spikes me. *He didn't*, I lie to myself. *He's just gone to sleep somewhere.*

I rush through the house, smashing my shins on furniture, my shoulders on doorframes. He's nowhere. Not dead, not alive. All I find is the clothing I gave him, folded neatly on the bathroom sink. His uniform is gone. The whole sword and the broken one, gone. I stand there, my head pounding, my whole body shivering like flu.

I am going to finish what she started.

He's out in the yard, I try to convince myself. He's gone back to the grave. I should have stayed awake. I should have kept an eye on him. *Please be alive, please be alive, please be alive.*

But when I open the door, something catches my eye. I look

down. There are words facing up at me from my feet, carved quickly and crudely into the wood of the porch. A message.

I HAVE TO

I take off running.

THE BIKE IS where I left it, lying in a faint blue patch of moonlight. I haul it into an about-face and start pedaling toward the city, battling my adrenaline-fueled way through the grass. It's cold enough to see my breath out here. Probably cold enough to snow. How long ago did he leave? How far ahead of me could he be? There's the slightest wash of light off in the distance. The sun is coming up.

I have no idea what I hope to accomplish here. Whatever he's gone back there to do, I'm not going to be able to do anything to—what? Help him? Stop him? Protect him? I'm not sure which of these notions is more outrageous. Maybe 22 has a solid game plan here, but I don't. All I know is I'm pedaling back toward Stellaxis HQ faster than I've ever pedaled anywhere before, dehydration or no, hangover or no, darkness or no. Because everything I've been moving toward since Jessa and I agreed to meet B in that coffee shop, it all points in one direction. I couldn't do anything to avenge Elena, to prevent 08's flare, to help old town get its water back, to save 06 from throwing herself on the gears of the machine to slow it down. It may be my last act on the face of this forsaken earth, but I *will* do anything and everything in my power to see this—whatever it is—through. I'm unarmed, unprepared, running on fumes. I don't know what's going to be happening at that building when I get there. Only that I have to get there before it does.

I try not to think about how awful I feel. I try not to think about leaving Jessa and the others behind to mourn my terrible decisions. I try not to think of what I'll find when I get to that building. Another massacre? Is there anyone even in the building at this hour to *be* massacred? Is he waiting for them to arrive in the morning? Are they waiting for him to? What the hell is he after? *Finish what she started*, sure. But does he have the first fucking clue how to do that? Can one lone superhuman end a war single-handed? For my money, 06's grave answers that question tidily. He said he wasn't going to avenge her, but from where I'm sitting, it looks pretty much like a death wish. Like another remembrance flare by nightfall. And nothing will have changed.

I try not to think that they'll be ready for him. That I'll get there as 22 is striding up the lawn into an ambush, his sword in one hand, 06's in the other, while the glowing dots of sniper sights swarm like fireflies on the black of his jacket. Arriving just in time to watch him fall.

I try not to think that the easiest way to break the SecOps program would be its last surviving operative walking through those black glass doors to die.

But when I get there, the grounds are quiet. It's early morning, the sky the color of blue milk. On the far horizon, some stars haven't yet winked out.

Everything at the checkpoint by the entrance to that long winding drive up the green lawn is dead. Humans and security bots, neatly dispatched. It looks to have been very fast. Most of them didn't even draw their weapons.

I can only hope that I woke up when he left the bombed-out house. I'm a light sleeper. Exhausted as I was, I obviously didn't wake up when he moved me to the couch or put the blanket over me, but it might've started the process. Closing the door behind him might have done it. A creak in the floorboards. The message he left.

I can't be too late. I *can't*.

I pedal hard through the busted checkpoint and up the hill, wincing. Expecting to get headshot straight off the bike. But if there were snipers, 22's either taken them out somehow or they missed their shot and have gone down into the building after him, because nobody fires on me, and I don't see his corpse.

I expect the front doors of the building to be similarly trashed, but they're not. They're pristine. The part of my brain that's watched too many movies goes, *It's quiet. Too quiet.* I push my way in cautiously.

There were more security guards posted down here this time. At least five. The way he's left them, I'd have to count their heads to be sure. Swallowing hard, I tiptoe over the body parts between me and the elevators. To my right, the water feature tinkles serenely. The sound of all those hoarded gallons— *decorative* gallons—hurries me past faster. I don't have much time to put something together here. Something that will save 22, help old town, protect Jessa and the others from ending up in an interrogation cell by association with my ineffectual ass. Something better than following 22 in order to bear witness to his death.

My toe bumps something hard. I look down. It's a semi-automatic rifle, like the ones the guards have for the water lines. I have no idea how to use one, if it's loaded, if it's broken. I pick it up anyway and head for the elevators, where my momentum hits a wall.

There's no trail of bloody footprints to follow this time, and this building has seventy-six floors. 22 could be anywhere.

"Okay," I whisper to myself. "Think."

This is harder than usual. My brain fog is thick enough to cut with a knife.

There's one of those maps on the wall by the elevators, this one with a separate set of plaques indicating the rooms on each floor. I skim the lists, my vision blurring like a migraine coming on. Public relations, human relations, research and development, marketing. It's just corporate word salad after a while. Nothing jumps out.

Then I realize the plaque for the four sublevels is off on the far side of the others, not before the lower levels but after the higher ones. There's MEDICAL BAY and DINING FACILITY and INTERROGATION, familiar from before. I keep reading.

I notice that the sublevels don't only have their own cafeteria and medical facilities. They also have their own air/water filtration, their own laundry, their own public relations office. Like, for whatever reason, these four floors are self-sufficient by design.

But they have some weirder stuff too.

OBSERVATION CELLS 1–30. QUARANTINE. DORMITORY A. DORMITORY B. COMBAT SIMULATOR. TRAINING HALL. MORGUE.

Not only that, but the sublevels are *huge.* Each one has as many entries on the plaque as any two or three upper floors. They must stretch for acres, past the manicured Stellaxis lawns, beneath the streets of New Liberty.

"What the *fuck*—" I whisper, and then my attention lands on something vaguely familiar.

DIANA REYES, DIRECTOR OF OPERATIONS

Now I don't *know* if this is the Director 06 and 22 referred to before. And I don't *know* what 22 meant exactly when he said he was going to finish what 06 started. But it's the best and only lead I've got.

Director Reyes's office is three floors down on sublevel C. Room C312. I make a note of it and punch the button.

While the elevator arrives, I check out the gun. It's like and not-like Jessa's Corviss A9 Devastator in the game, but now that I'm looking at it more closely, most of the differences might well be cosmetic. The way a citykiller mech is a TacSystems X10 in real life, but still recognizably the same machine.

I'm debating whether to test my theory by firing into a wall and possibly drawing unwanted attention—countered by the almost definite benefit of being able to *deal* with unwanted attention I run into below via knowing how to work my fucking weapon—when the elevator arrives.

22's been here, too. There are two dead guards crammed in here with me. I hesitate a second, eyeing their smart armor vests and helmets, before deciding against it. 22's going to be the most dangerous thing in this building by far, and if his pattern-seeking flags me as one of them, I'll be dead before I hit the floor. This armor, expensive though it looks, didn't do much to protect them against him.

There's a mess of blood smeared on the keypad touchscreen. I have to wipe it off with my sleeve before it will register my floor selection. It's only barely dried. It smells how your hand smells after holding loose change for a while. The guards' eyes are still open, and there's nothing for them to look at in this elevator but me. I hurry to wipe my sleeve on the elevator wall, keeping my stare glued to the front of the elevator so I don't have to make eye contact with the dead.

The cheery *ping* of the elevator is exactly as incongruous as the calming water feature upstairs.

I step out into carnage. At first I think it's left over from yesterday, but no. This is all fresh. Guards, sentry bots. A drone lying in clean halves, each piece landed in a different puddle of organic mess. There's so little clear space on the floor that I have to tiptoe. They must have been waiting to ambush him out of the elevator.

Although. I think back on the checkpoint, the security guards in the lobby. Nobody got a chance to raise an alarm.

They were already down here. There's something on this floor they were protecting.

I wish I was more confident I knew how this fucking gun worked.

I follow the hall around past C301, C302, C303. It branches after that, but it's easy enough to follow the sounds. Gunshots, screams. It's like yesterday all over again. Like I've rewound twenty-four hours. Or like I never left. To my compromised higher functions, the dream logic is bizarrely compelling.

I switch off what I hope to hell is the safety and make my way down the hall, gun first, hugging the wall, willing myself to be invisible. No Jessa to have my back here. I'm glad. I don't want her within five miles of this.

I reach room C312 as a body flies out through the open door. It connects with the far wall with a kind of wet crunching smack and slides to a heap on the floor. On top of another guard who landed there first.

Before I can stop myself, I throw myself into the room, slam the door, mash the locks, then move to the side of the door-frame in case somebody out there tries shooting through.

Stupid. I should have announced my presence first. Done something to alert 22 that it's just me and not another guard coming after him. If his reaction times are faster than his decision-making processes, I'm done.

But it turns out I had no need to worry. He just glances at me and turns back to whatever hasn't yet been dealt with in room C312. His expression changing only slightly when he realizes who he's looking at. Like he suspected I might follow. Like he's at least a little surprised I actually did.

"Go home," he says, his back to me. His uniform and boots are exactly as encrusted with dried blood and grave dirt as yesterday, except there's more fresh blood on top of it, and it's impossible to tell whether he's been injured somewhere under all that. "Get out of here. It isn't safe."

He doesn't bother looking to see whether I listen to this advice, which is fine by me because I have zero intention of doing so. His focus is elsewhere.

Beyond him is a desk with a woman behind it. The placard on the desk reads DIRECTOR D. REYES.

He's caught her in the midst of packing up her shit to get out of here, presumably before 22 came back to deal with her. She almost made it too. She must be really kicking herself right now for doing whatever she did to make her operatives move so fast.

There's an open box on her desk full of papers and devices and, weirdly, a paperweight snow globe of old San Francisco, where I'm not sure it ever snowed even before it was underwater.

Even now she's standing there with an armload of stuff, frozen in place, like if she stays *very* still, he might not notice her there. Like she's wearing a ten-second invisibility cloak and trying to figure out how to maneuver out of this situation before it expires.

A manila folder drops from her armload and falls to the floor, scattering papers. Reflexively she reaches for it, which sends a weird-looking pocket screen tumbling after.

22 shakes his head slightly at her, and she freezes again.

I expect her to be pleading for her life. I expect him to be explaining to her, patiently, levelly, almost lovingly, like a villain in a movie, why she deserves to die. But they're just looking at each other. Neither one moves. Whatever they had to say to each other, I think, was said some time ago. Or never needed saying in the first place.

22 holsters his gun and draws the sword instead. Begins to circle slowly around to the Director's side of the desk. He's moving a little unsteadily, he's got the half-lidded eyes of a person with a killer headache, but he's locked on and he keeps on coming. Whatever they're doing to him over that implant, he's run out of fucks to give today.

"Wait," I say.

22 ignores this. Advances another step. Slowly. It's not just the pain. He's toying with her. *Is this how I was able to catch up with him? Or did he save this tactic for this room?*

"Wait. Don't kill her. *Don't kill her.*"

It's like he can't even hear me. Like all his senses have narrowed to a point, and that point is making Director of Operations Diana Reyes pay for crimes I can't even begin to guess at.

There's a second, maybe two, during which all manner of stuff goes flashing through my head. B and her picture of Elena. Suit guy and his picture of B's dead sister. That dipshit on the bus with his *should've complied.* Old town dying slowly of thirst because I couldn't finish what I started. 06 murdered in cold blood because she tried to save some hypothetical next wave of stolen children from everything she'd spent twelve years enduring. 22 in the elevator, saying *There were forty-eight.*

Suit guy's voice in my head. *SecOps operatives 06 and 22 smuggling you into Stellaxis headquarters, your amateurish exposé, the riot in old town, and now this? These things are obviously connected. We need your help to figure out how.*

Well, they weren't connected before, not in the way he was thinking. But maybe they should be.

I launch myself over the desk and skid to a stop in a drift of paperwork, putting myself between Director Reyes and 22's sword.

"Move," 22 tells me.

I shake my head. My heart is pounding so hard my vision is going dark around the edges. I am all too aware that if he wanted me moved, he could move me. Easily. In pieces if he so chose. I don't know what I would do in his position. What I would have done already. I remember how young Elena looked in B's photo and think: If the woman behind this desk did to me and my people even a fraction of what she must have done to 22 and his, I'd have probably put a bullet in her head before I fully walked into the room. It's a measure of 22's exquisite control that he hasn't.

He pauses now to take me in: blood-smeared hoodie, deranged dawning-idea face, giant gun. "You of all people would try to stop me."

"What? *No.* I—"

22 moves, and before I know what's happened, he's reached past me and retrieved a pistol from Director Reyes's hand. I don't know if she was planning to fire it into my back or around the meat shield of me at 22, but that ship has definitely sailed. 22 looks like he's about to feed her that gun. I insert myself in his way as best I can.

"Hold up a fucking second and *listen to me.* You want to finish what Kit started? Really finish it? Or just get revenge?"

22 draws himself up and looks at me. If he's conceptualized the difference between these two outcomes, it's not obvious. His face twists, like something behind that welded-in-place calm demeanor is trying to leak out. "If you had any idea what this—*person*—put us through—"

"Okay, but . . . don't I? At least a little? Either of you, feel free to correct me if I'm wrong. She took you. All of you. Forty-eight of you. As children." I look at 22, then at the Director. I hold my giant gun where she can see it. "Sit *down.*"

The Director looks at me, then looks at the gun. She sits.

"She took you from the wreckage of your families and your homes. The recovery crews that found the survivors in the fallen buildings brought you here. You, and all the children they didn't end up taking. You were in a big bright room. Lots of kids running around. All of you were being observed. Asked questions. Given worksheets to do. Puzzles and things. You were being tested for candidate suitability somehow. While all any of you saw was a safe place. A roof over your head. A place to stay while your family was rescued too. I know. I know all of it. I was there."

The Director opens her mouth, shuts it. As well she fucking might.

"There must have been a hundred kids there the day I was brought in. When they were done with us, they sent us to the camps. Everything we'd ever owned was gone, but they gave each of us a plastic bag with the company logo on the side, with a toothbrush and a blanket and I forget what else." I twitch the gun toward the Director. "Help me out here."

She swallows. "That wasn't my department."

I want to clobber her. Instead I talk over her head at 22. "It wasn't her department. But here's what I think was. They put us on the news as they led us out of there. Big publicity stunt. Big distraction. Waving our company-logo plastic bags. Tell me, Director Reyes. Out of those hundred kids that day. Just that one day, when I was processed. How easy would it have been for a few to just . . . not leave?"

22's gripping his sword so hard that either his hand or the hilt is going to break. "Go on," he says. His voice is nothing. How can he still stand here, menacing her, when he can barely speak against the SecOps program aloud? He's going to black out. He's going to have an aneurysm. Hurry up, Mal.

"Nobody was left to come looking for you. Not in the camps, not in the lists of dead, not anywhere. That was probably part of the appeal of the four dozen kids she chose. She kept you in this building. Probably in this basement. Didn't let you out much. Something was done to you. Something to change you. Make you into weapons. It took a long time." I think of 17, the first to die, and of the damage under 22's gloves. I realize the next part aloud. "I'm not sure you all survived the experience."

"The biotechnology was bleeding edge, unprecedented," the Director protests. "As such the methodology was unavoidably uneven in its advancement. Unfortunately, hindsight is—"

"If you tell me *hindsight is twenty-twenty* in the context of systematically kidnapping and torturing children for profit, I am going to knock your fucking teeth in," I inform her. "Did any of them actually die in combat? Or was that just what we were told? Remembrance flares for those who were killed in action fighting for our economic freedom. It probably sells more mourning swag than if you say *slowly tortured to death in a basement over the span of a decade or more,* I guess."

The Director sits up a little straighter. "I never meant those children harm."

"And yet you never stopped harming them. Or letting the company and the media lie about what the operatives are. Where you got them in the first place. They're not some kind of biological robot thing that grows like a person but is conveniently too hard to replace when it dies. They're *children Stellaxis stole.* And gave to you. To change. To use. To cover for the lie. Because if people knew the truth, there'd be outrage. And that'd look real, real bad for the company. Just like it does now. Because I put the truth out there. And I'll keep—"

The barest noise reaches us from farther up the hall. A tiny scrape, like someone's armored elbow brushing a wall. More security guards, maybe, trickled down from the building somewhere, coordinating an assault on this room.

I raise the gun, but 22's holding up one gloved finger: *Wait.* He listens for a second, then strides straight across the Director's office, throws the door open, walks out. There come panicked shouts, bursts of gunfire, wet slumps as bodies hit the tiled floor. 22 returns. The sword is still unsheathed. He stalks toward the Director's desk, and I scramble back around it and walk up at him until he's forced to either go around me or through.

He does neither. He stops.

"She knows what she did," he says, not taking his eyes off the Director past my head. "I know what she did. It doesn't—"

"Listen to me. Our goal here is the same. Just hear me out. How did 17 die?" I ask over a shoulder.

"He drowned," the Director says, too startled by the change of subject to prevaricate. "In his blood. In his sleep. I believe it to have been painless. We were still fine-tuning the—"

"How many were actually killed in action? Not deployed. Not *saw* action. Killed. In combat."

The Director squirms a little. "Does it really—"

"Yes," I say, at the same time 22 says, "Two."

"Two?" The Director's brow furrows. Even here, even now, a discrepancy in her data is enough to snag her attention from imminent death. "38, certainly. Who's the—"

"Catherine," 22 says, his voice terrible. He's passed beyond murderous rage and into something far quieter, colder, held perilously in abeyance. At the moment it's working out well for me, but whatever's at the end of this tunnel isn't going to be pretty. "Catherine was killed in action. At war with you."

This hits home. "Catherine was—"

"Catherine," 22 practically whispers, "was *what*?"

"Two out of forty-eight," I say loudly. "As an experiment goes, those aren't great results. You're running out of subjects. What about the next batch?"

"There won't be a next batch," the Director says. "They axed the funding years ago. The project's done." Her face does something I can't place. If Jessa were here she could. I've never been able to read people like she can. But from where I'm standing it looks a lot like anger. "There were any *number* of phases of this project I never approved. My concerns were overruled. But I was always . . ."

When she trails off, I turn in time to see her eyes widening. I track her stricken gaze to 22. I don't even know how to describe the look on his face. But I know what it means.

The project is done. It was over anyway, it would die with the last of the twelve, and she never told them. Which means 06's death stopped nothing. No more SecOps machine for her corpse to jam the gears of. The war trundles on without her, without 22 or 08 or anyone, no matter how special they were raised to think they were. And my chance of keeping the Director alive has just evaporated.

I push the air in front of me with both palms, a futile gesture with a decidedly nonzero chance of ending with my hands getting lopped off. "Wait. Please. Just—"

The door cracks open behind me, and something rolls into the room. 22 moves so fast he practically vanishes, and the next thing I know he's opening the door and throwing something back out, then slamming the door and locking it. "Gas grenade," he tells me.

Not resonance grenades. Not frag grenades. Not any number of awful things it could have been. For one pants-shitting second I imagine being stuck in a room with a hallucinogen burst and 22.

I look at the Director. "Guess they don't want you dead either." Even as I'm saying it, I wonder. If the SecOps program is over, is it her they're protecting? Or the last remaining part of their investment?

Do they actually think he's going to let them take him alive?

The Director perks up a little at the *either.* Then looks confused. Glances from me to 22, who very obviously doesn't share the sentiment.

"She can't help us if you kill her," I tell him.

"Help us," 22 says, voice curdled with hate. "The furthest thing possible from anything she has ever done is *help—*"

"Well, today she's going to broadcast a live confession. Everything she just told us. She's going to take us to wherever in this godforsaken building she can do that from."

I look the question at her. The gun looks too.

"I don't know," she says. "Communications?"

I nod. "I think I saw that on the list for the sublevels."

"No," she says. "Ours is for internal communications. Reporting results back upstairs, that kind of thing. You'll need theirs. I don't know the floor. I don't get out of the basement much either." A watered-down smile. Then an idea hits her. "Actually. I have a map."

The glassy-eyed stare comes over her as she accesses something on her lenses. Within about a nanosecond 22 is beside her, the point of his sword set just below her right eye. "Careful."

But she only gestures, throwing the map up on the wall.

Lenses. Lenses that interface. I could make her get word out to old town. Tell Jessa I'm sorry, but I might not be coming home. I don't want to leave her wondering what happened to me. Most of our families' bodies were never found, or at least not identifiably. I can't put that kind of question on her all over again.

Shit. I could have asked 22. If his implant will even let him access anyone who lacks high-level Stellaxis clearance, which I doubt. They've got him on a tighter leash than that.

Or thought they did.

The Director runs a search on *COMMUNICATIONS* and finds it, way up on the fifty-third floor.

"There," I say. "Okay. Let's move out."

22 doesn't budge.

"Look," I tell him. "You kill her, they replace her, end of story. The program's done. They barely need her anymore." The Director makes a face at this but knows well enough to keep her trap shut. I ignore her. "But we air the company's dirty laundry in public? They don't like that shit *at all*. Why do you think they put me in that cell? Exposing Stellaxis's lies got old town's water rations cut. It got my implant put on lockout. It got me thrown into interrogation. And most people didn't even believe me. But they'll believe it when it's coming from her. Being broadcast from this building. With the only surviving operative to corroborate her story. This is a *major corporation*," I add, because for all I know this is news to 22. "Kill their people, they send more people. Destroy the building, they build another. But my way? We burn this fucking place down from the inside. And *that* is how we're going to finish what Kit started."

22 studies me for a long evaluating moment. Then he nods once at the box on the Director's desk. "There are files in there? On us?"

The Director touches the box unconsciously, protectively. "Yes."

"Then pick it up and start walking."

She doesn't protest. While the Director retrieves the papers from the floor and stuffs them in the box, 22 draws me aside. "I'll take point. You follow with her. Whatever she says, whatever she does, don't trust her. Not for a second. Maybe she didn't want to hurt us, but she still took notes while she watched us die. We'll do it your way, but after that, she's mine."

I swallow. "Maybe she's trying to make it right."

"She can't," 22 says simply. "But it's as good a use of her last minutes as any."

"WAIT," 22 SAYS. HE'S OPENED THE DOOR to the hall and is standing half in, half out of it, pistol in hand, listening to something I don't have a hope in hell of hearing. "They're at the elevators. They're waiting for us." He smiles coldly. "I imagine they got tired of sending their people down the hall to die."

"So they're going to ambush us instead?" I say.

He holsters his pistol and draws both swords, the whole one and the broken. "No. They're going to die there instead."

I glance back at the map on the wall. "Show me this sublevel?"

The Director complies.

There are emergency exits from sublevel A up to the ground floor. Four huge, round hatches, set into the ceiling. Like the lower floors of Stellaxis HQ are more of a bunker than a basement. And maybe they are. This building was put here with the expectation of a corporate turf war, after all.

But all four of those are situated at some distance from the elevators. We either fight our way to one of them and then back across the ground floor to the elevator up, or we fight through to the elevators here.

"Don't let her out of your sight," 22 tells me. "If she tries to run, shoot her. If she tries to call for help, shoot her. Take your lenses out." This part is pretty clearly aimed at the Director. She obeys.

"Put them on the floor."

She does, and 22 grinds them to jelly beneath his heel. "Anything suspicious," he tells me. "Take the shot."

"We need her," I say. "Alive. Remember?"

"Then shoot her in the stomach," he says, "and tell her to walk faster."

The Director blanches.

"They weren't like this as eight-year-olds, huh?" I murmur to her. I poke her in the back with the rifle. "Let's go."

Backtracking along the halls to the elevator is uneventful. But 22 stops me before I lead the Director around the final corner. He holds one gloved finger to his mouth. *Quiet.* Then gestures *wait here.* The unspoken threat he glances at the Director looks elaborate. I press the gun against her spine for good measure.

A sword in each hand, 22 takes off running.

The second he turns the corner there's a deafening rattling noise as easily two hundred bullets gnaw a hole in the wall to our left. Perimeter gun. Fully automatic. Motion sensors. It's all I can do not to do something stupid. Attempting to provide cover fire will just get me reduced to stew within seconds. I've never seen perimeter guns in real life, but in the game, my semiautomatic would be about as effective as a water gun against one.

I drag the Director back and down into a crouch just as a spray of bullets clips the cinder-block corner less than a foot from her face.

Then I realize the burst of gunfire didn't come from the perimeter gun. Or anything else out of sight by the elevators. It came from behind.

I whirl around, still crouched, already strafing with the rifle. My aim is for shit, but the safety's been switched off since before the Director's office, and it's just point and shoot, ridiculously easy. A few shots catch my attacker across the middle of the body, most of them absorbed by the smart armor, but not all. Something takes me over. Panic? Anger? Protectiveness? I don't know. I keep firing until he stops moving.

Stops moving.

I stare at him a second. He doesn't get up.

"Fuck," I whisper. The gun falls from my hands. Only the strap around my neck keeps it from clattering.

Behind me, the noise at the elevators stops. A hand reaches around the corner and grabs the Director by the arm, dragging her forward so hard she goes flying, the box skidding across the floor.

I sprint over, gun at the ready—but it's 22, now in the process of bundling the Director and her box of stuff into the elevator. There are more dead soldiers here, along with the mangled wreckage of the perimeter gun, which looks to have been picked up, sentry tripod and all, and *twisted* into a one-ton heap of legs and barrels, then flung into the ceiling. 22 catches me staring up at this like some kind of war tourist and makes a *hurry-up* gesture with one hand. I hustle over as, down the hall, booted footsteps close the distance. 22 covers me with the pistol as I get into the elevator, and smart armor or no, each shot is a kill. When he runs out of ammo, he draws 06's broken sword and *hurls* it, like some kind of oversized throwing knife. It goes end over end and buries itself in somebody's faceplate, thirty yards down the hall. 22 stares fixedly after it, like he's only just now realizing what he's thrown.

"Come on!" I shout at him because there are now a dozen or so live soldiers running past the dead one in our direction, and he's standing there, out of ammo, presenting them with the clearest shot they could have asked for on all their birthdays combined. Even if by some miracle he gets past them to retrieve 06's sword, it's a delay that gives more company goons a chance to catch up with us on our way upstairs, or worse, just freeze the elevators and strand us. "We'll come back for it after, let's *go.*"

Bullets whistle past his head. A drone tries to dive-bomb the open elevator, spraying fléchettes. 22 shears it from the air, then sprints down the hallway and plows into the oncoming enemy. He cuts one down, then another, slides under a spray of bullets, and before I know it he's beside me in the elevator, 06's sword in his hand.

I eye him. "Really."

"I can't leave it," he says. To his credit he looks at least somewhat repentant. "Long story."

He closes the doors and inputs *53* on the touchscreen. The elevator climbs and climbs. No knowing what will be waiting when those doors open. I push the Director behind me.

"No," 22 tells me. "Keep her in front of you. Back up into the corner."

This seems backward to me. "The hell? I'm not using her as cover. We need her alive."

"You are probably the only person in this entire building who doesn't deserve to die," 22 says. "I am *asking* you—"

"What about you? You deserve to die?"

It takes him a second to reply. The Director is watching this exchange like her fingers are itching to take notes on it. "I should have died a long time ago," he says eventually.

"That isn't—" I start to say, but the elevator pings and the doors open.

Onto an empty hallway.

I look at the Director. Her lenses are out now, but she still had them in when she realized where we were going. She could have contacted whoever's been sending these guards and soldiers after us, told them to set a trap for us when we arrived. But she didn't.

She shrugs. "I told you. I never meant any of them harm."

22 gestures. We follow him out into the hall. Communications is room 5302, within easy sight of the elevator. Lenses or no, the Director's implant still works, so she gives her thumbprint and retinal scans to the biometrics reader on the lock, and it releases with a click. 22 opens the door and rushes in like a wind. Someone yelps, then silence.

We hurry in after. Communications is about twice the size of the Director's office. A wall of windows overlooks the green lawns, the city beyond. I've never been this high up before.

There's a man sitting in a chair facing an incomprehensible bank of dashboards and panels in front of a smart-surface wall. He's in the process of removing his lenses, with shaking hands, at swordpoint. 22 holds out a hand, and the comms guy surrenders them without protest.

"We have a video to broadcast," 22 tells him. "You're going to help us do it."

Comms guy blinks up at him. "Broadcast? Like, on the company news channel?"

"There are four company news channels," I say, "and you know it. You're going to simulcast this across all of them. Nationally. Farther, if you can. However far it goes."

He looks at us, the confusion in his face deepening as he places each of us in turn: first 22, then the Director, then me. He stops just shy of saying *what the fuck is going on*. Apparently having a sword in your face is a great demotivator.

"Okay," he says shakily. "I'll set that right up."

No idea what would have happened if this room had been empty. Communications doesn't really seem to be the Director's field, and it sure as hell isn't mine, and 22's probably the only person on the planet worse at it than me.

But this guy's powering up the smart surface, and the Director is gesturing her login credentials over via the interface chip in her palm.

"Do, um. Do you need help making the video?" he asks, his whole body cringing away from the potential answer. I can't really blame him. He has no idea what we're doing here, but it's not rocket science to figure out that it's every shade of illegal.

"I make video reports all the time," the Director says, to the guy's obvious relief. "It's not like the people up here come down to the basement to see how things are going. All I need is access to the broadcast channels. Then you can be on your way."

Comms guy blinks his way through a few windows on the smart surface. "There. Done. You're in. Can I go?"

"No," 22 says. "You stay."

The Director pulls up another chair in front of the wall.

"Everything you said downstairs," I remind her.

"No tricks," 22 adds. He runs the point of the sword slowly along the top few inches of her spine between her shirt collar and the back of her skull, raising the thinnest possible line of blood. "I can keep you alive for days." He turns his gaze fractionally to the guy in the chair.

"Hey, man," the guy says. "Of course. No tricks. Look." He clasps his hands behind his neck like we're here to arrest him.

"There's no need to threaten me," the Director says. "Did you have to drag me here? I came willingly." The wall changes to reflect the room as she throws up a recording surface. She makes a doorknob-twisting motion in midair, bringing the smart wall in tighter focus on her face. "There are many decisions I have had to make over the past twelve years that I regret," she says as she works. "I can't undo them. But I can do this. Now shut up and let me."

She starts broadcasting.

"This is Director of Operations Diana Reyes," she says, as 22 stands by a wall offscreen and keeps an eye on the door. "I have worked for Stellaxis Innovations since September 2115. In the first quarter of 2122 I was put in command of a program with the goal of designing a new breed of soldier. I warn you that what I have to show you may be graphic."

I expected somebody to shut us down by now. Maybe they've run out of guards to send in here, or they're wary to throw more into the meat grinder of 22's sword when it's already single-handedly taken out everything they've sent so far, but they also haven't cut or jammed the broadcast.

Unless they can't. Unless there's no failsafe for if a SecOps operative goes rogue and locks himself in this exact room. Certainly nothing they've done to prevent him getting here has had the least effect. They're fucked.

I go over to 22. He hasn't taken his eyes off the door, but I know he's listening. I sidle up next to him, still watching the wall, shoulder to shoulder just like in the elevator a million billion years ago. "See?" I whisper. "It's working. They'll try to do damage control after, but now they're trapped. It's coming from their own house. We *got* them."

"And you really think," 22 murmurs back, "that this will make any kind of difference."

Fuck if I know. Part of me wants to say yes. Wants to trust that people will be galvanized enough to effect change. An overlapping part of me points out that it's their beloved operatives we're talking about. 06 martyred for what we came here to resolve. Maybe that will mean more to them than a town with its water rations cut. Which is pretty fucked up in and of itself. I wonder how much it matters what the catalyst is, as long as there is one. Not that I can begin to say which is more important or worthy of attention. A few thousand people without water, or four dozen children stolen, tortured, used? We should never have let either of those things happen. We should be fighting both.

"I don't know," I say. "But do I think it's the best play we have? Yeah." I nod. "I do."

He leans back against the wall and folds his arms. "Good enough."

Now the Director is gesturing something from her implant over to the screen. It's a photo of a girl, maybe fifteen years old. Lying on some kind of hospital table. Instantly recognizable as 05. Elena.

Did the Director choose 05 deliberately because of my videos? Impossible to say. I'm not even thinking about that yet. I'm wondering what happened to the girl in the photo. She's very obviously dead and very obviously did not get there by being killed in action. Or by drowning in her blood in her sleep. Whatever happened to her is the furthest possible point from painless.

She looks burned. Almost. What it's more like is the footage you see when a nuclear reactor explodes and they have to evacuate towns, and then they bring reporters around in hazmat suits to show the viewers at home what advanced radiation sickness looks like. But it's something else, too. I have no comparison for what this dead girl looks like, except maybe a zombie, but that's not right either. Whatever it is, she's very, very sick. Her skin looks blistery and loose and weirdly gray. Her eyes are open and red-rimmed and just *red*, like all the capillaries in both of them have ruptured all at once. There's blood crusted around her nostrils and tracked in dried paths down from both ears. The skin you can see is mottled, bruised, covered with weeping lesions and places where patches have shed damply away. I can't get a good look at her hands to see if they bear the same weird old damage as 22's, but I can make out similar evidence on her arms and shoulders. A network of scar tissue, ridges and valleys, like something has burrowed underneath her skin.

22 doesn't turn to look, even when my breath catches audibly. He doesn't need to. He'll have witnessed the play-by-play, up close, inescapably, forty-six times already.

"One by one, the subjects' bodies rejected the treatment. Very few survived the crisis period, pictured here. We lost three-quarters of our subjects before they could be released for duty. One promising subject, known to you as 17, almost made it through the crisis period before dying in his sleep, age nine. Those who survived this period—the eleven remaining SecOps operatives with whom you are familiar—were not immune to further damage. Their life expectancies were . . . severely curtailed. They were subject to periodic flare-ups of debilitating illness. Autoimmune responses. Organ replacement and skin grafts slowed the process, and blood transfusions met with moderate success, but we were unable to find a permanent solution. The treatment ate away at them, month by month, year by year, and one by one it overcame them."

So this is the *occupational hazard* that killed 08. That would have gotten 06 eventually. That will get 22.

06 was wrong. I was wrong. There was never any escape for any of them.

"Stellaxis was aware of this and did not allow my staff to discontinue the treatment. Though I petitioned them for years in my monthly progress reports. I called for conferences with every department I could think of. The marketing people laughed in my face. I have transcripts of all of this."

This comes as something of a surprise. I had the Director tagged as some kind of paint-by-numbers evil scientist. But now I'm not so sure. She's certainly not the highest rung on the ladder of who stands to gain. Does it make it better, what she did, if she was only following orders when she did it? Fuck if I know that, either.

If 22's body language is any indication, he's not inclined to think so. He's got his arms folded like he's holding himself together. Like how you'd hold a detonation shield over a grenade. It's a wonder I don't hear his ribs breaking.

"This is a complete list of the subjects of this project. Some numbers you will recognize. Most you will not. Before now they were never publicly released. The operatives you do know, thanks to the efforts of our marketing department, are simply the ones who lived long enough to be deployed." She clears her throat. "Subject 2122-01-B, Torres, Inéz. Subject 2122-02-C, Khoury, Safiyah. Subject 2122-03-C, Geissler, Colin. Subject 2122-04-A, Nguyen, April. Subject—"

The helicopter appears from nowhere. On the smart wall it's a dark shape behind the Director's head, hovering outside the window maybe fifteen feet from the building.

A dark shape with a pale logo. A tiny two-lobed sprouting leaf.

Not a Stellaxis helicopter. A Greenleaf helicopter.

It adjusts a degree or two, making sure of its angle. Then it fires.

"Get—" I scream, but either the next word never comes out or it's lost in the explosion when the missile strikes. Either way, too late.

So this is it. After everything, this is how I go. Blown up in Stellaxis HQ by a Greenleaf Industries missile alongside 22 and the Director and some poor fucking guy just trying to do his job.

Faster than dying of thirst anyway.

I don't have time to turn away from the blast. I barely have time to flinch before the room is swallowed in white-hot billowing flame. The force of the explosion blows me backward through the wall so violently that at first I don't even feel the pain of all my bones on that side shattering.

Fleetingly I wonder if falling to my death fifty-three floors down will be more pleasant than burning alive.

But I'm not tumbling through the air. All my bones aren't broken. I'm being propelled sideways by some sustained force that takes me past the smashed-in wall and now sets me on my feet on the carpeted hallway of the fifty-third floor.

"You look like shit," I tell 22 because the part of my brain that makes words has been utterly short-circuited while the rest of me struggles to piece together how I haven't been incinerated. He must have grabbed me, shielded me with his body, and run us both straight through the fucking wall. Faster even than the fireball that devoured that room.

Almost.

He's badly burned. His jacket is still on fire. He doesn't seem to notice.

"Wait for my signal," he says. "Then jump."

Jump?

He vanishes back into the room. No fucking way am I abandoning him in there. I follow.

There was little in this room to burn. What there was—the carpet, the chairs, the bodies of the Director and the comms guy—burned quickly, and the blown-out giant window lets the cool spring air inside. The floor is sticky, which turns out to be the soles of my sneakers melting. It smells like a nightmare. But I can breathe without scorching my lungs.

I have about half a second to register all of this. And then 22 is launching himself *out* of the shattered window and straight at the helicopter, whose pilot has committed the tactical error of taking more than two seconds to peel away from SecOps leaping range. 22 grabs the skids one-handed, reaches up, and rips the door off its hinges. Then he lifts himself up and inside.

One body goes flailing out the open door and falls, screaming. Then another. 22 says something to the pilot, which I have no chance of hearing against the wind and the buffeting of the blades, but whatever it is, that helicopter stays put.

22 reappears in the space where the door used to be. He holds on to the doorframe of the fuselage with one hand and reaches the other out to me.

It's at least ten feet of nothing between the wrecked window and him. I go over to the window and make the mistake of looking down. That close, the rotors are deafening, but I can clearly see that he can't make the pilot bring it closer without clipping the side of the building.

I'm not a fucking supersoldier. Not even a dead one. I'm one of the orphaned kids Stellaxis had no use for, and I can't make that jump. I will fall fifty-three floors and probably land on that stupid fountain. Behind me, back in the hall, the elevator is pinging.

22 adjusts his grip on the helicopter, leans out another inch. It looks painful. From here I can see how the skin has sloughed off with the burning sleeve of his uniform, leaving something not-skin, something oozing and red.

The elevator doors swish open.

Fuck it.

I back up for a running jump and tear ass across that room while gunfire crackles from the hall. My half-melted sneaker strikes the bare edge of the drop, and I leap, my arms windmilling in front of me. I'm going to wreck hell out of that fountain when I land.

22 catches me, wrist to wrist, and hauls me up. He must have yelled orders to the pilot previously, because the helicopter is already taking off fast over the city.

I barely have time to register the troubling pain constellation that's mapped itself across my body—shoulder, side, leg—before I black out.

I JERK AWAKE to gunshots and struggle to sit. Thinking: *22's gun was out of ammo.* Thinking: *I left my rifle in that room.*

Out the door-hole, the city banks and wheels. We're higher than I thought, spinning erratically above all but the tallest buildings. One more gunshot and then a scream as the pilot tumbles out into the air. Guess he thought he'd take out the last remaining SecOps survivor. Catch him by surprise. Go home a war hero. So much for that.

"Do you know how to fly this thing?" I yell up at 22. It hurts to yell. It hurts to breathe. It hurts to live.

"Not really," 22 calls back. "You?"

"Of course I fucking don't!"

I drag myself into the cockpit anyway, like I'm going to pick this up by looking at the controls. He's managed to straighten us out, at least a little, but we need a plan before we crash or someone shoots us down. "What do we do?"

22 shrugs a little. "I didn't expect to make it this far."

"Okay. Okay. Lots of these buildings have helipads, right? If you can land us on one . . ." I trail off. Almost half of these buildings will belong, in one way or another, to Stellaxis Innovations, who just tried to kill us. Most of the other half will belong to Greenleaf Industries, who also just tried to kill us.

I catch sight of a Stellaxis building with a giant screen on the side. Then another. Then another. All playing static, as of a signal that's just been cut. Like by a missile sent to stop a video. That, up until a minute ago, had been playing on these screens.

Huh.

"No. Wait. Outside the city. The woods where we were yesterday. Nobody goes there. Maybe you can land us in the trees."

"Worth a try." His tone strongly suggests he wouldn't bet on himself sticking that landing. But he knows the way. *You could see this place from the roof of the building. The woods. She always wanted to go.*

Which is good for me because my vision's starting to go hazy again, darkening to a tunnel, then a point. From some vast distance someone says *stay with me, hey, stay with me,* and something shakes my bad shoulder. Pain bobs me back up to wakefulness, a cork on dark water. An outrageous amount of pain. It's only when 22 withdraws his hand that I see the fresh blood on his palm.

The glove burned too, I note fuzzily. My thoughts feel like someone sank them in cement and pitched them in a river. My whole body has broken out in cold sweat. It occurs to me I'm shivering.

22 looks at his palm, then at me, eyes narrowed. He touches something on my shoulder that feels like a laser boring through me, front to back. "Fuck," he whispers.

"Hey," I mumble deliriously. "You finally said—"

And the leftover scraps of my consciousness drop me bang on the doorstep of whatever happens next.

0 0 2 1

I DREAM OF BEING BURIED ALIVE AND wake to the smell of dirt. I'm clawing at a grave that's not there when something grabs me by both hands. I can tell the grip is meant to be gentle. It isn't.

"Just a dream," 22 says, and lets go. His hands drop out of my field of vision. The pain resumes. I struggle to look down. I can't even orient myself. 22 is kneeling beside me, both swords on the ground at his side. Am I sitting? Am I lying down? Where's the helicopter?

"What are you—"

"You were shot." He holds up a plastic first aid kit. It has the same leaf logo on it as the helicopter. The box rattles when he shakes it. Opening it reveals four bullets, slimy with clotting blood. "Several times." He drops a fifth one in, applies a smart bandage to somewhere on my ribs. "Done."

I blink. This seems to take several seconds. The gunshots as I ran the length of the communications room, preparing to jump. Guess they didn't miss after all.

I try to ask him how it's possible that I'm still alive, that people who have been shot any times, let alone five, are lucky if they survive in a hospital, let alone being field surgeried or whatever you call it in a—wherever the fuck we are.

But what comes out is "Not dead?"

"Not quite. You were lucky."

Too fast for bullets, I think. Then I realize I said it aloud.

"Smart of you to hide that," he says. "Twelve years ago. You would've ended up like me."

Laughing hurts. It hurts a lot.

It's worth it.

I struggle to get a grip on my situation, but all my senses are muddled. We're under trees, at the edge of the woods. Through bare branches I can see the fields beyond. The dirt smell is because I'm lying on dirt, propped up on something that feels an awful lot like a rock. At a guess, it's midmorning.

"You weren't awake to see me land the helicopter," he says. "Pity." He lifts his chin toward something to the left, where the trees fade into abandoned farmland.

I try to prop myself up on my elbows and at once regret this intensely. He raises me up to see.

Out in the fields, something's burning. Something big.

"They don't have helicopter piloting in your combat simulator, huh?"

"They do," he says deadpan. "My landings look like this there, too."

His breath catches in a way I've only heard it do once before, but I know at once means *pain.* Too much of it to hide. Of course. The burns. For all I know he's been shot too. It's been that kind of fucking day. He held it together long enough to dig the bullets out of me, but now he's visibly spiraling.

22 reaches out, sets one hand against the earth to steady himself. There is very little skin left on that hand. I can't tell how much of the blood is his versus mine.

"In the house," he says. "Emergency kit. Flare gun. They'll come for you. You need a—hospital."

"Fuck a hospital. They'll just arrest me anyway. Stay still."

I grit my teeth and push myself upright.

Whatever was in that first aid kit, he hasn't used a bit of it on himself. He's burned horrifically. The jacket of his uniform is pretty much of a piece with his body. There is nothing between the insides of his hands and the air. *You flew a helicopter like that*, I think. *You caught me when I jumped. You pulled bullets out of me.*

I look around for the rest of the first aid stuff. Whatever he dumped out of the box and rifled through to find the things he used on me. I don't see much. There are a few smart bandages, a nearly empty tube of antibiotic cream, a splint, a few pain-killer dermal patches, and some insta-stitches that turn out to be mostly wrappers. He must have used those up on me.

There's nothing here I can heal him with. I mean. There's nothing in a hundred untouched mint-in-box first aid kits that could heal him. He needs a medbot. A long stay in a good hospital. Whatever that thing was 06 used on those injured people a lifetime ago. But I could have at least tried. If he hadn't used it all up helping me.

"What the *fuck*," I whisper, "did you do."

"Told you," he says. "Should've died a long time ago. You heard what the Director said. All borrowed time now. Makes no difference."

"Bullshit," I say. "Blood transfusions, remember? Organ transplants. I could crowdfund that for you in five seconds flat." Remembering the look on his face, seeing the SecOps posters in that dead kid's room. *You have no idea who you are,* I almost say, but what comes out is: "You have no idea how many people you have behind you. And we are not letting—you die—in some—fucking—field." I get one knee under me, shove myself to standing. It hurts. Way worse than laughing. It feels like someone is drilling holes in me, and someone else is putting out cigarettes in them. It gets worse when I reach back down and try to drag 22 up with me.

I can't lift him. He's deadweight. Worse, he's starting to look like he's about to pass out. Whatever reserve of will that's carried him this far ended when he pulled that fifth bullet out of me. The dry humor from a minute ago was the last light left in a sinking ship. He's dying.

"Get the fuck up," I grit at him, categorically failing once more to heave him to his feet. Something in my side gives way. I ignore it. "You're not done."

He blinks up at me in bleary surprise. Somehow, seeing him like this—all the sharp edges of him dulled to mush—is almost worse than the evidence of injury. It isn't that he's unrecognizable. It's the opposite. It's that he's recognizable and broken.

"Of course I am," he says, in a voice like sleeptalking. "The Director is dead. The project is dead. I finished what she started." Effortfully he draws me into focus. "*We*. Finished what she started. The Director's confession is out in the world. You were right about that. It is exactly what Kit would have wanted. Not just killing the people behind it. Shutting it down. You—"

He stops moving. His eyes close. He doesn't even fall over. He's still kneeling in the dirt, like a decommissioned mech. Switched off.

"No." It rips out of me more breath than voice. "No you fucking well do *not*."

He's breathing. I see that now. Still breathing. Shallowly, erratically, but there.

I start rummaging through the pile of scattered first aid supplies. Ripping smart bandages open with trembling hands. *Put them on the worst of the burns*, I think, and then almost start laughing hysterically. The worst of the burns cover probably forty percent of his body.

I apply them as best I can. His back, which he put between the burning room and me, is the worst of it. I crawl around behind and stick smart bandages to the red mess of him.

They won't even stick. They need skin around the edges to adhere to. They shift wetly and peel back at the corners.

And right then, right at that moment, is when it starts to rain.

There's no cover. The trees do nothing to stop it. A few degrees colder and it'd be sleet.

The ground liquefies to mud beneath me instantly. My feet skid as I try once more to pull him to his feet. My field of vision darkens and slews ominously. White sparklers fall through it. I might be in less rough shape than 22, but not by much. I have to watch out. We both pass out in this, we die. Either from hypothermia or blood loss or shock or because the company—*either* company—comes back and finds us. At least the downpour will put out the helicopter fire, making us harder to spot.

If it's not too late. If this area was visible from the Stellaxis building rooftop, then the fireball definitely is. It's too much to hope they'll assume we burned up in the wreckage. Far more likely there was a tracker in the helicopter, and they're on their way right now.

Who is *they*? I don't even know anymore. That was a Greenleaf helicopter. Maybe it was just taking potshots at its enemy's HQ. At the exact moment Stellaxis stumbled into a trap it couldn't get out of on its own.

Sure.

I need to get in front of this. Throw them off the scent. In the slim-to-nil chance we actually make it out of this field alive.

I can't go back home. Not after what I've done. I can't do that to Jessa. To any of them. But I can't let them catch me either. Me, or 22. Will they track his implant? Or mine? Almost definitely. But I'm not a brain surgeon. I have to do what I can.

What if I leave something at the crash site that makes it look like we burned? Something that we wouldn't leave behind.

It might give them pause, anyway. Buy a little time. I have to try.

Taking quick inventory of our possessions doesn't turn up much. A nearly empty first aid kit. Some bullets. Our clothes. 22's weapons.

06's broken sword.

I half expect him to snap awake and grab it from me when I pick it up from the ground beside him. After all, he refused to leave it behind in the Stellaxis building. But he doesn't move.

There's no room here for sentimentality. I don't know 06—Kit—very well, of course, but I can't see her wanting 22 to get himself killed over some relic of her service to the company.

Carrying it across those few hundred yards toward the guttering blaze of the helicopter feels like miles, but I get it there. I can't bring myself to pitch it in the fire, so I drop it nearby, hoping it looks like it was flung free in the blast. Hoping the rain will erase my footprints. Hoping I can get 22 to cover before it's too late for him, or for me, or for us both. If it's not too late already.

We're dangerously close to city limits. In the middle of a field. A drone could pop out of nowhere and shoot my bloodstream full of two dozen separate biohazards before I make it to the trees.

I have to find the trail. That busted house is the only cover I know out here.

Squinting through the rain, I maybe catch a glimpse of the trailhead, a gap in the trees about a quarter mile off. The crumpled shape of something that might be the remains of the sign.

It'll be hard going through the woods, suicidal going out here over open ground.

Fast as I can, I limp back to where I left 22 and kneel in the mud beside him. I can't carry him. He's going to have to walk.

"Sorry," I whisper, and jam my thumb into the burned flesh of his arm.

It works pretty much exactly as well as it did when suit guy did it to me in the white room. 22 jolts awake, grabbing my wrist hard enough that my bones creak, then letting go when he sees it's just me.

"Sorry," I say again, now that he can hear it. I'm already gathering up the first aid garbage, shoveling the sodden lump of it back into the plastic case. No evidence left behind. "I had to wake you up. We have to walk." I point vaguely in what I hope is the direction of the trail. "Over there."

"I won't make it. Leave me here and go."

"Yeah, that's going to happen. Come on. I know the way."

Slowly, laboriously, like a couple of shambling undead corpses, we hold each other up and make our way through the trees. There's no footing and no path and the world is thorns and rain and everything hurts, and where my hand hits 22's arm it comes away sticky, and we must both be running out of blood to bleed, but neither one of us quite passes out again, and eventually, long past when we're soaked through and shivering and I'm certain we're irreparably lost, we hit the trail.

It's still over a mile to the house, though, and we're both fading fast. I black out a few times, coming to as I stumble in the mud. Judging by 22's weight on my shoulder, he's faring similarly.

"Hey," I say. My voice sounds like it's been tied to the back of a truck and dragged cross-country. I force words out all the same. We fall asleep, we die. Or we wake up back in the company basement, which is worse. "Why don't you ever see elephants hiding in trees?"

A bit of 22's weight lifts off me as he rouses a little. Still, there's a space of silence before he wakes up enough to speak. "What?"

"Because they're really good at it."

Silence.

"Get it? My mom told me that joke. Right before she died." My voice is slurring worse now. I sound drunk. We both sound drunk. We stagger down the trail, only stubbornness and momentum keeping us upright. I understand what the phrase *dead on my feet* means now. I'm going to be dead in the mud if we can't keep each other awake. "Your turn."

There's a long enough pause that I'm sure he's fainted again. "Did you hear about the restaurant on the moon?" he says at last.

"Wait," I mumble. "Don't tell me." I'm sure I've heard this one before. I just can't bring it to mind. My brain is a sponge full of glue. I'm going to fall asleep waiting for it to cough up the answer. "I give up."

"Great food," he says. "No atmosphere."

I try to groan.

"One of the guards used to tell them to us, and we'd pass them around. Kit told me that one. A long time ago."

"That's truly awful."

"That's what I told her."

"Do you remember any—" I trip over my own feet, land hands and knees in the mud of the trail. White fire lances up my side. 22 drags me up. I lift my left foot, plant it. Then the right. "Any others?"

"Hmm." Another dangerously long silence. "Two goldfish are in a tank."

I don't even bother trying. "I give up."

"One of them says to the other, 'Do you know how to drive this thing?'"

"Oh my god. That's even worse than the first one."

He sounds almost pleased. "I know."

"Thanks, Kit," I say, immediately wondering if I've overstepped.

"That one," 22 says, "I told her."

We carry on like this the whole way up the trail. Not just terrible jokes but whatever random shit falls through our minds. Our favorite foods. Weird dreams we've had. The best kinds of weather. Games we've played. ("Would a combat simulator count as a game?" 22 asks. "Sure," I say. "Why not.") Movies we've liked. Turns out 22 hasn't seen any since he was little, and he's not entirely sure whether he actually saw any then or only imagined it in hindsight, so I promise to take him to see one when we get out of here, which we both know is a lie but the best kind of lie, the kind of lie that keeps you walking when your everything is shutting down around you, like a house's lights being turned off, one by one.

After forever, we reach the overgrown yard, slog through the tall grass, drag ourselves up the porch, somehow make it through the door, and immediately collapse. Right there on the floor. We don't even make it to the couch.

If I can get to the bathroom, there might be more first aid stuff in the medicine cabinet. I have a vague memory of seeing it there. Was that just *yesterday*?

But I can't get up. I can't even reach over to the first aid kit I dropped when I fell over in this entryway. We just slump there against the wall, breathing. All our injured places smushed against one another. We don't even have the energy to move the inch or so that would change this. To do anything. Say anything. Keep our eyes open.

I'm sorry, Jessa. But everybody has to die sometime. I hope you're not too pissed at me. I hope my plan worked. I hope you get your water back. I hope you find the third option I never figured out. No Stellaxis, no Greenleaf. Something else. Something new.

I had a real-life adventure, Jessa. And I saw it the fuck through.

I'm almost asleep when 22 says something. I can't quite make it out. It sounds like it might be *thank you*, which strikes me as ridiculous. As if I have somewhere else to be, something else I could be doing that's more the culmination of all my life's pitiful desires than sitting in this spreading puddle on this floor beside him, free, awake, alive.

Later, when I wake up and find his corpse cooling against me, his head lolled on my shoulder like he fell asleep beside me on the bus—later, when I try to shake him awake and part of his burned flesh peels off against me and stays there—later, when I drag myself to the kitchen of the fallen house to find the fucking pie server I'll use to dig 06's grave back up, and out to the shed to find the can of gasoline I'll pour over them both once I've dragged 22's corpse through that tall grass in the lightening rain, and back through the house to find the match—later, when I sit in the dirt under a clearing sky and set the fire that will keep them both out of company hands forever—I'll wish I'd somehow maintained consciousness just long enough to reply.

0 0 2 2

I DON'T KNOW WHAT TIME IT IS, what day it is, how long it's been since the white room, the Director's confession, the crash, the house, any of it, when I finally stagger off the trail and into old town. It's dark, and it's raining again, and I don't feel the cold anymore, and it smells almost like spring.

It's past power curfew, whenever it is, so I make my way through empty streets, one hand trailing on the buildings like it's a maze I'm trying to find my way out of, one hand dragging 22's sword behind me because I haven't figured out yet how to let it go.

Nobody stops me. Nobody sees me. Maybe I died out there and I'm a ghost, walking home because there's nowhere else for me to return to. Certainly I don't feel like anything more substantial than that. I may as well be made out of the rain.

I can't stay. I can't ask anyone to hide me. I shouldn't even be here at all. But there are bandages and water and clean clothes and food in our room, and as much as I hate the idea of letting Jessa see me like this, I owe her at least the decency of a proper goodbye.

For a while I stood over the pit of flame that was 06's grave and now is 22's also, and weighed the pain of burning against whatever the company will do to me when it gets hold of me again. I held 22's sword to my throat and weighed that quicker pain against the same. How much blood could possibly be left in me? It'd take seconds at most.

But then I remembered what 22 had said. *I am going to finish what she started.*

And I lowered the sword, and turned, and walked away.

Not knowing what I'll do. What I can even do. Only that doing nothing isn't an option anymore. The entire fucking world is burning. Jessa and Keisha and Tegan and the rest of us, we tried to draw a line to stop it. *Firebreak*, Keisha said. But the fire jumped right over. Over us, and 06, and 22. And it'll probably amount to nothing, but with whatever life is left to me, I'm going to plant myself right in the path of it and yell my fucking head off.

The Director's video. It's out there. It's not getting put back in the box. I have to hope that someone will connect it to the videos Jessa and I made. What 22 told me in Stellaxis HQ. Fake Nycorix in her RESIST shirt. Old town's rations cut. That mech on my doorstep, showing up in the internet blackout of an impromptu power curfew to threaten me. A mech of Greenleaf design.

Like that helicopter.

I hope to all fuck that its cute little leaf logo was visible through the window behind the Director's head just before the broadcast cut out forever—right before the precision strike that just so happened to occur in the exact room, at the exact moment, that something inconvenient needed shutting down.

All this long walk I've been wondering, nine-tenths out of my head with blood loss and exhaustion and thirst and bereavement: If you were Stellaxis Innovations, and you wanted to nip a problem in the bud without getting caught holding the shears—what would you do?

A stalemate, 22 called it. Stellaxis's and Greenleaf's control of New Liberty. What exactly, in the face of that stalemate, in the one supercity in which they both still had influence, did they agree on? If I were a major corporation, which would be the least of evils to my mind? To keep on fighting, throwing money down the pit of this war, at the risk of losing tens of millions of customer-citizens if I don't eventually manage to win? Or to make a deal with a fellow corporation with similar goals, and periodically knock down just enough low-priority buildings to keep up appearances? Would that deal look maybe a bit like the Neutralities Accord? Might *keeping up appearances* look a bit like the SecOps program and its resulting multibillion-dollar marketing campaigns?

I can't help but think that if I were a corporation like Stellaxis or like Greenleaf, this would all look like a pretty sweet deal to me. I can't help but think of these data points like an unfamiliar constellation: once you know what to look for, impossible to unsee.

The SecOps program is dead, but that's only the beginning. A symptom addressed, but the disease remains. Stellaxis took our water. At the very least we have to make enough noise to get it back. Or better yet, think bigger. Remove the water readers. Deactivate the accounts. Let it come out of the tap for free, just like the old days. If it works in New Liberty, it can fucking well work elsewhere.

Has it ever, in my lifetime, been anything but lies? The resource scarcity. The operatives.

I'll probably never live to see these answers. And that's okay. There's no hospital or clinic that will take me. My lenses are locked out, and I won't be able to sign in to the system. Even if I could, I wouldn't be able to pay. Even if I had the cash, I'd be arrested on sight.

This is my message in a bottle. Somebody, somewhere, please: use it. All of it. 06's death. 22's death. Mine. Politicize the shit out of us. What we did. What was done to us. To the operatives. To old town. To B's family. To ours. Let us mark the line that others will go on to hold.

But.

If 22 managed to save my life out there—twice—and the field surgery and smart bandages are somehow enough to see me through this? I won't ever stop. I'll keep making noise, keep pissing off the people in power, keep exposing every secret I can get my hands on, keep yelling until they come and shut me up for good. I'll find somewhere beyond New Liberty, beyond old town, and I'll make my way there. I'll keep walking until I find it. If I don't find it, I'll make it myself, and I'll tell Jessa and Keisha and Tegan and all the others where to find me whenever they're ready to try something new. I'll find a house like that one in the woods. I'll hang the sword above the mantel, plant a garden, share my rainwater with anyone who asks. I probably won't heal, not in all the ways I need to, but I'll live. And I'll remember.

I'll tell 06's story, and 22's, to anyone who'll listen. I don't know these stories, not really, and they're only mine to tell because there's nobody left to tell them. A woman like a burning ember. A dead man running on borrowed time. Both heroes, in the end, of nothing they were expected to be. The last of their kind. The beginning, I hope, of the changes to come. A spark that starts a fire of our own.

It's a nice thought anyway.

For now, I'm walking. Falling. Standing back up. Time stutters around me. No 22 here to wake me if I black out. But it's precisely because there isn't that I can't. I'm dragging this sword, and I'm putting one foot in front of the other, and I'm coming home. The skittering of that blade point on the pavement is the only thing keeping me awake.

One street, then another, and I'm rounding the last corner that brings me within sight of the hotel, and—

—it's different. There's a crowd. They're surrounding something. Some kind of light? It's like an in-game SecOps NPC beacon, only dimmer, with less upward reach. I stagger closer, through the crowd, and even up close I have no idea what I'm looking at. A huge array of flashlights, headlamps, candles, handheld lanterns. Anything with enough charge. All pointing at the sky.

It *is* like a beacon. But also like a remembrance flare. At the base of it, people have put flowers. Photos. A mountain of SecOps merch. Lists of something. Names. Not only of the forty-eight that would have been in the Director's video, though those are probably in there too, but hundreds more as well. Thousands. Missing families. Dead friends. The collateral damage of New Liberty's profit margins.

And standing to the sides: reporters. Talking into microphones and cameras, some of them, and some narrating over their implants. They must have brought their own power supplies, their own broadcast capabilities. They certainly brought water. I can see it, a literal bus full of it, pallets of bottles with people handing them out at the door. One of those people is a company guard, helmet off. Ex-guard, I suppose.

I glance down, and there's a water bottle in my hand. When did that get there?

Then I see who's talking to the reporters, standing in a semicircle of them, holding court. Keisha. Suresh. Tegan.

Jessa. Raising her eyes across the crowd toward me like I've called her name aloud.

Time skips and Jessa's beside me, both hands on my shoulders, and the reporters have followed. I catch the words *medical attention*, and *thought you were dead*, and *a fucking doctor*. But it's hard to connect those things together. Thoughts drift apart like continents. Darkness edges in.

"—hell have you been all this time?" Jessa's asking me, and everyone is staring and there are microphones in my face and I don't quite know how they got there.

But it's a question I know how to answer, a question I was maybe born to answer, a question that I owe it to the dead to answer, a question that every step along my path has brought me here to answer.

So I do.

ACKNOWLEDGMENTS

I don't even know where to start with this one. Way back in 2015, just after *Archivist Wasp* was published, the concept for this book landed in my head almost fully formed. I then proceeded to spend the next three years refusing to let myself write it. Telling myself I wasn't good enough to do it justice. It was too complicated, it had too much stuff going on, I'd probably screw up the characters, it'd comprehensively suck, etc. Maybe someday I could manage not to ruin it, but not yet. So I pushed it to the back and tried to ignore it while I wrote other stuff instead.

It didn't listen.

In spring of 2018 I realized it'd just been getting louder and more insistent the longer I tried to put it off. Further, my kid was very close to being out of school for the summer, and I know from experience that I am really unpleasant to be around when I have an idea chewing a hole in my brain and no time to let it out.

So over the next five or so weeks I panic-drafted this book. I'm used to being a lot slower than that, and to have a hundred and ten thousand words just *fall out of me* with zero prompting in a little over a month was a really strange experience.

My thanks go first and foremost to Navah Wolfe, who first decided to take a chance on a book I should by no means have gotten away with and then gave me latitude to double down on a lot of plot elements I had initially glossed over for fear the draft was too long. (I have heard so many horror stories of writers receiving edits along the lines of *ok, cool, now chop out twenty thousand words.* Navah told me to *add that many.* Almost every single scene in this book got stronger because of it.) Her edit letter was the most thought-provoking, thorough, incisive, yet somehow non-despair-inducing one I've ever received. Navah is, and I do not say this lightly, the ideal editor. Working with her on this ridiculous labor of love has been an honor and a privilege.

Big thanks also to Joe Monti and everyone at Saga for doing such a great job shepherding this book into the world. I've loved Saga's books for a long time and it's a pleasure to be part of their lineup.

Kate McKean, best agent, not only found me a dream home for this one, but put up with a truly heroic amount of my bullshit throughout the process. Turns out that after you spend three years talking yourself out of writing something and then finally let yourself do it, you get really attached, and every little bump in the road looks like apocalypse. Everything I write is personal, but I gave this one everything I've got, and having Kate there as the voice of reason was more helpful than I can articulate. She is the greatest and I almost certainly don't deserve her.

My five-week panic-draft would have crashed and burned if it weren't for my amazing neighbor, Margaret Stevens, who let my kid hang out at her place after school for a couple of weeks when I was in full-on antisocial up-to-my-eyeballs-in-a-project mode and really, really, *really* needed that time. Thank you.

Thanks also to my first readers: Caitlyn Paxson, Ysabeau Wilce, Tiffany Trent, Patty Templeton, Grey Walker, and Autumn Canter. You guys made some great points that made the book a lot stronger, while also being really reassuringly encouraging that the plot made any kind of sense to anyone who wasn't me. Gili Bar-Hillel read it later and gave me some really useful insights into the ending, which is one of the few things that's been entirely restructured since the first draft and I needed an outside perspective. I owe you all drinks.

I'd drafted this entire book with Stellaris as the company name before I bothered to google it and realized that it was already the name of a video game and mine would need to be changed. Dan Stace suggested Stellaxis, which was an immediate keeper. He also remains scarily good at finding all the typos and things when I'm too close to a project to make out those details. I probably owe him drinks too.

There's a lot of myself in a lot of my characters, and Mal has all my awkward antisociability. Antisociableness? Being bad at people. I'm writing this deep in coronavirus lockdown, and I can honestly say Leitha Ortiz and Jon Pesner are two humans who aren't related to me that I actually miss hanging out with. Thanks to them and also to my family for the support, game nights (*wistful sigh*), etc.

When I realized I needed a lot of gamer handles for BestLife, I knew I didn't want them all to sound like they came out of the head of one person. I wanted stylistic variety. So I crowdsourced them. Thanks so much to Eric Henn, Jessica Wick, Reina Hardy, Anthony John Woo, Shawna Jacques, Karina Sumner-Smith, Jeanine Marie Vaughn, Sita Aluna, Robyn Egwene Young, Lori LoSchiavo Canter, S. Brackett Robinson, and Zhi Zhu Saathoff! I tried to fit in all your suggestions, but believe me when I say I loved them all.

Big thanks to my Patreon subscribers, who are helping me get away with writing exactly what I want to write, which is honestly everything I've ever wanted. Your support is *so* extremely appreciated.

Also to all the librarians and booksellers and bloggers and enthusiastic readers who've championed my earlier books so loudly, both online and in real life. Word of mouth can make or break a novel, especially a small press one, and if you've heard of my previous books, it's probably because of amazing people like these.

This was the first time that a book has made me feel like I had to really do a deep research dive into some aspects if I had any hope of doing the story even the tiniest bit of justice. Some books that were instrumental here included: *No Logo* and *The Shock Doctrine: The Rise of Disaster Capitalism*, both by Naomi Klein; *Water Wars: Privatization, Pollution, and Profit* by Vandana Shiva; *Mind Wars: Brain Science and the Military in the 21st Century* by Jonathan D. Moreno; *The Future of Violence* by Benjamin Wittes and Gabriella Blum; and *LikeWar: The Weaponization of Social Media* by P. W. Singer and Emerson T. Brooking. I recommend all of these wholeheartedly.

And thanks most of all to you for reading. Honestly. Writing this book felt like letting out a scream I'd been holding in for years, which sounds obnoxious but is true, and I'm still a little stunned I got away with it. I can't even tell you how much it means to me that you've stuck it out with me this far.

I wrote this book in solidarity with all who struggle against oppression, corruption, fuckery, and greed, whatever face it wears. Let's never stop fighting for a better world.